By J[illegible]

Last Dance with Mary Jane

TALES FROM FOSTER HIGH
Tales From Foster High
The End of the Innocence
151 Days
Going the Distance
Taking Chances
What About Everything?
By Robert Halliwell: A Way Back to Then
Save Yourself
When I Grow Up

Published by Harmony Ink Press

Jordan vs. All the Boys

LORDS OF ARCADIA
Distant Rumblings
Eye of the Storm
With J.G. Morgan: The Unseen Tempest
With J.G. Morgan: Stormfront

Published by DREAMSPINNER PRESS
www.dreamspinnerpress.com

JOHN
GOODE

END OF THE INNOCENCE

DREAMSPINNER
PRESS

Published by
DREAMSPINNER PRESS

5032 Capital Circle SW, Suite 2, PMB# 279, Tallahassee, FL 32305-7886 USA
www.dreamspinnerpress.com

Trade Paperback ISBN: 978-1-64405-840-4
Digital ISBN: 978-1-64405-839-8
Library of Congress Control Number: 2020935001
Trade Paperback published October 2020
Second Edition
v. 2.0
First Edition published by Harmony Ink Press, November 2012.

Printed in the United States of America

This paper meets the requirements of
ANSI/NISO Z39.48-1992 (Permanence of Paper).

Part One

Plus ça change, plus c'est la même chose

Kyle

THERE IS an old French quote that goes: *Plus ça change, plus c'est la même chose*. It's usually translated as: *The more things change, the more they stay the same*. Jean-Baptiste Alphonse Karr wrote it in the 1800s, and it has become a common phrase people use when they are complaining about life or by adults who want to instill the feeling that no matter how weird things get, they have seen it all before.

Have I lost you already? Like one paragraph in and you're all, "I just can't with this kid." But bear with me. I'm going somewhere with this, okay?

So the French quote, the actual translation is: *The more it changes, the more it's the same thing.* And that, my friend, is completely different.

See, the one we use, the more they stay the same, that really isn't true, is it? I mean when something changes, that shit is changed. It's like diffusion. You know, the process that happens when you add a drop of red ink to a glass of water. At first the red drop is super obvious and you can see it is clearly different than the rest. So if we go by an inaccurate translation, the more red we add to the water, the more it stays the same.

But that isn't true.

Sure, the water is still water, but it isn't what it was before. One, no one wants to drink it. People want crystal clear water, and if you have some weird red water that has ink it, you're going to pass real quick. Two, you can't get the ink out of the water either. What was once pristine water is now ruined with ink, and everyone knows it. You can't hide the red; you can't pretend it isn't there. What was a glass of water is now ruined, so what use does it have anymore?

So the more things change, the more they are not the same.

So let's try the actual translation, okay?

You have a glass of water, sitting there on the table. You're either going to drink it or not. That is determined in your mind by looking at it, and there are a lot of factors that will influence that. How thirsty are you? Are you hot? Did you just work out? So many things that have nothing to do with the water.

Now someone comes by and adds a drop of red ink into the glass and it's changed. Changed forever, never to be that clear glass of water again. The question is not what's wrong with the water or why did someone put ink in it. The question is, how thirsty are you?

See, people didn't know me before all this. I had spent so much time being invisible that I was used to not being considered a person. So I was a glass of water sitting on the table, being ignored because who gives a damn about a lone glass of water. But then Brad kisses me and suddenly I'm seen, and I'm not just seen, but they figure out I'm gay.

And one drop of ink falls.

Nothing has changed. I am still the same person I was before he kissed me, but am I? I am now gay and will always be gay. I could get struck with a lightning bolt sent by Brocules, the patron god of heterosexuals, and have my entire brain rewired. I would wake up and like boobs and stuff, care about the color of girls' panties, and spit more. And fart I guess, I don't know. I'd make a bad straight.

But the point is, even after that lightning bolt, I'd still be the gay guy to those people. They'd go, "Did you hear Kyle got struck by lightning?" and then ask, "Who?" and they'd say, "You know, the gay guy."

I haven't changed. Brad hasn't changed. Yet we can never be the people we were before last week.

And here comes more of the same thing.

I was still ignored because no one wanted to be caught talking to the gay guy in public, only this time they were doing it on purpose. They knew I was there, they knew who I was, but they made a point not to even glance at me. Completely changed, more of the same crap.

Brad had always been the center of attention. People talked about him, watched him as he walked by. He was someone everyone knew. But he had always been envied and scorned by the people who were never going to be as cool or handsome as he was. They thought about how much they disliked him; they talked among themselves about how fake he was and why people couldn't see through his bullshit. They just didn't say it to his face because he was that guy, and no one wanted to talk shit about that guy.

Brad kisses me and suddenly their thoughts became words and their words became weapons, and instantly, Brad was the center of attention in a completely different way.

Nothing in his life stayed the same, nothing at all. He was kicked off the baseball team, and though they were willing to let him play to save face, he wasn't going to go back unless they changed the rules about how they treat gay people at Foster High. The people who used to be his friends openly scorned him, and a few were very vocal about it if they ran into him in the halls or whatever. He used to date the prettiest girl in the school, and now he was dating me, who was not the prettiest anything in the world. He was no longer the person people thought he was, although he hadn't changed one thing about himself.

Yet according to Brad, this was all just more of the same.

He had always known these people didn't really like him, and the only thing that had changed was they were being honest about it. I thought he'd miss being popular and everything that came with it, but he said he honestly didn't miss it. He did say he hated being spit at in the hall, but besides that, he was relieved he was out.

The more it changes, the more it's the same thing.

So as another week passed, the next part of our diffusion happened.

People stopped seeing the red ink and started seeing red water.

Brad explained that most of the people he knew didn't have the attention span to dislike someone for very long. It didn't sound right to me, and one night, at his house, he laid it out for me.

"See, you think everyone is like you," he explained as we lay on his bed. "You think that people have the ability to focus on something and not let it go. You have that crazy elephant memory, so once you dislike something, you keep disliking it for… well, forever, I guess."

"You know elephants do have great memories, but they forget stuff."

"Fine, but you're elephant-like in more than just your memory."

He glanced down at my crotch, and I blushed instantly.

"Brad!" I whined.

"Okay, but my point is, these people don't have the endurance to care about anything for long. I mean, look at memes. They are everything for, like, five seconds, and then they're gone. You know why? Because people find something else and move on. They hate me—"

"Us," I interjected.

"Us," he added. "But that was like two weeks ago. We're gay. Who cares? They all hate us and that's a law now, so going out of their way to show it is too much for them. They'll never like us, but they will start to ignore us."

"Well, that's normal for me," I said, going over what he said in my mind. It was scary how smart Brad could be about people. It was like he had access to the machine code of people's minds. He didn't know the formality of psychology or the technical terms for things, but he understood the motivations of people like no one I had ever met.

He scooted over toward me. "And I still don't understand how anyone could ignore you." He moved closer. "You're just too cute for words." He leaned in to kiss me.

"Knock it off, Romeo," his dad said, walking by the open door, a rule his parents had insisted on once they accepted we were dating.

Brad smiled and gave me a quick peck as he pulled back. "Sorry, Dad."

"You're going to get us in trouble," I scolded him.

Another grin that could charm the pants off a nun and he adds, "You're worth the trouble."

And sure enough he was right. As we headed into the third week, things just… stopped.

People stopped yelling things at us at lunch, people stopped moving as far away from me as possible in the hall, and Brad said he hadn't had his books knocked out of his hands two days in a row. And then I made a friend.

I think.

Well, let me explain.

See, normally when I walk into a class, I take my backpack off, sit down, pull my notebook out, make sure I have a clean page ready and have the textbook on hand if I have to read out loud or something. I sit near the side of the classroom, next to a wall, and usually in front since I want to actually hear the teacher instead of a bunch of idiots drooling on their desks.

No one ever really talked to me unless they were in deep shit.

Maybe once a month since I had been a freshman. someone would come up to my desk and beg to see my notes on whatever since they were dead fucking asleep when we covered it. I knew with my memory I didn't need them, but I liked making detailed notes because it gave my brain another way to memorize the stuff and pass the time in class. So I was used to someone wanting me to share what I wrote down now and then.

When I walked into trig, the blue-haired girl from the drama club waved at me.

Yes, I turned around to see if she was waving at someone else, and she nodded and said she was waving at me. I walked over and pulled my notebook out. "This is everything this week. For anything older, I'd have to check my locker."

She glanced at my notebook like I had offered her a dead bird or something.

"What's that?" she asked.

"My notes."

"On?"

"On trig. Hurry before the teacher comes in."

She laughed. "Kyle, I'm not asking to see your notes."

I looked at her, completely confused. "Then what do you want?"

"I was saying hi?"

Confused.

"You know, like a human being?"

More confused.

"Trying to be nice?"

Yeah, something was off.

"You can sit here," she said, gesturing to the seat next to her.

"What's wrong with it?" I asked, giving the seat a stern look.

"Um, nothing? What do you think would be wrong with it?"

Sighing, I explained, "It's just this is my last good pair of pants, and I can't get them torn on a tack or stained with something."

Now it was her turn to be confused. "Who would put those things on your seat?"

"Tommy Lopez, seventh grade. It was some kind of soda that made my pants stick when it dried. I had to go home and change and miss the rest of the day."

She looked horrified.

"So what's with the chair?"

"I was just offering you the seat, to sit together? Like, I don't know, people?"

Yep, not understanding one word.

"Jeremy was an asshole to you guys and I wanted to say sorry. I didn't know you'd be this paranoid."

My confusion turned to ire. "Three different people spit gum into my boyfriend's hair last week because they were having a contest on who could make the bigger mess. It's not paranoia if they're out to get you."

Now she was completely shaken. "I didn't know. I am so sorry."

And she did seem sorry. I didn't see pity on her face or even just sympathy. She really looked like she was distressed by the way we were being treated.

"The chair is safe. I'll sit in it if you don't believe me." She started to stand up.

"Okay, I believe you," I said, sitting down gently, just in case.

"I'm Sammy," she said, holding her hand out.

"Kyle," I replied, shaking it.

"I knew that."

That made me smile. "Sorry, habit. I'm not used to people knowing my name."

She shook her head. "Well, they know it now."

I got my books out. "Tell me about it."

"She just told you to sit next to her?" Brad asked as we sat in Nancy's, waiting for our food.

I nodded as I took a sip of my Coke. "Out of nowhere, she was really nice and said that Jeremy is an asshole and we shouldn't take it personally."

He laughed. "Well, you shouldn't. I should take it very personally. Like don't walk down a dark alley with Jeremy kind of personally. He hates me."

He was trying to make it sound like he was joking and that he didn't care, but he wasn't and he did. I reached across the table and grabbed his hand. "He hated the person you were."

He gave me a weak smile, not even a real smile but a reflex of one. It was a tic of his when he was trying to cover being upset. The corners of his mouth would twitch upward like a smile, but you could see by the sadness in his eyes that there was nothing smiley about his smile.

"I'm still me, Kyle. I still did those things. Trust me," he said, looking toward the kitchen, to see if our food was coming. "He hates me, all of me."

We had been skating around this sinkhole of a problem since the night after the school council, and it looked like he had fallen in finally.

See, Brad was having a hangover of sorts, waking up to dealing with all the shit he and his friends did when he was popular. He hadn't actually realized how hurt people were about the things that had been done to them, and he was taking it all to heart. I had been trying to remind him that he wasn't like that anymore, but he had been blowing me off pretty bad.

"To steal from Thomas Merton, I think the fact that you feel bad about those things proves you aren't that person anymore. The guilt you're feeling is something the old you would never acknowledge."

He stared at me from across the table, a what-the-fuck look on his face. "Thomas who?"

"Forget it," I said, shaking my head. "You're punishing yourself for things that are in the past and you can't change."

"No, Kyle, *they* are punishing me for things in the past, and they have every right to."

Our food showed up, and though I wanted to keep pressing him on this point, we had fifteen minutes to eat and get back to campus, and I was so fucking hungry I could eat my backpack.

Books included.

When the burgers were devoured and his plate of fries was gone and mine were almost finished, I said, "Okay, so let's say you deserve all this."

"I do," he quipped, smearing a fry in ketchup before popping it in his mouth.

"So what does feeling bad get you?"

He stared at me as he chewed. "What does feeling bad…. What does it ever get you?"

"Exactly. Guilt is a reflex, your conscience trying to tell you that you did wrong. You know that. So what is gained by continuing to beat yourself up over it?"

He leaned across the table and said in a low voice, "I was a douchebag to these people. When I was with the guys, I picked on them, laughed at them, made fun of them. And yes, even threw empty beer bottles at people we thought were freaks. How am I supposed to feel about that?"

"Bad."

"Well, there you go. I feel bad."

"No, you're beating yourself up over nothing."

"That wasn't nothing!" he said, raising his voice.

"I know that, but does kicking yourself in the balls make things better? Does it change anything?"

He sighed and pulled at the top of his hair, another habit he had when he was upset. I told him if he didn't learn to calm down, he'd be bald by forty. He told me I worried so much that my heart would explode in the middle of college if I didn't learn to chill.

We were both right.

"Okay, fine, Kyle. If I shouldn't beat myself up over it, what should I do about it?"

"Make it better."

Neither one of us spoke as we just sat there, my words sprawled out between us, neither one knowing how to handle them.

"How do I make it better?" he asked honestly, not an iota of spite or sarcasm in his tone.

Sighing, I took the last sip of my Coke. "I don't know, Brad, but beating yourself up? That isn't it." I could tell he wanted to keep arguing by the way he was searching for an answer to my rhetorical question, but the alarm went off on his phone, telling us we were both out of time.

Brad

EVERY TIME I think I understand how smart he is, he says something new, and I realize I might never know how big his brain is.

He was right, like he usually is. I had been wasting my time beating the shit out of myself in my own head, thinking if I felt bad, then that was something. But leave it to Kyle, over a cheeseburger, to tell me that I had in fact been doing nothing but making myself feel like shit.

I did need to make things better. I just didn't know how.

That ain't true. I did. I just didn't want to do it.

I mean, look at the library nerds, who I need to come up with a new name for because they're actually pretty cool guys. I showed them I wasn't an asshole and they accepted me, despite everything that my friends had done to them. They didn't blame me for things in the past; they just accepted that I had changed and moved on from there. If everything was that simple, I'd be on easy street.

I was nowhere near easy street.

More like Fucking Impossible Boulevard at the intersection with Dude, Just Give Up Already Avenue. Most of the people who hated me would always hate me, so my first impulse is to say, what's the point?

But that is the point, isn't it?

It doesn't matter if they forgive me or if they even listen to me. I need to let them know I was wrong for doing that and was really sorry about it. I needed to try, even if I knew it was a waste of time.

When I walked into my science class, I saw my first chance.

Jennifer and I had been lab partners, because why not? We shared a table and pretty much goofed off most of the class while everyone we knew did the same. Since the kiss, I had been sitting in the back, just lying as low as possible, giving her as much space as I could.

That was me being a chickenshit.

There was some guy sitting next to her, no one I knew, and as I approached, my first impulse was to tell him to fuck off and move.

An impulse that I realized was garbage the moment I opened my mouth.

Instead I looked at him and said, "Dude, I need to talk to her real fast. You mind switching? If not, that's cool, but it's important."

The guy stared up at me like he was waiting to get hit. My words hadn't even gotten to his ears, he was so scared.

Sighing, I said, "Really, man, I'm just asking. If it's a no, then don't worry."

He glanced at Jennifer, who was busy staring at me with a surprised look on her face. He grabbed his books and scrambled to the back of the room.

"Thanks, man…," I tried to say, but he was gone.

"It is okay to sit here?" I asked her.

She was pissed. I mean, who wouldn't be? But I knew Jennifer. No matter how pissed she was, she'd be more curious about what made me come and talk to her. She shrugged and I sat down. I opened my book up to make it look like we were actually paying attention, and then I turned to her.

"So, I owe you an apology."

She was silent, but her eyebrows were about to head into orbit.

"That was majorly uncool of me, and I shouldn't put you in that position. You're smart, beautiful, and no one should have ever treated you like that. So I understand why you hate me, but it needs to be said. This had nothing to do with you. It was all my garbage, and I'm sorry I dragged you into it."

She was silent for, like, forever. The only acknowledgment she even heard me was the circles she drew on the cover of her book. When Jennifer was caught by surprise or had no idea what to say, she'd do this. Grab a pencil and aimlessly doodle as she tried to gain her mental footing. From the scribbles I saw, she was really out there.

Maybe about twenty minutes into class, she turned and whispered, "Tell me the truth."

I nodded, already knowing I would never lie to her again.

"Did Tony and some guys hold you down in the locker room and beat you up?"

I looked away, which was all the answer she needed. I could feel the flush on my face as the humiliation of that moment replayed in my mind. My stomach clenched as a phantom pain ached through it, and though no one in the world would be able to tell, my eyes misted up for a moment because I wanted to cry so bad.

The moment passed as I was able to pull myself together and just nod. "It was no big deal."

It was the biggest of deals.

"Goddammit, he was right," she said, obviously to herself since I had no idea what she was talking about.

"Who was right?"

She shook her head and gave me a mathematics smile. "Look, you're an asshole for what you did. I get why you did it, but you should have given me a heads-up beforehand."

I nodded, agreeing with all that.

"But beating you up? Those guys wouldn't even be popular if you hadn't been friends with them, so where do they get off holding you down for that?"

Was she really saying this?

"Brad, I'm mad, not because you're gay but because you lied to me. If you had just told me beforehand…."

She trailed off, and I waited.

"Okay, I can see why you didn't tell me either. I would have lost my shit. But I had to find out that you kissed a guy from other people! You didn't even call to tell me what happened."

"Didn't think you'd want to talk to me," I said, knowing that was a shitty answer.

"I didn't, but you should have at least tried."

I knew that too, but had been simply too afraid to try.

"You're right, and I am so sorry. I didn't mean to bring all this down on you, but as always, I was only thinking of myself and other people got hurt because of it."

Story of my life right there.

I knew I could talk myself out of some shit. I had made a reputation out of it, in fact. The local cops always just gave me an *awww shucks, be careful next time*, instead of *you're fifteen and have no right being this fucking drunk in public*. If I was late to class or turned in homework late, I could always give them a sad look and say I didn't realize it, and like clockwork, I'd be okay. It sounds like I'm bragging, but I'm not.

See, I might have gotten away with that shit, but my friends didn't.

The cops weren't so kind to people who were drunk with me. I'd get sent home while they got their parents called. I might have skipped being tardy, but the guy behind me would be asked, "And what was your excuse?" It used to make me feel slick that I was so untouchable.

It wasn't until recently that I understood it was also incredibly selfish.

"Wow, you really are different," she said, sounding amazed.

"I am." At least I thought I was.

"I heard you were playing some game with the library nerds. I assumed it was so you could get them to do your homework or something."

"No, it's D&D and they aren't nerds." I paused. "Okay, they are nerds, but if they are, so am I."

She just started at me like I had grown a second head.

"So anyways, I am sorry. I will always be sorry, and if you never want to talk to me again, I understand."

We were silent for the rest of the class, and then the bell rang and we went our separate ways.

Kyle and I ended up at my house, as we normally did after school.

He was self-conscious about his place, and I know his mother was a subject he did not want to deal with. At my house we had a room to ourselves, food, and a bigger bed to lie down on. So it was an all-around win for us.

We had taken our shoes off downstairs, tossed our backpacks on the floor, and he was leaning back on me as we both stared at my ceiling.

"So I talked to Jennifer today."

He instantly sat up and turned around. "I knew this was going to happen."

"That I was going to talk to her? Well, yeah, I had to, man."

He sighed and began to get up. "I should have known better," he said, grabbing his backpack. "I wish you would have given me a warning."

I was so confused.

"That I was going to talk to her? I didn't even know I was until I saw her."

He stood there, looking like he was ready to leave. “Fine, can I get a ride home at least?”

Now I stood up. “You’re leaving?”

He nodded.

“Why?”

His voice cracked like he was about to cry. “I told you I wasn’t going to be your sidepiece, Brad. If you won’t take me home, just let me know so I can start walking.”

“Sidepiece? Who? Huh?”

“I am not going to be your DL!” he nearly screamed. “I know we didn’t say we were exclusive yet, but I thought boyfriend covered that.”

“We are exclusive! Wait, what the hell are you talking about?”

“You talked to Jennifer!”

I nodded.

“I know what that means.”

I didn’t.

He looked away. “I know you’re going to get back together with her, so just take me home.”

I was gonna what?

“Hold on,” I said, sitting back down on my bed. “You thought because I talked to Jennifer that meant we were getting back together?”

“Doesn’t it?”

“Fuck no.” Now I was getting angry. “I gave you my class ring. I called you my boyfriend. I mean, have a little faith in me, man. You really thought I was just going to dump you like that?”

“Why wouldn’t you?”

And now we were both close to crying.

“Because I want to be with you, dumbass.” I was raging now. “I didn’t kiss you in front of the whole school on a whim. I didn’t just decide one day to like guys. I chose to be with you, a conscious choice. When I told you you were my boyfriend, I meant that.”

He stared at me like I was speaking another language.

“Have you been sitting there this whole time, waiting for me to turn straight again or something?”

He didn't say anything, which said everything.

"Has Billy been talking to you again?" The personification of Kyle's fears and worries for some reason looked like Billy Porter to him. I loved Kyle to death, but I had to admit, trying to convince his inner Billy was exhausting at times.

He nodded.

"Okay, time out," I said making a T with my hands. "Put your backpack down and sit."

He didn't move at first but then slowly dropped it to the ground.

"Now sit," I said, patting the space next to me.

He sat down like he was waiting for the bed to explode.

"I know this is new for you," I began in the kindest voice I could muster. "And it's new for me too, but we have to at least trust in each other. If I say I like you, and that you're my boyfriend, you can't assume I would dump you out of nowhere by talking to Jennifer."

He seemed unconvinced.

I took his hand. "I'm crazy about you. I said that already. Why can't you believe that?"

A tear fell from his right eye.

"Because...," he said, barely above a whisper.

"Because why?"

Another tear.

"Because why would someone like you like someone like me?"

Yeah, that was classic Billy all right.

I thought he had been making a judgment on me. That he was saying I was the type of guy who would just bail on something out of nowhere, but in fact his own insecurities had been chasing him around at night again.

"Because I do," I said, taking his other hand. "I like everything about you. You're the last thing I think of when I close my eyes, and you're the first image that pops into my head when I get up. I almost literally count the seconds between classes when I can see you again, and the best part of my day is lying here with you, just talking. I know you don't think that highly of yourself, but that's because you're stupid."

He gave me a look.

"Super stupid, because I'm nuts for you. And I would never do what I did to Jennifer again. That was bullshit, and I told her so today when we talked. I apologized to her, that was it. I told her what I had done was fucking wrong and she didn't deserve it."

Now he was crying.

"I don't want to get back with her. I don't want to do anything but be with you, dummy."

I pulled him in, and he threw his arms around me and held on for dear life.

"I'm not going anywhere," I promised him.

And I meant it.

Kyle

SO I'M a weepy bitch, sue me.

But honestly, if you had someone like Brad saying they liked you, how long would you expect it to last?

Thank you.

So anyways, after my 'sode—short for episode, thank you—I settled down some.

Sammy asked me in class what was wrong, and at first I was hesitant to share anything. I mean, up to this point, the most I had ever talked to someone at school was a book report I gave on *Call of the Wild* in junior high, and even then I had dry heaves when I was done. Brad had cautioned me that people would be looking for gossip about us, but I didn't feel like Sammy was the gossip type.

And it would be nice to have someone besides my own inner voices to talk to.

So I explained to her what had happened, and she just nodded.

"Oh yeah, I would be worried about the same thing. I'd keep wondering if this was a bet with one of his friends to make me seem cool or not."

I laughed. "He is not She's All That-ing me. I know that for a fact."

She shrugged. "Then what are you worried about?"

"Um, look at him and then look at me."

She looked me up and down and then met my eyes. "Okay, and what?"

"I am nowhere in his league!"

She scoffed. "What league? He's an… he was an asshole. You're a way better person than he is."

Wow, that just pissed me off something fierce.

"One, he is an awesome person. You don't know what he's really like, so that's not fair."

She looked surprised by my response but recovered quickly. "Well, one thing Jeremy forgot to add to his story is that I was there with him the night they threw the beer bottles. So yeah, I kinda know the person he is."

"Was."

"Fine, was, but besides kiss you, I haven't seen anything new from him."

"He is not like that," I insisted.

"Says you." When she saw I was going to argue with her, she held up a hand to stop me. "Kyle, look. I believe what you're saying, but you know it isn't your job to walk around defending him, right?"

"He doesn't need me to defend him."

"Then why are you?"

She had a good point.

"Brad's a big boy. He can apologize all on his own, and if you talked to him, I bet he would in a second," I answered neutrally, trying not to sound like I was defending him.

She smiled. “Okay, but I thought we were talking about how you were worried he’d break up with you. You seem pretty defensive for a person you think can dump you at a moment’s notice.”

I stopped because she was right.

If Brad had changed so much and if I believed he wasn’t that guy anymore, why would I ever think he would just dump me in the middle of nowhere?

When we went to Nancy’s for lunch, I told him as much.

“So I’m sorry for losing it in your room yesterday.”

He looked at me over his menu and smiled. “It’s okay, this is new for both of us.”

He put the menu back up and I pulled it down.

“No, I am sorry for doubting you.”

He looked at me, confused. “Um, okay. You’re forgiven?”

“No, you don’t get it. I am sorry I doubted you, because I know you’d never do that to me.”

He nodded slowly.

“You’ve changed. You aren’t that guy anymore.”

“I hope so.”

“I know so,” I said firmly. “We have to stop doubting ourselves.”

“You shouldn’t listen to Billy that I’d leave you,” he added quickly.

“And you should stop thinking that you’re the type of guy who could.”

He paused, and then I saw realization dawn on his face.

“I’m not that kind of guy anymore, am I?”

“Not even a little,” I said, smiling.

He smiled back. “I’m not that guy anymore.”

I was so glad we could agree on something.

Brad

AS THE days passed, things got easier and easier.

Kyle thought it was because of some water thing and that people were accepting us more. I knew it was a little simpler than that.

Winter break was coming up.

Remember what I said about people's attention spans—they were already losing their will to go out of their way to fuck with us because it was too much effort. But heading into Christmas, it was hard to think about anything but being off until the end of the year.

There were places to go, days to sleep, presents to wish for. Who cared if Kyle and I were hitting it, school was going away for a few weeks! Nothing else mattered.

He had made a friend in that blue-haired girl, which was cool. He needed someone besides me to talk to. Half of the stuff he liked I'd never heard of, and the other half, which I had, just seemed weird to me. I mean, I was trying, but man, it was hard. Having someone who was into the same things as he was would help him realize that he wasn't as much of a freak as he thought he was.

I mean, we were all freaks; he hadn't figured that out yet.

Jennifer, on the other hand, seemed ready to be friends really fast.

Really fast here meaning at all, since I imagined the only time she'd think of me was when she was shoving needles into my voodoo doll. But to my surprise, she was keeping the seat next to her open and seemed genuinely happy to see me in science every day. She always asked about Kyle and if I had heard anything about the baseball situation.

He was good and no.

Finally, by the end of the week, I had to know.

"So why are you being nice to me?"

It came out of nowhere. We had been putting some liquid into some other liquid so we were wearing those plastic goggles. She had been in the process of using an eyedropper when I asked.

"What?" she asked, sounding like that came out of left field for her.

"Why are you being so nice to me? If the roles were reversed, I would have hated the ground I walked on."

She put the eyedropper down. "You would have hated me or yourself? I'm confused."

"I'm saying if you had dumped me out of nowhere, I would have hated you."

"What if I had been a lesbian? Would you hate me then?"

"I… would… not have," I answered honestly.

"Why?"

"Because I'd know it wasn't about me, it was… oh."

She smiled at me. "Yeah, oh." She went back to the experiment. "Sure, I was pissed at first. Who wouldn't be? But I had a talk with a friend and realized that besides the shame, this really didn't have anything to do with me. You weren't trying to be mean. You weren't trying to hurt me. You were probably terrified about coming out, and the thought of your imaginary girlfriend didn't even cross your mind."

"I'm sorry," I said reflexively.

"I know," she said softly. "So I decided to get to know you. The real you. Not the you who lied to me, the you who was gay this entire time and was afraid anyone would find out."

There was a smile on my face that I felt would never go away.

"Well then," I said once she was done. I held my hand out. "I'm Brad, and I'm gay."

She laughed and took my hand, "Hi, Brad. I'm Jennifer and hate that all the cute guys are gay."

We both laughed, and I felt a million times better.

"You should meet him," I blurted out.

"Who, Kyle? I have."

"No, I mean the real him. He's amazing."

She just stared at me in wonderment.

"What?" I asked. "Is something on my face?"

She nodded. "Yeah. Love."

"Wha…?"

"Don't deny it. I've never seen you like this before. I'm not going to lie. If I knew you could feel like this, I would have known in a second you weren't into me."

I felt good and bad at the same time.

"The difference is night and day, Brad. I mean it, he looks good on you. And I would love to meet him."

I just nodded, not trusting myself to even speak at the moment.

Kyle

SO AS I was sitting on the steps of the music building, I saw my worst nightmare walking toward me.

No, it wasn't Nicolas Cage as Ghost Rider trying to show me another sequel. It wasn't Tim Gunn coming to talk to me about what I was wearing, and it wasn't John Wick coming to ask about the dog I agreed to watch.

It was Brad and Jennifer, smiling and laughing, walking across the quad.

Now I am sure there wasn't a light breeze blowing that made their hair move as if alive, and I am fairly certain there wasn't a diffused glow around them that made them look like deities, but I damn well know they were walking in slow motion.

I know Brad and I just had this huge fight about if he would ever leave me for her, and I was as at peace with the outcome as I could get, but this was nightmare fuel. They looked like they belonged together. If you saw these two on a movie poster, you'd know instantly who the love story was about. They'd use a shot like this to promote the new CW show, *Locker Love*: A tale of drama and lust set in a North Texas town. Including several other photogenic guys who were jocks and introducing Kyle Stilleno, the token gay who sits in the background saying, "Guurrrll!" and "Uh-huh," and then snaps his fingers or some shit.

I think I stopped breathing at some point.

"Kyle?" Brad asked, suddenly standing over me. "Babe, you okay?"

Slowly my vision cleared, and I saw the look of concern on Brad's face that made me feel so fucking loved and so completely embarrassed at the same time.

"What happened?" I asked, not sure what just happened.

"You kind of swayed and then looked like you nodded off."

"He was hyperventilating from a panic attack," a girl's voice said from behind him.

And just like that, my memory came back online and hundreds of flashing red lights went off in my brain as Majel Barrett, the voice of Star Trek's computer, announced the All Fucked-Up Alert.

Brad looked back at Jennifer and then to me. "Were you having a panic attack?"

Still was, if I'm honest, which we all know I'm not.

"No," my voice squeaked, sounding like I was on helium or possibly a cartoon mouse. "I mean no, I'm good."

Yeah, that sounded so much better.

I stood up and she was looking at me, concerned. She was… God, she was so fucking pretty. I mean, there were girls who were, like, slutty hot, just trying too hard? But not Jennifer. She seemed naturally beautiful, and I couldn't tell how much was simply her and how much was careful preparation each morning.

"Jennifer, right?" I asked, holding my hand out.

She took it and gave me a small smile. "And you're the history whore."

You could have cooked an egg on my face.

"That's okay, I'm the beard formerly known as Jennifer."

We shook hands, and I felt myself smiling.

"You sure you're okay?" Brad asked, hovering within arm's reach in case I fainted or puked.

"He's fine," Jennifer said, never looking away from me. "Get us something to drink. We'll wait."

He instantly started to move and then paused, looking at me. An impulse from years of dating, I assumed.

"A Pepsi?" I asked.

He smiled and nodded. "And Diet Coke," he said to Jennifer, who nodded.

He jogged off, and we both watched him cross the quad.

"That boy is cute as hell, but he is even better-looking going away," she said, which made me lose it.

"I keep meaning to tell him to stop wearing those damn baggy jeans but haven't figured out how to bring it up," I admitted.

"I tried, but he said skinny jeans were gay, so you might have better luck now."

I knew it was a joke, but it still made me sad.

"I am so sorry all this came down on you," I told her honestly. "He just kissed me out of nowhere. I told him not to…."

She held her hand up to stop me and then sat down on the steps. "One, you have nothing to apologize for, and two, once Brad has something in his mind, there is nothing short of an act of Congress to stop him. If he wants to kiss you, plan on getting kissed."

I sat down next to her. "Still, I can't imagine what you've been going through."

She had a slight shocked look on her face. "You guys have it a thousand times worse and you're worried about me?"

I shrugged. "I'm gay, I expected it."

Her expression changed to sad, and she said, "Well, it's bullshit, and trust me, I am not upset at all."

I arched one eyebrow at her and she laughed. "I mean I'm upset that these fuckers won't stop asking me how I feel because they want some new drama, but I have no problem with the two of you. In fact I was telling Brad, you look good on him."

"When did you see me on top of him?" I blurted out.

She stared at me for a long second and then started laughing her ass off.

"Oh my God," she said between gasps, "I didn't—" More laughing. "—it was an expression."

Yeah, I got that now.

"What's so funny?" Brad asked, walking up with three cans of soda.

"Kyle was just telling me about how he mounts you," she said, taking the Diet Coke.

"Why would you tell her that?" he said, looking at me, and her laughing started up again, and I have to admit I joined in.

"We're really bad at this," I said as I tried to catch my breath.

"I can tell," she gasped, trying to gain her breath.

"I still don't know what's so funny," Brad said, sitting down.

Once we settled down, I took a sip of my Pepsi and felt a million times better.

"So was your panic attack about seeing us together?" she asked.

I nodded. "You guys look perfect together."

"Maybe on paper, but I see the way you make him smile and I see the true love here."

"Love?" I sputtered. "I mean, we like each other, sure, but no one has said love yet." I looked at Brad. "Right? I mean, it could be, but it's, like, soon…."

Brad's eyes were wide with panic. "Right! I mean, no one said love yet 'cause that would be nuts. I mean, who says I love you this fast? I mean, it's not that I don't, it's just…."

"Oh God, get a room, you two," Jennifer interrupted us. "It's nice to know that gay boys are as stupid as straight ones."

We both looked at each other and then away, as neither one wanted to broach that subject yet.

"So," she said, looking out across the quad. "This is nice. I wanna do more of it."

Brad leaned forward and asked her, "Drink on the music steps?"

She glanced back at him. "Hanging with you guys. You all need friends, and I happen to be sick of the ones I have."

Brad looked at me and I just sat there, not sure what he wanted me to say.

"You wanna hang with us?" Brad asked, obviously not believing what she was saying.

"Look at them," she said, gesturing toward the Round Table but not looking over there. "All they are doing is watching us talk. If I walked over there, those bitches would be, 'What did he say, did you tell him off, how horrible are they?' Those idiots had nothing done to them, but they're coopting my situation for their own amusement. I mean, did you know they were that bad before this?"

Brad nodded, which seemed to surprise Jennifer.

"Remember, I hung out with them with the knowledge that if they ever found out about me, they'd turn on me in a second. Which they did, so yeah, I always knew they were two-faced dicks, but it was just the game I had to play."

She looked sad again. "God, the last four years had to be horrible."

Brad didn't say anything, but we knew they were.

"Okay, so fuck them," she said. "We don't need them, and we never did. Let's start a new group, right here."

"The three of us?" I asked, not sure if she meant me.

"Yeah, for now. Trust me, if we stand together, I bet other people come around."

"I don't want those people coming around. I don't want those people anywhere near Kyle," Brad said in the most menacing tone I'd ever heard.

"No, no, I don't mean them. I mean if we hang out and just ignore it, other people who don't care will join us. Trust me, I am not trying to get those idiots to do anything."

"I have a friend," I said quickly. "She's in the drama club and super cool."

"See?" Jennifer looked at Brad. "That's four, and you have your library friends. That sounds like a group right there."

"You're going to hang out with those guys?" Brad asked in disbelief.

Her face hardened. "Look, Brad, let's try this. I never knew who you really were, so let's not pretend you ever knew who I was either. If you say those guys are cool, then sure, I'd hang out with them. I am not the stuck-up bitch that people make me out to be."

He looked chastised, and I said, "I never thought you were like that."

She laughed and finished her Coke. "Oh, I was completely that, but what you guys have done has reminded me that I didn't ever want to become that person. Somewhere I lost my way and gave in to the popularity and peer pressure. Seeing you two buck the whole system has given me faith I can do the same thing."

"You can," Brad said instantly.

She smiled. "I know."

And just like that, we were a group.

Brad

IT WAS the end of the week where things got… weird.

Jennifer and me were in science and things had been great. Kyle had gotten over being worried I was going to suddenly degay myself and get back with her, and Jennifer seemed to really like him. The rest of the school didn't know what to make of it, but this close to the end of the year, no one really cared enough to bug us.

So I guess we all had a false sense of security.

"So, Christmas break's coming up," she said casually.

"Yeah, can't wait," I answered, wondering what the hell we were supposed to be doing in this class. The people next to us had a Bunsen burner going, which made me think we might have missed something.

"So you know what that means," she said, still in that halting tone.

"Um, yeah, no school, no school, and oh yeah, no fucking school. Sleeping in, staying up late, and then food and presents. I mean, it's the best time of the year."

"And Kelly's having the Party…." She trailed off.

And that was when the wheels fell off the bus.

While my brain scrambled to find the ability to make words again, let me explain that Kelly's parents are some of the worst people I have ever met. People have to get a license to fire a gun, drive a car, even to sell lemonade on the corner, but any idiot can have a kid. If there were two people less suited to be parents than mine, they were Kelly's.

His mother was one of those ladies who had no idea how to act her age. She still wore clothes that would have looked tacky on girls with half her mileage. She dressed like Ariana while looking like Ms. Swan from *MADtv*. Her hair looked like it was out of fashion in the '60s, but it was okay 'cause it was a color that in no way ever occurred in nature. Worse, she took every opportunity to try and talk up any of Kelly's friends like she was our age. Her language was laced with "What's up, dawg?" and "How's it hanging?" There was cringe, and then there was Mrs. Aimes.

His father was even worse.

There is a certain type of man who can only judge his value based on how many women find him attractive. He keeps count of how many girls he thinks he can have, even if he could never actually get them. That number translates exactly to how much of a man he is. I was used to seeing this behavior in guys my own age, but to see it in a man as old as my father was just gross. And that was Kelly's father in a word: gross.

I don't know if he was oblivious to the fact his toupee was bad and the waist strap he wore under his clothes didn't hide his weight. He was at least three times the age of the girls Kelly knew, but his dad would leer at any girl, no matter how old she might be. That kind of thing was sick. Kelly wasn't a girl magnet to begin with, and after it got out how pervy his dad was, it was near impossible to get a girl to come over to his house at all. The only exception was the Party.

I heard how Kelly conned his parents into it once, but I have no idea how much of it was true. See, Kelly's parents were the ultimate wannabes. They wanted to be cool, young, and hip, though they were tragic, old, and just the worst. From what my dad said, Mr. Aimes had gotten in on some internet company early and cashed out for the kind of money that should come on an oversized check or something. Instead of investing it and making a stable life, they used the money to try to play ball with Foster's wealthy.

I know it might not seem like it to you, but Foster has some rich-ass motherfuckers in it that no normal people got to see. They all hung out at that fancy restaurant outside of town or over at Cole's Club, a country club so exclusive that the entry fee was more than most people make in ten years. Those people are old money, oil, land, dark magic, whatever they used, but they had real money. Kelly's parents just had chump change. So they were the ultimate freaks when it came to networking and outside appearances.

Anyways, Kelly brought up once that Randy Osborne, son of the mayor, threw a huge party every year where the kids of the most influential people in Foster went to and that if he threw a party like it, he bet that he could get in good with some of those guys.

It was complete bullshit; no one at Foster High had real money. Granada was the newer school, so the best kids went there while the rest of us were stuck at Foster. My parents were considered well-off at Foster, and I can assure you, the real rich parents of kids at Granada didn't make less than six figures a month. So Kelly's idea was so much a lie that anyone with half a brain would know it wasn't true.

It seemed that Mr. and Mrs. Aimes had less than that.

Every year, his parents went out of town right before the break and left Kelly alone at their place. They'd leave him some money and make sure there was enough booze to handle the party so he didn't have to get someone else to buy it. Yes, you heard me right, grown-ass adults bought a shit-ton of alcohol for their teenage son's party that would have no adult supervision. I wish I was making this up, but in the last two years, the Party had become a force of nature.

All moral objections aside, the Party had become known as the low-rent version of what the rich kids had been having the entire time, and now that it was Kelly's senior year, it was rumored to be the best one yet. I had known all this, of course, but since everything with Kyle and me had gone down, going to the Party had been the last thing on my mind.

Until, you know, like now.

"Did I lose you?"

I looked up and saw Jennifer staring back at me. I wondered how long I had spaced out and shook my head. "No, just completely forgot about it."

"Color me shocked! Brad Graymark actually forgetting a party!" She was teasing me, but she was still telling the truth. I had been the first person to bring up having a party. I loved being able to drink, hang out with my friends, and not have to clean up after the chaos, so of course I pushed for other people to throw them all the time.

I pretended to skim through my textbook, turning pages at random as I ignored her gaze. "Yeah, I've been in the middle of other things; parties I can't go to aren't that important to me now."

"So you didn't plan on going?"

"Oh yeah, I'll show up with my boyfriend and be all, hey guys who held me down in the locker room, now that there are more of you, would you like to take turns beating the shit out of my boyfriend and me? Give me a break."

"You don't go and they win."

"Win? They already won, Jennifer!" I snapped. Mr. Olsen shushed us and I lowered my voice. "I'm not interested in winning anything. I'm focusing on surviving. I'm more interested in getting through the rest of the year without a broken bone than I am in winning. And I am sure in the hell am not putting Kyle through that."

"You guys wouldn't be alone."

"Right, so us three, the library guys, and Kyle's blue-haired chick against the varsity football starting lineup. I think they got us."

"I don't think everyone would be like that."

"And if you're wrong?"

She paused, not sure how to answer that.

"It's too dangerous," I added.

"It doesn't have to be," she said.

"Why?"

"I'll have your back."

I laughed despite how serious she'd become. "And what exactly are you going to do to them? Make them over to death?"

Remember, I have known this girl since we were kids, and I had been intimate with her for the last three and a half years, so when I say I thought I knew who she was, I am not making an idle comment. I had been there when her grandmother died, when her dog got hit by some asshole speeding on her block. I was there the night her dad said she looked like a whore for wearing a miniskirt on a date with me. I really had thought I'd seen every facet there was to her. But I assure you, there was a stranger staring back at me when she said, "Because my dad made sure I never leave the house without protection. And he didn't mean condoms." The smile she gave me was a predator's.

"You're serious?" I asked, more to myself than to her, because it was obvious from the look on her face she was more than serious. "You think guys will stop just because you're the sheriff's daughter? And you think I want to be saved by that?"

She sighed.

"You fucked them up with that little speech at the school board. If you don't move now, by the time we come back from the break, no one will remember what you said and did. You and Kyle will go back to being second-class citizens and it's over." She leaned across the desk toward me. "You want to change this town? You wanna make a point? Show up with Kyle on your arm and force them to accept it. And if you go, I promise you, you'll have at least one person standing there with you, and I bet a lot more."

I was stunned.

"You've been thinking about this."

"I have," she said with an evil smile.

"Why are you trying to start shit?"

She shrugged and said in a tone of voice that made me wonder if I ever knew her, "I don't want to start anything." She locked eyes with me. "But I sure in the hell want to finish some things. You guys show up and everything changes."

"Yeah, but for good or bad?"

She did not have an answer to that.

Kyle

WHEN CLASS let out, Sammy and I walked out together.

"So you should eat lunch with us," I said before she could walk away.

"Where do you eat lunch?" she asked casually.

"Normally, the music room steps in the quad." Brad and I had decided, though there were less public places to eat together, we were making a statement in plain sight of everyone. It was bad at first, but it had gotten a lot better since Jennifer started sitting with us. The other day, one of Brad's friends actually gave him a head nod as he walked by us. Brad said it didn't mean anything to him, but I could tell it really meant the world.

"Oh, I usually eat in the theater," she admitted as we walked out of the math building.

"Sit with us," I offered immediately. "Your hair looks way better out in the light anyways."

I saw her give a slight pause before asking, "Are you sure?"

"Of course," I answered, nodding. "Unless you don't want to be seen with the gay couple, then I'd totally understand." She stopped walking. About three steps more and I realized she wasn't following anymore. I turned back and asked her, "What?"

"Dude, I have zero problems with you and Wonder Jock being gay. Hell, if you want the truth, I think it's kind of hot. I just... I never had someone ask me to, like, sit with them with other people around."

I could feel the grin break out across my face. "Well, now you have." I headed back to her and hooked my arm into hers. "Come on. Brad will be waiting."

Brad and Jennifer were already there, deep in conversation.

"Is that his ex?" Sammy asked.

"Yeah, she's super cool."

"The head cheerleader is super cool?" Her voice made it pretty clear she thought I was high.

"She is. Trust me, she's not like you think."

Sammy said nothing and followed me, but she was wary.

As we got closer, I didn't think they were in a conversation; it sounded like a quiet argument. As we walked up, Brad told her to drop it and stood up to hug me. "Well, my day just got better," he said, putting arms around me.

"So what's going on?" I said, not returning the hug.

Brad took a step back and shot a dirty look to Jennifer. He looked back to me and smiled. "Nothing. You must be Sammy," he said, putting his hand out.

She took it. "And you must be the guy whispering to his ex-girlfriend and then not telling his boyfriend what it was about."

Brad dropped his hand. "Um, okay."

"I'm Jennifer," she said, standing up.

"Sammy," she said, her tone of voice broadcasting she had no idea what the hell was going on but didn't like it.

"And Sammy," Jennifer finished, "I love your hair, by the way." And she really did; I could hear the truth in her voice.

"Thanks," she answered quietly.

"So what was that about?" I asked him.

"Can we just have lunch?" he said, sounding exhausted. "I'll tell you after school."

"That's because he doesn't want me around," Jennifer chimed in.

"She isn't wrong," Brad muttered under his breath.

I stared at him.

"It's nothing about breaking up with you or anything. I don't want to get into it on the music hall steps, okay?"

"Okay," I agreed slowly. I mean, of course I wanted to know what was going on, but I could wait. *I think.*

Yeah, no, this was going to kill me.

"You both know that not telling him is a thousand times worse than whatever you're going to tell him," Sammy said to Brad.

"What I have to say isn't bad!"

"Then why can't you tell him now?" she pressed; she was like Lois Lane, up in his grill.

He sighed. "Well, for one, girl I don't know, it is something I want to talk to him about in private. Two, I am more than aware of how wound up he gets about things like that, which is why I assured him that it wasn't the things he was worried about." He looked at me. "Are you really okay with this? Because if you aren't, we can go talk now...."

I shook my head before Billy—the manifestation of all my negative thoughts, who was sitting on the steps, dressed in a pair of salmon capri pants and white sun hat—spoke up.

"I am okay. Yes, I can wait. And her name is Sammy and not 'girl I don't know.'"

He turned to her. "Hello, Sammy, I am Brad," he said and held out his hand again. "I am super sensitive about people judging Kyle and mine's relationship, so I apologize for being all aggro."

She shook his hand. "Hello, Brad, I am Sammy, and I don't care how sensitive you are about things, I don't like people doing shitty things to my friends."

I could tell Brad knew she wasn't just talking about this, and he nodded. I don't know if he recognized her from the bottle-throwing incident, but he knew he had done something to piss her off in the past.

And then, like a stage magician, his face lit up with a smile and he asked, "So we gonna sit down and eat or stand around introducing each other?"

So that was what it looked like when he was faking emotions.

"You grabbing something?" Jennifer asked Brad.

"Yeah, they got pizza. Want a slice?" Jennifer nodded, and he looked at me and Sammy.

"I have lunch," Sammy said, holding up her backpack, and then he looked at me.

"I'm okay," I said, pulling out my paper bag.

"Right, four slices, who wants a Pepsi?"

Jennifer and me raised our hands, and we all looked at Sammy.

"I didn't bring any change."

"Four slices and four Pepsis, got it," he said, running off.

"Are those new pants?" Jennifer asked me.

I nodded. "When I said they showed off his ass, he bought three pairs."

Jennifer laughed. "Well, I never thought of that."

"You guys talk about his ass a lot?" Sammy asked.

Jennifer and me chuckled. "It's a work in progress."

Sammy kind of smiled. "I was not expecting this."

I smiled at both Sammy and Jennifer and sat down. "So…," I began to say, then realized I had absolutely no idea what to say.

"So I thought you were pretty mad at Brad," Sammy said to Jennifer when it became clear I wasn't going to say anything of importance. "I heard some ugly rumors."

I'm not sure how she asked that and didn't sound like a complete bitch, but somehow she managed. Maybe it was the lack of hostility in her voice, or maybe it was because it sounded like she was actually asking a question instead of implying she already knew the answer. All I knew was it was the last thing I would have asked Jennifer.

"I was," Jennifer answered; her smile was not quite as wide as it had been. "But I've had time to think about everything, and I don't like the way people are coming down against the two of them." She was talking about Brad and me as if we'd *both* gone to grab something. I relaxed and listened.

"Yeah, but weren't you one of those people a couple of weeks ago?" Again, Sammy asked and didn't demand. It was impressive to watch her stare down one of the most popular girls in school like she was Nancy Grace all of a sudden.

"My problems with Brad had more to do with him lying than with his actual sexuality." For the first time, Jennifer looked at me. "I have zero problems with you guys being gay, seriously. I think it takes a huge amount of courage to do what you did."

"Thanks," I mumbled, my entire body half-numb from shock.

She looked back to Sammy and locked eyes with the other girl. "I had a friend explain to me what they might be going through, and I realized that this whole thing didn't have much to do with me. Brad didn't go out of his way to hurt me, it just happened. So I decided to see if the three of us could be friends." She didn't ask "Is that okay with you?" but she implied the question when she paused and arched one eyebrow.

An uncomfortable silence plugged itself into the next few seconds. The three of us sat there, not sure what came next. Tony Wright and his friends walked by, their heads turning like they were watching a car accident or something. "Hey, Wednesday Adams! Wash some of that shit off your eyes! You look like a fucking raccoon!"

His friends and the people around us in the quad laughed, and Sammy's whole body stiffened in embarrassed shock.

My mouth was half-open when Jennifer stood up and yelled, "Hey, Wright! Shut the fuck up before I tell everyone you have a tiny dick!" The three jocks froze in place just before she clapped a hand over her mouth—a little—and added in a stage whisper, "Oops. Too late." The laughter that erupted from the quad this time was thunderous in comparison to what Tony's insult had garnered. Sitting back down, Jennifer looked over at Sammy. "Ignore him. All his rage comes from trying to compensate." She held up her hands a few inches apart. Sammy burst out laughing as I stared in confusion.

Then I got it.

"Seriously?" I asked much too loudly. I glanced over and saw the trio of letterman jackets and their humans flee away from the steps. I looked back at Jennifer, and she just smiled and nodded. Without even thinking, I muttered, "I'm bigger than that, soft."

"Oh really?" Jennifer asked, leaning toward me.

Oh my God! I said that out loud.

"So how big is that?" Sammy asked behind me. The grin on her face made her look like a cat about to eat a bird.

Thankfully, at the last possible instant, Brad walked up with a tray of food and drinks. "What's so funny?"

The two girls laughed. I willed myself to melt into the concrete, where I could die of embarrassment unnoticed.

"What did I miss?" Brad asked, setting the tray down.

Jennifer chortled as she opened her Pepsi. "Well, we learned that your boyfriend has a bigger package soft than Tony Wright does hard."

Brad gave me a double take and then gaped back at her. "I was gone for, like, a minute. How did the topic of his junk come up?"

"Please talk about something else," I said under my breath, more as a prayer than an actual protest.

"From the way he sulked off, it looked like what you said was true," Sammy commented, opening her drink.

"His junk is tragic," Brad said, sitting down next to me. We all froze and looked at him. He casually took a drink before he realized he was the center of attention. "What?" he exclaimed. "I've taken showers with him. Everyone looks! Anyone who says they don't is a liar."

Even I had to laugh at that despite my mortification.

"So just ask him," Jennifer said as we began to pick at the food Brad had bought.

The hair on the back of my neck stood up as I realized she was talking about me. "Ask me what?" I asked Brad instead of her.

"Real subtle," he grumbled to her after seeing my look. "Nothing. We can talk about it after school."

My stomach started hurting again from stress. "Tell me now." I hadn't meant for those words to sound like a demand, but from the way Sammy and Jennifer looked over at us with concerned expressions on their faces, I could tell it had. I cleared my throat and tried again. "I mean, why wait?"

Yeah, that didn't sound lame at all.

"It ain't important," Brad said, not meeting my eyes.

I honestly felt like I was going to throw up.

"If it isn't important, then just ask me."

"Jesus, you're stupid," Jennifer said, pushing Brad out of the way. She sat down in front of me and her eyes locked with mine. "He's an idiot, and this is nothing serious. Do you know about the Party?"

I heard the way she inflected the words to indicate they should be capitalized. Obviously she hadn't learned much more about me since the last time we met, back when I had no idea who she was, much less what the hell the Party was. I shook my head, which kept me from answering with something sarcastic.

"Kelly has this party every year, and it is just crazy, and I was thinking we should all go this year."

She sounded so kind and compassionate that I instantly felt bad for coming back with "Why? Do you want us to be killed?" She recoiled like she had been slapped; that might have been less from my words and more from the coldness in my voice. "If Kelly can't stand me walking around the school, how do you think he'd handle me walking into his house? That's not even mentioning the rest of the Neanderthals Brad plays ball with. Suggesting we show up either means you are trying to get us beat up or just completely naïve about how bad it has been for us."

I saw Brad's mouth open in shock as Sammy tried not to laugh out loud.

Jennifer's face moved from surprise to hurt to unreadable in a manner of seconds. "Suggesting you show up was my way of trying to make people accept you two, because I think the way you've been treated has been bullshit. I understand that might scare you, but do me a favor and try not to assign motives on my part, since you don't know me."

And suddenly everything I had been sitting on the past few weeks came spewing out of my mouth like a broken sewage pipe.

"Sorry, but I've heard a lot of the same things you said about Brad that Sammy had," I countered.

"And I've heard from half a dozen guys you've made passes at them since you came out, but you don't see me believing random gossip, do you?" Her voice wasn't harsh, but she was obviously challenging me.

"Um, guys," Brad said, trying to interrupt us, but we ignored him.

"So you didn't say all that about Brad after you guys broke up?" I'd wanted to ask her that since the moment Brad brought her over with us. I know that might make me a horrible person, but someone had to ask.

"I said stuff, yeah. I was angry. But I went back and told people I was just talking shit because I realized it was unfair to him and you." Again, she wasn't angry, but she sure as hell wasn't backing down.

"And you think showing up to this stupid party will change minds?" I tried to match her tone, but it was hard because I was still kinda pissed.

"I think showing up proves you aren't afraid of them."

"Can I say something?" Brad asked behind her.

"Hold on," I said to him and then looked back to her. "And if they do try to kick our asses?"

She gave a smile that was nothing like a pretty-girl smile. If anything, it looked like a villain's leer, something given to remind people how dangerous she was. "Then they have to kick my ass too."

And damned if I didn't believe her.

"You're serious?" I asked after a few seconds.

"Completely," she shot back instantly. No hesitation, no thinking about it.

If we'd been playing poker, she would have just called my bluff.

"Fine, we'll go," I said with all the force I could muster.

"Good." She nodded and smiled and held her hand out to me. I took it like we were making a business deal. "This is going to be fun."

"Do I get a say?" Brad asked in a small voice.

"No," we both said, looking at him and then laughing out loud.

And that was how we ended up going to the Party.

Brad

OKAY THEN, having my ex-girlfriend and current boyfriend sit down and talk seemed like a good idea at the time. But in class after lunch, it began to dawn on me that I might have made a mistake. After agreeing to go to the Party, they seemed to get along okay, eating and talking about nothing in particular. The girl with the weird hair even got into it after a while, leaving me to wonder if I had created a monster.

I tried not to be jealous when Jennifer and Kyle talked like they were lifelong friends. Up to that point, I had been Kyle's only friend, and I hadn't realized how much I liked all his attention. Seeing him open up to Jennifer and what's-her-name was cool, but I couldn't stop wishing it was just the two of us sitting on those steps.

God, I was the worst person in the world.

When school let out, I headed toward the gym so I could change out for practice. No one had lost their mind about me being on the field with them so far, but the way the team behaved had changed. It was obvious, at least to me, that I was one of the stronger players this year, which was going to make their choice about keeping me on the team that much harder. Normally it would be a mortal lock that I was playing, but after everything that had gone down and the fact I wasn't sure if they offered me a position I'd take it, I played as hard as I could to stack the deck in my favor. I hadn't been bluffing when I told Principal Raymond and his good ol' boy buddies I wouldn't play for them if they didn't change their attitude toward bullying. Though my dad had been spitting fire about what I'd said, my mom supported my decision to transfer to Granada if things didn't change.

But none of that compared to how the other guys treated me.

So I liked being popular, I think we all know that by now, but when I walked into the locker room, it was just painful. Before I would be welcomed by people saying hi, guys asking me what's up, and a couple of freshmen had taken to shouting "Big guy on deck!" when I walked in.

I swear I didn't tell them to say it.

But now, now it was quiet as a grave. As soon as I entered, all conversations stopped, and people froze and covered themselves with anything they could find. Guys would hold their shirts up to cover their nipples, and if they had their jeans off, they'd grab a towel or part of their uniform and cover their crotch. God forbid one of them was actually nude. I walked in last Tuesday and Roger Lakes had just taken his underwear off and was slipping his jock on, but then he saw me, screamed, and literally threw himself on the ground, face-first.

I hadn't even seen him, so all I heard was a scream, the sound of meat hitting pavement, and then a low moaning as the pain of his reaction slowly started to dawn on him. Everyone shot me dirty looks as I made my way to the coach's office, like I had pushed him down myself.

So the normal dread I had walking toward the gym instantly vanished when I saw Kyle standing there waiting for me.

And then tempered when I saw Jennifer was waiting with him.

"Hey," I said, not sure what was going on this time.

"Hey," he answered back, stepping into my arms.

The moments when we hugged, the world stopped moving for me and everything went away. The thousand thoughts usually lurking in my mind disappeared the second I leaned into Kyle. It was like diving in a pool after a long summer day. My entire day restarted every time we touched.

"What's up?" I asked as he pulled back.

Jennifer answered for him. "I was going to kidnap Kyle while you practice. I always hated sitting, waiting around for you to get done."

"But I don't hate it," Kyle added quickly.

"Um, sure," I said, confused about what was going on. "I mean, I don't want you to just sit around waiting for me if you don't want to."

"I don't mind!" Kyle said again, but Jennifer was already talking over him.

"Sweet. So I'll have him back by the time you're done," she assured me. I wanted to ask Kyle if he wanted to go with her, but I didn't know how to ask that without telling Jennifer to go away so I could talk to him.

"Okay," I said, confused as they walked away. Why did that bug me so much? Did Jennifer just steal my boyfriend from me?

I tried to ignore all those thoughts as I walked into the gym. Why was I so wound up about this? I mean, I wanted Jennifer and Kyle to be friends, right? As I got into the coach's office and changed out, I knew I had to grab my brain and shake it up and down like an Etch A Sketch until it was blank. The worst thing any player can do is walk onto a baseball diamond with something other than baseball in mind.

To the people in the stands, the game might look slow and leisurely, but I assure you that, out on the field, baseball is anything but. Reacting to the crack of a ball when it hits the bat means you are already too late. You should know the moment the ball leaves the pitcher's hand whether the batter will get a piece of it or not. If your mind is wandering, then there is no chance for you to react in time.

As I put on my uniform, I realized life was a lot like that.

I mean, you're out there, just chilling, being yourself when—wham! A line drive slams into your face, and you're on the ground screaming in pain because you lost focus or figured you were safe and there was no way you could end up on the ground bleeding. Because most people can't resist looking at a car crash, there are people standing over you, looking down at you as you try to look up. Some guys will feel bad for you, and others might not even care, but there will always be a few who enjoy seeing you caught off guard and slammed to the ground. They like seeing the blood flowing from your nose, and though they aren't going to laugh out loud at you, you can see the glee in their eyes as they watch you stumble to your feet.

So yeah, that's a metaphor for the past month or so of my life in a nutshell.

I walked onto the field, and the stress of the day evaporated. It was getting colder, as North Texas does close to Christmas. Of course, the cold wouldn't matter once we started laps and then drills, but right now I felt the chill of the oncoming winter and wondered if it was an omen.

Practice breezed by, and before I knew it, I was heading back to the locker room. I had no idea how much time had passed or even how well I had done. Baseball was like meditation in a way—I go somewhere else and a whole other me takes over and plays the best he can. I stopped to pick up my glove, and when I got to the doors, I saw Kelly standing next to the stands. My heart began to race as I searched the shadows to see if he had brought company. All of a sudden, however, I stopped being scared and moved straight into fury. When exactly had the sight of a person standing in the shadows begun to scare me? I was not becoming that guy.

"What do you want?" I asked, still unsure if he was alone but ready to throw down if needed.

He held up his hands in surrender as he realized how pissed-off I really was. "I just wanted to talk. It's okay, I'm alone," he added quickly, and I knew he was telling the truth. Kelly was a lot of things, but a master liar was not one of them.

The steps to the locker room led under the stands, so there was a small alcove made of cement before the locker room doors. I leaned against the wall across from him to escape the growing winds as the air got colder and colder. "Okay, then talk."

He shoved his hands into his jacket pockets and looked like he was trying to work up the nerve to say something. "So how you been?" he threw out after a few seconds.

"Fuck this," I said, moving toward the doors again. He knew how I had been; everyone knew how I had been. He spends the last few weeks fucking taking every chance to lord over me and he wants to come up and ask how I am?

"Okayokayokayokay wait!" he called out, moving between the door and me. "I wanted to ask if you were coming to the Party."

As Kyle would put it, my spider sense began to tingle. I wondered if the timing of Jennifer's decision to talk had anything to do with Kelly's appearance, and suddenly I needed to know if Kyle was okay. "Did you think I would go?" I shot back. Where was Kelly going with his questions?

He stomped his feet as he walked around in a circle. "Fuck, it's cold." His breath was fogging now. "Okay, look, things got weird and a lot of shit went down, but we're still cool, right?" He paused like he was expecting me to say something. Instead, I just stared at him. "Anyways, some people have asked about you, and I told them I didn't know…."

He took a deep breath.

"Look, if you were to come, it would be okay. Nothing would happen, and no one would do anything." He looked at me, and I could see the old pleading Kelly peering back at me in his eyes. "I would like you to come."

"We're okay?" I asked, my tone of voice far colder than the wind. "Did you just ask if we are okay?"

He said nothing.

"No, Kelly, *we* are not okay. You attacked Kyle, twice, you've taunted me for the past couple of weeks nonstop, my life has been a living hell, and we both know you're behind a lot of that. So no, Kelly, we are not okay. We are way fucking far from okay, you couldn't find it with a damn atlas. What would make you think we were okay enough for me to consider going to your fucking party? In what world, after everything that's gone down, did you think the answer would anything but Hell. Fucking. No?"

He swallowed hard, and I think his hands were shaking, or he could have been losing feeling in them like I was in mine.

"Doing all that was wrong. I know that now. Nothing's been the same since. All anyone does is go on and on about how they missed all the signs and they suspected the whole time when that's bullshit. No one knew. No one even dreamed of it. They aren't mad or upset, they are just looking for someone to hate because *Game of Thrones* ended."

"And you?"

He sighed and stomped his feet again. "Look, we both know the truth, and I never once told anyone about you, about us. Not once!

And even though I think you were an idiot for kissing him in the middle of everyone, it doesn't mean I want to keep… I don't…."

He stopped and swallowed. "I don't want to be mad at you anymore. Please come to the party. Nothing will happen. I swear!"

I gave him a few seconds to add anything else, but he didn't. "I'll think about it," I said curtly. "Anything else?"

There was a ton more he wanted to say. I could tell from the way he hesitated, but expressing his feelings through long, drawn-out speeches was not one of Kelly's strong points. He shifted from one foot to the other as he struggled with something to say. "You looked good out there," he said finally, gesturing toward the field.

"Anything else?" I repeated.

He moved away from the door. "No. Thanks for listening."

I rushed inside, partly because I was freezing now and partly because the feeling that someone was going to rush out of the shadows at me wouldn't go away. Coach Gunn was standing at the door of his office. "You coming, Graymark, or what?"

I squashed the feeling and rushed into his office so I could change before he kicked me out of the gym.

Kyle

WHEN I got up this morning, I had no idea I would go off on an adventure with my boyfriend's ex, but here I was. She owned a sky-blue Accord that fit her the same way that Brad's car fit him. It was cute yet practical, flashy but not so much it distracted from the car itself. It was incredibly girly but at the same time, I liked it a lot.

Until Taylor Swift came screaming out of her speakers.

It isn't that I don't like T-Swizzle, but no one liked it at 9,000 decibels.

She lunged for the radio, accidentally hitting the windshield controls with her elbow at the same time her seat belt, triggered by the driver's side door closing, tried to wrap itself around her. For a moment, her car looked like it was trying to swallow her, and I just had to laugh out loud at the image. She spun to look at me quickly, I think she was checking to see if I was making fun of her, but when she saw half the things on her car going off, she started to chuckle too.

"Some days I think this car is out to get me," she admitted after she turned off the windshield wipers.

"It's nice, though," I said, wishing I had a car, any car.

"Yeah, it's great until your grades start to suck. Then your dad threatens you with it. Then it's an albatross around your neck." I tried not to look shocked that she even knew that reference but obviously was pretty bad at it. She gave me a small smile and said, "Yeah, I've read a book or two."

"Actually it's a poem. But still, nice use."

She turned the music up louder. "Okay, you're smart. I get it. No one likes a show-off."

I was still laughing when we pulled out of the parking lot.

As she turned onto First Street, I pointed to the radio. "I love this song!"

She nodded in agreement. "She has the best breakup songs on earth!"

And suddenly I felt like shit again.

I didn't say anything for, like, two songs. She didn't notice until we drove up to the light at East Avenue. "You got quiet," she said, turning the music down.

"You must have really hated me," I said, wishing I was anywhere else but here.

"'Cause of Brad?" she asked. I nodded. "No, I hated him; you, I didn't know. And once I did, I felt sorry for you."

That made my head spin. "Why would you feel sorry for me?"

She shrugged. "Because I assumed Brad would be with you like he was with me, and I had to feel sorry for anyone going through that."

Okay, not feeling so bad now and moving toward annoyed. "Go through what?" I asked in a voice that was harsher than I meant.

She must have caught the hint because she quickly added, "No! I meant the way he and I treated each other. We were horrible when we were together. In fact, when I saw you guys together, I realized how wrong I was."

And now on to confused. "I don't understand."

She pulled over, parking in front of a small thrift store I'd never been in before. I waited for her to turn the car off and think her words out. "Brad and I dated each other because we were supposed to. When he was a freshman, he ended up hitting this home run that won an important game, and suddenly, he was the most popular guy in the world. My friends told me I had to go out with him, not because I liked him, but because I was *supposed* to." She took a deep breath, and I felt sorry for her. "We didn't so much date as we used each other as accessories. I was a pretty girl to take to parties, and he was a cute boy to walk around school with. And I really think we hated each other for it."

"Did you know about him?" I asked softly.

"That he liked guys?" she more asked herself than me. "Not really. Well… most guys who play sports are always all over each other after three beers. Every party I've ever been to has ended up with two or three guys on the ground wrestling each other for no real reason, so he wasn't gayer than anyone else. But I'll be honest; even when he's with you, he doesn't seem gay."

I felt my chest seize up as she began to voice all my inner fears out loud.

"Oh, that was shitty of me to say. I'm sorry, I'm new to all this. I meant that neither one of you seems like the gay I've been exposed to."

"What kind of gay have you met?"

She smiled. "That's why I brought you here." Now I was confused all over again.

"But to answer your first question, no, I am not mad at him or you anymore."

"But you were." That wasn't a question.

Her sigh pretty much said it all. "Of course I was, but I'm trying not to be." And then she gave me that thousand-watt smile, and it was easy to believe she was the best-looking girl in this town.

She had that same aura of believability Brad had when she talked. There was a quality about her that made you want to like her, and it was easy to see how the two of them made a couple. But I knew how much of Brad's façade was complete crap, so I wondered how much of hers was just as insincere. "Did you really drop a bucket of Coke on him?" I asked, smiling a little.

She covered her mouth, but she barked out a laugh before she could suppress it. "One of those huge cups they sell at the Vine!" she confirmed. "He looked like a drowned rat."

That image made me laugh with her.

"And then I threw his ring at his head, and it bounced off across the lobby." Her voice was getting higher as she began to laugh more and more.

I held up my hand. "This one?"

She nodded as she struggled for breath. "There was no blood on it when he gave it to you? Because I chucked that thing at him pretty hard."

It shouldn't have been funny, but it was. It was part imagining cock-of-the-walk Brad Graymark getting dowsed with a Coke and then hit in the head with a ring by a girl, and part having someone else to talk to about this stuff. Sitting there in her car, it became painfully obvious to me that I had no other friends, period, much less ones I could talk to about being gay.

How sad was that?

"God, it's nice to be able to laugh about that with someone," she said once we could talk and breathe again. "All my friends just start trash-talking Brad every time he comes up, and that gets old fast."

The most popular girl in the school didn't have anyone to talk to? She had more friends on Facebook than I had ever even seen in real life. It was surreal to think someone with that many people wanting to be near her would have trouble finding someone to talk to. I couldn't put it into words, but I felt the world shift beneath me when my horizons widened a bit. I realized things were tough all over.

"Okay, enough of that," she said, dispelling the mood instantly. "Come on." She gestured for me to follow her as she got out of the car.

Again, I had no idea what we were doing.

I guess the store would be considered more consignment than thrift, but it was all the same in my mind. It was a place where you bought other people's shit. I honestly had never once thought about shopping at a place like this, no matter how financially challenged I was. I followed her, but I was concerned why someone like her would be in a place like this. The store was called Twice Upon a Time. A small bell rang in the back when we walked in.

I will admit, I expected it to smell like a thrift store, that weird stale smell that made walking into them as unappealing as possible. Instead, it smelled just like any other store downtown.

Well, downtown in a real town.

A skinny guy stood behind the counter. He was thirtyish or so, maybe older. His thinning hair made it pretty clear he wasn't young but by no means was he old.

Oh yeah, and he was gay. Like obviously gay.

Damn, I know that sounds bad, so let me back it up some. See, the only way you can be gay in Foster is by not giving any indication of it whatsoever. Jeremy was the only openly gay guy our age I knew, and he got trashed constantly over it. If anything, he was the cautionary tale why you never showed any gay traits to anyone at all. So when I see someone as gay as this guy, every alarm goes off in my lizard brain. He is in danger and dangerous to me, so my first impulse is to think it's negative, when it isn't. Don't like my reaction? Blame evolution and millions of years of being eaten by bigger things. I'm trying to get over it.

I really am. He knew Jennifer, since he called out to her across the store. "Girl! You did not cut that hair!" He didn't exactly shriek, but from the inflection in his voice, he obviously gave no fucks who knew he was gay.

Jennifer cupped the back of her hair as she struck a pose like a model. "You like?"

He eased around the end of the counter, and I saw he was wearing the skinniest pair of black jeans I had ever seen on a person before. He wore a pair of steel-toed boots made of black leather that just screamed "I am not from Foster!" I know I am harping on this, but I had never seen an actual gay adult this close before.

"You bitch!" he said, walking around her in a circle to see the whole haircut at once. "I would kill for locks like this."

"You would look horrible as a blond!" she said, swatting his hands playfully.

"I hate you," he replied, laughing. "So what brings you into my domain of your own free will?"

"Dracula," I blurted out before I could stop myself. They both looked over at me, and it felt like a spotlight was thrown down on me from on high. "That's from Bram Stoker's *Dracula*," I said, trying to explain myself.

"Oh look, this year's model is out," he said with a smirk on his face.

I felt myself begin to slowly sink into the floor.

"Be nice. He is still adjusting, and I don't want you to warp him before he has a chance to live."

She put her arm around my shoulder. "Robbie, this is Kyle, Kyle, this is an old drag queen."

"Fuck off, Mean Girls Barbie." He moved over to me with a hand extended. "I'm Robbie; pleased to meet you, Kyle."

I shook it and mumbled a "Hi" under my breath.

"Oh, and he blushes!" he exclaimed, laughing.

"Ignore him," Jennifer whispered, knowing Robbie could hear us. "That part of the brain that allows people to edit what comes out of their mouth was killed long ago by alcohol poisoning, so just nod and pretend to be nice."

"Nod and pretend to be nice," he said, sounding shocked. "Don't you have that tattooed somewhere on you?"

She flipped him off, and they both laughed.

"So seriously, what are you looking for today?" he asked, gesturing to the displays behind him.

"Well, the Party is this weekend, so I need something that doesn't look like a laundry bag." She looked over to me. "What are you going to wear?"

I paused, not sure what she was asking for a moment. "To the party?" I asked, not putting the emphasis on the words. She nodded. "Clothes?"

"And show me something to make him look cute," she said, turning back to him.

"Well, he already has that covered," Robbie said, heading toward a rack of blouses. "You look through here and see if you can find something that doesn't make you look like a total bitch." He gave her a small grin. "I'd suggest something that covers your face."

"I hope you die in a fire," she said, pushing him out of the way.

"You," he said, pointing at me. "Come with me."

I looked over at her, and she nodded. "Go ahead, he's all bark."

I followed him to the other side of the store, where the men's clothes were. "So what is your style? Preppie? Hick?" He gave me a look over. "You are rocking that whole nerd thing something fierce. You want to go with that?"

I shrugged, not knowing what he was talking about. What was my *style*? Did I even have a style? I put on clothes and hoped they didn't fall off in front of people; that summarized my thoughts about clothes.

He took my silence as an answer, I guess.

"Okay," he said, looking back at the racks. "Let's just build on what we already have." He flipped through a few shirts before pulling out a white shirt with thin blue stripes. "Hmm—let's start with this." He handed it to me and then walked over to another rack and pulled out a black vest with a gray back on it. "With this." I grabbed it too, as he walked over to some pants. "And then let's go with some slacks…." He looked at me again and then back to the pants. "You're what, a twenty-eight waist?"

"How did you know that?" I asked, shocked.

"It's one of my superpowers," he said, pulling out a nice pair of pleated black slacks. "And these." He put them over my arm with the rest of the clothes. "Okay, so go try them on."

"Here?" I asked, forcing myself not to stammer.

"No, as I do not like teenage boys stripping down in my store. Because of that, we have dressing rooms." He nodded to the back of the store.

"Oh," I said, feeling stupid now. "All of them?"

He laughed. "Well, yes, they are meant to be worn together, but that's up to you."

I wasn't sure what to do. My first instinct was to tell him there was no way I could afford any of these clothes, but that sounded so pathetic I could have cried. I half shuffled toward the dressing room, and when I hesitated, he shooed me into motion again. "Well, they aren't going to try themselves on."

I had no argument for that and went inside the room.

I put the clothes down on the small shelf and wondered if I put them on, would I have to buy them? I'd never really had to try on clothes before; my mom knew what size I wore and just bought me clothes at the start of the year. She knew I didn't much care how I looked in them, therefore she didn't much care. Apathetic though it was, our system had served me well for the last few years, so I was reluctant to change it now.

Of course, I had never been to an actual party before either.

Well, that's not true. The one and only party I had gone to was when I was in the first grade and went to Ed Herget's sixth birthday party. I showed up late because my mom had overslept. Of course we had not bought him a gift yet, so we ended up at Value Giant trying to find the cheapest action figure they had. We didn't have time to go home and wrap it, so Mom tossed it in a gift bag and took off out of the parking lot like a bat out of hell. By the time I showed up, they had already broken open the piñata and were in the process of giving gifts. I was so embarrassed by the whole thing I ate half a piece of cake and then asked my mom to take me home.

When I looked back on that day, I noticed that Ed didn't say anything about the toy. I was too young to be aware if anyone was shocked by my mother, yet I remember being horribly embarrassed. How weird is that? It's like I didn't even need a reason to be ashamed, I could do it all on my own.

And did that guy really say I was cute?

I took my pants off and was in the process of pulling the new ones on when there was a knock.

"You still breathing in there?" Robbie asked from the other side.

I slammed myself against the door so it couldn't open. "Don't come in!" I screamed, one hand clutching the pants like they were a life preserver.

Silence fell on the other side in the wake of my hysteria, and then I heard him say in an overly formal tone, "Just let me know when you're done."

I tried to catch my breath before I pulled the pants all the way up. I hauled the shirt on over my T-shirt and buttoned it up. I wasn't sure if I was supposed to tuck the tail in or not, but I was thinking not. The pants were tighter than the ones I normally wore, and I understood why Brad didn't like skinny jeans. The vest went on last and easiest. When I was done I felt like I was wearing a straitjacket, there were so many clothes. The urge to rip them off came to mind, but instead I opened the door and walked out slowly.

Robbie leaned with his back against the wall across from the dressing room, texting someone. At first he didn't even look over at me and just started to ask, "So everything fit all right?" and then turned toward me. "Oh my" were his only words. Shoving the phone in his pocket, he faced me and looked me up and down. "Well, that is one way to wear it," he said quietly. The sarcasm in his words practically dripped from his mouth. "Can I try?" he asked, holding his hands up to the vest.

I nodded, trying not to gulp.

As he buttoned the vest, he said in a quiet voice, "Look, you're the one who stole her moose, right?"

I just stared at him, dumbfounded.

"Her boyfriend, Archie? You're the one who finally got the purse out of his mouth, right?"

"Brad?"

He sighed and said like he was a caveman, "You gay? You like the pee-pee?" I nodded, my stomach cramping up. I was so stressed. "And you have to be from Foster, right?" Another nod. "Okay, then let me give you some free advice. What I have been doing is called being nice. It can also be interpreted as flirting by some people. Flirting is, to most people, a compliment. Complimenting you makes me social and a pleasant guy to be around." He buttoned the top button of the vest and then smoothed the front down. "What it doesn't make me is some lecherous child molester who breaks into dressing rooms to cop a feel from a high school kid. I'd expect that from some of these hicks, but from a fellow Mo, it's insulting."

I felt like I was going to throw up.

"So next time, take the compliment or tell me to fuck off. But don't act like I have a windowless van out back with your name on it, okay?" He smiled at me, but I could tell he was pissed.

"I'm sorry," I said quietly.

"I know you are, and it's adorable on you," he replied, turning me around to face the mirror. "Now look, Cinderella, you're ready for the ball." I began to tell him I hated fairy tales, but I stopped when I saw my reflection.

I honestly did not recognize myself in the mirror.

"Wow" was all I could say. The vest made me look super skinny, which would have sucked, but the shirt helped make my chest stand out so I didn't look like I was seven. The pants actually hugged my legs so they weren't just huge, shapeless blobs that ended in my sneakers. At first I couldn't describe it, but then it hit me. I looked my age for once.

"See?" he said over my shoulder. "That was what I was complimenting you on earlier." I honestly couldn't talk. "So take them off so we can ring you up."

That got my tongue working in a flash. "I can't afford these!" I said quickly. "I live at the end of East Avenue in trash apartments, and my mom would kill me if I asked her for clothes I was only buying to wear to a party!" I was horrified that I was saying all this out loud, but once my mouth opened, I couldn't stop. "I didn't even want to go to this stupid party, but my boyfriend wants to, bad, and I don't want to go and make him look like an idiot, which is what I'll do if I dress normal!" I leaned up against the dressing room wall. "I wish I was dead!"

Robbie waited for me to draw breath and then asked, "You done?" I nodded as I forced myself not to cry. "Okay, good. Look, if you don't want to go to this party, then don't go. It's that simple. And if your boyfriend is embarrassed to be out with you unless you're dressed to suit him, he is an idiot."

"It's not like that," I tried to explain. "It's just Brad lost everything because of me, and I know he wants to get some of it back, and if I go to this party dressed like a reject, then everyone is going to look at him and go, 'He went gay for that? Ugh!' I couldn't take that." He stood there staring at me for a long time. Finally he asked, "You have a job?"

"Like a paying job?" I asked stupidly.

"If you ain't getting paid, it's not a job. Yeah, that kind of job." I shook my head. "Look, I need someone to help go through inventory and pricing. How about you start after school and work off those clothes, and if you work out, we can move on to an actual paycheck. Sound good?"

"You're offering me a job?" I blurted in amazement.

He paused and then raised one eyebrow. "I was under the impression you were smart for around here. Clearly that was fake news. Didn't I just offer you a job?"

"That would be wicked!" I said, overjoyed.

"Calm down, newbie. It's a job as a stock clerk, not a slot on *American Idol*. Take those off so I can ring them up. Can you start Monday?" I nodded quickly. "And tell no one I did this, or my reputation as a bitch would be ruined."

"Thank you!" I said. Overcome with emotion, I hugged him.

"Oh, see? Now this, this is sexual harassment," he remarked, not hugging me back. "Get off me before people think I'm molesting you back here."

"Sorry," I said, letting go of him.

"Oh jeez," he groaned, rolling his eyes. "It's a joke, Kyle. You are going to need to learn how to take that stick out of your ass or you'll drop dead at thirty." He turned to walk away. "Now get in there and change. Shoo!"

I looked at myself in the mirror again.

"Can I wear them now?" I asked, praying.

He shrugged. "Wear them all you want, they're not mine." And he walked away.

He was right; they were mine. I owned actual clothes.

Brad

WHEN I came down off my baseball high, I realized today's practice wasn't the worst I've had, but it was easily in the bottom ten.

I had been so distracted by everything going on that I would have caught more fly balls sitting in the stands than I did out on the field. Thankfully, we were on the last week before Christmas break, so everyone sucked equally, but I knew I was sucking for completely different reasons than the rest of the guys. I waited in the coach's office for the showers to open up, another way my life had changed since Kyle. My whole gym experience had gained about twenty minutes on either side since I had to change out in the coach's office beforehand and then wait after practice for the showers to open up so I could rinse myself off and not head out smelling like a dirty sock.

I wondered every day what they thought I was going to do differently than I had for the past ten years.

Coach Gunn came into his office and jerked a thumb toward the shower. "All yours. Hurry it up. I want to get out of here."

I forced myself not to point out that if he was so damn stressed about time, he could have saved a good half hour by letting me shower like a regular person, but I refrained since it would fall on deaf ears. As I soaped up, I wondered if Kyle would be out there waiting for me. It was an odd thought because before today, I had never worried about it. I would come out, and he would be leaning against my car like he had always been there. I was sad for a moment because if he wasn't there, I had no idea what to do. Should I go home? Should I go to his house? I used to have a life where I did whatever I wanted, but now it was all different shades of Kyle, and I didn't want that to change.

Of course, those thoughts led to the future and what happened after high school, but that was too terrifying to contemplate, and I shoved them away as fast as I could.

"Quit stroking and move it, Graymark!" the coach shouted from the locker room. I quickly finished up and changed into my street clothes. I left the locker room with my duffel bag over one shoulder, Coach Gunn right behind me, ready to lock up. As we walked out into the dying afternoon sun, he warned, "And don't think I didn't notice you wandering around like a zombie on the field today. If you want them to take your threat seriously, you need to play as good as I know you can."

I froze, not sure what I just heard. Slowly I turned to look at him, and he gave me the ghost of a smile. "You have to do better if you want to prove to them you're worth listening to."

"Yes, sir," I replied in a low voice.

"Get out of here," he ordered gruffly, but I could see he wasn't really mad.

I turned to my car, and I honestly caught my breath as I saw Kyle standing there.

He held up his arms and asked with a smile, "How do I look?"

He looked fucking incredible.

Now before I get ahead of myself, let me state I was the head of the Kyle Stilleno is Hot fan club. His baggy pants and oversized T-shirts drove me crazy. They went with his shaggy hair and clown-sized Converse shoes, making him look like a cartoon character sometimes. A hot, ridiculously cute, skater cartoon, but a cartoon nonetheless. But there he was, all dressed up in actual clothes, and let me tell you....

Oh, fuck it. I instantly threw wood.

He had on a pair of black slacks with a vest over a button-up shirt, the tails sticking out... I can't even describe it properly. He looked two years older and a thousand times hotter. He suddenly had a waist and a chest and... man, I am screwing this up something fierce.

He looked hot. Well, hotter than normal. Hotter than I could have imagined. I must have just stood there gaping, because his face got serious, and he asked in a halting voice, "You hate it, right?"

"I hate the clothes so much I want to rip them off your body," I said, rushing toward him. "You look *hot*!"

I saw him blush, and I knew he liked them too but would never admit it. I had spent most of our time together trying to convince Kyle how hot he was, and he always ignored me, but I could tell the way he wore these clothes that he liked them. A lot.

"Seriously?" he asked in a warning tone. "'Cause if you're just being nice, I swear I will get you back...."

I dropped my bag and scooped him into my arms. "If I toss you in the back seat and take you right now, would that be proof enough?"

He murmured a quiet "Shut up," but I felt him lean into me and hug me back.

"You really like it?" he asked after a few seconds of—oh hell, snuggling. There, I said it.

I nodded eagerly. "Smoking hot. What's the occasion?"

"Jennifer said I should have something to wear to the Party." His eyes got wide after a second, and he asked me, "Is it okay or too much?"

I hadn't even thought about what he would wear. Leave it to Jennifer to be three steps ahead of me when it came to social crap. The people who would be at the Party would tear Kyle apart if he showed up dressed like he normally did. I mean, I had no problem with his clothes, but baggy jeans and a worn T-shirt was not party apparel. I guess I could have lent him some of my stuff, but Kyle is way skinner than me, and they would have just looked like crap.

"They're perfect," I said and saw him hide his face in my chest again. "Do you like them?"

He looked up and nodded, his face exploding with a smile.

"Then that's all that counts." Which wasn't the truth, but it was close enough for this discussion. I didn't want Kyle's first introduction to an actual social life to be a room full of assholes laughing at his clothes. "You hungry?"

"Am I ever not hungry?" he replied with a grin.

"No, and I am still trying to figure out where it all goes," I said, squeezing his sides and waist, looking for mass.

"Brad, stop!" he cried out as my touches became tickles.

I hadn't seen him this happy… well, ever.

I took him to Nancy's. We found a booth in the back where we could sit together and no one would stare at us. Gayle, the waitress who had waited on us that first day we came there, was there as usual. She had taken a keen interest in us as a couple ever since she found out that had been our first date. She put a menu on the table and gave us a wide smile. "And what can I start you two lovebirds out with?" There was a thrill from hearing someone refer to Kyle and me as a couple in public that I couldn't deny.

"Coke and iced tea?" I said, checking Kyle to see if that was okay. He nodded, and I added, "And a huge plate of onion rings."

"Let me put that in while you guys figure out what you want for dinner." She took a few steps away from the table before turning back. "And I have to add, you're looking mighty sharp there with your vest." Kyle buried his face in my arm in response.

"He's shy about it. Tell him how good he looks in it," I said, teasing him.

"I almost didn't recognize him at first. Then I saw the hair and realized one of you dressed up for date night."

I waited for her to walk off before I whispered to him, "So, need any more proof? You're a bona fide hottie."

He peeked out to make sure we were alone. "Does it look that good?"

I leaned in toward him. "You are going to have to admit it," I said before my lips touched his. "You're officially cute."

I lost track of time while we were kissing because the next thing I knew, Gayle was clearing her throat. I looked over, and she was holding our drinks. "You guys coming up for air to eat, or you gonna make out all night?"

I began to answer "Make out," but Kyle ordered us two burgers before I could say anything.

"Coming right up," she said, taking our menus.

"You were going to say 'make out,'" he said, his voice just slightly louder than a whisper.

"Well, duh," I said, leaning in for another kiss.

It was rudely interrupted by a male's voice calling out, "Why in the fuck are those queers in here?"

Kyle pushed off of me in a flash as I turned to see what the drama was this time. Standing in the middle of the diner was Tony Wright's father. I hadn't said one word to Tony since he beat me down in the locker room. We kept our distance since there was nothing much to say. In fact, him standing behind his dad right now was the closest we had been since that day. I'd never noticed Mr. Wright before, but as he glared at us, I realized for the first time how big he really was. Where my dad had grown soft and fat, Mr. Wright looked like he was still a linebacker. His fists looked like shaved ape paws as they trembled at his sides.

I began to stand up, but Kyle's hand clasped on my jacket prevented me. I looked over at him. His eyes were wide with fear, and he shook his head very quickly.

"I'm talking to you two!" the man said, slamming his hand down on the table.

My head spun around as I readied myself to kick this old man's ass. I didn't have an idea how to do that since he was built like a brick house, but I was too mad to even care at this point. "What is your problem?" I asked, trying to keep my temper under control before I said something we would all regret.

"You are." He sneered at me. "You and your queer boyfriend here making everyone sick to their stomachs."

Tony pulled at his dad's sleeve again, and this time I could hear him. "Come on, Dad, let it go."

But Dad was not the least bit Elsa about this. In fact, Dad was doing the exact opposite of Elsa by looking over at Kyle and then to me. "No one wants to watch you and your fancy fag girlfriend kiss. You aren't welcome here!"

I pulled away from Kyle's grip and got to my feet. "But they allow you and your mutt in here without a leash; go figure!" I started toward him, and he pushed me with the palms of both hands. I was expecting King Kong over there to take a swing or something; the slap fight was straight out of a nine-year-old girl's playbook and caught me completely by surprise. I tumbled back onto the table but caught my balance quickly and came up ready to swing.

Which was when Gayle appeared out of nowhere.

I mean it. It was like watching *Bewitched.* One second she wasn't between us, and the next she was. I had never seen the older woman twitch her nose or anything, but from that point on, she was on the list as a possible witch. I towered over her, and Mr. Wright was even taller than I was, so when I say she was looking up at him, it isn't a joke. If she was aware of the size difference, it didn't show in her voice as she began to berate the man. "Lincoln Wright, you should be ashamed of yourself! What do you think you're doing?" You could visibly see the gears in the man's mind try to downshift as he looked at the wagging finger of the woman as she dressed him down. "Where do you get off coming in here harassing my customers?"

"Th-they're queer!" he cried out, as if even saying it out loud was a threat to his manhood.

"And you're an asshole, but I've served you for fifteen years," she shot back in a flash. "But that is about to change. Listen to your boy and get out of here. And never return."

She said it in the same tone that old guy in *Lord of the Rings* said "You shall not pass." I mean, I think I heard echoes and everything.

Mr. Wright just stood there in slack-jawed shock for several seconds.

"And shame on you, Tony!" she said to the now cowering figure behind his dad. "Of all people, you want to come in here and start something?"

Tony looked like he was going to puke. Luckily his dad covered for him. "Don't talk to my boy! And you can't kick me out of here!"

"Oh, watch me, you homophobic piece of crap," she said, pointing a lone finger at him. "Do not ever come back in here again. Ever." She then looked around him and addressed the entire diner. "That goes for anyone else as well. This diner is a place couples have come and eaten since before most of you were born. In fact, looking at a few of you, I can tell you with some certainty if it wasn't for this diner, y'all wouldn't be here to bitch. I have never once stopped a couple from stealing a kiss now and then, and I am not going to start now."

She paused and looked right at Tony before continuing, "So if you are like this idiot and have a small mind when it comes to what makes a couple, then start eating somewhere else." She looked back at Mr. Wright. "What are you still doing here? Get out!" she barked at him.

"You're serious," he said numbly.

"In a second I am going to be past serious and move right on into pissed, and at that point I will go in the back, and when I come out, I will have my shotgun. Get. Out. And. Never. Return."

"Let's go, Tony," he said, not taking his eyes off of her. "I don't want to eat anywhere they'd serve queers."

"Then don't go over to the Rusty Kettle, because Paul has a gay nephew, and he won't serve you after I call." Gayle began listing off places on her fingers. "And I suggest finding breakfast somewhere other than Joanne's because her brother is gay, and she will spit in your coffee as you watch once she hears about this." With every place she mentioned, his eyes grew wider and wider in outrage. "And Bobby Richards has a gay brother-in-law, and once I tell his wife what an asshole you are, I will put money on the next time you pull up into Starr's, you'll get your car keyed. So good luck with that."

"Fucking bitch," he said under his breath as he made his way to the door.

She took one step toward him and he took a step back. "Call me that to my face."

Mr. Wright took another half step back and said loudly, "Well then, fuck this place!"

Someone in the back of the restaurant shouted, "Get the fuck out, asshole!" which got some people laughing and then clapping. By the time he slammed the door behind them, the entire place was clapping and hollering at him as he got into his car out front.

"Can we go, please?" I heard Kyle ask softly behind me. I turned with a smile, about to ask him why, since these people were so obviously on our side.

The front of his vest was soaked with both of our drinks.

He looked like he was about to start crying when he added, "I haven't even paid for it yet…."

"Do you want me to get a towel or something?" I asked as I turned toward Gayle, who was making sure Mr. Wright was truly gone.

"Brad, please," he said, on the verge of losing it. "I just want to go."

I slipped off my jacket and handed it to him as he got out of the booth. "Okay, come on." He huddled into it, trying to cover the fact it looked like he had said "I don't know" on a Nickelodeon show. Gayle saw us walking past her. "You boys don't have to leave," she said, concerned.

"That was epic," I said to her as Kyle hurried out. "Thank you."

She looked at Kyle, who made a beeline to my car. "He okay?"

I nodded. "He doesn't do well with attention," I said, opting out of explaining that his new clothes were ruined.

Her face got serious for a moment. "Tell him he's not the first person Lincoln Wright has attacked before and he won't be the last. This wasn't about Kyle—"

"I know that," I said, cutting her off, "and I'll try to tell him."

She just smiled. "Go on, see if he's okay."

I gave her a hug; it was nice to know there were some people on our side. "Thank you, Gayle. You rock."

I took off after Kyle, hoping I could make him feel better.

Kyle

I HUDDLED in his car, miserable.

I could say I was mortified, but honestly, the word was not strong enough to convey how horrible I felt at the moment. I was heading into a panic attack, so I began to list all the different ways I could say how I felt. Abased. Abashed. Belittled. Disgraced. Humiliated. Ridiculed. Shamed.

"You know," my feeling of impending doom said from the back seat, "sometimes I told you so isn't a strong enough phrase to convey how much *I told you so*!"

I winced from the shout.

"What did I say?" my newly resurfaced pessimism remarked. "Don't do this. Don't come out. Don't let people see you. And what happened when they saw you?"

I sat silent.

"They hated you!" my ego, pleased at being right, screamed. Brad slid into the driver's seat.

"You okay?" he asked. I knew he was concerned, but he had asked the stupidest question I had ever heard in my life.

"Oh, he's peachy," my sarcasm answered, sticking its head forward. "You told him things were going to be okay, and things are not okay." It looked at me. "You know this guy is making you dumber by the minute, right?"

"I just want to go home," I answered, trying to keep the thunderous chorus of voices from my sanity. I wasn't mad at Brad, but obviously parts of me were blaming him for this, so I kept my mouth shut before one of those assholes in my head said it for me.

"Kyle," he said softly, "you can't let people like that get to you. There are always—"

"*Take me home*!" I screamed. In my head there were scores of voices at once. I imagine if I had pulled a gun on him, he would have the exact same look on his face he did at that moment. Forcing my emotions down, I said, "Please, Brad, take me home."

Without another word, he drove me home.

If you are curious, my guilt was now sitting next to my horror at being exposed, telling me I was an asshole, because he hadn't done a thing to warrant it, but there was no way to stop myself. I felt like I was falling apart. Falling apart has always been something I did by myself. I didn't want him to see me cry because some pop got spilled on my fucking clothes. I mean, just saying it like that showed how stupid it was. I was going to cry because my clothes were wet? It wasn't about the clothes, and it wasn't about the embarrassment of some redneck humiliating me in public.

It was something worse than that.

"Do you want me to come in?"

I looked up, and we were in front of my house.

I shook my head and began to get out but stopped myself. I turned to him, and I could see the confusion and fear in his face. "I am not mad at you, and you didn't do anything wrong. I'm just broken."

I went to slide out of the car, and he grabbed my hand. "Then be broken with me," he pleaded.

I squeezed his hand back and then pulled away. "I can't right now, Brad. I'm sorry."

"Don't let Billy make this more than it is," he pleaded with me.

"More than it is?" a voice asked from my mouth. "More than it is?"

I scrambled to stop my mortification from speaking, but it was too late.

"That was literally my worst nightmare, Brad. No joke, literally being attacked in public for being gay was the exact reason I didn't talk to people for the past three years. Being verbally attacked, in a room full of people, that is what wakes me up in cold sweats at night.

So when you say don't make this more than it is, I assure you I am making this exactly what it is!"

He said nothing, because honestly, what was there to say?

"I'm sorry…," I began to explain and then just fled the car.

And then I ran into my house like a fucking fool wearing one glass slipper who knew in about ten seconds she'd be wearing a flour sack. My mom sat in the living room with some friends. I ignored them as I rushed into my room and slammed my door. I could imagine what my mom was saying. "Ignore my daughter; it's that time of the month."

I started to rip the clothes off.

"You know your dumb ass hasn't paid for them, right?" my personified sense of worthlessness and self-loathing asked.

If you're curious, it still looked like Billy Porter, except now he was dressed as Angela from *The Office*, cat and all. That shocked some sense into me, and I slowly took the clothes off before I tossed them into the corner. The vest was ruined; I was pretty sure the front was silk or something. The shirt was stained. I had no idea if it would come out, but I did know I couldn't bleach it or the stripes would fade. Finally I gave up and just left everything sitting there.

"It's like someone threw a bucket of water at you and all your little dreams melted," my cruelness commented.

Grabbing a towel, I ducked into the bathroom and turned on the shower.

I waited until the water was this side of scalding before crawling in. I sat in the tub and watched the pop drain out of my hair as the inevitable tears began to fall. So like I said before, it wasn't the clothes, and it wasn't the humiliation that drove me to cry. It was something much worse.

See, I cried because I should have known what had happened had been coming at me. None of it should have come as a surprise. This is what happened when I dared to be happy in my life. When I stuck my head out of my turtle shell and dared to smile, fate made sure to lay the smackdown to remind me I was not allowed a life like everyone else. Good things didn't happen to me, and that was for a reason. I wasn't allowed to be with a great guy without getting attacked at school for it, I couldn't own good clothes without them being ruined, and I wasn't meant to go to parties like normal kids were. Not me, that wasn't my lot in life.

It didn't matter if I got out of this town or if Brad and I ended up working out. I was always going to miserable because that was the only way life wanted me to be. As the water fell on me, I decided to just stop fighting it.

By the time I got out, my mom said Brad had called, and he was worried about me. I was too far into my funk to actually say anything. I fell into bed and hauled the covers over my head. I didn't care if I ever got up again. I fell asleep for a while and then heard my mom open my door, talking on the phone. "No, Brad, he's already asleep." Her voice faded away as she closed it behind her.

The next time I woke up, it was morning because the sun was streaming through my windows like the beginning of a fucking Disney movie. You know that really bright and aggressively cheerful sunlight that tries to get you to do dishes with cartoon bluebirds and shit? Yeah, well, that was what I saw when I poked my head out of my covers. Like every other Emo Teenage Groundhog in the world, I knew an overly cheery sun meant eighteen more years of misery. I promptly ducked back under the covers.

"Yeah," my self-loathing said with a smile, "you still suck." I jumped up and locked my door, and then I went back to my blanket coffin.

I woke up when my mom tried to open my door. She knocked twice. "Kyle, are you up?"

"Feel sick!" I yelled from under my covers. "Not going to school."

I could hear her sigh on the other side, but what could she say? I was acing all my classes, and before this whole gay thing, I had been a model student. If I wanted to cut a day or two, she really couldn't scream at me; I had a few banked by now. "Did you tell Brad that? Because he's outside waiting for you."

Fuck.

I threw on some clothes and unlocked my door. My mom stood there, and I could tell she was forcing herself not to laugh out loud at the way I looked. "Did you go to bed with wet hair?"

I touched the top of my hair and could feel most of it standing straight up. One look in the bathroom mirror showed me I looked more like a troll doll than I cared to admit. I threw water on my bedhead until it calmed down before walking to the front door. I swung it open and saw Brad leaning on his car with his phone in hand. He broke into a huge smile when he saw me walk out. When he saw I wasn't dressed, his smile broke.

"I'm not going," I said as he walked over to the door.

"Kyle!" he half whined. "Come on, you can't let them—"

I had heard this too many times already. You can't let Them get you down. You can't let Them win. You can't let Them make you the victim. I had heard every single motivational statement about being gay and not letting assholes do this and that to me, and I was sick of it. "I'm not letting them do anything," I said, cutting him off. My skin felt like it had been pulled too tight, I was so upset. I still wanted to scream out loud, I still wanted to break down and cry, and I didn't want to be having this conversation. "I just need a day off. One day to collect my thoughts."

"Well, then we take a day off," he said quickly.

"Alone."

Damn, I sounded like a dick.

"Please, Brad, I am in a foul mood, and if you were here, I would take it out on you, and I don't want to do that. Just let me be miserable for a day and I will be okay. I promise." He looked at me like his puppy had died, and it was killing me, but I knew how my mind worked. I was in the mood to beat myself up, and Brad wouldn't let me, which would lead to me beating *him* up. And neither one of us wanted that.

"It feels like you're mad at me," he said. His eyes were bright green, and he looked like he was on the verge of crying.

"I swear," I said, walking closer to him so I could hug him. "I am not at all mad at you. I am just in a mood." He cocked his head questioningly, and I kissed him on the cheek. "I just can't handle it today. Tomorrow I will be back bright and early, ready to be spit on and kicked and everything. Give me one day to lick my wounds, okay?"

He put his arms around me, and I felt a chill go through me as if the rest of the world faded away and it was the two of us alone in the middle of nowhere. And though I longed to stay safely under the Brad force field, I knew I had shit to work through in my head, so I took a half step back and gave him a smile. "I'm sorry I'm like this."

"I understand," he said miserably. "I wish you'd let me in, because you sitting here all day listening to Billy tear you apart isn't healthy."

He was right.

"I'll ignore him. Call me when you get out of practice," I said, backing toward the door, not wanting to turn away from him.

"Can I call you at lunch?" he asked, and it broke my heart.

I nodded. "Call me at lunch." I walked inside, hating the expression of abject sorrow on his face but knowing I was doing the right thing. He raised one hand to wave at me as I closed the door. As I leaned against it, I let out a sigh. That was the hardest thing I ever had to do.

"You wanna talk about it?" my mom asked after a few seconds.

I forced back the automatic sarcasm that came flooding to my mouth, because she was really trying to help. "No, I just want to sleep," I said, heading back to my room.

"What happened at the diner?" she asked to my back.

"Just another day in Foster!" I yelled as I slammed my door.

And that was how my day was supposed to end. Me falling into my bed and waiting for life to pass me by, at least this one day of it. But as with the best laid plans of mice and men… that didn't happen.

A little over an hour later, I heard the front door open and my mom talking to someone. I ignored it since her friends came over anytime they felt like it. But as I listened, the voices got closer and closer to my room until the door came swinging open.

Robbie stood there in the doorframe like a vampire waiting for permission to enter my room. My mom was right behind him, not looking anything close to happy. “He said he knows you,” she said.

“He knows me,” Robbie said, walking slowly into my room. “He just won’t admit it out loud.” He tossed my backpack off my chair and sat down like it was his personal throne, sitting exactly where Billy normally sat. “We’re good,” he said to my mom, clearly dismissing her.

“He’s okay,” I said to her before she exploded on him. She did not take her eyes off him as she closed the door.

“I am far more than okay, but we will let that one slide,” he said, looking around the room slowly. “I love what you’ve done with the place; postapocalyptic Target, right?”

I buried my head in my pillow. “What do you want?”

“What I want is another ten years of *Charmed* with the original cast, but we all know that isn’t going to happen.” He paused and then asked, “Is that what happened when you got a bucket of water thrown on you?”

“I’ve already done that joke,” I said miserably.

“Right, so this is what happened at Nancy’s?”

I sat up. “What did you hear?”

“I heard there was an asshole at the diner, and Gayle almost shot him. So what, did he throw something at you?”

“I really don’t want to talk about it,” I pleaded with him.

“Did he spit at you? Try to hit you?” he kept asking.

“Please, just drop it.”

“Did he try to drag you into the middle of the street and tie you to the back of his car?” His tone had not changed a bit. The same kind of sarcastic, conversational tone he’d had when we talked in the store still was there, but there was a new coldness under it. I stared up at him, and he sat, expressionless, watching me. “Did he try to tie you to a fence and throw rocks at your head while he made you recite the Lord’s Prayer?” I shook my head slowly. “Then I guess it wasn’t that bad a day, was it?” He stood up, walked over to the heap in the corner, and kicked at the clothes. “Get up, get dressed, and meet me outside.”

He paused before he opened the door. "And put the clothes in a bag or something."

"I am not in the mood to go anywhere," I told him.

"Oh good. Because I didn't ask you," he replied. "Five minutes. Then I *am* throwing water into your bed." He closed the door, then opened it again. "That was not a joke." And he was gone.

"What the fuck?" I asked myself as I got out of bed. I had no idea what had happened beyond the fact that I was confused.

In less than five minutes I was outside, carrying the ruined clothes in a plastic grocery bag.

He stood smoking in front of a lime-green VW bug with the top down. Normally I would have said a lime-green any kind of car would be extremely gay, but somehow the bug worked for him. He offered me the pack in his other hand. "You smoke?"

"Uh, no," I answered, waving them off.

"Good, don't start. They are an ugly, ugly habit." He tossed his cigarette away and got into the car. I got into the passenger seat, although I had no idea where we were heading. He turned off the loud house music that had started the minute he turned the key in the ignition. "Buckle up," he ordered as he backed the car out of its parking space. "This is the only neon green car people can't seem to see coming a mile away. Already been in two accidents in it. I'm just waiting for the front end to fall off one day."

I slowly put the seat belt on as I examined the car's structural integrity.

We headed left on East Avenue, traveling farther out of Foster instead of toward downtown. "Where are we going?" I asked after a few minutes.

"To the past," he answered cryptically and lit another smoke.

"I doubt you can get this thing over eighty-eight miles an hour," I mumbled, looking out the window.

"That's cute, McFly. Very topical," he said, turning the music back on. "I speak fluent nerd."

I settled in and stopped talking.

My thoughts began to wander as I waited for us to end up wherever we were going. If you'd asked me if I would end up driving in the car of a guy I had just met to the surface of Mars, I would have told you no way. But here I was trusting someone based on nothing more than the word of my boyfriend's ex-girlfriend that the guy driving was to be trusted.

"Hey," I said, sitting up suddenly. "Tell me about Jennifer."

He gave me a quick glance to see if I was joking. "What about her?" he asked cautiously.

"Why doesn't she hate me?" I asked, getting to the heart of the matter.

He laughed at that. "Oh, she did. Trust me. She hated you both something fierce."

"So then why the one-eighty?"

He paused for a moment. "You mean three-sixty."

"No, if she did a three-sixty, she'd end up in the same place she started. A one-eighty is ending up facing the opposite way," I explained to him.

He did a slow double take and then shook his head. "You really are a complete brain, aren't you?" I nodded but prompted him to continue. "Well, she was obviously thrown by the whole 'My boyfriend is now gay' thing, but I talked her down from climbing a water tower."

I didn't get the reference, but I figured it out enough to know she had been mad. "What did you say?"

He kept his eyes on the road as he began to explain. "I told her that in towns like Foster, being gay was akin to being a vampire, and not the sparkly kind. Which means you hide yourself deep underground or risk a pack of villagers trying to hunt you down with pitchforks and torches to burn you alive."

I was about to comment on the fact he mixed his Dracula metaphor up with Frankenstein, but in the end, a monster was a monster.

"So I explained to her that if Brad had the guts to come out in front of everyone, then the least she could do is try to imagine what it must have been like to force himself to be something he wasn't for so long. When she didn't like that, I told her to imagine she had to pretend to like girls for the past eighteen years and see how she felt about it."

I was equally impressed and humbled that he had our back even before he knew us.

"So why haven't I ever heard of you before?" It was something that had been bugging me since Jennifer introduced us. I was under the impression that there were no gay guys in Foster at all. Yet here was what could politely be referred to as an openly gay person, and yet he had never been mentioned before.

He glanced once and then again at me like he was waiting for me to add something else onto my question. "Okay, really?" he asked. "You really want to ask that?" I nodded, and he sighed. "Well, let's count down the reasons, shall we? One, because the world does not start and end in Foster High. There is a lot going on in this town that doesn't get mentioned during study hall. Two, it isn't exactly like you have your finger on the gay pulse of North Texas, so the fact you have never heard of me before isn't as shocking as you make it sound. And three, I keep mainly to myself when I'm in town. Hanging out on Second Street getting wasted at the Rodeo Club is not my idea of a good time." He looked over at me. "That cover it?"

"Do you know Tyler Parker?" I asked, and his expression immediately went sour.

"Pick another question. I am not answering that one." It was the first time I heard real anger in his voice.

"Wait. Tyler is pretty cool. What's wrong with him?" Which, of course, was the absolute wrong thing to ask.

"Tyler Parker is not the handsome, all-American man he looks like. He is not the awww shucks guy who sits in his little shop and sings for true love. Tyler Parker is a blight. He is a leftover plague from when God cursed the Egyptians. He is a polyester jumpsuit on a summer day, he is the last season of *Game of Thrones*, and if there is a thing called karma in the universe, he will get hit crossing the street while the whole town watches." He raised his knee up to steer as he lit another cigarette. When the car weaved a little, I reached over and steadied it.

"Why do you hate him so much?" I said as he flicked his ashes out the window.

He gave me a quick glance. "Hate is such a small word for what I feel."

"He stood up for Brad at the school board meeting."

"And who paid him to do that?"

"He came with my mom, but he wanted to help."

"Yeah, by invoking a name that should burn his tongue whenever it leaves his mouth," he muttered.

"Who?"

"Drop it," he said pitching the butt out the window. "Tyler Parker only cares about one thing, his dick. If something can't get fucked, find someone for him to fuck, or knows someone he can fuck, it doesn't matter to him, and he will slit your throat in a second if you let him." He kept staring at the road. "And close your mouth. You look like a damn fish."

I closed my mouth and decided not to say another word.

We ended up out in the middle of nowhere, which is a feat since most of Foster was nowhere to begin with. On a stretch of road that went even farther nowhere stood a little dive bar. It looked like every other dive bar within fifty miles of Foster—all wood, no windows, more like a chicken coop with delusions of grandeur. Weeds pocked the dry, dull dirt all around and made the bar even uglier. I almost choked when he pulled into the "parking lot."

"Did you bring me out here to harvest my kidney or something?" I asked, half joking.

He gave me a half grin to match my half joke, I had a feeling. "I bet other people find that sarcastic wit just oh so cute." He turned off the car. "I am not other people."

"You show up, practically kidnap me, and bring me to what I think every serial killer's hideout looks like, and I am not supposed to wonder?" I shot back, slamming my door. "So far I am the dumb blond in every horror movie I've ever seen."

He spun on me with a passion that shocked me out of my funk. "Look, you want to live in New York or West Hollywood and have that attitude, great. But until then, try to remember you live in Mayberry, and that means not everything is nice and shiny like you see on *Queer as Folk*. So before you start throwing around attitude, learn a little history first. Got it?" I wasn't sure what had pissed him off so much, but I nodded nonetheless.

I really was going to lose a kidney.

He stalked around back and knocked on the door, which looked like the kitchen exit, with a few trash cans and empty crates. "If you can't say anything nice, do me a favor and just fake it, okay?" he asked quietly. I nodded again, still not sure what I had stumbled into. Robbie pounded again.

A few seconds later, the door half opened, and I could see an older man's face peeking out. "Robbie?" he asked in shock. "What the hell you doing out here so early?"

"Guided tour," he quipped, jerking a thumb at me.

The old guy looked at me. "He's new." He closed the door, undid the chain, and opened it all the way. "Well, come in, if you're coming."

We walked into a small diner-style kitchen with a stove on one side and an industrial dishwasher on the other. As soon as the door closed, I took a look at the guy who had let us in and almost choked when I saw the rifle in his hand. He explained as he reracked it by the door, "Sorry 'bout that. Can't be too careful when someone comes knocking this early."

"Tom, this is Kyle," Robbie said to the man.

"Howdy, Kyle." He put out a huge paw of a hand. "Welcome to the Bear's Den."

I looked around the small kitchen as I shook his hand and asked, "This is what, now?"

He laughed and led me through the kitchen with a hand on my back. "This is where we make what little food we serve." We passed through two swinging doors, like the ones in an old Western saloon, and walked into a huge bar. A pool table stood in the corner, there was a jukebox, and between the table and the jukebox, a space had been cleared out to make a small dance floor as well. What caught my eye, though, were the pictures on the wall. There had to have been a hundred of them. The first—and from their sepia tones, the oldest—ones were black-and-white and grainy, while others were Polaroids and 35mm. The newest were digital photos printed out from a computer. They were all guys, almost all of them were young, and they all had a slightly bewildered look on their face.

I turned around to ask what they had in common, when a flash from a camera blinded me.

"What the…?" I said, rubbing my eyes.

"That's a keeper!" I heard Tom say with an evil laugh.

"A little warning next time!" I said as I squinted, trying to kill the afterimages.

"That's not the tradition," Robbie said when my eyes cleared a bit. "First-timers always get their picture taken." He pointed at a photo a couple of years old. A younger Robbie and a stupid hot guy next to him stared out from the picture. They both looked like deer caught in the headlights. "That was my first night here," he said with a wistful tone. "And you know him, of course?" he asked sarcastically, pointing to another picture. It was Tyler. He couldn't have been more than a year older than Brad in the picture.

"Wow, he was hot," I said out loud.

"Who's that?'" Tom asked from behind the bar.

"Fucking Tyler," Robbie called back to him.

"Yeah, he was a little stuck-up when he first came in here, but he grew out of it." I could hear a printer going off.

"My ass he did," Robbie muttered under his breath.

"So this is a gay bar?" I asked, trying to change the subject. I began looking around in wonder, trying to take the place in.

"No. This is *the* gay bar. Only gay bar for almost eighty-five miles," Robbie said with some pride. "Trust me, when you're gay, places like this are like gold." I didn't know about that. It seemed a little run-down to be gold. I didn't say anything, but he could see the look on my face. He held up one finger, reminding me of my promise. I nodded and tried to look neutral.

"And done," Tom said, holding up a piece of photo paper. On it was a picture of me, looking half-stoned. "Welcome to the club," he said, pinning it to the wall.

It seemed like a moment for him, so I smiled and said, "Thanks."

His laugh was so loud it seemed to fill the entire room. "They're all the same at first, aren't they?" he asked Robbie.

"I wasn't any better," Robbie admitted.

"No, but you made up for it."

I still had no idea what was going on.

"I still have no idea what's going on," I said out loud. "You wanted to show me a wall of photos?"

"Yeah," Robbie said. "But not that wall, this one." He led me over to the wall across from it.

It was a wall full of funeral notices.

Some were from the actual service; others were cut out from the newspaper. It wasn't the fact that there was a wall of dead people smiling out at me. It was that there were twice as many death notices as welcome photographs. I walked up to the wall, and I began to skim the articles one by one. Some were hospital deaths, AIDS-related kind of stuff; others were just random accidents like car crashes and the like.

The majority of them were assaults.

Robbie stood behind me and pointed. "He was stabbed, beaten, and then lit on fire." His voice was thick with emotion. "They followed him home from a party and attacked him." He pointed to another one. "He was attacked by two guys in a car. They beat him with a baseball bat, and once he tried to fight back, they tried to pull him into their car, closed the door on his arm, and dragged him for over a block before they let his body go." He pointed to another one. "This one was jumped, and they took him—"

I pushed him away as my stomach threatened to expel its contents at high velocity. "Stop!" I screamed. "What the fuck is wrong with you?" My breath was heaving as I struggled not to vomit. "Why would you bring me out here to show me this?"

"Because it is our history," Tom said, sitting at the bar quietly. "It is part of being gay in Texas."

"What is wrong with you?" I raged, taking a few steps back from them. "I don't want to know this crap!"

"Neither did I," Robbie said, a deep sadness entering his voice. "I'm not from Foster, if you couldn't tell." I nodded but didn't trust myself to say anything. "I lived near New York and met a great guy. We ended up dating and eventually got together." His voice was a mix between anger and sorrow, and it was hard to listen to without reacting. "Riley's family grew up around here, so I moved back with him." He walked past me up to the wall. "I thought the same thing you did, that all of this had nothing to do with me." He put his hand up to one of the pictures. "One night he walked out of the bar, got hit by a truck full of guys who yelled fag as they drove off." His voice dropped, and I almost walked over toward him to give him some support.

Before I could, he turned around. "This town sucks when it comes to being gay. I know that from experience. But you need to know the history of all of this. You need to be prepared."

Tom said from behind me, "This the one Gayle was talking about?" I saw Robbie nod and heard the sigh from behind me. "Lincoln Wright's been an asshole since the day he was born. His son isn't much better. He and his friends were always driving around here seeing what kind of trouble they could cause."

"Now do you see?" Robbie asked me.

I did.

"You're crazy!" I almost shouted when I could speak. "None of that has to do with me!" I said, gesturing toward the wall. "I am sorry about what happened to you, but that has nothing to do with what happened at the diner. In fact, my whole life has nothing to do with any of this! I didn't ask to be gay, and I didn't ask to be raised in Foster. The fact that both happened just means life sucks, and I am pretty sure Fate hates me. But there is nothing I can do about any of that."

I felt out of breath, and I expected Robbie to explode.

Robbie stared silently for what seemed like forever. Finally he asked, "So do you still plan on going to that party?"

My answer barreled out of nowhere; I didn't even stop to think. "Fuck no! Why would I go to the house of someone who hates me so I can be there with a bunch of his friends, who also hate me, and who are just going to get drunk and eventually realize I am there? I couldn't go to a public diner without getting attacked. What makes you think I'd go into someone's house? Does that sound like something I should do?"

"Yes," Robbie and Tom said at the same time.

"This is crazy!" I said, throwing my hands up in frustration.

"No. This is the real world, and you are now a part of it," Robbie fired back.

"Why does it matter if I go to a stupid party or not?" I could feel *pissed off* changing rapidly into *blind fury*.

"Because they never will!" Robbie shouted, pointing at the wall. "Because if you just run away, then those people will continue to torture the next batch of gays and the next." He composed himself. "Someone has to stand their ground. Someone has to say no. You get that, right?"

I hadn't, but I was starting to.

Brad

IN SHOCK, I watched Kyle walk into his house.

I know he said he wasn't mad at me, but as I stood there wishing he would come out again, it sure felt like I had fucked up. When it was obvious he wasn't going to come back out, I got into my car and took off. The thought of ditching school for the day crossed my mind, but all I would end up doing would be going nuts wanting to talk to Kyle about a hundred times and forcing myself to stop. I might as well sit in school and hope it distracted me. I was halfway to my first class when Jennifer found me in the hall.

"What the hell happened?" she asked without even a hello. I gave her a confused look, since my mind was still standing outside of Kyle's door instead of in the hall talking to her. "At the diner?" she prompted me. "Everyone is yakking about it, but no one knows what happened."

As we headed toward class, I talked her through our run-in with Tony's father. She seemed to be more shocked at what happened than I did, because when I got to Kyle losing his mind over having the Coke spilled on him, she stopped and pulled out her cell.

"Who are you calling?" I asked her, wondering when the day had gone 'round the bend.

She held a finger up to me, which was Jennifer for "Shut the fuck up, I am on the phone." "Robbie?" she asked into the phone. "Kyle got his clothes ruined by some homophobe at Nancy's last night." Whoever the hell Robbie was said something because she nodded and said, "Yeah, I thought the same thing. Hold on." She looked at me. "What's Kyle's address?"

"What?" I practically choked. "Why would I give his address to someone I don't know?"

She sighed and gave me her "Don't be stupid, Brad" look. "You know Robbie. He owns that clothing store off East Avenue."

"*That* guy?" I didn't even want to talk about that guy.

She sighed. "Look, Brad, I have some bad news, okay?"

I nodded.

"You're gay."

"Huh?"

She went on, "You're gay, so that means you don't get to have an attitude when it comes to other gay people. Robbie is a friend, so just give me the damn address." I gave her the address, and she rattled it off. "Okay. Call me back," she told him and then hung up. "We're going to be late. I'll tell you during study period." I followed her into the classroom in the same way Alice followed that stupid rabbit down its hole.

As I wait for the teacher to walk in, so Jennifer and I can talk, let me explain Robbie to you.

He was this older… wow. I was about to say fag. I literally had the word on the tip of my tongue. Jesus Christ, what was wrong with me? I want people to treat Kyle and me with respect but all I can do is trash talk another gay guy? Nice, Graymark, real nice.

Anyways, he's a homosexual man who runs this used clothing store out on East Avenue. Jennifer calls it consignment, but the fact of the matter is he sells clothes other people have worn, so sorry, used clothes is all they will ever be to me. Jennifer brought me in there once and it was super obvious that this guy was gay and I freaked. I mean, what if he could sense me? What if whatever gaydar is works and he can, like, ping me, which I assume means he would know I'm gay. He's friends with Jennifer. Would he out me? Would he hit on me?

I was so flustered I said something rude and waited in the car for her. She came out, like, ten minutes later, which led to a fight between us that I was an intolerant hick who needed to get my head out of my ass and that she was a bitch for making me be that close to a gay.

Yes, I know, I was a horrible person, still am I'm sure. I'm trying to get better here, okay?

So yeah, I did know who Robbie was, but my knee-jerk reaction was still not to like him. What does that say about me? I don't know. But I had no idea why Jennifer told him about Kyle's situation, and I wanted to know pretty badly.

Hold up, my phone just vibrated. That means the conversation is about to go down.

Jennifer: Ok, so U remember Robbie?

Brad: Yeah, why would U send him 2 Kyle's house?

Jennifer: Because he was the 1 who gave Kyle those clothes. U should have seen Kyle's face when he wore them, he was over the moon. I'm willing to bet that getting attacked & having the clothes ruined in the same day has Kyle fucked up. Robbie knows about being gay & fucked up in Foster.

Brad: How?

Jennifer: It's a long story, but from what I gather he was dating the Mathisons' son, the 1 that got killed?

Everyone had heard of that accident, but no one my age really knew what went down. All we knew was that the richest family in Foster had their kid run over. But no one said he was gay.

Brad: So THAT guy was dating the richest guy in town?

Jennifer: He was b4 he was killed. So maybe he can cheer Kyle up since he's gone through worse.

I got that Kyle was upset. I didn't get why the clothes were so important.

Brad: So Robbie is going to help get Kyle over having his clothes ruined?

She physically looked over at me and sighed, and then began typing.

Jennifer: They weren't just clothes. I don't think U'd understand.

Brad: Try me.

Jennifer: U never worried about how U looked. I don't think U would understand the frame of mind.

Brad: What does looks have 2 do w/it? Kyle is cute @ fck.

Jennifer: U do know Kyle doesn't know that, right?

I did, but I couldn't connect that fact with Kyle's reaction at all.

Brad: I still don't get it.

Jennifer: Those clothes were the 1st time he felt attractive. And they got ruined in public.

Brad: That's not Kyle's fault!

Jennifer: Brad, it doesn't matter. Trust me, he was crushed.

He was crushed, and I missed that? My girlfriend, who had known Kyle for a total of one minute, knew he was crushed, and the guy who was supposed to be in love with him was clueless? What the fuck?

Brad: Was I that bad a boyfriend to U?

She gave me a sad smile.

Jennifer: Have U ever, 4 1 second ever once worried that people would think U were ugly?

I thought about it and shook my head at her.

Jennifer: Then trust me, U don't get it. Kyle will B fine.

I did trust her, but I still felt like a pile of crap.

For the rest of the class, I sat there and thought about it. Was there something wrong with me? She was right. I had never once worried about how I looked or if people thought I was ugly or not. I was always too worried they'd see the gay inside me and be far more repulsed. Was I stuck-up? Did everyone know I was stuck-up?

When the bell rang Jennifer and I walked out together. Turning to her, I asked, "Am I that fucked-up of a person?"

She laughed and shook her head. "No." She put a hand on my cheek. "You just have no idea how insanely beautiful you are to other people. You're like a millionaire who has no idea what money problems are like to the rest of the world. You have never had to worry about it."

I knew she was trying to give me a compliment, but it made me feel worse.

"We're going to be late for next period," I said, looking at the clock.

"I have Prom Committee," she said, heading off the other way. "Meet you on the steps for lunch?" I nodded. "Smile. He's going to be fine."

I smiled, but it was just one more mask on top of the others.

I sat alone in my next class and tried to pay attention. Of course, concentration off the ball field had never been my strong point, so my thoughts drifted to where they normally stopped. Toward hating myself a little more. I honestly could not connect to the emotion Kyle was feeling over the diner. So we knew Tony learned to be an asshole from his father. What did it matter? They were only clothes. People can always get new clothes.

I felt like Pinocchio without my cute shaggy-haired cricket telling me what was right and wrong. I laughed at the visual, but I realized I'd felt that way for most of my life, like I was a person-shaped thing going through the motions without understanding what everything was about. I'd built a wall around myself a long time ago to protect me from what other people thought. It'd started with my dad and his constant berating of me and my failures at being what he wanted in a son, from picking baseball over football to being gay. To survive, I had long ago removed my feelings from the equation, and now I was worried I might have gone too far.

But everyone I knew had done that to survive, sooner or later. Of course, that was what made everyone I had called friends jaded and stuck-up douchebags, but I understood why it had to be done. From the way Jennifer was talking, though, I thought I had done something different. I hadn't just walled off my emotions but buried them somewhere I couldn't get to anymore, and the thought of that scared the hell out of me.

I wandered off toward the quad, my mind a million miles away.

"Um, Brad?" a voice asked from behind me.

I turned around and saw the girl with blue hair who had joined us for lunch yesterday running up to me. "Hey…." I searched for her name.

"Sammy," she said, saving me from saying something stupid.

"Right, sorry. I'm bad with names," I said lamely.

She paused for a moment and then asked, "Who has the record for most stolen bases on the Rangers?"

"Elvis Andrus," I answered automatically.

"And behind him?" she asked.

"Ian Kinsler," I said in a defeated voice.

"So you are great with names. Let's not start lying to each other so soon, okay?" She didn't sound angry, but it was obvious she was calling me on my bullshit.

I sighed and nodded, holding out my hand. "Hi, I'm Brad and you're Sammy."

She took my hand and shook it. "Pleasure to meet you again, Brad. Where's Kyle?"

I laughed at the complete lack of pause she took before asking me about Kyle. "He took a mental health day," I answered neutrally.

"I heard he got jumped at Nancy's." Her tone wasn't openly accusatory, but she obviously didn't fully trust my answer.

"There was an incident." I wasn't sure how much Kyle wanted people to know about what happened, but I knew I wasn't going to be the one spreading rumors.

I expected her to just walk away or to at least let it go. Instead, she took a step into my face and pointed one finger up at me. "Look, dude, if you don't start telling me what happened to Kyle, I will find a way to kick your ass. No joke."

The girl was five-foot-nothing and maybe a buck-oh-five soaking wet, and still I believed she would find a way to hurt me.

Luckily we didn't need to find out, because Jennifer walked up. "What's going on?" she asked, concerned.

"Something happened with Kyle and this jackass won't tell me if he's okay," Sammy replied, never taking her attention off me.

"Why didn't you just tell her?" Jennifer snapped as she smacked me in the chest.

"What'd I do?" I sputtered.

"Come on," Jennifer said, taking Sammy's arm. "Let's grab some food, and I'll fill you in." Both of them shot me a dirty look as they walked off.

"And this is why I'm gay," I said to myself, more confused than ever. I waited until they were out of sight before pulling out my cell and calling Kyle. I got his mother telling me he left the house this morning and hadn't been back since.

He left with Robbie?

"Older guy, gay?" I asked her.

"That's him. He said he was a friend of Kyle's."

"Friend of Dorothy's more like it," I mumbled, "Did they say where they were going?"

"No, but the Robbie guy left me his number in case I needed to get a hold of Kyle."

"Can I have that number?"

Oh please, oh please, oh please.

"Yeah, ready?"

I put her on speaker and added the number to a blank contact.

"Thanks, Mrs. S.," I said and hung up.

The phone rang twice before Robbie, I assumed, answered, "If this is a telemarketer, be warned, I have an air horn on me."

"Um, Robbie?"

"Who is this?" he snapped.

"Brad? Kyle's boyfriend."

"Jesus, Kathleen, he's been gone for a couple of hours. Are you going to be this clingy the whole relationship?"

I was about to answer when I heard Kyle ask who it was.

"No one," Robbie told him.

"Let me talk to him, please."

"Is that Brad?" Kyle asked.

"Wouldn't it be a little creepy if it was?" Robbie told Kyle.

"Give me the phone," Kyle demanded, and I heard the phone change hands. "Brad?"

And just like that my anxiety and worry was gone and a smile drifted across my face. "Are you okay?"

He sounded like he had been eating. "I'm fine. I got shanghaied but am being treated well enough."

"Oh, shut up," Robbie's voice rang out. "This isn't a prison camp!"

"Hold on," Kyle said, obviously moving somewhere outside. I could hear the wind and the buzz of power lines. "Okay, I'm back."

I actually felt my chest tighten some when I heard his voice. "Where are you?"

"You would not believe me if I told you." He sounded as sad as I did. "He dragged me out in the middle of nowhere to talk to me about being gay in Texas."

"What?"

"Please don't ask. I'm as confused as you are."

"This sucks without you," I said in a whisper. I was holding the phone with both hands now like it would somehow help me get closer to him. "When are you coming home?" I sounded exactly like every single girl in every romance movie ever made.

"Soon, I think," he whispered back. "I hope we're almost done here."

"Where?" I asked again.

"Middle of nowhere. Like where they went to make meth in *Breaking Bad*? Past that."

That made me chuckle.

"I miss you too." I could hear the smile in his voice, and just like that, my day got better.

"Call me when you get home?" I asked anxiously.

"The very second," he promised.

"I miss you so much," I heard myself say over the phone. I hadn't even meant to say it, but the words came spilling out before I could stop them.

There was a small pause before he answered, "Not as much as I miss you."

I'm pretty sure we both knew the word *miss* was standing in for another word neither one of us wanted to say first.

I hung up before I said something even dumber.

When I got to the steps, Jennifer and Sammy were picking at a tray of food and talking to each other. "So am I still an asshole?" I asked, sitting next to them.

"Yes, but we forgive you," Jennifer said, handing me a burger. "So, call Kyle?" I nodded with my mouth full. She looked over at Sammy. "Told you." Then to me she added, "You are so his bitch."

I flipped her off as I took another bite.

"I'm sorry I came off so aggro," Sammy said between bites. "It's my default setting when dealing with jocks."

I waved her off. "I understand. I'm just not used to sharing information. My last group of friends would take the smallest piece of gossip and turn it into something the size of Everest by the end of the day."

"Man, you aren't kidding," Jennifer muttered as she took a sip of Pepsi.

We sat in relative silence for a while, each one of us taking the day in the best we could. It was as nice as it could be without Kyle there, so, of course, the peace wasn't going to last.

Tony walked toward me with Josh Walker right behind him.

I heard Jennifer sigh as they climbed up the first couple of steps to us.

"What?" I called out to him, hoping to end this before it became anything.

He paused, the scowl on his face deepening. "I wanted to say that was uncool, what my dad did." I saw Jennifer and Sammy pause, and I knew how they felt because, if I was completely blown away by his admission, I knew they had to be almost speechless.

There was a pregnant pause as we all waited for someone to say something else. So I just ended up deciding it was going to be me. "Yeah, it was."

He had been in the process of walking away when I said it. Josh had tapped him on the shoulder and no doubt gave him a quiet "Dude, let it go," which was the teenage guy's version of a hostage negotiator defusing a bank holdup. You can be Incredible Hulk angry, but if one of your bros puts his hand on your shoulder and says, "Dude, let it go," you are then given a free pass to walk away without being called a pussy by other people. You can leave and tell your friends that you "would have pounded that guy into paste if Josh wasn't there to calm me down," and no one could call bullshit on you. He was about to walk away, and I fucked it up.

He spun back around and shouted at me, "What did you say?"

This is where I made things worse.

I say that because I could have just shrugged and said nothing, and it would have been over. This was him trying to toss me a bone and do the bare minimum it took for him to not come off like an asshole. He wasn't happy with what went down, and he was coming to me to say "Hey, that wasn't me." I could have let it go. I could have taken it and gone on with my lunch.

And I might have done that if Kyle had been with me.

But I'd had a shitty enough day, and I could lay it right at the feet of this asshole. I got to my feet as I snarled back, "You heard me. It was fucked-up." Jennifer and Sammy backed away as Tony got in my face.

"Well, it wouldn't have happened if you and your freak weren't locking lips in public!" His chest was pressed up against mine; from another view it could look like we were going to kiss.

"I've seen you and the dogs you take on dates making out since I was fourteen! What's the difference?" I pushed against him but didn't use my hands. This was like soccer; the first person to use their hands was the first person to actually throw a foul. The point now was to say something to make the other guy push first, and from there we'd ride the inevitable-fight escalator.

Trust me; that was where we were heading.

"The difference is, that fag shit is gross!" He bumped me back.

Josh, who was behind him, let out a "Dude, knock it off."

"No. What's gross is me having to see your redneck ass try to shove your tongue down any girl's throat every Friday night after a game." Bump and a step forward.

"Least it's a girl!" Harder bump back into me.

"You're a fucking girl." I saw his eyes twitch at that, and I knew we were about to go.

I pulled my fist back, ready to watch the side of his face cave in, when Tony just vanished. One second he was in front of me; the next he was gone. I looked around like an idiot before I realized he was on the ground with someone on top of him. It took me another second to realize that the someone was Kelly.

What the fuck?

Kelly had pinned Tony down and was whaling on him. Tony was technically bigger than Kelly in height and build, but right then he was on his back with Kelly on top of him, not giving Tony the time to remember he had an advantage, much less use it. I was so shocked to see Kelly beating him, it took a second to actually realize what he was saying to Tony.

"Why can't you just let it go?" he snarled, slamming Tony onto the ground. "What the fuck is wrong with you? Why do we have to keep making excuses to attack them?" Kelly seemed more upset than actually angry; his voice sounded almost panicked. "We've done enough to them! Fuck, haven't we done enough?"

He was on the verge of crying, and seeing that freaked me out. I went for Kelly the same time Josh did, and we pulled him off Tony. He was still swinging when we got him to his feet. Josh looked at me and silently asked if I had him, because Kelly was in no way calming down. I nodded at him and stepped right in front of Kelly. "Hey. *Hey*!" I shouted in his face.

He blinked twice before his eyes slowly focused on me.

"What the fuck?" I asked, confused. "What are you doing?"

His eyes were as red as if he had been crying, but there were no tears yet. "I told you, I'm tired of hating you," he said, clearly exhausted. "I'm tired of all of it."

I had no answer to that. I froze because it was the most emotion that had come out of Kelly's mouth… well, ever, and I didn't have a clue how to deal with it. I turned when Jennifer ran up and tugged at Kelly until he leaned on her. "Come on, stud," she urged him, her voice overly cheerful. "Let's take a walk somewhere else."

She began to lead him off when Tony, who had been helped up by Josh, shouted, "Yeah, you better get your faggot ass out of here!" He glared at me. "You need your boyfriends to fight your—"

I am going to go with "battles," but we will never know because Josh just hauled off and punched him across the jaw. Tony's knees buckled, and he went down like a tree crashing to the ground, the punch was so unexpected. Jennifer and I both looked over at Josh, who was rubbing his hand. He glared down at Tony and snapped, "Jesus Christ, give it a fucking rest already. We get it, you don't like gay people. You made that pretty clear." Tony looked like Josh was breaking up with him or something. "What the hell do you think you're proving, doing all this? You've moved from 'giving the fag a hard time' into 'asshole bigot' territory. If Kyle and Brad bug you that much, stay away from them. In fact, if gay stuff makes you this nuts, stay away from all of them."

There was an emphasis there, but I didn't catch it.

Shaking his head, Josh stormed off, leaving Tony rubbing his jaw, the center of everyone's attention. I held my hand out to help him up. He stared at it for a few seconds and then took it. Seeing there was no further bloodshed to be had, the onlookers began to walk away.

Tony and I stood there, neither one of us knowing what to say next.

"You shouldn't do that shit in public, man," he said in a low voice. I opened my mouth to complain, and he kept talking. "Look, you want to kiss your boyfriend, that's great. You wanna be—" I saw him bite back the word *fags* and replace it."—gay and all that, then do it. But stop throwing it in people's faces. It makes people like my dad crazy."

"Are you one of those people?" I asked him, trying to keep the anger and loathing out of my voice.

"Dude, just don't do it in public."

I shrugged. "People do lots of things that bug me. I ignore them and look away."

"My dad won't ignore it, man." He almost sounded like he was warning me.

"Your dad didn't start *this* fight." I could see the realization sink in when I said that. He backed away a few steps and then turned and left. I think he was honestly confused.

He took off after Josh in a hurry. I sighed. This day just kept getting worse and worse.

Kyle

I HANDED Robbie's phone back to him.

"You know that is going to become a problem, right?" Robbie asked as he cut another slice of rib meat with his knife.

"Shut up," I muttered and picked up the rib on my plate with my fingers and took another bite out of it.

Tom had made us lunch, which turned out to be an incredible rack of BBQ ribs and fries. I swear it was easily the best thing I had eaten in recent memory. We had all dropped the topic of the wall, a temporary cease-fire called on account of food. But as the ribs vanished and the fries dwindled down to nothing, an uncomfortable silence lurked among us.

At least, it was uncomfortable to me.

"You looked like you enjoyed those," Tom said, his pride in his cooking clear in the tone of his voice. I gnawed the last of the meat off the bone and nodded while I glanced hopefully at the sad, empty place where the rack of ribs had been enthroned only a few minutes earlier. When nothing magically filled the platter, I examined the chaos on my plate, looking hopefully for some bits of meat. I also tried not to look like a dog guarding my dinner. Tom looked smugly back at Robbie. "See? Someone knows how to eat ribs."

Robbie tossed his napkin onto the plate. "I assure you, I have never once had a complaint about how I eat meat."

I almost choked at that polite statement, and both of them burst into laughter. Red, was my face red? No—it had definitely passed red and headed toward crimson. More laughter.

"So, you have time to think about it?" Robbie asked me point-blank. His abrupt change of focus should have caught me more off guard than it did.

I wiped my mouth and went over the answer I'd already framed in my mind. After a sip of pop, I nodded. "I've been thinking about it, yeah."

"So you understand what we're saying?" His voice had a hopeful tone.

"I understood when you first brought it up," I said as politely as I could. "I just don't agree with you." They both looked at me like I had grown a second head.

"Which part do you not agree with?" Tom asked before Robbie could say anything.

"The part where those people"—I pointed at the picture wall—"and what happened to them have anything to do with me or Brad and me going to that party." I felt like I was a kid trying to have a conversation with two adults and failing badly because I was talking about generalities, and they were talking about stuff that actually had happened to them. It almost made me lose my train of thought, but I pressed on. "What happened to those people is horrible, but it isn't relevant here. Whether or not Brad and I go to that party, people will still hate gay people, and they will still hurt us. I don't see how going to a party is all that important. I don't think it ever could be."

Robbie began to open his mouth, but Tom waved him off and started talking instead. "When I grew up around here, there was nothing for gay people. You couldn't come out, you couldn't have a boyfriend, and even if you wanted to go to a party, you wouldn't because the odds were you'd get your ass kicked."

He looked like he was going to keep going, but I interrupted him. "And a couple of months ago, I was told there was nothing anyone could do about people picking on me at school for being gay unless they hit me in front of someone who would report it. My boyfriend got thrown off the baseball team, even though he's a key player, and he's been beaten up. Odds are, if we go to this party, we will get our asses kicked. The more it changes, the more of the same thing it is. Now tell me again why Brad and I should risk our lives."

Tom looked confused, so Robbie jumped in. "Because someone has to say they aren't moving to the back of the bus."

"I'm not Rosa Parks," I replied confidently.

"You could be."

No one talked while the jukebox finished playing its last song. "I get you're scared—" Robbie began.

"Do you know Rosa Parks was a plant?" I interrupted.

He stopped and gave me a confused look. "A what?"

"A plant. She wasn't tired and didn't want to give up her seat. She worked for the NAACP and wanted to be arrested. People always say she was too tired to give up her seat and then got arrested, but that isn't the case. Other people had been arrested before her, but the NAACP didn't feel their case would hold up. Rosa Parks knew when she sat down on that bus her life was changing, and she did it on purpose. I am not Rosa Parks."

Robbie looked at me in shock and then back to Tom. "Did you know that?" Tom shook his head.

"You want me to be Rosa Parks. You want me to walk into that party representing those people," I said, nodding toward the wall of obituaries. "And I am telling you I can't. I don't even know if I am going. And do you know why?" They both shook their heads. "Because neither one of you can say with any certainty that going to that party won't be the reason Brad or I or maybe both of us end up being up there was well."

I just wanted to go home to Brad. Turning to Robbie, I added, "Whenever you want to take me back, I'm ready." And then I looked at Tom. "Bathroom?" He pointed over toward the other side of the bar. I got up feeling every inch of the tired person I was. I made sure not to make eye contact with any of the pictures as I passed them.

I stayed in bathroom for a while, giving Tom and Robbie more than enough time to digest what I said and to come to terms with the fact I wasn't their guy. Worse than that, I didn't even *want* to be their guy. I wanted to finish this year and get the hell out of Foster, out of Texas, as fast as I could.

"That's because you possess a brain," Billy said, pushing me aside to look at himself in the mirror. "Girl, just keep your head down and shut up. You've done it for three and a half years. What's a couple of months compared to that?"

It worried me that I agreed with everything he said.

"It bugs you because you know they're right," my sense of right and wrong said. "You know that if no one does anything, nothing will change. How can you look at that wall and do nothing about it?"

"Why me?" I asked. "What can I do?"

"You can do something," my decency answered. "You can do something, which is a million times more than the ones on that wall can do now."

"Don't listen to these bitches," Billy said. "They gonna get you killed."

"Why is it my responsibility?"

"It isn't," my common sense said. "But you know that things have already changed. The school board is forced to look at LGBT issues now. Other people have been exposed to a real, live pair of homosexuals. Just seeing Brad and you are normal kills a lot of stereotypes they have in their mind. And Gayle stood up for you in the diner, and the rest of the people did too. That's changing things by showing up. So don't play stupid that you don't know what to do."

Billy made a tsking sound. "Ignore her, she thinks she's in JFK or some shit."

Can I say how much it was bugging me that Billy was saying what I was thinking for once?

When I left the restroom and looked across the bar, the table had been cleared, and Robbie had his keys out. "You ready?" he asked brusquely. When I nodded, he looked to Tom. "Thank you for the hospitality."

Tom nodded and walked over to me. "You and your guy are welcome here any time. Since we serve food, we can have minors in as long as they don't drink." I began to tell him that probably wouldn't happen, but then he held up a hand. "And before you tell me the probability of that happening, let me remind you manners dictate you say thank you for the invitation and move on."

I closed my mouth, smiled, and said, "Thank you for the invitation." He held out his hands, and I let him pull me into a hug. As I hugged him back, he whispered, "Don't let those brains make you stupid. Everyone needs someone sooner or later. We will always be here."

I wasn't sure how to take that, but I nodded and slowly pulled back.

"If you two need a room…," Robbie complained impatiently.

"You know, Ms. Thing, I remember when you were a hot mess as well. Don't make me read you right here in front of the kid."

I was going to make a comment about not being a kid, but I resisted.

Robbie walked out into the afternoon sun to his car with me following a little bit behind him.

The return was about as uneventful as the ride out there, except now there was a big, ugly silence in the car with us. There was no music this time, no idle conversation, just Robbie, me, and the ugly silence in the back seat sticking its head over the center console, daring us to talk. I wasn't sure if he was mad or disappointed, but either way, it was not a conversation I looked forward to having, so I ignored Robbie and the silence and watched the road again.

"I get it," he said after almost thirty minutes of nothing. I looked over at him silently. "I really do; I was the same way in high school. Keep my head down, don't call attention to myself, don't be the obvious fag, repeat until college." He cracked his window as he lit a cigarette. "I didn't want to be gay, I didn't want people to know I was gay, and the only way to do that was to pretend my gayness didn't exist. I just needed to get through those last four years, and then I'd be home-free." He took a long drag and flicked his ashes out the window.

"What happened?" I asked, curious.

He looked over at me and then looked away with a half smile. "Same thing that happens with every high school queen in the closet. I ended up having a crush on a straight guy I could never have and outing myself accidentally." He took another two drags to settle his nerves. "The boy hated me because he was embarrassed; I was humiliated because suddenly I was the high school's token homosexual, and I spent the last two years of high school alternating between being in a medical coma thanks to booze or flirting with the idea of killing myself."

I sat there stunned, staring stupidly at him rubbing the butt of his smoke out in the ashtray. I had never heard anyone just admit they thought about killing themselves before. I mean, you heard people say stuff like that, but they were either making a bad joke or desperately crying out for help. I think it was the matter-of-fact way Robbie spoke that eliminated any thoughts I might have had that he was being cynical. No one I had ever known would have said, "Oh yes, I had some breakfast, cleaned my room, and then thought about killing myself." My mind recoiled from his words.

"Oh, don't look at me that way. Trust me, every gay kid thinks about it at least once. Tell me you haven't." I looked away, and he let out a small, spiteful laugh. "Trust me, you don't even want to know what the suicide rate is for gay teens. So anyway, yeah, my Brad wasn't as nice as yours, so be thankful for what you got."

"I am," I said softly.

"Good."

We had come to an impasse again, and the silence stuck its ugly head between us once more. Robbie turned on the music. I watched the nothing that surrounded Foster and was visible all the way to the distant horizon rush past my window. It seemed impossible that I'd ever escape this place. It was just too big, and at this very moment… seemed like it was my everything.

"Where am I dropping you off?" he asked when we got into town.

I checked the time and saw school was almost getting out. "School. I need to talk with Brad before practice." He nodded and turned toward Foster High.

"So when do you want to start?" he asked as we pulled into the school parking lot. Startled out of my thoughts, confused, I looked over at him. "You still owe me for the clothes, and you're going to need another set of clothes if you are going to the party."

"Um, Monday, right? After school?" I offered, since there was no way in hell I could pay for the clothes I'd already ruined. The business about needing more to go to the party I just let slide away.

"Sounds good. I don't do mornings all that well, so any time after ten is good." He didn't sound upset now, but there was a difference in his demeanor from when he'd picked me up that morning.

"I'm sorry I'm not the person you thought I was," I said before getting out of the car. "I wish I was."

He stared straight ahead, both hands twisting around the steering wheel. "The thing is," he said finally, staring over at me, "you are. You don't know it yet." I opened my mouth to argue, but he held his hand up, stopping me. "I'm not in the mood for a debate. Just remember what I said." The dismissal bell rang, and he smiled. "You better grab Brad before practice."

As much as I wanted that debate, Robbie had also made a good point; if I didn't catch Brad before he got to the gym, I would have to wait until practice was over. "Thanks for lunch," I said, getting out of the car.

"See you Monday," he called back.

I watched him drive away, wondering why he thought I was someone I knew I wasn't and didn't want to be. I ignored the thought and jogged toward the gym. I caught up to Brad just as he pulled his gym bag out of his car.

When he saw me, he dropped his bag and scooped me up into a hug. You'd swear we hadn't seen each other for years instead of hours. I wrapped my arms around him and buried my face in his shoulder. The smell of his hair gel, cologne, and his letterman jacket made the stress of the day fade away as he whispered "I missed you" in my ear.

"Not as much as I missed you," I whispered back. "I should have gone to school with you."

He pulled back and looked into my eyes. "Are you okay?" I nodded. "I should have known that the clothes were—"

"Shut up," I said before kissing him.

My day got a thousand times better right then and there.

"We have to talk," he said after a few incredibly satisfying seconds of kissing.

"And this is where he dumps you!" Billy yelled from across the quad. "Hold up. I'm coming."

If I am ever made Overlord of the World, I'm going to make a few changes. After the whole world peace and wiping out bigotry things, I am going to make specific alterations to the way the world works. First on that list, after, you know, I make Tom Holland and Chris Hemsworth my servants, I am going to ban people from using the phrase "We have to talk" unless the end of the world truly comes. There is nothing more frightening than someone looking at you and, in a serious voice, announcing "We need to talk." I mean,

I would rather have someone say "You are on fire" than "We have to talk."

"We have to talk" was my mom's way of telling me that something bad—or worse—had happened. When I was nine, we had to pack our stuff and move out of the apartment we were currently living in. One of the guys she had been dating got out of jail and was coming back to town completely pissed. Mom started her explanation by saying, "We have to talk." When she told me she had taken my computer to a pawn shop so we could make rent, she started by saying, "We have to talk." And when I asked who my dad was, she got quiet, told me to sit down, and sighed, "We have to talk."

I hated those words. Well, not those specific words, because they have other uses. But those four words in that order just caused every nerve ending I had to pulse with fear.

So hearing those words coming out of Brad's mouth? I almost wet myself as I imagined the worst.

"What?" I asked as my mouth went dry.

"I just…," he began to say as he looked over at the locker room. "It's going to take more time than I got right now. You going home?"

I shrugged.

He tossed me his keys. "If you want to hang out, listen to music in the car or go sit in the stands and watch us practice." He leaned in and kissed me. "I promise to be fast."

He turned and ran into the locker room.

"Shit," Billy said, catching its breath from running all the way over here. "Gimme a second," it said, kneeling over gulping air. "You couldn't have imagined me as Grant Gustin so I could just whoosh over here?"

"I know what you're going to say," I said miserably as I walked over to Brad's car.

"Bitch, I know you know, doesn't mean you don't need to hear it."

I got in the car, closed and locked the door.

"Oh, that's cute," Billy said from the other side of the glass.

I closed my eyes and tried to calm down.

"You know what you did wrong?" Billy asked from the back seat.

"Give you a voice?" I answered numbly.

"Shut up. You know what you did wrong?"

"Everything?"

"Everything," it said, ignoring what I had said. "I mean, from the start you fucked this up. You should have let his ignorant ass walk away in the hall, let that fool flunk out. Is it your problem he can't read above a fourth-grade level?"

"He's not dumb," I said, reclining the seat back.

"He ain't Einstein either." Billy was now in the driver's seat, looking over at me. "That was your first mistake; then there was going to his house, kissing him, holding his hand on the way home...."

"I know all this," I said in a loud voice.

"If you knew all this, then why are you so shocked he's about to break up with you?"

I didn't have an answer until a small voice said from the back seat, "Um, that was me."

Didn't even need to turn around to know that was hope.

Hope used to be a little kid, because it was used so rarely, a tiny voice among all of the louder ones assuring me my life sucked royally.

It was still little, but it had grown up some.

"You should stop being mean to him, because Brad is nice," it said, berating Billy. "He is sweet and always there and would do anything for us."

"Uh-huh," Billy said, looking at its nails. "You keep telling yourself that."

"Leave Kyle alone!" it screamed in its ten-year-old voice.

"You should have slept with him," Billy said out of nowhere.

I sat up, real panic in my chest.

"You know that boy has had sex already with Jennifer. No way she was dating him for that long without putting a quarter in the horsey and riding it until time ran out."

God, my mind is fucked-up.

"He has had sex before, and all you do is get him all wound up and then a lousy hand job. Once you have had steak, why would you ever settle for Spam?"

Shitshitshit.

"Also, you're ugly," my self-destructive tendencies added. "I mean, you know he's just dating you 'cause you're the only other gay person in the world to him. Look at yourself!" I glanced at myself in the visor mirror and felt the normal wave of revulsion that engulfed me when I saw myself. Everything about my face was wrong to me. My eyes were too big, my nose pointy, and I didn't even want to go into the catastrophe that was my mouth. It felt like I had been constructed by a lot of leftover parts from the Handsome People Assembly Line. I'd been given the castoffs since I had to have some kind of face.

"Why would anyone who looks like he has walked out of the Spring A&F catalog have anything to do with you? You're the only other gay and he wanted sex. You screwed that up."

"No, he didn't screw it. That's the problem!" my inappropriate humor said, and the whole car roared with laughter.

I turned the AC to drown them out and leaned back again. I had started down a steeply angled spiral of negative thoughts. If I didn't try to level out now, I would just end up running home and locking my door for a year or so.

I fell asleep eventually. Images of Brad with his arm around Jennifer, laughing at me as they walked away, terrified me. I kept trying to run after him, but every time I did, I would trip and fall down. The third time I looked to see what was tripping me, and I saw I was wearing high heels and a dress. I heard laughing and realized all of Foster High's students stood in a circle surrounding me, all of them pointing as they roared at me. I tried to pull the shoes off but they wouldn't budge. Then I saw Brad standing in the crowd. "What do you expect? You're a fag. You should dress like one."

I woke up screaming. No laughing students, no dress, no shoes, and no Brad mocking me. No Brad— Dazed, I looked around and saw Brad frozen in midmotion next to the half-open driver's side door, gaping at me in shock. "Whoa!" he said carefully. "You just scared the living shit out of me."

I rubbed my face to banish the images of the nightmare from my mind. "I fell asleep...," I mumbled.

He tossed his bag into the back seat. "Jeez, you're lucky you didn't die of hypothermia," he exclaimed, turning the air-conditioning down. "Bad dream?"

I nodded and shakily pushed myself upright in the seat.

"So—" he began to say.

"I love you and want to have sex," I blurted so fast I somehow made it all one syllable.

He froze again, mouth hanging open. Eyes blinking slowly and brow furrowed, he stared at me.

"I mean it. I'm sorry I was an asshole this morning, and I shouldn't have done it, and I want to have sex with you badly, and please don't break up with me."

His mouth snapped shut, almost as if it was spring driven.

"I know I'm moody, and I know you can get someone better-looking, but please, you're all I have right now, and if I have to face people and have them ask me why we broke up, I think I'll die, and I love you, and I don't know why I kept putting off sex and... please?"

His eyes narrowed in anger, and he looked away as he started the car. "Buckle up" was all he said. I barely got the seat belt on before he threw the car into reverse. I heard the tires squeal as he turned the car with one hand and slammed it into Drive with the other. Smoke from the burned rubber trailed behind us as the Mustang peeled out of the parking lot.

"Um, where are we going?" I asked, trying not to grab the door handle and jump from a car rolling along at God knows what speed.

"Out to the woods to shoot you," some voice, not even sure who, said from the back seat.

Brad said nothing.

"Brad?" I asked, not liking the look on his face.

"Please. Stop. Talking," he asked in a voice that sounded to me like pure serial killer.

"Yep, we dead," said the voice.

This was the second time today I was stuck in a car, feeling I was going to have internal organs harvested in some out-of-the-way place.

We headed out past First Street toward the lake. The sun was almost down, which meant there wasn't much traffic at all. And it was deserted, a perfect place to bury a body. I tried to banish that thought as Brad pulled off into a small dirt road that would have been impossible to see unless a driver knew where to look. A tiny grove of cottonwood trees grew around the perimeter of a clearing that contained a fire pit for grilling. The place looked like an old discarded camping spot that hadn't been used in a long time.

We parked, and Brad got out of the car. I huddled there for a few seconds, not sure if I was supposed to follow. He looked at me through the front window and pointed for me to join him. I got out slowly, wondering if I could just go back to him breaking up with me instead of him kicking my ass before he dumped me.

I walked around the front of the car but kept out of arm's reach of him.

"Okay, look," he snarled. "I don't know what your fucking mom has done to you, and to be honest, I don't want to know, because if I did, then it would be impossible for me to resist the urge to punch her in the face. We need to get a few things straight if this is going to continue." He stopped, and I wasn't sure if I was supposed to answer, since there wasn't a question. Instead I nodded.

"I don't know how she convinced you that you were worthless, but it's bullshit. Plain bullshit. You are the most… just… you are the best person I have ever met, and I have shaken Nolan Ryan's hand. There is *nothing* about you that doesn't blow me away on every single level there is. You are smart, cute, brave, humble, and…." He swallowed as he tried to contain the emotion in his voice. "You are the only good thing that has ever happened to me. Ever. And if you can't get it through your skull how crazy I am about you—then we are going to have problems."

This didn't sound like anything I had imagined.

"I love you too. That isn't a like, isn't a puppy love, and it isn't a crush. The moment we kissed in my room, I was yours; it just took my stupid brain time to figure it out. You are everything I need in my life, but more importantly, you are everything I will ever need. I am *never* going to break up with you. Never. If we break up, and God, I hope that's a gigantic 'if,' it will be because you realized I was not the guy you thought I was and that *you* can do better. So no matter what happens between us, I will never break up with you. Got it?

"But I don't want the first time you say I love you to me being some kind of Hail Mary pass to keep us together. This should be about trust and acceptance, not about fear and panic, Kyle. So I am going to ignore the fact you said all that because I don't think you meant it the way it came out. But I am saying it, because I don't care if it's fast or rushed or whatever. I am falling in love with you, and that isn't a joke."

I knew what he was saying was supposed to be romantic, but he sounded so angry. I just nodded.

"If anyone should be scared, it's me. You're going to outgrow me, Kyle. I know that in my heart, and it terrifies me. But you should never, ever worry that I am going to break up with you. Because it will never happen." He was close to crying, and it was killing me.

I cleared the distance between us in two strides and wrapped my arms around him so tight my shoulders hurt. He clasped me back, and we stood there in front of his car, holding each other for dear life. "I am never not going to love you," I said to him when I could talk.

He swallowed and looked me straight in the eyes.

"I used to fool around with Kelly."

I felt a chill run up my spine and took a half step away from him.

Maybe I was hasty in saying never.

Brad

THERE ARE times I wish I was a douchebag.

I know that sounds like something no one would want to be, but there are times I wish I was missing a conscience or whatever those guys don't have. Not having a conscience or whatever allows them to be complete assholes to other people and never feel a thing afterward. I have seen Tony Wright be a complete shit to a girl. Then, within ten minutes of her confronting him with his fuckery, he could turn what he did around so completely that she was grateful to still be going out with him.

If I was a douche, I could have done that to Kyle and not been in trouble.

But I wasn't and I couldn't.

I could never have looked into his eyes and treated him like shit. I had a feeling even if I was one of those guys, I still couldn't hurt him. I could have assured him that I had no intention of breaking up with him and let it be, but I couldn't keep what Kelly and I had done away from him anymore.

"What did you say?" he asked me, taking a half step back.

"A long time ago, before you and I ever met, I fooled around with Kelly," I said, resisting the urge to move toward him. The worst thing I could do was crowd him. If I had learned anything from dating Kyle, it was when he needed his space, he *needed* it.

His face turned white, and he had a hand over his mouth like he was on the verge of throwing up. "Why didn't you tell me?" he asked after gaining some composure.

He'd asked a good question. Why hadn't I?

Well, I was embarrassed about it. That was at the top of the list. Followed closely by "I was afraid Kyle would one day realize I wasn't the guy he thought I was and leave." Good reasons, both.

In the end, though? In the end, the real answer was because, as I had since I was ten, I was deflecting attention away from my mistakes. Standing there looking at Kyle and realizing how truthful he had been to me since day one, I knew I needed to stop. I needed to man up.

In hesitating words, I began to explain how we started fooling around during football camp and how it was always Kelly doing the touching while I lay there. Then I described how when people started becoming suspicious of the way Kelly acted toward me, I just dropped him as a friend. And then I added that I thought Kelly might harbor some feelings toward me after all this time.

And then I waited for Kyle to hate me.

"Was that why he went apeshit on me in the quad?" he asked.

It was a good question, one I had asked myself more than once over the past few months. I shrugged because I didn't have any more of an answer than I did the day it happened.

"So wait, when you came out in front of everyone, you were telling the truth that Kelly used to…." He seemed to choke on his own words before he tried again. "Are you telling me that Kelly is not a homophobic asshole but might be a jealous ex-boyfriend?" He really sounded mad now.

"He was never my boyfriend," I said bluntly.

"Did he know that?" he raged back at me. "Or did you just smile at him and imply the whole thing?"

Now I was getting mad. "Are we still talking about Kelly?"

"I don't know." He was on the verge of yelling now. "How do I know you didn't say the same things to him that you've told me? How do I know you won't do the same thing to me you did to him?"

Something in my head snapped.

"Oh, for fuck's sake!" I screamed. "How many different ways can I say how I feel about you? Seriously, Kyle, is there a number somewhere that will quiet the voices in your head? Is it ten? Twenty? A hundred? Pick a number, and I will do it. Just let me know what it will take, and I swear to you I will not stop trying until you believe me, but this is getting old. I did not go out with Kelly; he sucked my dick for a week. I did not tell him anything I have told you. In fact, I didn't tell him a thing, which makes me a bigger asshole than the one you're imagining. Whatever! I'm tired of hiding it. I was scared and horny and I used him for sex and then ignored him. If you think that is what I am doing to you, then obviously we have different ideas about what is going on here."

I was trying to catch my breath, standing there staring at him. I had finished practice half an hour earlier, and I was more out of breath now than I had been running laps.

He let out half a laugh before stopping himself. Since there was nothing I had said that was funny, I frowned, which made him laugh even more. He held a hand up as he really started laughing. "I'm sorry, but that was the first time you've really yelled at me, and it was to tell me you love me." He guffawed some more. "I'm just thinking that all that screaming was the most romantic thing I've ever heard." And then he burst out like a hyena.

I had to admit, it was kind of funny.

"Well, you drive me crazy," I said, trying not to laugh.

He looked up, and I saw him almost crying, he was laughing so hard. "Yeah, I saw the crazy part."

"Shut up," I said quietly, but I was smiling.

He shook his head as he tried to stop laughing. "Give me a second." His hands were on his thighs as he tried to get his breath. "Okay… almost."

I sighed as I waited for him.

He stood up and looked at me. "One, you knew I was crazy when you kissed me, and if you didn't, that's on you. Two, I'm sorry, but there isn't a number because I cannot wrap my mind around why someone like you would go out with someone like me, so I can't help you there. And three, what you did to Kelly is exactly what I am terrified of, and you saying you've actually done it to someone is like admitting you're Freddy Krueger or something." He walked over to me and put his arms over my shoulders. "But I'm glad you told me."

I pretended to be mad, but he saw right through it.

"You can pout all you want, but you know everything I just said was the truth." He kissed my cheek. "So? Fight over?"

I couldn't hold it and let out a huge grin as I grabbed his waist and picked him up. "You are so lucky you're cute," I said, sitting him on the hood of the car. "So I never dated Kelly, and you get I do care about you?" He nodded. "Good. Because that wasn't even what I wanted to tell you."

His smile dropped.

"I know you are on the fence about it, but I changed my mind. I need to go to this party." I couldn't read his expression, but that was nothing new. "Kelly stood up for me today, and he practically begged me to go." I leaned my forehead against his. "I totally understand if you don't want to go, but I wish you would."

I felt him lean into me, and I held my breath as I waited for him to answer.

"Then we go," he whispered.

I looked up and saw him smile back at me. "You'll go with me?"

He rolled his eyes as he said, "I suppose, if I have to."

I began to tickle him, which turned into feeling him, which turned into kissing him.

I laid him on the hood of my car, and I felt him move under me.

"Were you serious about the whole sex thing?" I asked after a few minutes.

"I think so," he offered.

"Because if you did, I mean if you want to…." I took a deep breath. "Kelly's parents have, like, five empty bedrooms. We can take one of them over and lock the door." I leaned in and kissed his neck. "No parents, no interruptions." I felt him sigh as I moved up to his ear. "Just you and me…."

"You promise no one could walk in?" he asked, pulling my mouth off him.

I nodded. "We wouldn't be the first people who had sex at the Party, you know?"

He put a hand over my mouth. "I have heard enough today about who you have and have not been with. If you want to—"

"Do you?" I asked, interrupting him.

He hesitated and then nodded.

"You mean it?" I asked a little too eagerly.

He laughed. "Yes, yes, I want to."

I had to kiss him. No words could have expressed how excited I was.

And that was how we ended up going to the Party.

Something I don't think I will ever stop regretting as long as I live.

PART TWO

DEATH OF THE PARTY

Kyle

OVER THE next couple of days, a lot of things began to dawn on me.

Okay, more like they were screamed at me, but you know what I mean.

"So let me get this straight," Billy said, rummaging through my closet. "You wanna walk into the Lair of the White Worm, an action so insane it borders on suicidal, try to socialize with people who would literally spit on you for a couple of likes on IG, a feat you can't even accomplish with your imaginary friends, much less real people, and you're going to do all this dressed in what?"

It turned around and held up two shirts, "The lighter side of Sears or the shit Walmart marks down because no one in the world would buy it?"

I grabbed the shirts out of its hands and shoved them back into the closet. "I'll figure something out."

"May I suggest finding a rummage sale and hope for a lamp to rub?"

I walked over to my CD player and turned on *A-Teens Greatest Hits*.

"Bitch!" Billy hissed at me, "How can you let those attractive yet soulless kids butcher your people's music?"

"Can't hear you," I said, turning up "Dancing Queen," a rendition so corny it should have a high-fructose warning on it.

Billy shrieked and ran out of my room, hands over its ears.

Say whatever you want, I like A-Teens. It always cheers me up.

With my doubt out of the room, I looked at my closet and came up with the same conclusion I had the last three times I'd checked. I needed to beg Robbie for more clothes.

Or teach some mice how to sew a dress for me. I'll be honest, I was more inclined to obtain a grant to teach rodents how to manipulate a needle and thread before I actually went back and admitted to myself and to him that he had been right about me needing to face the Party head-on. Of course, I wasn't going for the reason he thought I should go, but I had a feeling he was just going to smile and nod and give me that look every adult gives kids when they disagree with them. That "Oh, isn't that cute! The baby can talk and wants to give his opinion. How adorable" look.

Sigh.

Today was Monday and the Party loomed on Friday. I worked today, which meant asking him at work or finding three rats somewhere. I breezed through the day at school, trying not to think how horrible it was going to be begging for new clothes. Brad noticed I was off, but he left it alone, no doubt thinking it was me trying to adjust to learning about him and Kelly. The thing was, I wasn't surprised they'd fooled around. If anything, knowing they had and that Brad had treated Kelly like crap helped explain a lot of things.

Kelly Aimes behaved like a complete asshole unless you looked at his actions from the perspective of him being a spurned lover. At some point, I actually started to feel sorry for him. It wasn't like I could blame him for having a crush on Brad. I mean, have you seen my boy's ass? There was no way the average human could spend more than a few days around him without getting at least a little crush on him.

But I have to be honest; I had absolutely no idea how to deal with this information.

I was just now almost getting my mind wrapped around the fact that Brad actually liked me; trying to expand that thinking to include the fact he liked me more than another person was too much for me. The way Billy was, if I tried to compare myself against any other person in the world, it would always end up with me walking away with a lifetime supply of Rice-A-Roni, the San Francisco treat. That, by the way, is an old game show reference for when the runners-up, or the losers on these shows, were given a lifetime supply of this rice product. I watch a lot of old game shows on YouTube; I have a thing for the '70s. Anyways, what I am saying is that Gollum from *Lord of the Rings* and me could be on a dating show and I would be going home alone. In my mind there is no way anyone, much less Brad, would pick me over anyone else, even Kelly.

For some reason I half expected Kelly to come by and sit with us at lunch, but it was just the four of us, Jennifer explaining the progress of the Prom Committee to Brad as Sammy and I ate in silence.

"So, you decided on that party?" she asked me quietly.

I nodded. "He wants to go, and I've never been before. It could be fun," I said in a voice so pathetic I didn't even believe it myself.

Sammy laughed. "You sound so convinced."

I stifled the groan of anxiety I felt about the party, making sure Brad couldn't hear me. "I am not going to know a soul; there will be all the popular people, and then me, sitting on the couch looking at my watch every fifteen minutes. You know what the worst part about that is?" I asked her. She shook her head. I held up my wrist. "I don't even own a watch."

She burst out laughing at that.

We both feigned innocence when Jennifer and Brad glanced at us. I elbowed her as they went back to talking. "You're going to get us busted!"

"I'm sorry. I was just imagining you looking at the freckles on your wrist," she said, smiling. "But it does sound horrible, though."

And then the Idea hit me.

"You should go," I said, almost jumping up in excitement.

She gave me a look I imagined I would get if I had offered her a fresh bowl of cow manure. "You're kidding, of course." I was surprised her words didn't drip acid into the concrete and leave pockmarks like alien blood.

"No! It's genius!" I said, ignoring her complete and utter disdain for the suggestion. "Look, the whole point of us going—well, I'm not clear on the *whole* point, but Jennifer seems to think me going is important. She said something about standing up and proving that different isn't bad. Am I right?" She nodded hesitantly. "So then why does that have to stop with me and Brad? Why can't it include you and Jeremy and everyone? If we want to make a statement, everyone should show up. The way to make it the Party is to make it a party for everyone." She didn't say anything, but at least she wasn't arguing anymore.

"Look, we've been here four years just like them, and the only people who go to that damn thing are them." I nodded toward Jennifer and Brad. "Let's show them they have been wrong this entire time. What are they going to do? Call the cops?"

"Kick our asses?" she countered.

Wow, she answered that fast.

"Not if there are more of us than them." I gave her a smile, and I saw her eyes light up. "Forget the Party… let's call it Occupy Foster."

"No more 1 percent?" She was grinning now.

"No, let them keep their 1 percent. I just want to show them the other 99 percent." The Idea felt right. Well, no, not right. It felt very, very Wrong, and that felt completely Right. If Jennifer thought Brad and I showing up would make a statement about equality, then we needed to make a real statement.

"Do we tell them?" she asked me, looking at Brad and Jennifer.

My first impulse was to say no, but I knew that was the wrong approach.

"Hey," I said, leaning forward toward Brad. "Isn't Friday night your D&D night with the council of nerds?"

He squinted and frowned at me, because he knew I knew Friday was D&D night. Though he liked his role-playing group, he didn't make it public knowledge. "Yeah, why?" he asked, trying to play off being a D&D nerd like it was no big deal.

"Did you tell them you weren't showing up this week?" I knew he hadn't.

"Um, not yet," he replied, hesitating, not really *sure* about the presence of a trap, but not really sure about his safety, either. He looked the same way a stalked deer might look before it ventured into a clearing. "Why?"

"Well, I was thinking. This whole 'going to the Party' thing is about us showing your ex-friends how wrong they were to exclude people for various reasons, right?" This time I asked Jennifer. She nodded slowly, no doubt sharing Brad's building sense of impending doom. "So then why don't we bring them to the party too?" Neither one of them even blinked. "In fact, why don't we bring a lot of people? Like Sammy and her drama friends, the library guys, heck, anyone who wants to go."

Brad's face remained neutral, but Jennifer automatically rejected it. "But they weren't invited," she tried.

"So? Neither were Brad or me, for that matter." Jennifer winced microscopically; she did not like where this was going.

Sammy chimed in. "Didn't you say it wasn't that kind of party? That people just showed up? So what if we all showed up?"

You could see the wheels turning in Jennifer's mind as she tried to find words that wouldn't come out sounding like she was insulting us. "I am saying, I have no problem bringing people I know to a party, but strangers who I don't know at all—"

"I know the drama crew," Sammy interrupted her. "And Brad obviously knows the library guys."

"Brad," she said, looking over at him desperately. "Help me out here."

He glanced at me, silently asking me if I knew what I was doing.

I did not, but I gave him a smile like I did. I saw him smile. Then, turning back to her, he shrugged. "I'm with them. If we're going to do this, why not do this right? We aren't talking about posting an open invite on Craigslist. We are just saying to invite a few of our friends who would never get to go."

"Do you know what they would do if all those kinds of people showed up?" she asked.

"What kind?" Sammy asked. I imagined fog coming out of her mouth, the tone was so cold.

"I mean, people who normally don't go," Jennifer added quickly.

"No, you didn't," Brad said, not giving Sammy the chance to get started. "And we know it," he said in a softer tone. "Look, Jen, you were right. Those people are assholes, and we both knew it when we were part of the asshole group. It's time to shake things up. Let's do this right and invite everyone who never got a chance to go. You wanted to make a statement, let's make one."

She shook her head. "You do know most of the people there will just leave."

"Let them," I said, resisting the urge to leap up and hug Brad because I was so proud of him. "We'll have our own party."

She looked at the three of us and then laughed. "Okay, I know when I'm outvoted. But I would suggest not telling Kelly." She thought for a second and amended that to "No. Don't tell a soul. If word gets out, everything will be over before it starts. The only way this works is if we all show up out of nowhere."

I was about to say something when Sammy burst out with "Wait. So you're going to go along with it?" She stared intently at Jennifer.

She thought about it a second and nodded. "Yeah. I mean, I was trying to make a statement, not ruin the whole party, but if we have to ruin the party to make the statement, fuck it."

"Wow, you really aren't a bitch." As soon as Sammy said it, she clasped both hands over her mouth. "I am so sorry. That was mean."

Jennifer laughed. "I am a bitch, born and bred." She looked at Brad and smiled. "Maybe it's time I aspire to be more than that, huh?"

SAMMY TOLD her friends and swore them to secrecy, and Brad talked to Andy, Jeff, and Mike, who, of course, turned him down. It took him the better part of an hour to convince them he wasn't setting them up, and he really wanted them to come to an actual party. Finally I had to cut in and talk to them in a way they would understand.

"Look, guys," I said, interrupting Brad. "This is your moment. You have the opportunity to show everyone else that you are real people and are cool. Or you can refuse and spend the rest of your high school life as Morlocks." They got the reference, but Brad looked at me, confused. "Subterranean race of mutants that live under New York City." To the guys, I continued, "Or you come out of the dark and become X-Men. That's your choice. But you don't get to complain later and tell your friends you never get invited anywhere. This is your invitation. Take it or don't, but you lose the right to bitch about it forever."

The one with the curly hair—Jeff, I think—asked me, "Are you going?"

I nodded.

"We're in," he said, speaking for all of them.

Brad looked dumbfounded. "Just like that?"

The one with black hair, Mike, said, "Well, we didn't know Kyle was going. And he made the very cool X-Men reference."

Brad shook his head and wrote down Kelly's address. "Don't spread this around, okay? It's kind of a surprise."

The biggest of the three—that one was Andy—took the paper and added, "Who would we tell?"

I saw Brad had forgotten who he was talking to.

"Well, make sure you're there no earlier than nine. No one shows up early," he added as we were leaving.

"Should we bring something to eat?" one of them asked.

He shook his head and looked over at me. "I am so blaming you if this goes south."

I smiled and gave him a kiss on the cheek. "You worry too much."

Turns out, I did not worry nearly enough.

Brad

I AM a lousy liar.

You would think that wouldn't be the case since I spent most of my life pretending to be someone I'm not, but it was true. When it came to lying, I sucked. I think it was the fact I only had so much space in my head to keep Fake Brad running, so there was no room for me to learn how to lie about little things. I also think subconsciously it helped people believe there was no way I could be lying about my sexuality if I couldn't keep my mouth shut about a surprise party.

So when Kyle and I left the library, it was just a matter of time before I broke.

The last few periods, I kept to myself, which wasn't hard since I hadn't been let back into the pack of popular guys who sat together. For once I didn't mind because I knew they were talking about the Party, and that was a subject I needed to stay away from. So by the time school was over, I found myself half sprinting to practice before someone asked me whether I was going.

I slammed into Kelly because I was too busy looking behind me.

We both crashed back onto our respective asses, stunned from the impact.

"Hey," I said, getting up quickly. "Practice," I added, pointing at the gym.

He scrambled to his feet and grabbed my shirt before I could take off. "Hold on, I need to ask you something."

Damn.

I turned back toward him. "What's up?"

Please don't ask me about the Party. Please don't ask me about the Party. Please don't ask me about the Party.

"It's about the Party," he said.

Fuck.

"Um, okay," I said, looking for an escape route.

"You're coming, right?" he asked. The emotion in his voice made me feel uncomfortable because it reminded me of how shittily I had treated him in the past. I nodded, keeping my mouth shut. "And you're not bringing anyone, right?"

Fuck. *Fuck!*

"No. No, I'm not. Who told you I was bringing someone? Why would I do that? I mean… what?" The words came shooting out my mouth like verbal diarrhea, and I just couldn't stop them. "Whoever told you that is wrong, really wrong. I mean, why would I lie? What was the question again?"

See what I mean? I was never going to be James Bond.

"I wanted to make sure," he said, confused by the vocal explosion of words. "So we're good?"

"Good. Great. Perfect. Yeah—" I forced my mouth shut before "okey-dokey" escaped.

"Cool," he said, taking a half step away from me. "Uh, you okay?"

I nodded and commanded my mouth to stay shut.

"Well, okay… good practice," he finished, backing up a few steps.

I held up a hand and nodded. I waited until he turned and walked away before I let out a huge sigh. "Okey-dokey?" I berated myself. "What the hell, man?"

I shook the memory of my general idiocy off, and I jogged into the locker room and changed for practice.

Kyle

IT TOOK very little effort on my part to convince Sammy to skip her last class and head over to Robbie's for work, and to beg for mercy.

I figured if I had a civilian with me, he wouldn't make me beg as much as if I showed up alone. I was counting on the fact that Robbie would understand the social convention that involved not making a scene in front of strangers and abide by it. Both points were long shots, given the way Jennifer had described him to me, but I had to try.

As soon as I pushed open the door of the store, I knew my plan was for shit.

"J'accuse!" he proclaimed loudly from behind the counter.

My first impulse was to turn around and walk out.

Sammy pushed me from behind. "Come on! Go in or move!"

I had no choice but to walk in, which was definitely the wrong move.

Robbie charged around the counter and pointed a finger at me. "J'accuse! Mon petit citron!"

I paused. "Did you just call me your little lemon?"

He stopped and thought about it. "Perhaps, but it's the only French I know. So… j'accuse!"

I sighed as I rubbed my temples. "Sammy, that is Robbie; he's crazy. Robbie, this is Sammy; be nice."

He put a hand to his chest and did a pretty convincing display of being wounded. "Moi? You ask moi to be nice? When am I ever not nice?" he protested, taking Sammy's hand and kissing it lightly. "When have I ever been anything but the sweetest, most delightful person you ever met?"

"Every day I have ever known you," I said, trying to get him off Sammy's hand.

"You wound me," he proclaimed loudly. "To the very quick, sir, to the very quick." When he realized I wasn't going to respond to his theatrics, he stood up straight and asked, "So, ready to work?"

I nodded.

"Okay, I have some boxes in the back, you need to… what?"

He had noticed me just standing there, staring at him.

"I need to ask you something."

"What?"

I said nothing.

He waited and then sighed, "Well?"

My mouth refused to open.

"Oh, for fuck's sake, what could be so horrible you can't just…." His voice trailed off.

Please don't guess. Please don't guess. Please don't….

A smile broke out across his face as he shook a finger at me. "I knew you were listening."

"I am not going because of you," I shot back instantly. "This has nothing to do with you!"

Oh yeah, Kyle, that's the way to get him to give you free clothes.

"Uh-huh," he said, casually examining his nails. "Tell me another one."

"Do you guys, like, need some time alone?" Sammy asked uncomfortably.

"He needs meds," I said, glaring at Robbie.

"And you need clothes, Cinderella," he retorted, leaning toward me. "So I would lose the 'tude and get with the kissing." To solidify his point, he smacked the left cheek of his ass.

"Screw this. I'll go naked," I said, turning around.

"Least that decision shows courage!" he shouted back at me.

I spun back to look at him. "I have courage! I just don't believe in what you believe in. Why is that so bad?"

I expected him to shout back and say something sarcastic, but instead his face got somber. "You'll figure it out. The hard way, but you will figure it out." He looked over at Sammy and smiled. "And that is easily the coolest color blue I have ever seen in Foster." He gave me an exaggerated glance and then, in a stage whisper, he said to her, "You are way too cool to be with him."

I closed the store door, knowing this round of drama was over.

She laughed at him and did a small pose as she cupped her hair with a hand. "What can I say? I was in a blue mood."

"Well, we should all be so blue," he said, leading her toward a rack of dresses. "I call this rack of dresses my Helena Bonham Carter collection. They are dresses that are too dark for anyone normal to wear." He pulled out a raven-black dress that had been slashed diagonally across the front as if it had been attacked by a giant wolverine. Inside the cuts, though, a shocking blue lining of satin gave the illusion that a second dress fitted underneath the outer layer.

Sammy actually covered her mouth when she saw it.

"Try this on," he said, handing it over to her reverently. She took it like it was made of spun crystal instead of cloth and thread. He pointed to the girls' dressing room, and she took off like an Olympic sprinter. As soon as the door closed, he turned back to me. "And you were looking for something in a flour sack?"

I bit the inside of my cheek to prevent me from saying something I would regret. "Can you help me or not?"

He rolled his eyes as he walked toward the men's clothing. "Well, I am not a miracle worker, but I can find you clothes."

"Why are you so shitty toward me?" I asked as he looked through the racks.

He looked over at me, saw the look on my face, and realized I wasn't joking. "Well… because I am willing to bet no one has ever talked to you like this."

"That is a good thing."

He had never met Billy.

He shook his head. "No, it's not. You never had a big brother, and you need one. I mean, look at you," he said, gesturing at me. "You're smarter than anyone in this town, you have a brain that can think circles around the best minds I've ever met, and you waste it stumbling over your own feet and hiding in your boyfriend's shadow." I opened my mouth to argue, but he ignored me. "You have the opportunity to really change things around here, and instead you're going to waste time trying to be normal." He grabbed a shirt off the rack. "Trust me on this, Kyle, normal is highly overrated." He handed me a pair of pants and a jacket. "You spend your life trying to be average, and you might end up succeeding." He pointed toward the changing room. "And then you'll be just like everyone else. Won't that be nice?"

I took the clothes and beat a retreat to the changing room.

I angrily began to put them on as I finished the argument safely in my head.

"There is nothing wrong with normal," I muttered to myself.

"You tell him," Billy said, sitting on the small bench in the changing room. "Normal is going to save your fucking life."

"Yeah, but is it going to be a life worth living?" my stubbornness asked.

Billy clapped back quick. "I don't know, stupid. How about you tell me what a death worth dying for is like?"

"Will the both of you shut up?" I said, buttoning up the shirt. "We aren't normal and we know it. So fuck off and argue somewhere else."

When I looked back they were gone.

I stomped out of the dressing room and looked in the mirror.

"Fuck, he did it *again*!" I muttered as I stared at myself in the clothes.

I had no idea how he did it, but once again the clothes had somehow transformed me from being mild-mannered Kyle Stilleno into, well, a real teenage boy. I wouldn't go so far as to say I looked good, I would never get myself there in regards to my self-esteem, but I had to admit I looked better than I had.

"You know, if you were serious about your convictions, you'd throw those clothes off and refuse to take them from me." Robbie was leaning against the door to the dressing rooms with a shit-eating grin on his face.

I tried not to look him in the eyes; I hear they have no power if you refuse to look them in the eyes.

"So do I look okay?" I asked, keeping my eyes fixed on the clothes in the mirror.

"Close," he said with a critical eye. "How much do you trust me?"

I made the mistake of looking him in the eyes.

The next thing I knew, I was perched on a stool in the back of the shop with a towel over my shoulders. Sammy watched in her dress, looking like something out of a nightmare Walt Disney might have had when he was alive. "You are crazy," she said to me. "And that is coming from someone who has a primary color in her hair."

Robbie stood behind me with scissors in his hand and a leer of what I was sure was pure evil on his lips. "Quiet, you," he ordered, accenting his words with the snipping of blades. "And you? Head down," he added as he pushed my chin to my chest. "This takes concentration."

"Why do I feel I am going to regret this?" I asked, trying not to sound as scared as I felt.

"You'll regret me cutting that pretty face if you keep squirming," he threatened before he sprayed my hair with water. "I used to make a pretty good living cutting hair before I was sentenced to twenty-to-life in this one-horse town."

"Did they pay you to cut hair or pay you not to?" I asked, trying to glance over my shoulder.

He pushed my head down again. "One more word out of you and I will have you with pigtails. No joke."

I did not think he was joking.

For the next fifteen minutes, I tried not to wince every time he snipped off another piece of hair. Sammy had gotten bored with the whole thing and was looking through clothes.

"By the way," Robbie said, barely above a whisper, "if you're going to argue with yourself, may I suggest doing it silently? Because other people will think you're nuts."

I turned around and looked at him.

"We all do it, but seriously, kid, do it in private. My great aunt used to argue with herself, and she ended up eating pudding upstate in a place where people don't get to keep their shoelaces. You get me?"

I nodded, and he turned my head back around. "You aren't crazy, by the way. You're probably the only person who's smart enough to follow your train of thought."

That didn't do much to cheer me up.

Robbie had assured me the only thing I needed was a trim to make the look complete, and like an idiot, I believed him. Over the years I had learned to love my shaggy hair because, one, it was easy to maintain; two, it didn't require a lot of money for haircuts; and three, it hid my eyes. It was my very own veil of privacy, and I was giving it up for a stupid party.

I saw more and more hair fall to the floor around me, and I felt my stomach start to convulse. "I do like my hair, you know."

"Then shut up," he said, standing in front of me and studying my bangs. He made three more cuts and then took a step back. "Okay, look left." I turned my head. "And right." I looked the other way. "Now stick your right hand out." I looked at him, confused, and held my hand out. "Okay, put it down." I put it down. "No," he said, shaking his head. "Put your hand out again." I slowly stuck it out. "Now shake it all about."

I flipped him off, and he started laughing.

I ripped the towel off and headed toward a mirror. "It's still wet!" he called after me. "It's going to look a lot better when it's styled!"

I envisioned my hair looking like I was in the late stages of radiation poisoning, the ones where there are just patches of hair sticking out of a balding headscape.

One look in the mirror and the breath I'd been holding left me in one shocked "Oh!" I honestly did not recognize the guy staring back at me.

"You hate it?" Robbie asked from behind me.

"I don't," I said, half-stunned. "I really don't."

The bad part was, I really didn't. He'd cut my sides short and left my bangs kind of long. The result made my whole face look different, longer. I looked older, but in a good way.

"See?" Robbie stated. "There was a handsome kid under all of that hair and insecurity after all."

Between the haircut and the new clothes, I looked 1,000 percent better, more like I imagined everyone else my age looked. "I can't believe that's me," I said, not even sure if I'd said anything aloud.

"Believe it, kiddo," he whispered.

I looked over to Sammy, and she gave me a thumbs-up. "But then, I never had a problem with your hair before," she added.

"All right, missy, a good haircut does a body good," he said, shooing at her. "Now go pack that dress up or I might charge you for it."

She gave him a double take before she took off toward the dressing room.

When we were alone, he began putting the new clothes in a bag. "Now remember—"

"Yeah, yeah," I said, cutting him off as I slipped on my shirt. "Make sure not to wear them to Nancy's."

He froze, his hand halfway in the bag.

"No," he said sternly. He dropped the bag and walked over to me, then put a hand on each of my shoulders. "No, I wasn't going to say that at all. I want you to wear them to Nancy's. I want you to wear them everywhere. And if some asshole throws a Coke on them, come back, and I will give you another set and another and another. And you will wear those in there too, and if he keeps throwing Cokes at you, then I'll buy you a raincoat. But you are not going to stop going to Nancy's or anywhere else you want to go, and you are not going to stop dressing nice. That's not the point."

I was shocked, and I knew my face was pale. "Then what is the point?" I asked, dazed by the strength of his conviction.

"The point is that They don't win. Sooner or later, someone is going to tell him to knock it off with the Cokes, and after that, he is going to get kicked out. And after that he is going to get banned, and then sooner or later someone will make it illegal for him to do that. And that, young man, is how change happens. One immaculately dressed boy at a time."

I felt my eyes stinging, and I realized no matter how sarcastic or rude Robbie got, he was always on my side. "Why are you so nice to me?" I asked him, wiping at my tears.

He ruffled my hair and went back to putting my clothes in a bag. "You mean you haven't figured it out yet?" I shook my head. "I'm your fairy godmother, bitch. Get used to it."

Brad

THE REST of the week was insane.

Winter Break on the horizon created its own excitement, but for us seniors, the fact that this Winter Break was our last one at Foster High made everything seem a little out of whack. The Party was also a "last," our last one as high school students. Between the two, our whack-out got worse by the day.

So far Kyle's plan to secretly invite people who never had a chance to go to one of these events seemed to be doing well. At least it hadn't become public knowledge yet.

And that fact continued to bug me.

Nothing moved faster through Foster High than gossip. Yet the fact that several dozen people knew what we were planning and none of them talked seemed impossible. It wasn't until I brought it up to Kyle that I understood why. He had been distracting as hell with his new haircut. I thought I had liked his shaggy hair, but this new look was just pushing all of my buttons, and I almost forgot to ask my question.

"No one you used to know listens to these people," he explained over lunch. "Even if they shouted what they knew in the middle of the quad, all they'd get is milk thrown at them. Gossip only works if the people hearing care about who is talking."

I suddenly understood why he wanted these people to show up to the Party.

By Friday the school was a mess. What little control the teachers had over us during the year vanished on days like these. Any work that needed to be done had been finished days before, giving way to period upon period of movies or free time where the teachers sat behind their desks and watched the clock as closely as we did. I wasn't even sure why we came to school except for the fact that if we had been given Friday off, we would have been completely useless on Thursday instead.

I sat in the back of the classroom with Jennifer while the rest of the class pretended to play hangman or slept.

"I am actually excited about tonight," she said, leaning in toward me. "I can't remember the last time I felt that way about one of Kelly's parties."

"Yeah, it's weird," I commented, watching the pack of jocks who used to be my friends play paper football on their desks. "Last year I would have been over there, not giving a shit about anything."

"And now you have Kyle," she said softly. I looked over at her and smiled. "He's good for you." She went back to making endless circles in her notebook. "He makes you a different person."

"I don't feel all that different, though."

She looked up to see if I was joking. "Oh, you are. Trust me, the difference is like night and day." She traced a few more circles. "But then, if you asked me last year if I was planning on smuggling a couple dozen nerds into the Party, I would have told you to fuck yourself sideways. So he seems to have that effect on people."

I put my hand on hers. "If it means anything, I like you a lot more like this than I ever did before."

She put her hand over mine. "You know, it does." She squeezed my hand and smiled. "It means a lot."

We sat through the rest of the class in comfortable silence.

I was telling the truth. I didn't feel all that different. I felt like I was the person I always wanted to be inside. The only real difference was I stopped editing who I was to fit in with people. I cared more about Kyle than I did about being liked, and that had made all the difference in the world. I walked out of the English building and saw Kyle coming toward me, and my face lit up. I strode to him, picked him up by the waist, and gave him a huge kiss right there in the middle of everyone. He looked at me, shocked. "What was that for?"

"For being you," I whispered to him. "And if I haven't said it enough, I am crazy about you."

This time he kissed me back.

He kept his arms around me and pulled a little away to beam a smile at me. "I'm not sure where all that came from, but we should do it some more."

"Get a room," Jennifer snarked, walking by us. I playfully kicked at her as she dodged out of the way, laughing. "So, we meeting up beforehand or just meeting at Aimes's?"

Good question. With parties like this, no one wanted to be the first one who showed up. Only lame people stood around doing nothing in the first uncomfortable minutes of a party. At the same time, no one ever wanted to be the last to arrive, because odds were everyone there would probably be talking about you. All of us showing up together would mean the party started when we showed up, since there were more of us than the jocks and their girlfriends. It was also a show of strength, proving to the people we invited that they weren't on their own.

"We could meet up at your place," I said to Jennifer. "You could catch a ride with us to Kelly's house."

"Um, yeah." She hesitated. "But what if you guys wanna go and be… oh, you know, by yourselves? How am I getting home?"

I started laughing while Kyle looked at me, confused. "We'll get you home," I said through my chuckles.

"I don't understand," Kyle asked. "Where would we go during a party?"

I leaned in and whispered in Kyle's ear, "She means what if we go upstairs and have wild monkey sex in an empty room."

It embarrassed me to admit how much I loved watching him blush.

"Trust me," I told her while I wrapped my arm around Kyle and tugged him close. "You have a ride home."

She looked at Kyle and then back to me. "Okay, if you promise."

"We promise!" Kyle blurted out.

I really resisted the urge to just break down laughing and instead nodded at her. "What he said."

"Be over by seven," she said, walking away.

I nodded as I tried not to cry from holding back my laughter.

"Shut up," Kyle said to me, seeing my face. "I mean it! Shut up."

I couldn't hold out and started to laugh as loud as I could.

"I hate you so much right now," he mumbled under his breath.

I jumped up and grabbed him from behind, picking him up in a bear hug as I twirled him around. "Don't blame me. Your new haircut drives me crazy!" I was rewarded by his laughter as I spun him around a few times. The fact that no one paused or even looked twice at us showed how distracted everyone was about Winter Break.

I put him down and caught my breath.

"You're crazy!" he said, hitting my back.

"That's a word for it," I said, turning toward him.

"Brad," he warned me, laughing, but I kept coming at him. "*Brad*!" He turned to run as I chased him to my car.

When I got there, I took the time to kiss him a couple more times before letting him go. "You know we can just skip the party and head out to the lake. You, me, the back seat…."

"We are going to that party!" he said seriously. "We promised people that we would—"

I kissed him again. He was so cute when he got worked up.

"We're going. Calm yourself, spaz," I replied, pushing him up against the driver's side door. "I'm thinking about what we are going to do at the party." I saw him get all shy for a moment, but then I felt his hips buck against mine.

"Are you sure you want to?" he asked in a whisper, like someone was close enough to hear us.

"I'm pretty sure you can feel how ready I am," I said, bucking my hips back. That got me a small blush.

"I mean, are you sure we won't get caught? How do you know someone else won't walk in or—"

I kissed him again.

"Don't worry, I got this," I said, giving him a reassuring smile. I waited for him to come to terms with the decision. The last thing I wanted to do was rush him into sex. Well, I wanted to rush him a *little*, but only if he wanted to do it, because I had a pretty serious case of blue balls going on. "Look, we don't have to do anything. I'm just saying that a party like that is the perfect place to get some alone time with no parents or anything bugging us. But if you don't want to—"

"I do!" he practically screamed, his voice cracking from the strain. He cleared his throat and tried again. "I do want to do that with you. I'm…." He sighed and leaned against my car. "I'm just scared about doing it somewhere weird like that."

"Then we don't do it," I reassured him, trying not to sound disappointed as I did so.

"But I want to!" he protested and sighed again. "I don't know…." He looked down, depressed, shuffling his feet.

I put a finger under his chin and tilted his face up until he was looking at me. "We don't have to do anything you don't want to or do it anywhere you don't want to. If you aren't into it, then don't worry."

"But I do want to." He half pouted. "I'm kinda chickenshit."

I laughed and pulled him into a hug. "No, you're completely normal. Don't worry about it." I tried not to make it obvious that my hard-on was killing me.

"No," he said, standing up suddenly. "No." He said it stronger. "I'm tired of being scared. You want to have sex, I want to have sex. We are going to that party and having sex!"

A guy walking by our car held up a hand and called out, "Hell yeah, get some!"

Kyle's head pressed into my chest as he moaned, "Oh God. I just yelled that out loud, didn't I?"

I nodded to a few girls who were laughing as they walked by. In a low voice, I said to him, "No, I'm sure no one heard that at all." I waved to another couple of people who were slowly turning away from where we were standing. Thank God this was the day before the break, or what Kyle had said would have been everywhere by Monday.

"I'm serious, though," he said, looking up at me. "I'm tired of being scared."

I smiled and kissed him on the forehead. "Then don't be scared. I'm here."

He hugged me back while I tried not to think about the fact I was going to have sex with my boyfriend tonight. I did try, but trust me when I say it had no effect on my junk whatsoever.

"So, are you coming over to change at my house?" I asked after a few minutes of holding him.

"No, I'm changing at my house, and you're picking me up like a proper date and everything," he said, smiling. "And you better not be late."

"Hey, if you're putting out, I'll rent a limo and have fireworks ready," I said, making him laugh.

"I, I mean… this is going to be our first real date, you know?" he explained softly.

And it hit me. Tonight would be our first date.

We had been together for months, and I had never actually asked him to go out with me. I was kind of shocked because if he had been a girl, I would have made a big thing about asking her out to a movie and all that, but with Kyle we just… happened. Suddenly I felt really weird about our relationship for some reason.

"Okay, then," I said aloud, trying to clear the confusion from my head. "Let's do it right." I grabbed his hand and slid my ring off his finger. I did it so fast he barely had time to acknowledge it was gone. I put it in my pocket. "Hi," I said, sticking out my hand. "My name is Brad."

He looked at my hand for a few seconds, shot a glance at my face, and then smiled and shook my hand. "I'm Kyle."

I gave him a huge smile. "Oh, trust me, I know who you are. I've been watching you for a while now."

He arched one eyebrow. "Yeah, that doesn't sound like a creeper at all."

"I mean, I've seen you around school. I've just been too shy to talk to you," I clarified quickly.

"Oh. You, shy?" he said skeptically. "I find that hard to believe."

I took a half step closer to him. "No really, in public I am like one person, but inside I am a really shy person." I tried to play it up, looking down as I spoke, sneaking a quick glance at him as I talked. "And I kinda like you."

"Kinda, huh?" he asked.

"Maybe," I said, taking another half step.

"I've heard that 'maybe' before." We stood face-to-face now.

"Okay. I definitely like you." I was so close he could hear me whispering.

"And?" he whispered back. I pressed a kiss to his forehead.

"And go out with me." I paused for a moment. "Tonight."

"On a date?" I could hear the smile in his voice.

"Very much on a date. You dress up, I dress up, we go to a party together…." I licked the outside of his ear and felt him shiver.

"Pick me up around six." He sounded like every ounce of his concentration was focused on not humping me there in the parking lot.

I pulled back and said in a chipper voice, "Six it is."

He almost fell onto his face. "You're a jerk," he growled as he regained his balance before he actually did get parking lot rash on his chin.

"I'm your jerk." I laughed and gave him a quick peck on the nose. "See ya at six," I said before I got into my car and hit the ignition.

"You're not dropping me off at my house?" he called out to me.

"Isn't it bad luck to see you before the date or something?" I called over the sound of the engine starting.

"That's the bride before a wedding, you goof!" he called after me.

I revved the engine over his voice and cupped a hand around my ear. "Huh? I can't hear you." He tried again, and I revved the Mustang even louder. Shrugging, I shouted, "Sorry, Kyle, it's too loud in here! See you soon!"

I let him think for about five seconds I was leaving before stopping and opening his door. He was laughing when he got in the car. "You are so cruel to me."

I stuck my tongue out at him and pulled out of the parking lot.

"You are so not getting any tonight with that attitude." I glanced over at him; he ignored me. I glanced over at him again; he ignored me some more. I stared at him with full-on puppy-dog eyes. He continued to ignore me.

For those of you coming in late, the score is Kyle 1, Brad 0.

Kyle

IF YOU had asked me one year ago what the chances were I would be getting ready to go to a party with Brad Graymark as my date,

I would have calmly explained to you that you were crazy. If you had insisted on making me come up with realistic odds, I would have told you to knock it off. If you had persisted, I probably would have thrown something at your face and run while you were distracted.

What? Did you expect me to actually lie and say I would have hit you?

Once when I was showering and twice while I was drying off, I had to fight the urge to pinch myself to make sure I wasn't dreaming. I settled for a fake slap to the one cheek. Nope, not dreaming.

Robbie had given me a bottle of gel so I could style my hair. "Style my hair," of course, had meant nothing to me, so he spent another twenty minutes showing me what styling my hair meant. Turns out styling involves a lot of putting some kind of goop in my hair and then moving the hair around with a comb until I liked what I saw in the mirror.

Since I never liked what I saw in the mirror, I just screwed around with my hair until it looked close to what it had when I walked out of Robbie's.

Next came the clothes. The jeans were skinnier than the ones I normally wore but weren't as skintight as the ones I've seen on some guys at school. This time the button-up shirt was royal blue with black stripes. Robbie also gave me a pair of dark-brown leather shoes; they were the first shoes I had owned as a teenager that weren't sneakers. The last piece of clothing was my favorite. It was a black blazer that fit over the shirt perfectly. Robbie told me when I walked in I should have one button closed, but when I started to talk to people I should unbutton it.

I took a deep breath before looking in the mirror. This was going to be the first time I had seen the whole outfit with the hair combined. I prayed I wouldn't look like some little kid dressing up in his dad's clothes.

An American teenager stared back at me.

"Well, look at this suave motherfucker," Billy remarked behind me. "When they show your body on the news, everyone will say how well dressed you were when you got beaten to death by a pack of wild Neanderthals."

"Leave him alone," my self-esteem said. "He looks good."

Billy turned to face it. "Did I say he didn't look good? Did those words ever get near to dropping out of my mouth? No, ma'am, they did not. So why don't you twist yourself into a position where you can try to pull your head out of your ass."

My self-esteem shut up.

"Why you trying to scare the boy?" my defiance asked. "This is supposed to be a fun night."

"Yeah, and the Donner party were supposed to be vegan. Things don't always work out like they're supposed to."

"He does have a point," my fear said, coming from behind my chair. "We could get hurt."

This was getting out of hand.

"Look, everything will be okay. Brad will be with me," I said with way too much confidence.

"Oh, superjock is cosplaying Kevin Costner, is he? Well, let me tell you." Billy looked me up and down. "You ain't fucking Whitney Houston."

I might have stayed in there even longer if my mom hadn't pounded on the door. "Okay, come on, Cinderella! Let's see the goods."

I counted to ten in my head before opening my door.

And was instantly blinded by the flash of a camera.

"Oh my God! You look adorable!" she enthused. I rubbed my eyes vigorously, trying to clear the afterimages, and didn't respond.

"That is a sharp jacket," a male voice remarked. Wait. What?

I squinted and blinked a few times. Tyler stood next to Mom. For some reason, I had the impulse to cover myself, even though I was fully dressed. "Oh, hey, Tyler."

"Well, I know you weren't going to take my word for it that you looked good, so I brought a gay man over to prove it," my mom explained as she half blinded me again.

Tyler gave me a small smile. "There is no way I can comment on the way you look without sounding like a complete pervert, so I will just say, you look more than presentable."

For some reason, hearing those words from a man made me feel good. "Thank you," I replied. My mom clicked and blinded me again, although the third time I was ready for her and got my eyes shut. Mostly. "Mom, I think we have captured this particular Kodak moment." Tyler cocked his head and chuckled.

"If I remember correctly, Linda, you said something pretty close to that to your mom the night we went to the prom." She gave him an ugly look in response.

"You took my mom to prom?" I asked, shocked at the idea that there had been proms when Mom had been a teenager and at my incredibly bad poetry.

"No, *I* took *him* because he was terrified the other girls who wanted to go with him would want him to put out, so he begged me to be his date to protect him from girl cooties." She grinned slyly at Tyler. He face-palmed.

"Ignore her," he advised casually. "She lies."

Mom and Tyler were talking like regular people instead of adults. I could almost see the kids they used to be peeking behind their eyes as they ragged on each other. It was cool but unsettling as hell.

Thankfully, a knock on the door saved me from further embarrassment.

"Oh God, he's here," I said. All the courage I had saved up in my life to spend in a moment like this spiraled down an imaginary drain. "I look like crap," I said. I spun on my heel, turning to head back into the bathroom.

I did not expect two hands to grab me by my shoulders and do a one-eighty with me. Tyler stared me in the face. "You look great. You do not look stupid. And he is waiting for you to answer the door." His voice was calm yet stern. His words carried weight, and I could feel myself quieting. "You have made it ninety-nine yards so far. All you have to do is walk to the door and you score." His smile made him look ten years younger. "Don't chicken out now."

I took a deep breath and calmed myself. In a voice that seemed to come from outside of myself, I said, "I understood everything but the ninety-nine yards part, but I will assume it's a sports reference and leave it at that."

He smiled and nodded.

"Have fun," my mom called after me as I walked to the door. "But not that much fun!" she added after a second.

I turned the doorknob and held my breath.

You know those moments in movies where the camera falls on the leading man and then pulls back to reveal the rest of the scene? That was exactly what happened in my head. I saw Brad and his smile and all my nervousness fled as quickly as it had come. And then I saw he was leaning against his car, his arms crossed, with a dozen roses clutched in one hand. He wore a pair of khakis that clung in all the right places. His green V-neck sweatshirt over a white T-shirt also did some very right clinging.

He looked perfect.

Brad's grin faltered, then faded when I walked out. He stood up straight, looking dazed, his arms dropping to his sides. Shaken, rose petals fell to the parking lot. I glanced over my shoulder just to make sure there wasn't a lunatic wielding a knife behind me.

Then it hit me; I looked hideous.

"Oh God, you hate it!" I choked, wheeling in panic back toward my house.

"Stop!" he called out in a voice that was way louder than I think either of us expected. The word echoed across the apartment complex, and we both ducked our heads and looked at each other like little kids who'd done something seriously wrong. "Get over here!" he whispered loudly enough for me to hear.

"You don't like the way I look," I repeated, not moving.

"Are you insane?" he said, almost dropping the flowers. "I didn't say that." He walked over to me.

"Your face did," I said miserably.

"Uh-huh, my face—well, congratulations, you are officially off my list of people who could possibly be Batman. You suck at reading body language; you'd never figure out who the guilty party was. If you were Batman, you'd know that my face was trying to figure out how to make my eyeballs pop out of my head at the same time as rolling out my tongue like a carpet when I saw you." I felt myself begin to blush. "You look… just wow," he mumbled, too stunned for complete words, much less sentences.

"So then you do like it?" I asked, smiling; it was a little smile, ready to run for cover at the first sign of trouble.

"It is easily the second-best look you've rocked so far," he answered easily.

It took me half a second. "Wait! Second-best? You liked the vest better?" He shook his head. "Then the way I normally dress?" Another shake of the head. "Uhm, so how is this second-best?"

"Well, I think you look your hottest when you're wearing nothing but a blanket, but that's just my opinion."

I felt every inch of my body blush. *Another topic, quick, another topic or I'll jump him*, I thought desperately. The flowers—I latched on to the noun "roses" and swam away from imminent jumping on the boyfriend.

"Are those for me?" I asked, looking at the roses.

"They are, if you don't think it's too gay for me to give you flowers," Brad added clumsily.

"How can we be too gay?" I asked him.

"I don't know," he whined. "I have no idea how to do this whole dating thing with another guy! Give me a break!"

"What would you do if I gave you flowers?" I asked him.

He thought about it for a moment. "Um, thank you and then wonder what I was supposed to do with them."

"Yahtzee! We'd do exactly the same thing!" I said, laughing. I took the flowers and kissed him on the cheek. "Thank you."

He kissed me back. "So now I hold the door open for you and stuff?" he asked, worried.

"How about we make it up as we go along?" I offered as we walked over to his car.

"Okay, cool," he said as I opened my own door. I put the flowers in the back seat since I wasn't going to walk around like I had won the Miss Foster Pageant all night. "So, are you hungry?" he asked once we were buckled up.

"What about Jennifer?"

"We have time," he assured me as he flashed me his Tom Cruise, Everything is Peachy Keen smile.

As soon as we pulled onto East Avenue, my nervousness faded and my brain began to work again. I looked over to him. "You are such a dork."

He gave me a double take. "What did I do now?"

"You actually knocked on the door and then ran back to lean on your car just so you could look all pimp, didn't you?" It was one of the few times I had ever seen *him* blush. "Oh my God, you did!" I burst out laughing.

"I was trying to set the scene," he said, attempting some dignity and failing pretty spectacularly.

"I am dating a Grade A cheese ball!" I shouted out the window as we turned onto First Avenue.

"But seriously…," he said, clearing his throat. "I did look cool, didn't I?"

I almost started crying, I was laughing so hard.

Then Brad parked in front of Nancy's, and I felt my stomach tighten. Before I could start thinking, he covered my hand with his and squeezed. "Trust me?"

I nodded.

He got out of the car and ran around to my side to open my door. "Then come with me," he said, holding his hand out to me.

If one of you haters out there says one thing about me being a princess, I swear I will hunt you down and punch you in the face. I am not joking.

I took his hand, and he led me up the steps to the diner's front door. There were no lights on, so I started to say something about it being closed. But he had asked me to trust him, so trust he got. He opened the door. The sound of the small bell over the doorway was a thousand times louder than normal with no one inside.

When we got in, I could see a pale flickering light coming from the far front corner. A mysterious smile on his face, Brad nodded in that direction and tugged me along. Gayle stood waiting for us, two menus held textbook style across her chest. A white tablecloth covered the table, and the lone candle in the middle cast a warm light that glimmered off the plates and the silverware set for two. "Your table is ready, gentlemen," she said, winking at me. I literally had no words and couldn't think enough to object when Brad helped me slip into the seat before he slid into the booth opposite me. His eyes sparkled mischievously as he watched me fumbling for words. Evidently, that was the right reaction if his grin was any indication. Gayle put the menus down in front of us. "If you're willing, may I suggest the chef's specialties tonight? Yes? Excellent. The first course will only be a moment." As she walked away, another waiter appeared and put two glasses of soda in front of us.

"How did you…?" I began to ask, but he held up one finger, asking me to wait.

I heard the metallic clink of coins being dropped into a machine across the room. Gayle leaned a bit over the restored 1950s jukebox, pushing buttons. The music of Lifehouse began to play softly in the background.

He put down his finger. "You wanted a date," he said, smiling. "You get a date." He reached across the table and grabbed my hand.

"You never cease to amaze me," I managed lamely, completely astounded by the green-eyed boy who had taken my heart.

"If I ever do, let me know," he asked, tracing his fingers over the top of my hand. "I'll step up my game."

I shook my head. "Your game is pretty good right now, trust me."

He gave me his Ferris Bueller know-it-all grin. "You haven't seen anything yet."

Gayle reappeared carrying a plate of chili cheese fries that looked and smelled so perfect that I knew they had been handmade. She set the plate on the table and smiled at both of us. "Frites à mozzarella fromage et chili," she announced; after bowing slightly, she backed away from the table.

"I love these fries!" I said, grabbing one, watching gleefully when the cheese stretched off the plate. He laughed as I cut the cheese with a bite and popped the fry into my mouth. "Oh my God!" I said as I chewed. "You have to try these!"

We devoured the entire plate before the song had even finished.

"This is the best…." I struggled to find words. "I mean, you are…." I shook my head and settled for "Just wow."

The music changed to Edwin McCain.

Brad slid out of the booth. "Come on," he said, holding his hand out. "Dance with me."

I mean it, guys: one princess joke and you're dead.

We slow danced in the middle of the diner as he sang that he would be the biggest fan of my life in my ear. I had never felt so happy… ever. In fact, if you were to take all the happy moments of my life and add them up, they wouldn't even equal the fries, much less this dance. He assured me he would be my crying shoulder, and I leaned into him as we swayed. His voice was deep and imperfect, but it expressed each emotion so perfectly that I knew I would never hear this song again without hearing his voice singing along with it.

I was eighteen years old, and I finally knew what the word "love" meant.

When the song ended, we sat down again and were surprised to find two perfect bacon cheeseburgers waiting for us. "You seriously thought of everything, didn't you?"

He shrugged as he took a bite, but I could see the laughter in his eyes.

We finished the burgers in silence; both of us knew we couldn't carry on a conversation with one of Gayle's burgers sitting in all its tempting glory right in front of us. Like magic, as soon as we were finished, the second waiter materialized from the shadows to take our plates away. Once he had retreated, Gayle arrived, with the same Cheshire cat grin on her face. "Are the gentlemen ready for dessert?"

"Oh God!" I puffed, wiping my mouth. "I am stuffed."

Brad nodded. "Yeah, we're ready."

"I seriously don't think I can eat anything else," I said, trying and failing to stop her.

"You'll want this," he assured me with his Chris Evans grin that meant he had something else planned.

"This is really enough, you know." I tried to reason with him, but it was no use. He had set this whole thing up, and we weren't leaving until Vanna turned all the letters around. "So, any clues?" He just looked at me with that same smile. I sat back and waited.

I didn't have to wait long, because Gayle came out holding a small chocolate cupcake with some whipped cream on top of it. Instead of a cherry, though, on top sat Brad's class ring, polished and sparkling like new.

And I was speechless for the second time in an hour.

He removed the ring from its cakey throne and licked the whipped cream off. "So now you've had a real date," he said, getting up out of the booth. A light tug on my hand was all Brad needed to propel me to my feet and face him. "We had our first dance," he added, getting down on one knee. "And now I am going to ask you to be my boyfriend." He took my hand. "That is, if you want to be." And there was that smile again. "Kyle Stilleno, will you be my boyfriend?"

My eyes started to sting as they teared up.

I just nodded since I was incapable of actually making any sounds resembling speech. He slipped the ring on my finger and pulled me into a hug. "I love you," he whispered in my ear, and I had never believed it so much as I did right then and there.

Gayle and the waitstaff were clapping and offering congratulations, but I honestly couldn't hear them over the sound of Brad's voice in my ear telling me again and again that he loved me.

It was the first perfect moment I could ever recall having.

Brad

THE PERSON I was before I met Kyle would have tried to convince you that setting up our first date was more for him than for me. He would have assured you that it was a means to an end that led to me having sex with him. The guy I was before would have told you a lot of things, most of them flat-out lies.

The person I am now can tell you, watching him sneaking glances at that ring on his finger as we drove over to pick up Jennifer made me so happy I could burst. Kyle's such a good guy—no! a great guy—and up to this point he had never had one break in life. He had never had someone trip over themselves to go out with him or go through all the trouble of having someone cook all his favorite foods. He should have had that, but he hadn't until tonight.

He had been worse than ugly; he had been invisible, one of the countless unknown people no one noticed as they wandered through high school on their own unnoticed missions in life.

As I held his other hand, I was so fucking glad I noticed.

"So it's official, right?" I asked as we turned onto Jennifer's street. "You're my guy now?"

His smile could have warded off vampires, it was so bright. "Only if you're mine."

I laughed and glanced out at the street to check for traffic before I turned my attention back to him. "You know I am not just your boyfriend, right?" He was puzzled and looked like he had no idea what I meant. "I am 100 percent your love slave. I am now and will always be your bitch." His mouth dropped half open at my words. "I want you to be sure where we stand. I am so in love with you that I would do anything you asked. Anything."

I knew I had shared too much when he withdrew all the way to his side window for a moment. Next would be some self-deprecating statement he was going to treat like a joke but would actually be a pretty good sign of how he was really feeling.

"You're just saying that 'cause of the blazer," he tossed out.

I parked in front of Jennifer's house and turned the car off. I leaned over until I could look him directly in the eyes and said, my voice raspy with emotion, "You do know you didn't have to change a thing about the way you looked, right?" He blinked quickly but said nothing, which told me that was exactly what he had been thinking. "I am not going to lie and say you don't look incredible in those clothes, but I was crazy about you before. I don't want you thinking I want you to look or dress a certain way, because I don't. I am turned-on by Kyle, any kind of Kyle I can get. Dressed up, shaggy-haired, blanket-wearing, all Kyles are welcome." I could see the relief in his eyes even though he would deny it if I asked him. "All you have to do is walk in the room and I'm turned-on, no matter how you're dressed."

"What did I do to deserve you?" he murmured, nearly breathless from keeping his feelings inside.

I wrapped my right arm around his shoulder, and he slid toward me. I kissed him and explained, "You charged in and saved me from the monster."

"What monster?" he asked, bewildered.

"Myself," I answered. My phone rang just then and startled us both. I looked down and there was a text waiting.

Jennifer: Are you two making out in front of my house or am I being stalked by another two gay guys?

I showed Kyle the text, and we both started laughing our asses off.

Two minutes later Jennifer plunked down in the back seat. "You guys going to sit out here all night or what?"

I jerked a thumb toward Kyle. "Blame him, he was getting all handsy."

Kyle shot me a glance. "Say what?"

"I mean, I am not just a piece of meat, Kyle."

He glared at me and opened his mouth to say something....

So I turned the car on quickly before he could. "We all ready?"

She nodded, but Kyle was still giving me a look. "I was handsy? What happened to love slave?"

"And we're gone," I said, shifting into Drive.

Jennifer was rummaging in her purse. "I am not even going to ask what that meant," she said, moving stuff around, "but I did bring reinforcements." She pulled a small bottle of schnapps out of her purse and held it up.

Kyle's eyes almost fell out of his head. "You're drinking?" He was looking at Jennifer, but from the way he glanced over at me, I knew he was asking me.

And right then it occurred to me I hadn't honestly thought things through very well.

"Are you drinking tonight?" Kyle asked again, this time looking at me.

See, I hadn't deduced everything about Kyle's past, but figuring out his mom was a mean drunk had been pretty easy. I don't mean to say Linda Stilleno is Foster's town drunk, but in a postage stamp of a town like Foster, once someone earned a reputation, that person became gossip fodder. And Kyle's mom had a reputation. I didn't know squat about children of alcoholics, but that was no excuse. I should have thought things through better.

Jennifer and I always frontloaded before a party.

Frontloading is getting drunk before you go out in case wherever you end up doesn't have the right kind of drink or even might not have any alcohol at all. Dealing with the Drama Olympics that come with a party like the one we were about to go to had always been easier if I walked in already lit. Frontloading's like Novocain before a root canal. It just numbs the parts that are going to cause you excruciating pain later on.

I should have known Kyle would be worried about people drinking, especially me.

"No," I said after a second. "No, I'm not drinking tonight." I looked in the rearview mirror at Jennifer. "And I wish you wouldn't either."

She paused with the bottle to her lips. "Why?"

Good question. How did I get her to not drink without exposing Kyle's home life?

"Because when things go south tonight, I'd like someone who these guys respect by my side to talk some sense into them." I saw her eyes looking back at mine in the mirror. She knew me too well to just buy what I was saying, but she was letting me go on. "And when that happens, I really need you sober."

"Why do you automatically think there is going to be drama?" she asked, still not drinking.

"Because I know these people as well as you do, and I know Tony is going to be there. And what do you put the odds on that he won't say something? What about Kelly deciding to be a dick tonight, *and* this is Foster, Texas. Do I have to say more?"

She sighed and put the bottle in her purse. "First we invite the Island of Misfit Toys to the Party, and now I'm going sober. Never let it be said, Kyle, that you haven't made a difference around here."

He didn't say anything, but I saw Kyle smile and relax into his seat. Only then did I understand what he'd been going through. I hadn't even factored in that Kyle might not equate parties with something positive. And as always, he said nothing and went along with it.

How had no one noticed him?

Kelly lived in a much better neighborhood than the rest of his friends, something his dad made sure to bring up every time he spoke to our parents. A fact that pissed my dad off so much that he usually walked away before he hit someone.

"I could afford to live in a better neighborhood if I had a cousin who tipped me off on a good stock too. Fucking asshole wouldn't know a blue-chip stock from a poker chip."

And then my mom would say, "Of course, dear," which was adult for "Sure, Jan," and they'd start fighting.

Good times.

When we got to Kelly's house, there were a few cars already parked outside, which meant we weren't the first people to arrive. That was a good thing, because it also meant there would be people inside bored silly just waiting for other people to arrive. Jennifer must have thought the same thing because she leaned up from the back seat and said, "I bet the people sitting in there now are so bored they wouldn't care if we had the Rose Bowl Parade with us."

I parked the car some distance away from the house. "I have a feeling they would prefer the Rose Bowl to who we brought." My words sounded sour in my own ears, and I realized I was reverting to old habits. Sarcasm, apathy, self-deprecating talk….

That wasn't who I was anymore.

Before Kyle could say anything, I said, "No—we're going to make this fun. It will most likely be just this side of a three-ring circus, but we are going to have fun no matter what. Right, guys?" I turned to the two of them. They stared back at me, owl-eyed, like I had started speaking in Farsi. "Right, well, let's try to have fun at the very least, okay?" I said in a much lower tone of voice.

Kyle opened his mouth to say something, but then the sound of someone knocking on his window from outside interrupted him. When I say interrupted him, I really mean scared the living shit out of us.

"What the fuck?" Kyle yelled, trying to jerk away from the window. The seat belt stopped him and threw him back into his seat. He started fighting with his buckle, but I put a hand over his to calm him.

"I think that's Andy," I said, nodding toward the window.

Kyle rolled his window down, and sure enough Andy, leader of the library nerds, stood there with Jeff and Mike behind him. "We didn't know what the definition of too early was," Andy said apologetically. "We were hoping you hadn't shown up yet and already gone inside."

"We're here, might as well walk up with us."

They nodded and waited for us to get out of the car.

"Why do you all have tablets?" Kyle asked.

"Um, in case no one will talk to us, we thought having Hearthstone on hand would pass the time."

I could hear Kyle's eyes rolling. "Give them to me."

They all looked at him, shocked, clutching their tablets.

"I'm serious, if you guys have those, all you're going to do is sit somewhere and play with each other. You're not here to do that."

"We're not?" Jeff asked, confused.

"No, you're here to socialize," he said firmly.

"But they are just going to tease us and say nasty things," Mike said.

"And spit," Jeff added.

"And spit at us," Mike added.

"Bullshit," I said, getting angry. "No one is going to spit on you while I'm around. You guys are my friends now. No one will bully you. I promise."

They all stared at me in silence before Andy asked, "We're your friends?"

"Of course, what did you think we were?"

"Um, a distraction?" he said.

"A mistake," Jeff answered.

"Slumming until you got popular again," Mike admitted.

I had never hated myself more than I did at that moment.

"He isn't like that," Kyle said, coming to my defense. "Brad would never just hang out with you guys and then ignore you. He has fun with you guys, and I think you really hurt his feelings 'cause he thought you all were friends."

They looked at me, stricken, but I didn't trust myself not to say anything to make it worse.

Andy took a step forward. "Look, we're sorry. Just a lot of guys who… well, that are like you were fuck with us. They pretend to be friends to get homework done, figure out how to fix something on their phone, and then in public trash us. We weren't sure what you were doing with us."

"Trying to make friends," I said miserably.

Andy looked back at the other guys, and they nodded. "Okay, go down on one knee."

He asked me to what?

"Huh?"

"Go down on one knee," Andy said again.

I glanced at Kyle, who just shrugged.

I went down slowly, wondering if this was a mistake.

"Bradley Graymark, thoust were a douchebag of the highest order."

I heard Jennifer chuckle.

"You failed not only your school but yourself. Your honor is stained."

Yeah, this was a mistake.

"But though you have wandered through the darkness of jockdom, you can still be saved."

"Um, my knee is starting to hurt," I muttered.

He tapped his hand on each of my shoulders and said, "Right, so with all graces and powers bestowed upon me by the Council of the Three, rise and be known as Sir Graymark, Knight of the Realm."

I looked at him, and he nodded.

I stood up, and the three of them cheered.

"I guess it's the Council of Four now," Andy said as Jeff bowed to me.

It was all very corny, but I have to admit, it made me feel good.

"Kyle!" Sammy's voice called from down the street. "Is that you?" Kyle waved back, and Sammy and the rest of the drama crew came walking behind her.

"You wanna get on your horse and escort them over?" Jennifer asked.

I flipped her off.

Sammy had a dramatic black dress on with slashes across it showing an electric blue lining underneath. Her friends were dressed like they had walked out of the movie *Underworld*, with pale white makeup and leather coats for all. One half of my brain thought they looked completely badass; the other half thought this was just an inferno waiting for a lit match.

"Someone didn't think you were actually coming," Sammy said, not looking at Jeremy. "So we were waiting until we saw you show up."

"You wanted me to be here, right?" Jeremy asked Kyle.

"Yeah, all of you," Kyle answered quickly.

The way Jeremy was looking at Kyle was… off.

"So we're all here?" Kyle asked, looking at the collected group of people who had surrounded us. I wasn't sure if he was counting or not, but he looked them over and then nodded to me. "I think we're good."

He looked at me with those bright blue eyes with all the trust one person can have for another, and I just melted inside. "Okay, then," I said, smiling at him. "Then let's go to a party."

We walked across the street like we were reenacting a scene from *Braveheart* as done by the cast of *Revenge of the Nerds*. Part of my mind told me I should be worried or at the very least embarrassed by showing up with these people behind me, but as Kyle's arm looped around mine, those thoughts went away.

I was one of these people now, and there was nothing wrong with that.

One deep breath later, I knocked on the door.

The thumping of the bass could be heard from here; no one behind me said a word. I knocked again louder, and Kelly's voice screamed, "Coming!" from the other side.

The look of joy and excitement on Kelly's face lasted all of six seconds from the moment he opened the door and then saw I wasn't alone. "Brad?" he asked, his voice cracking in surprise. "What the hell?"

I tried to keep the most neutral look on my face. "You invited me, remember?"

He said something as he turned away from the door and stomped back into the house. I turned to Jennifer and asked, "What did he say?"

"He said he only invited you," she said in a quiet voice as we began to stream inside.

"Oh. Well, *that* can only mean the rest of the night will go well," I said, making sure everyone else didn't hear.

"What's wrong?" Kyle asked when he saw Jennifer and me talking.

"Kelly opened his door and saw a couple dozen strangers; what do you think is wrong?" I tried not to sound sarcastic, but I couldn't pull it off, since all I could imagine was these people blaming me for them being harassed all night. I shook my head and added, "I'm sorry; I just have a bad feeling about this."

Kyle smiled for a second and then tried to hide it.

"What's funny?" I asked, desperate for anything to laugh at before this night got sideways.

"It's a *Star Wars* thing," he explained, sounding half embarrassed. "Never mind," he added when he saw I didn't get the reference. "Come on. It'll be fine."

Though there were several dozen outcomes I could imagine for tonight, none of them even got close to fine.

"Sure you don't want to drink?" Jennifer asked as we headed toward the living room.

I said no, but I was lying my ass off.

Despite our effort to show up late, we were still some of the first ones there. You could tell because the four guys who had been there before us were now huddled together near the kitchen, as if the unpopular guys were carrying a communicable disease or something. This was exactly what I had been worried about. Kyle had imagined some kind of great communing between the groups, but this was exactly the situation I had been dreading. Both groups had more than enough opportunities to mingle at school; just because they were in the same house wouldn't change the way they acted toward each other. Sammy and her friends were huddled together by the stereo, almost instinctively circling their wagons against attack. Andy and the library crew sat on the couch, looking around aimlessly. Since

Kelly's friends were standing by the refreshments, no one dared to approach them to grab something to drink.

It honestly looked like a junior high party with all these different cliques hovering around each other, no one saying a word.

"If looks could kill, you'd be one of the Beatles," Jennifer whispered to me, pointing out Kelly in the kitchen, glaring at me. She was right. He was boring a hole through my face that would have blown out the back of my head like a hollow-point bullet if emotions could be made real.

"I should talk to him," I said, not making the smallest effort to move.

"Better you than me," she remarked, also not making any attempt to move. "I don't think I've ever seen him that mad before."

I sighed mentally. "I have," I said, making the decision to talk to him. Looking over to Kyle, I said, "You going to be okay out here by yourself? I think I need to talk to Kelly."

He nodded and gave me a small smile. "He looks really mad." I had to agree, taking another glance at Kelly out of the corner of my eye. "Here's for luck," Kyle said, giving me a small kiss on the cheek.

"Fuck!" Kelly screamed, throwing his beer bottle across the kitchen. The sound of breaking glass was like a bomb exploding. He stormed off deeper into the house.

"Yeah, that's my cue," I said to Jennifer and Kyle. "Wish me luck."

"Don't get killed," Jennifer said, smiling.

"What she said," Kyle added.

I walked into the kitchen and grabbed a couple of closed beers before following Kelly's trail across the house. I hadn't been here in a while, but I remembered the general layout well enough. He wasn't in the living room or the bathroom, which only left upstairs. I climbed the stairs two at a time, hoping he wasn't up there grabbing a gun from his father's rack or something. The door to his bedroom was open, and I could see someone pacing around.

"Kelly?" I called out, peeking into the room.

The door flew all the way open, and he stood there raging at me. "What the fuck do you want?"

I held up the beers. "I come in peace?"

He thought about it for a few seconds before grabbing one of the beers and falling back onto his bed. "What the fuck, man?"

I turned his desk chair around and straddled it. "I can explain."

"I asked you if you were coming alone," he accused me angrily.

"I know, and I couldn't tell you I was bringing them or you would have said no." It was a lame excuse, but it had the rare merit of being the truth.

Kelly paused, his features twisted in confusion for a moment. "What *them*?"

"The drama guys, the nerds, the people I walked in with?" I asked, now confused myself. "What are you talking about?"

"I asked you if you were coming alone!" he fumed. I slowly nodded. "And you said you were coming alone." Another small nod. "So then why would you show up with him?"

We stared at each other in silence for a second before I admitted, "I have no idea what you're talking about."

"*Kyle*!" Kelly shouted. "Why would you bring Kyle when I asked you not to?"

"Kyle?" I repeated, shocked. "Wait! You wanted me to show up without Kyle?"

"I asked if you were coming alone! What did you think I meant?" His voice was strained, almost soundless. I had never seen Kelly cry before, but I suddenly understood that he was close to doing just that.

"I thought you meant don't invite a bunch of people you thought were lame," I answered slowly.

He waved a hand, dismissing the party as a whole. "I don't give a fuck about them. I wanted to talk to you alone," he said, sounding really upset.

"Okay, well, I'm here alone," I said, trying to get him to turn a few more letters over so I could guess at what he was talking about.

"*No*, you aren't!" he yelled. "You're here with him, so it doesn't fucking matter now! None of it matters." He threw himself back down flat on the bed, taking one of his pillows and putting it over his face as he screamed. His unopened beer bottle rolled off the edge of the bed and under it.

"Dude, what is wrong?" I asked, now kind of worried about how much he was losing it.

"Just go," he said, pillow still over his head.

"Kelly, I'm serious. What's wrong?"

He sat up like a jack-in-the-box, his eyes red with tears. "*Get the fuck out of my room*!"

There was literally nothing else I could say. I moved slowly and deliberately, hoping that me being calm might chill him. I got up and made my way to the door before I tried again. "If I did something wrong, man…."

"No, I'm the idiot," he said, wiping his eyes. "Just go, please!"

I turned around and walked out, pretty sure I'd missed something serious.

Kyle

I WAS beginning to wonder if this was such a good idea.

No one was talking to anyone. The people who had arrived before we had were pretty much hiding in the kitchen. Everyone else sat or stood in the living room, looking like they were waiting for a bus. Over on the couch by the door to the dining room, the library guys were talking to each other, no doubt having some kind of debate about comic book characters. Sammy and her friends just stared around the room, trying not to look as bored as they were.

"This is bad," I commented.

Jennifer nodded. "That's a word for it."

"We have to do something," I said to her, pretty much meaning I had to do something.

"When you say 'we,' I assume you're speaking French?" she asked, pretty much saying this was my bed to lie in and if I wanted to change it, I was the one who needed to change it.

I did not have an answer for that.

The music stopped all of a sudden, and Jeff's voice thundered through the silence. "—but no way Hulk could take Loki if he was ready." Everyone in the room looked over to the couch. Jeff shrank from the attention. No one dared speak.

I saw an opportunity.

"Anyone have any good music? A Spotify playlist? Anything?" I asked everyone. No one said a word; the guys in the kitchen ignored me altogether. "Seriously? No one has anything?"

Jeremy raised his hand. "I have some mash-ups on mine."

"Sweet," I said, pushing him toward the music setup. He handed me his iPhone. Something like thirty seconds later, I'd changed the setup from the CD player to Jeremy's playlist. I crossed my fingers and prayed there was some halfway decent music on there.

The first one was this insane mash-up of Britney Spears and Linkin Park that seemed to please everyone. With the music flowing, the conversations started back up again. The drama crew looked somewhat pleased as Jeremy explained he made most of the mash-ups on his computer at home.

One group of people satisfied.

I sat down on the couch with Andy and his boys. "Okay, you guys ready to shine?" Mike nodded. "Go grab your tablets and start playing against each other."

Mike and Jeff ran out to grab their tablets; Andy gave me a puzzled look. "Do you really think these guys will want to play Hearthstone?"

I shook my head as I stood up. "No, but I'm willing to bet they have never seen the game played before." I walked over to the dining room table, which was littered with some empty beer cans and a bowl of chips. Kelly's friends had abandoned the table when they huddled in the kitchen, so I felt safe claiming it for my own purposes.

Jeff, Mike, and Andy sat down and loaded up the game.

"Make sure the sound is on and try to use as many legendaries as possible—anything with a big graphic."

For those not in the know, Hearthstone is an electronic card game where you play against each other and the cards all have these sounds and graphics that are too cool for words. I didn't know anyone my age who could see someone else playing a video game and not want to see what it was about.

The thing was, Hearthstone was impossible to understand from just watching; you needed to be shown and told how to play, and again, no one my age wouldn't want to try at least once.

The three of them set up a game while the guys in the kitchen looked on from the doorway. "If they ask you to explain what you're doing, use the simplest words possible," I said quietly. "Pretend you're explaining the game to your mom." Andy nodded in assurance as they began to pick their decks. "And if one of them gets into it, make them an account and have them play the tutorial against the Innkeeper. That's when you know they're hooked."

The three of them nodded and started challenging each other to matches.

There was a cooler of ice by the kitchen filled with beers, wine coolers, and some Cokes. I grabbed two cans of Coke and headed back to Jennifer and saw Brad was back. They were deep in conversation when I walked up.

"…just yelled at me to get out." Brad took the Coke I offered him and downed half of it in one gulp.

"What happened?" I asked.

"Kelly," Jennifer answered with a grimace.

"He's pissed we're here?" I asked Brad.

He shrugged. "I don't know!" he exclaimed, frustrated. "He went on about how I was supposed to come alone and then said he didn't care about all of them." He gestured toward the drama crowd.

That was the very moment I knew what was wrong.

"He's upstairs?" I asked, putting my Coke down.

Both Brad and Jennifer gave me a strange look. "Yeah, his room is on the left," Brad answered, confused.

"Be right back." I turned and headed up the stairs. I heard Brad call after me, but I ignored him. I didn't know much about high school social situations; in fact, I didn't know anything about them. I had spent the last seventeen years with my nose pressed up against life's glass, looking at everyone else walking by having a blast while I begged for someone to notice me, even if I did try to stay invisible. If there was anything I did understand, it was unfulfilled longing.

"Abandon all hope ye who…," my fear started to say as I walked up the stairs.

"Unsubscribe," I said, dismissing it with a wave of my hand.

Kelly was lying on his bed with a pillow over his face when I walked in.

"Can we talk?" I asked him loudly.

He threw the pillow off his head and sat up in a flash. "Get the fuck out of my room." His voice was angry and harsh, but I could tell he had just finished crying.

I ignored his threat, kicked his door with my foot to close it, and sat down. "We need to talk."

"Do you want me to kick your ass?" he threatened, standing up.

"Are you in love with Brad?" I asked back. All the blood in his face drained away, making him look like a ghost staring at me with his mouth half-open. That was answer enough for me. "When you asked Brad if he was coming alone, you were asking if he was bringing me or not, right?"

He slowly sat back down on his bed. I waited until I knew Kelly was hearing me.

"Does Brad know how you feel about him?" Kelly shrank in on himself. I could see how much pain he was in.

"I don't… I never said…," he started to say; then he stopped. In a very small voice, he pleaded, "Please don't tell him."

I forced myself to stay where I was, because I wasn't sure how he would take me going over to sit next to him. "Kelly, you can't live like this," I said softly. "Sooner or later it's going to kill you."

"Not if you don't tell him," he assured me quickly. "If you just shut up, then no one needs to know." The sound of desperation in his voice was like nails on a chalkboard.

"*You* know it." I shook my head. "You know how you feel, Kelly, and look at you." He said nothing, but I could see him silently sobbing. "You were going to tell him tonight, right?" I already knew the answer. "If he showed up without me, you were going to tell him how you felt. And then what?" Kelly looked up at me with those bloodshot eyes. "He came out. Everyone knows he's gay. Even if he said that he liked you that way too, what then? Are you willing to come out too? Do you want people to know how you feel?" I spoke as gently as I knew how because I knew he hadn't thought that far. I knew it.

One gasping cry broke free of his control when he imagined having to come out.

"This is what I'm talking about; this is what's going to kill you," I said with as much sympathy as I could express. "Even if you got what you wanted tonight, come tomorrow, how could you live with it?"

He was crying audibly, staring blindly down at his feet, his hands limp in his lap like he had no idea what to do with them.

I bit my bottom lip as I balanced between the feeling of abject terror at what he could do to me with those hands and the overwhelming instinct to give him comfort.

"Don't do it," Billy said as I moved toward Kelly.

I ignored it.

"I'm serious, bitch. That dog will bite you."

I took a deep breath and knelt down in front of him. I slowly reached out and took one of his hands. "Kelly, you at least have to admit it to yourself."

He refused to look up as he sobbed even harder.

"Are you in love with Brad?" I asked him again.

I wish there were words to convey the raw pain in his face as he looked back at me and exclaimed, "I don't want to be gay!" before he broke down in hysterics.

I put my arms around him and gave him a hug, not because I was trying to be nice to him, but because there was no way to hear the emotion in his voice and not be moved to help him. "No one is saying you have to be gay."

He clung to me, his face buried in my shoulder. "But I love him so much!" he wailed. "I always have, since we were in junior high. Before he ever met you, I was in love with him." His entire body shook with his anguish. "I would have done anything for him… anything! But he started dating girls, and I thought I was a freak."

"And then he started going out with me," I said, knowing now where all his hatred had come from.

"Why you?" he asked, looking up at me. "What's wrong with me?"

There was no answer to that, at least not one that would make him feel better.

"I don't want to be gay. I don't want to have these feelings!" he said savagely as his voice turned to rage. "I wanna… I wanna be normal. I just want to go get married and have kids and be… and be…."

"And be someone you aren't," I finished for him.

He collapsed into my arms again as a new round of tears began to pour out.

"No one is telling you to be gay, you know."

He looked up at me with outright confusion on his face.

"So you like Brad. That doesn't mean you're gay. It just means you have good taste." I smiled, and he choked back a laugh.

"It's more than Brad," he said, barely above a whisper.

I nodded, because I had already known that answer. "It's not the end of the world." I tried to assure him. "So you like guys; no one is telling you to do anything about it now. We're less than six months away from graduating, and then you'll be gone. And if I have learned anything from *Girls Gone Wild*, it's that college is where people get to experiment with all sorts of things and get a free pass."

He laughed again, this one a little less miserable than the last.

"But I'm serious—you have to at least be able to say it to yourself. Even if you are never going to tell anyone else, you need to admit it to yourself."

We stared at each other for almost a minute. Finally he asked, "You mean now?"

I tried not to laugh. "You doing anything else just this minute?"

He leaned away from me, sighing heavily as if the weight of the world was crashing down on him. I said nothing, knowing this was the hardest thing in the world for him to say out loud. Especially with me kneeling there.

"I like guys," he said, mumbling.

"You like fries?" I asked, cupping my hand to my ear.

"I like guys," he said a little louder.

"You like pies?" I asked, smiling.

"I fucking like guys," he answered angrily. "Happy? I think I might be gay." His eyes narrowed at me. "And that is the most I am going to say."

I laughed and held my hands up in surrender. "Okay, okay! You said it. Happy?"

His expression didn't change all that much. "No." But we both knew he was lying.

Neither one of us knew what to say for a long time. Finally he asked me, "Are you going to tell Brad?"

"Do you want me to?" I asked back.

"No!" He took a deep breath and tried to calm himself. "Please don't," he added.

I shrugged. "Then I won't. It's none of his business."

He looked down at his shoes for a moment, relieved. He glanced up at me, an evil smile on his face. "Any chance you could share?"

I flipped him off, and we both burst out laughing.

That was when we heard the screaming from downstairs.

We both stood at the same time. "What the fuck now?" he asked rhetorically.

I heard Brad's voice screaming over the party and then another voice I was getting more and more used to hearing screaming back.

"Tony," I said, knowing the night had just taken a hairpin turn for the worse.

We both ran out of Kelly's room to see what was wrong.

There are a lot of things I look back on and regret in my life, wishing I could change. Suffice it to say the list is long and distinguished, and it covers a variety of embarrassing moments. But right there on the top of the list, the thing I wish I could go back and change the most?

I wish I had noticed that Kelly's door had been slightly ajar when we ran out. It might have changed everything that happened after.

Brad

THIS WAS turning out to be the weirdest-ass party I had ever been to.

The drama group was sticking together near the computer Kelly was using for music. For the first time in Foster history, there wasn't an annoying mixture of country, rap, and hard rock being played way too loud. Instead, the music sounded like it was being spun by an actual DJ, which made conversation flow a little easier. Sammy seemed to be watching over an iPod while her friends half swayed to the music. A couple of Kelly's friends had asked them what song was playing or where they got the mix, which was about 1,000 percent more conversation than those two groups had shared in the last four years. Andy and his crew had begun playing that card game, which, of course, drew some attention from the guys hiding in the kitchen. One by one they walked over to see what they were doing and watch the game until there were half a dozen guys surrounding the table. They hadn't asked them yet how the game was played, but it was just a matter of time.

"Did he really pull this off?" I asked Jennifer.

She seemed as shocked as I felt. "Sure seems that way, doesn't it?" She looked over at me. "There is no way you deserve someone like him."

She was making a joke, but we both knew it was the truth.

I let the breath I hadn't even known I was holding the whole night go and began to believe we might just get through this night intact.

Which was the exact moment the front door slammed open and Tony came walking in with Josh Walker and a few other guys behind him. "The party has officially starte—" Then he saw who else had showed up.

"What in the fuck is going on?" he raged. The six-pack he was carrying fell to the ground.

Someone paused the music as Tony began to circle the living room. "Who in the hell invited you dweebs?"

Inches from a clean getaway.

I moved past Jennifer and intercepted him before he got to either group of people. "Okay, Tony, calm down."

He turned toward me, which was a good and bad thing all at once.

Good, because he was no longer looking at Andy and his friends or the drama group. Bad, because now he was looking directly at me. "And who the fuck said your fairy ass could show up?" I could smell the alcohol on his breath and knew we weren't the only people who practiced frontloading before a party. "This is a no-fag party." He accented the word fag by poking me in the chest with one finger.

I slapped his hand away. "And yet you're here," I almost growled back. "Don't come in starting shit, Tony."

He got right in my face. "I ain't afraid of you, Graymark. I've kicked your ass before."

"Yeah, you wanna try it without your boys holding me down?" I was done with this guy's shit. In fact, I was done with this entire town's problem with me. We weren't at school. There wasn't any risk of an adult coming and breaking this up. It was time people around here understood that—what I said to Kyle aside—I was no one's bitch.

Josh tried to pull Tony away from me. "Come on, Tony… chill out for a sec…."

I turned and shot him a death look. "Fuck off, Walker. I'm tired of you defending this asshole." It looked like he was going to say something but never got the chance as Tony's fist collided with the side of my face.

It took me back a few steps, but I had been hit harder before.

He lunged at me exactly the way he charged a defensive line in a game, and let me tell you, it was a little bit intimidating. Not so intimidating that I didn't bring my knee up under his chin, but impressive nonetheless. His head snapped back when chin and knee collided, and he fell into me. Then we went down in a mass of swinging arms and legs.

I had the presence of mind to throw him off me while he tried to regain his senses. Once he was on his ass, I knew the fight was over.

And then, out of nowhere, I lost it. I straddled his waist and began to swing at his face. His arms came up instinctively but not enough to stop the full impact of my punches. "Call me a faggot again, asshole!" I urged him as I swung. "Call me a motherfucking faggot one more time." He tried to curl up into a ball, but there was no way he could protect himself with me literally sitting on top of him.

I heard the people around me screaming, but they made no sense whatsoever through the sound of pounding blood in my head.

I hit him for beating me up in the locker room. I hit him for ruining Kyle's clothes. I hit him for being an intolerant asshole, and I hit him for living in a town that was so backward it couldn't let people be. I hit him again for his bigoted father, one more for ruining the party, and then after that I just hit him. I heard my name shouted a few more times, but I ignored everything.

And then someone kicked me in the back, throwing me forward off Tony. I couldn't have been ready for an attack from the rear and landed face-first into the carpet. I scrambled to get to my feet, whirling to defend against a second kick.

Kyle stood there, his face flushed with emotion.

"Did you just kick me off him?" I demanded, dumbfounded.

"What are you doing?" he asked me, his eyes wide in outrage.

"Did you just kick me off him?" I asked again, straightening slowly.

He took a step toward me. "Yeah, I did. Why? You going to take a swing at me now?" His chin jutted out in defiance, his hands balled up into fists.

I took a deep, halting breath as I tried to calm down.

"What is wrong with you?" he asked me in a low voice. "You can't go around hitting people."

I froze because Tony had risen to his feet and was standing behind Kyle, his face red and beginning to swell, distorted in rage. "Mind your own business, faggot," Tony snarled. He slammed Kyle in the back of the head—hard. Kyle went flying to the side, and Tony took a step toward me. "That the best you got?" he asked, putting his fists up. "Let's dance."

Kyle lay on the dining room floor, moaning.

I glared at him. "You're dead." And right then, I meant my words, and Tony knew it.

He took a half step toward me before he began to shake in place. He looked like he was having a stroke when his arms balled up involuntarily. Drool spilled out of his mouth, and his eyes rolled back into his head.

Like a giant redwood being chopped down, he slowly crashed to the floor.

Jennifer stood behind him, the lines of her Taser still connected to the back of his shirt. Everyone gaped at her in shock, but she just rolled her eyes. "Oh please, 'Let's dance'? Who even *says* that?"

Seeing Tony wasn't getting up, I rushed over to where Andy and his friends were helping Kyle. Jeremy pushed past us. How did he get in the kitchen? I thought he was by the music.

"You okay?" I asked, my voice cracking with emotion. "Get him some ice," I sort of asked, sort of ordered Jeff as I propped Kyle up in my lap. "Kyle, please say something."

He sounded drunk as he mumbled, "Fighting is bad, m'okay?"

I felt a tear fall from my eye as I pulled him close. "Fighting bad, I got it." Jeff handed me a towel full of ice, and I gently touched the back of Kyle's head with it.

"Goddamn!" he screamed as the cold towel made contact with the growing lump.

I looked up and saw Kelly watching the two of us, his expression hard to read, although I thought he might have been sad. Before I could think about it anymore, Kelly glared over at Tony, who had started to make some disjointed moves. Kelly's expression hardened. Two strides brought him up alongside Tony's prone body.

"Get up," Kelly said, pushing Tony with the toe of his shoe. He groaned slightly when Kelly toed him over onto his back. "Can you hear me?" Kelly snapped, looking down at Tony. "Nod if you can." Tony nodded slightly. "Good. Get the fuck out of my house." He looked over to Josh and his friends. "That goes for you too." Then he glared at everyone. "In fact, that goes for everybody. If you have a problem with who is here, feel free to leave now. But I warn you now, you stay and start anything"—he jerked a thumb at Jennifer—"and she will taser your asses."

Jennifer held her industrial-strength Taser up. "He is not joking."

Tony slowly got up. "Fuck it. I wouldn't want to stay anyway." He looked around at Kyle and me and made a face. "I don't go to fag parties." Turning to Josh, he nodded and said, "Let's get out of here."

Josh looked away, not saying a word.

"Walker," Tony said, snapping his fingers. "You coming?"

Josh looked over at him. "You know what, Tony? I'm done." Tony's face grew pale as Josh went on. "I warned you not to start shit and it is the *first* thing you do. So no, I am not going anywhere with you ever again." He looked over at Kelly. "Is it okay if I stay?" Kelly nodded, and Josh looked back at Tony. "Get lost."

They glowered at each other in silence, and I swore I could hear Tony say, "C'mon, Josh, I'm sorry," and Josh shook his head. Tony scoffed at him. "Screw you, then. Stay here with the other fags." He looked to Cody and his friend. "You guys coming?" They both refused to look at him. "Fuck all of you, then!" he screamed and stormed out of the house.

The whole party was silent as we heard the agonizing sound of a car's tires shredding on asphalt as Tony's Jeep sped away.

Jeremy pushed a button and a dance mix of "Ding-Dong! The Witch Is Dead" came blaring from the speakers.

It was the first real laugh I'd had all night.

The music seemed to be the icebreaker everyone was waiting for. The tension that had been suffocating the room was gone and people actually started talking. The kitchen guys finally asked Andy and the guys how to play Hearthstone. Other people went over and asked Jeremy how he made his mash-ups. Slowly, and then more easily, the night stopped being separate groups of people in the same house and started to become a party.

Looking down at Kyle, I said, "Look at this, look at what you did." He glanced around, making sure not to move his head too much. "These people never, and I mean *never*, talk to each other, dude. You really did it."

He looked up at me, and I could tell he was still pissed. "And you almost killed Tony." I looked away, but he kept talking. "Hitting people is not the answer; you have to start getting that."

I looked back at him, and in a voice that was cold even to me, I said, "No, you're wrong. I wish I could see the world like you do, Kyle. I wish I could look around and see the potential in everyone, but I don't. I look around, and I see people threatening the things I care about. Threatening you." He opened his mouth to object, but I kept talking. "I'm sorry you don't like it, but it is who I am. Someone comes at you, they have to deal with me. And that isn't because I don't think you can handle yourself. It's because no one hurts the people I love. You can be as mad at me as you want, but that is never going to change. No one gets away with hurting you. Ever."

He waited a few seconds. "Can I talk now?" I nodded and shut up. "I get everything you just said, but I wasn't in the room when you started that fight. I wasn't in danger when you started hitting him. You were mad." I tried to object, but he talked over me. "And yes, you deserve the right to be mad, but hitting someone isn't the way to express it. You may think it is, but it isn't. You think Tony got your point of view? You think he left here understanding why what he was doing was wrong? Or do you think he left even madder and having even more reasons to hate us?" He reached up and touched my face, and I felt myself starting to fall apart inside. "You beat him half to death because you didn't like him, which is the same reason he beat you up before. You think he thought his reasons were any less valid than the ones you are feeling now?"

I was literally stunned into silence as his words penetrated my brain.

"Thank you for standing up for me, seriously. You have no idea how happy it makes me. But please don't lie to yourself, trying to convince yourself the reason you were sitting on top of him punching him into a concussion was about me. Don't be that guy." He smiled at me, and I had never felt less worthy to have his affection. "I know you're better than that."

I laid my head against his hair and felt my eyes start to burn with tears. "I'm sorry," I whispered to him.

He tried to sit up but instantly regretted it. "Ouch! Fuck, that hurts!" He held the ice against his head. "Don't be sorry. Just be honest," he added, lying back in my lap.

"How do you do that?" I asked, completely unaware of anyone else around us.

"Do what?" he asked, honestly confused.

"Turn the entire world upside down with just words?"

He smiled. "Dude, I got mad skills."

I laughed and held him close.

Jennifer plopped down next to us and handed each of us a Coke. "Well, I think that was the funnest thing I have done at any party."

"You looked total Lara Croft standing there," I agreed as I opened the Coke.

"Where did you get a Taser that strong? I thought those were illegal for civilians to own?" Kyle asked, sitting up slowly.

"My dad is sheriff. Tony is lucky I didn't aim it where my dad taught me to taser first," she answered with a small smile.

Kyle looked up at me. "You broke up with the sheriff's daughter to go out with me?" He took a small sip and shook his head. "You're braver than I thought."

There was some yelling from around the dining room table, and I saw a couple of Kelly's friends had sat back down to play Hearthstone while they taught the library crew how to take shots. "You ever thought you'd see that?" Jennifer asked me.

"I don't believe it now, and I'm looking right at it," I admitted.

Jennifer raised her Coke toward Kyle. "I will admit it. You were right, and I was wrong." Kyle smiled, and they tapped Cokes. "I have known these people forever and never once thought they were capable of just being human."

"Everyone is human," Kyle said, taking a small sip. "I found if you treat someone like a person, it encourages them to treat you the same back."

She looked over at me and shook her head. "You so do not deserve him."

"I will drink to that," I said, holding up my Coke.

Kyle

MY HEAD hurt as if Tony had hit me with a sledgehammer.

Even though I knew breaking up the fight had been the right thing to do, my head was telling me something completely different. However, as the three of us sat there and watched the party begin to pick up, I knew it was worth it. I noticed Kelly wandering around looking over to us once in a while. I got my feet under me and very slowly straightened up; Brad and Jennifer looked at me like I was Bambi learning to walk. "Be right back," I told them and wobbled over to Kelly.

"How's your head?" he asked as I got closer.

"You ever see those hippos dance in *Fantasia*?" I asked him. He nodded. "Like I was their dance floor."

He barked out a laugh that looked like it was as unexpected to him as it was for me. "You're kinda funny."

I laughed as I took another sip of my drink. "I think that was the nicest thing you ever said to me."

He chuckled. "Yeah, well, don't get used to it. I still don't like you," he said with no meanness in his voice at all.

"You can come and sit with us, you know," I offered, gesturing toward where Brad and Jennifer were.

He shook his head. "Nah, I don't… I ain't ready for that yet," he stammered.

"You can't avoid him forever, Kelly."

"You're not going to tell him, are you?" he asked me in a panic. "'Cause I don't want him to know!"

"Calm down," I said quickly. "Seriously, keep acting like that and you won't need to tell anyone." Kelly calmed down, but I could see the lurking panic in his eyes. "I am not going to say anything to anyone. Just like I told you upstairs. Who you tell is your choice. But Kelly, I'm serious when I say you should tell him how you feel."

"Why?" he asked me back. "What good would that do?"

I tried to compress the thousand or so thoughts that were racing through my mind into words so I could get him to understand what I was saying, but all I could come up with was "You will feel better after, Kelly. You have to trust me on that."

I expected him to say something ugly or sarcastic in return, but instead he looked at me in silence before he said, "I don't want to say anything to him about it."

"Okay. You're still welcome to sit with us," I repeated as I wobbled back to the couch and Brad.

"Hey, geek," Kelly called back to me. I sort of hunched around and looked at him. "Thanks for this," he said, gesturing to the party. "It's kinda cool."

"You're welcome," I said, smiling around the headache.

"Don't let it go to your egghead," he said bitterly, but he was smiling when he said it.

"How's your head?" Brad asked when I sat down.

"Sore, but I've had worse." I saw his expression change slightly, and I realized that was probably the wrong answer. "I never told you I practiced MMA when no one was looking?" I tried to joke. Jennifer chuckled, but I could see Brad didn't buy it at all.

"We should go check it out to be sure," he said casually.

"It's good," I assured him.

"We can't be too sure," he insisted.

"No, I am pretty sure it's all good," I said, confused.

"We should go upstairs and make sure your head is okay," he said, gesturing to the stairs.

"Are you okay?" I asked.

"Oh, for Christ's sake, he wants to go upstairs and fool around," Jennifer said, standing up. "You need to buy a clue," she said to me. "And you need to learn how to give better clues," she said to Brad. "You boys have fun."

As she walked away, both of us were red.

"We don't have to," he said quietly.

I took a deep breath to settle my stomach. "No, come on, let's go," I said, standing up quickly. Much too quickly. He just sat there staring at me, shocked. I held my hand out. "Before I change my mind," I added.

He leaped to his feet like he was on strings.

"Okay," he said, grabbing my hand.

Brad

AS WE climbed the stairs, my heart threatened to explode in my chest.

My mouth was dry as Kyle led me toward one of the guest rooms. I realized I hadn't been this nervous losing my virginity. All the other times I'd had sex, my reasons had always been a mixture of something I needed to do to cover my tracks combined with the raw animal enjoyment of getting off. The few times I wasn't too drunk to remember, I had wished it was a guy with me instead of the girl under me. Now that I was about to get my wish, I felt like I was going to pass out. Kyle opened the door, and though I was sure the room was tastefully adorned with all sorts of little touches that made it homey, it might as well have been empty.

All I could see was the bed.

"This work?" Kyle asked, no expression on his face at all. I nodded mutely, wondering at what point I had lost the ability to talk. "Lock the door," he said, kicking his shoes off. I turned around and made sure the door would not open by accident. When I looked back at him, he had taken his jacket off and was halfway done with unbuttoning his shirt.

"Wait!" I said louder than I expected. "Hold on," I added in a much lower voice.

His fingers paused. "What? We don't have a lot of time."

I took his hands in mine and wasn't surprised to feel them shaking. "We don't have to rush."

His sigh spoke volumes to me.

What he said out loud was "Sooner or later someone is going to come looking for us."

What he didn't repeat was "I need to do this before I lose my nerve."

"Hey," I said in my most reassuring voice. "What's wrong?"

"Nothing," he lied. "Let's get undressed." He tried to pull his hands away. I say tried, because I didn't let him.

I looked into his eyes, and all I could see was fear.

"You do know we don't have to do this, right?" I asked, my nervousness turning into concern.

He nodded, but it was not the nod I had been looking for. It wasn't a nod that said, "Yes, I do know I have the option of not doing this but still want to." It wasn't even the nod of "We are at the edge of a cliff and I would rather jump off with you than face the guys with guns behind us." This was a nod of "Dear God, please stop asking me questions and let's get this over before I change my mind."

"Kyle," I said, trying to get through to him. "I mean it! We don't have to do anything if you aren't ready." He looked down, breaking eye contact with me, and all I could see was the top of his head. "I mean it. I don't want you to feel pressured…."

He looked up, and I saw the tears running down his cheeks. "I don't want you to dump me, so let's do it, and everything will be fine."

He could have kneed me in the balls and it wouldn't have caught me as shocked as much as those words did. To be honest, I wished he had kneed me, because it would have hurt less. "Leave you? Who said I was leaving you?"

He choked back a sob, disguising it as a laugh. "Oh, come on, Brad. I know you've done it before, lots of times. I'm a guy too. I know what it's like to be horny all the time. So let's do this, and then it's all good."

I moved him to sit down on the edge of the bed and just stared at him for a long time, not sure what to say.

"What?" he asked, annoyed. "Don't sit there looking at me like I'm speaking another language."

I slowly began to shake my head. "You are the dumbest smart guy I have ever met." That stopped him cold. "I mean it. There are times I think I'm dating Sherlock Holmes, and then there are times like this when you are dumber than Forrest Gump."

"Hey!" he exclaimed, pissed.

"Nope. You had your chance to talk and messed it up. Now it's time for the grown-up to talk," I said, a little more smugly than I intended.

"I am a grown-up," he said, gritting his teeth.

I shot back with a quick "No, you're not, and let me tell you why. If you were a grown-up, you'd have told me how freaked-out you were about this instead of nodding every time I brought it up." He opened his mouth, but I ignored that. "I have had sex. Yes, I like having sex. And yes, I want to have sex with you—very, very much."

He looked like he was going to interrupt again, but I ignored that too. "Yes, I am a guy, and yes, I am always horny, but you know what else I am? Not so desperate for sex that I would pressure the person I love—*love*, you moron—into having it. And there's no way I'd ever think about dumping you. Didn't we already talk about that earlier tonight?" Kyle nodded a tiny bit. "I have two good hands, and let me tell you, I am *really* good at jerking off. So if you aren't ready to have sex, that's great. Well, not great, but it's acceptable, and I will totally respect that. But if you think I am some sex-crazed maniac who needs to get off so badly that he'd get mad if we didn't have sex right now, then honestly, Kyle, I'm not sure who you think I am."

His mouth had closed, and his expression again gave away nothing about what was going through his mind. I made a mental note to try to teach him how to play poker someday. I bet he'd clean up at bluffing. More quietly, I added a little more, something I had never said to anyone.

"I know what it's like being pressured into having sex before you're ready. The first time I did it was only because everyone expected me to. I couldn't find a way for me to explain why I would turn down a sure thing. I was so scared…." I could feel my body kicking out adrenaline from just the memory. "I remember it feeling good and almost throwing up because I didn't know if that was a good thing or not. I just ended up doing it because I wanted it to be over." I got quiet, and he took my hand. "I almost raced out of her house to my car. I don't remember how I made it home, but I sat in the shower for, like, an hour trying to get the smell of her off me." I looked at him, and I could see the compassion in his eyes. "Trust me, Kyle; make your first time count."

Neither one of us said a word as the music downstairs drifted up to us. I could make out the song. It was a mash-up of Katy Perry and Rebecca Black. I smiled at him and asked, "Besides, do you really want to think of the lyrics to 'Friday' every time you remember your first time?" His mouth bent up slightly. I moved in, carefully laid him back on the bed, and sang in a whisper, "It's Friday, Friday! Gotta get down on Friday." A small laugh escaped his mouth. "Oh, does that turn you on?" I asked, smiling even more. "Gotta have my bowl, gotta have cereal…."

He finally cracked and started laughing for real. Then his head must have hurt, because he went still and made the worst face he'd ever shown me.

"I love you," I said, lying down next to him and pulling him in close, "even if you are a half-wit."

He punched me lightly, but I felt him curl up closer.

"I was more nervous walking up those stairs with you than I had ever been with any girl. And I can wait as long as it takes for you to be comfortable, because I want it to be the right time for both of us." He smiled and nuzzled in even closer to me. "I want it to be perfect, because I am warning you, once we have sex, I am not going to want to stop." He stared up at me, faking shock. "No joke. I might just walk around town humping your leg."

We both chuckled at that image as we relaxed.

"I want you to be my first," he said in a low voice after a while.

"I wanna be your first, last, and only," I replied, looking at him. "So stop worrying that I am going to dump you."

"Or what?" he asked with a smartass smile. "You're gonna dump me?"

There was no way I could not kiss him repeatedly for a long, long time.

After a while we settled in and just lay there holding each other. It was so weird not worrying about someone walking in or having to be somewhere. We had all the time in the world, and we took advantage of it. We talked about everything. He asked if I always knew I wanted to play baseball (no, I knew I didn't want to play football like my dad), and I asked him what he wanted to be when he grew up (happy). He asked what it was like to be the center of attention (kind of a head trip until you realize that people only like you if you are the person they think you are), and I asked him what it was like to be smart (not as fun as you'd think because people expect you to be smart about everything). He asked how old I was when I first realized I liked guys (I came home at six and told my dad I had met a boyfriend at school), and I asked him how old he was (he doesn't remember a time he didn't like guys).

We talked until our mouths were sore, and after that, we lay there, enjoying having each other so close. It was easily one of the most perfect nights of my entire life.

It makes me wish we had never woken up.

Kyle

WHEN I woke up, I had a panic attack.

I had no idea where I was or how I got there. The only thing that stopped me from losing it completely was the fact Brad was asleep next to me. It was morning because the sun was shining through the windows, all that cheery brightness making my brain hurt. My mind finally engaged, and I remembered last night. Then I wondered what had happened. Brad and I had been talking, and then—we fell asleep? Well, obviously we fell asleep, but why didn't anyone wake us up?

I looked over at the door. It was cracked open, which meant someone had checked in on us, since I knew it was locked last night.

I thought about waking Brad up, but he looked so damn cute asleep, I didn't have the heart to bother him. Someone had dropped a blanket over us while we had been sleeping.

If Kelly knew we were in here, why didn't he wake us up? I padded out of the room in my socks, wondering exactly what we had missed while we slept.

I passed Kelly's room and peeked inside. He was asleep facedown, still in his jeans, snoring. A few empty beer cans lay on the floor by his bed. I had had enough experience with my mom to know that waking him up would be a bad idea. So I backed out of his room and made my way downstairs.

Jennifer was sitting cross-legged on the couch with a bowl of cereal in her hand, devouring the flakes or squares or whatever while she watched TV. When she saw me, she held up her bowl in a mock toast. “The walk of shame after the Party, welcome to Foster High.” I was about to tell her we hadn’t done anything, but she gestured toward the kitchen. “Grab something to eat. Kelly has the best selection of cereals this side of the Mississippi.”

The mere mention of food made my mouth water.

The kitchen looked like a beer truck had hit a mountain and spilled its contents everywhere. Empties were scattered here and there, and a pretty impressive pyramid of cans was assembled on the table. I looked around its base and saw it was way sturdier than it should be, which told me Andy and the library crew had helped in making it.

Jennifer had not been lying; there were six boxes of cereal in the cabinet, each one a sugar-filled concoction made just for Saturday mornings. I poured a giant bowl with some Honeycomb, some Golden Crisp, and topped it off with Cap’n Crunch for good measure. After adding the milk, I walked back to the couch to sit next to Jennifer. She was laughing, watching *Adventure Time*, which made her instantly cooler in my book.

I ate half the bowl before I felt ready to start asking questions.

“So what did I miss?” I asked her during a commercial.

“Well, let’s see,” she began, turning toward me on the couch. “After a while Kelly turned on Rock Band, and we took turns being Freddie Mercury; then they”—she waved vaguely toward the dining room table—“put away the tablets, and we played beer pong until my dad showed up and told us to break up the party or he’d start calling parents. Then I had a huge fight with him because I said I was going to stay here instead of leaving with him, and then most of the people left, and Kelly and I dared each other to see if you guys were awake or not. Once we popped the lock and saw you were both asleep in your clothes, which was less exciting than we were expecting, I put Kelly to bed. He started crying, and you do know he is in love with Brad, right?”

It took me a few seconds to catch up with her words.

“He told you?” I asked her.

"Oh my God, you did know," she said, putting her bowl down. "And you didn't share!" She hit my arm.

"Well, I just figured it out last night, so there wasn't a lot of time to share," I said, pulling back in case she swung again.

"There is *always* time to share gossip. If you are going to be my gay BFF, you need to learn these things." She picked up her bowl again. "You tell me if what I am wearing looks like crap, you tell me which guys are most likely closet cases, and you *always* share gossip."

I looked at her in confusion for several seconds. "You do know I have no idea what looks good or not, and I didn't even know Brad liked guys until he kissed me, and even then it took me a few days to believe it." In a quiet voice I added, "I am a horrible gay."

She said nothing for so long I thought I had pissed her off. Finally she burst out laughing, almost spilling her milk as she rocked with the emotion. "You are too easy," she assured me. "Calm down, Kyle, you're doing fine." For some reason that made me feel a thousand times better.

We both settled in and went back to eating our cereals.

About halfway through *ThunderCats*, Brad lurched sleepily down the stairs, rubbing his eyes. "Food?" he croaked when he saw us on the couch. We both pointed at the kitchen, and he wandered off that way.

"You want some advice?" she asked me as the sound of bowls came crashing from the kitchen. I nodded. "Do not try to talk to him before he has food in him, because anything he says won't make any sense. Trust me."

"I heard that, and fuck you," Brad bellowed from the kitchen. She pointed toward him and gave me a "see what I mean?" look. I covered my mouth to stop from laughing out loud.

He came out, and I moved over to make room for him to sit. The three of us watched cartoons until our bowls were empty and our minds were awake. Jennifer described again to Brad what happened, minus the Kelly being in love with him part. It seemed she didn't think he needed to know that any more than I did.

"Your dad pissed?" Brad asked her.

She shrugged. "Is he ever not mad at me?" She sounded completely blasé, but I could see the way her forehead scrunched up when she remembered her and her father fighting. "I'm not trying to lay a guilt trip on you or anything, but he was pretty pissed when he heard about you being gay."

"I'm sorry," he said in that awkward way you use when you know you should say more than sorry to someone but have no idea what.

She stared at the TV, not even blinking for a few seconds; I imagined she was remembering some distant conversation. And just like that, she looked over at him and smiled. "Oh well, life sucks for everyone." It was easily the smoothest transition from a negative emotion to beaming smile I had ever seen. Academy Award winners wished they could fake emotion that well.

Brad looked like he was going to say something, but then Kelly came tripping down the last few stairs. His hair stuck straight up, and he looked like he hadn't quite woken up yet. He stared at us in confusion and then squinted to make sure he was seeing correctly. "What the fuck are you doing in my living room?" he asked in a half groan.

"Eating your cereal," Brad answered him, smiling brightly.

Kelly thought about it a second, nodded, and shambled into the kitchen himself.

"And you say I'm bad in the morning," Brad quipped.

"You are," Jennifer replied, sarcasm dripping from her words. "You fell asleep one night, and when I tried to wake you up to get out before my dad discovered you were there, you told me 'If he wants lemonade, then let him buy one.' To this day I have no idea what the hell that means."

I started laughing again while Brad tried to explain what he'd said that morning in Jennifer's room. "What does that mean?"

"You're asking me? I tell you my dad, who has a gun, is about to come in my room and you talk about lemonade? Trust me, Kelly's a Rhodes Scholar compared to that."

Brad flipped her off and went back to watching cartoons.

Kelly came over and sat down on the floor in front of the couch as we watched *Ben 10*. Halfway through, Brad stood up. "You have any clothes, man? I need to shower before I start having stink lines around me all Pigpen style."

Kelly nodded as he watched the show. "Mi closet es su closet," he said.

Brad looked over at me and raised one eyebrow, which was his way of asking, "Want to join me?"

I shook my head. My face had to be a portrait of complete panic. I felt Jennifer nudge me from behind, and when I looked at her, she nodded. I looked back to Brad, and he smiled, holding out his hand. "Hey, Kelly," Jennifer said, sliding to the floor. "Load up some COD so I can kick your ass."

Kelly looked at her incredulously, since everyone knew guys beat girls at Call of Duty.

Brad and I went upstairs like we were sneaking away. "Ten bucks she pounds him," Brad said once we were out of earshot. "I went shooting with her once, and she is like the Black Widow with a gun."

He was rummaging through Kelly's closet, looking for fresh clothes, while I stood there trying to calm myself. "What are we going to do?" I asked.

He poked his head out for a moment. "Um… I don't know. The day is still young. I was going to stick around and help Kelly clean up, but we can bail if you want."

I shook my head. "I mean right now."

He paused. "Um… look for clothes?"

I sighed. "I mean in the shower?"

"Oh," he said, suddenly getting what I was hinting at. "*Oh*!" he added once he really got it. "We can take a shower if you want. I thought it might be fun." He flashed me a smile that could melt ice at twenty yards, and I felt my stomach clench in distress while the rest of my body became aroused. "It's going to be okay, Kyle, it's just a shower."

I didn't say anything as he grabbed a handful of clothes for both of us and led me to Kelly's parents' room. Like the rest of the house, it was huge and way overdecorated. It struck me as the house of someone trying way too hard to prove they had money and ended up showing how little taste they had. But what the house lacked in style, it made up for with size, and the master bath was no exception.

There was a tub larger than Vermont on the right side of the room, while a shower that was bigger than my room at home stood on the left. In between them were two full-sized sinks, one for each of Kelly's parents. It wasn't as much a large bathroom as it was a small spa. "What the fuck?" I exclaimed out loud, not being able to handle such a waste of money. Brad set down the clothes and looked at me questioningly. "I'm sorry. I just think I've lived in smaller places than this bathroom."

Brad chuckled as he stripped off his shirt. I barely heard his words as I marveled at the flatness of his stomach. "Yeah, Kelly's parents grew up poor, so when they made their money, they kinda took a trip on the white trash express." He began to unbutton his slacks. "It takes some getting used to."

"Where should I change?" I asked, looking away from him in his boxers for some reason. I knew the question was stupid the moment it left my lips, but I was so flustered I couldn't help it. I could hear him throw his pants on the ground and walk over to me.

"Kyle, why are you so scared?" His voice was so low and so inviting that I relaxed some.

"I just…," I stammered. "I don't have any of that," I said, gesturing at his upper body. He looked down at himself, and it made me crazy. His pecs were so perfect that the charm on his chain rested perfectly between them. I had no idea how he got abs like that, but if I didn't know him, I would assume he spent all his spare time doing crunches. Everything about the way he looked made me feel even uglier than I usually did.

He gave me a look so damn reassuring it made me want to spit for some reason. "You have no idea how insanely hot you are, do you?" he asked. That was probably the stupidest question I had ever heard. "I mean it," he said, undoing the last buttons on my shirt. He slipped it over my shoulders and grasped the bottom of my T-shirt. I grabbed his hands as he tried to take it off. "Please," he whispered. "Let me see you."

I closed my eyes and let go.

He took my shirt off, and I half expected to hear laughing. His hands undid my belt, and my jeans fell to the ground. I stepped out of them, my hand resting on his forearm since I refused to open my eyes. His hands moved up from my waist, across my stomach, and paused on my chest. "So hot," he breathed into my ear as he traced circles around my nipples.

I laughed and pulled away a little, and when I opened my eyes, I saw him standing in front of me. He was naked now, his boxer briefs discarded at some point, and I half gasped as I took him in fully. It was like looking at a statue, the way all the lines of his muscles moved under his skin. He was hard, which surprised me more than anything else, since I had never really looked at it in actual light.

"Take them off." He looked at my underwear. "Please," he added, smiling.

I put my hands on either side of the elastic band, but they refused to move.

"Does this look like I don't like the way you look?" he asked, pointing at his hardness.

With the same conviction someone takes jumping into a freezing pool, I pushed them off and kicked them away. We stood next to each other, fully naked for the first time. He moved to me and pulled me close, the warmth of his skin as erotic as the feel of him pressing against me. "I love everything about you," he said as his hands moved down to cup my ass. "I wish you could see yourself the way I do."

I began to tremble and thought I was cold for a moment, but I realized I had broken out in a cold sweat. He pulled me even closer and held me. "Take a deep breath," he said, rubbing my back. "Just relax and breathe."

My hands clutched at each other around his back as I tried to calm myself down.

"Come on," he said, pulling away slightly, "let's get wet." He opened the shower door and turned on one of the two showerheads. Once he got the temperature right, he turned the other one on, and within a minute the room began to fill up with steam. He stood at the door smiling, his body looking even better wet. "Come on," he said, holding out a hand. "Come take a shower with me."

I stepped into the shower, praying at some point I would get relaxed with this or that my heart would burst and get my torture over with. Either one would be nice.

I stood under one of the showerheads and discovered that the water was hot but not intolerable. I rested my chin against my chest and let the water roll down my back. The steady wash of warm water felt awesome; the shower in my apartment had nowhere near as much pressure. Brad's hands moved over my shoulders, and I could feel him put some kind of lotion or soap on me. His grip got firmer, and he massaged the tension out of my muscles.

"Oh fuck," I said, catching myself with my hands before I fell forward and slammed into the marble wall of the shower. It was like an electric current was moving from his fingertips through me. "Where did you learn that?"

He chuckled as his hands moved toward my neck. "I've played sports since I was seven, dude. You know how many massages I've had? You pick up a trick or two along the way." His thumbs moved into the area right where my skull connected with my spine, and I felt another spark move through me.

"Oh my God," I half moaned. One, I wasn't the most comfortable person when it came to being touched. Yeah, don't look at me like that. I know you knew; I just need to say it out loud, okay? So the way his hands moved over my shoulders and neck was the best thing

I had ever felt, period, and that was including him going down on me. I knew I was a wound-up guy and had always wondered if a massage would help, but since I was never going to let a guy touch me like Brad was, to avoid going all sex crazy on him, I had never tried one. Two, he knew what he was doing. He hadn't learned a trick or two. This boy had a whole routine under his belt, and it was incredible. And though three shouldn't have to be said, I will anyway. He was fucking the best-looking guy I had ever seen, and he was rubbing me naked in a shower.

I guess what I am trying to say is, I got hard.

Since I was leaning into the shower wall with both my hands pressed to the tiles, I couldn't do a thing about it. Part of me hoped Brad couldn't tell; the other part wished he did.

His hands moved from my neck down the middle of my back and began pressing and kneading outward from my spine. With each passing second, I became more and more relaxed as I also became more and more turned-on. "See?" he asked softly. "Not so bad, is it?" I shook my head because I didn't trust myself not to shout out very, very loudly to *do me!* "All work and no play makes Kyle a basket case," he said, kissing my shoulders.

"Better?" he asked when I was almost purring. "What is there to be nervous about?"

As if to make his point, the bathroom door burst open and Jennifer called out, "Guys, get out here right now. We have a problem."

All the tension Brad had massaged out of me was back tenfold as I almost jumped out of my skin. The only thing that made it funny was the girl-like shriek Brad let out at the same time. "What the fuck, Jen?" he growled, knowing she couldn't see us through the steam.

"Not kidding, get out here." And she closed the door.

"If her dad wasn't a cop, and she couldn't, like, you know, kick my ass, I would kill her," he said, turning the water off.

I still felt like I was on the edge of a heart attack as we got out of the shower.

I threw on a sweatshirt that could have fit three of me while Brad just put on a pair of sweats and nothing else as he ran out. I followed him after slipping on my underwear and slacks.

I found Brad standing at Kelly's doorway, where the sound of Kelly's voice screaming "*Fuck fuck fuck*!" came echoing out of the room. I peeked in and could see he was sitting at his desk in front of his computer, pounding on his keyboard. Jennifer stood a few feet behind him, obviously too nervous to get any closer. I didn't understand what the problem was until I heard what was coming from the speakers.

"I don't want to be gay!"

I pushed past Brad as Kelly's words from last night came echoing from the computer. I saw the screen and my blood turned to ice water. It was Kelly and me talking last night. Someone had been standing with the door cracked, holding a cell phone, recording us. It had been edited and was looping almost everything Kelly had said over and over again. Someone had posted it on his Facebook wall with the title "Who's the fag now?"

There were over one hundred comments and twice as many likes on it.

"Oh God." Kelly began to cry when he saw it had been shared over forty times up and down his wall.

Someone had just publicly outed Kelly to the entire school.

Part Three

Somebody I Used to Know

Brad

YOU KNOW that whole thing people have about the zombie apocalypse? They are so sure the dead are going to rise again and get a taste for takeout that they have these plans. I know it isn't real, but it's like the worst thing in the world they could envision. Out of all the ways the world could end, the very worst to them is ending up a happy meal for a pack of dead guys. I've seen a few movies and watched that one show a couple of times, but it really didn't strike me as scary as everyone else thought it was.

That was because in my mind, the worst way for the world to end was what happened to Kelly.

I just stood there stunned as he tried to erase the video from his wall, knowing it had been seen by half the school already. His phone was on the desk next to him, vibrating like it was on speed with each new text that came in. I couldn't blame him for not checking them; after all, what was he going to say? No, that is not me crying about being gay on that clip. It is obviously a CGI Kelly. Can't you see how it looks like Jar Jar?

As we watched, more and more responses came streaming in from Facebook. It was obvious that most of Foster High was waking up and checking their emails. Within five minutes, the video popped up three more times on his wall; there was no putting that genie back in its bottle now.

I looked down at my phone, and sure enough, it was all over IG too. Every single person I knew from school had it on their wall, and the comments… well, never read the comments, but these were fucking horrible.

"Who sent it?" Jennifer asked between Kelly's vocal explosions.

"I don't know!" he raged. "I deleted the original post; these are repostings."

"It's a YouTube clip," Kyle said, pointing at the video. "Click that corner." Kelly didn't quite get what Kyle was saying, so Kyle clicked it himself. Another browser opened to YouTube. The video was titled "Kelly Aimes: who is the fag now?"

It had over a thousand views already.

"People are commenting here too!" Kelly exclaimed, pointing at the page.

"Turn it off," Kyle said quickly, reaching for the power switch.

"What are they saying?" Kelly asked, pushing his hand way.

"Don't read it," Kyle insisted, reaching with his other hand to shut the computer off.

"Knock it off, geek," Kelly snapped, pushing him away. Kyle pinwheeled back, hitting the floor with a thud.

"What's it say?" I asked, curiosity winning out over caution.

The second I read the words, I wished I could take it back.

"Fucking kill yourself, fag."

"All fags should die."

"God will laugh when you die."

"I always knew Kelly was a fucking fairy."

I reached over and turned the computer off myself; this time Kelly didn't stop me.

"I'm dead," he said in a voice that sounded like it was made with his last breath.

"No, you're not," Kyle said, getting up off the floor. "This will pass."

All three of us looked at him like he was nuts.

"It's just Facebook," Kyle said, obviously not aware of what he was saying. "And YouTube and Instagram…."

"It's on TikTok," Jennifer said, holding her phone up.

Kelly let out another scream.

Kyle went on talking like he didn't know how bad this all was. "You have a couple of weeks before school starts. By the time it starts up again, people will find something new to talk about."

"And if they don't?" Kelly demanded more than asked.

"Then we deal with it," he answered, his tone laced with steel. "This is not the end of the world." I didn't say anything, but I couldn't help feeling he was dead wrong. This was how the world ended, at least for guys like Kelly and me.

"Can you guys take off?" Kelly asked after a few minutes of silence.

"Do you want us to help clean…?" Jennifer started to ask.

"Go," he barked.

She looked at me, and I shrugged. "Let's give him some space," I said, and to Kelly, I added, "If you need us, just call, man."

Kelly didn't even look up. The only sound in his room was his phone vibrating again and again.

I followed Kyle out as Jennifer closed the door behind her.

"We're going to leave him alone?" Kyle asked, his voice straining with disbelief.

"He doesn't want us here," Jennifer answered.

"And we're going to do it?" Kyle asked, getting more upset.

I saw he was upset, but there wasn't much I could do about it. "We can't just stay here forever. He wants to be alone, he gets to be alone."

"He's in pain," Kyle said, pointing at the closed door.

"And he will be in pain until he lets someone help him," Jennifer said softly. She looked at me. "Let me grab my stuff and we can take off."

I nodded, and she went downstairs. As soon as she was gone, I said to Kyle in a lower tone of voice, "I know you want to do something, but he doesn't want our help. You can't force it on him." I saw he wanted to argue, but he knew I was right. "I love you for wanting to jump in and do the right thing, but some people need time to adjust."

Kyle looked back at the closed door and shook his head. "This isn't something you adjust to."

He let out a sigh and his shoulders slumped. "I'll go grab my clothes." He walked away with an aura of defeat around him. I felt like I'd kicked a puppy, but I knew if it was me in there, I would want to be able to cry in private. We gathered all our stuff, and I called up the stairs. "Hey, dude, we're taking off! Call if you need something!" Silence was the only response. I saw the worried look in Kyle's eyes. "He'll be fine. I'll call him later tonight on his parents' line." He accepted that answer, but I could see he didn't like it at all.

I closed the front door, ignoring the feeling of dread that passed through my mind momentarily.

Once we were on the road to Jennifer's house, Kyle started talking. "You guys know he is nowhere near okay, right?" I waited for Jennifer to answer, which was the wrong thing to do because I saw her look at me in the rearview mirror.

"Kyle…," I began to explain.

"No. Don't give me 'Kyle, everyone deals with it differently' or 'Kyle, you have to give people space.' That guy is in nine kinds of pain, and we are leaving him alone."

"So what would you have us do?" Jennifer asked from the back seat.

His answer was immediate. "I would sit on him until he realized the sky isn't falling down on his head."

"But it is," I said, correcting him gently. He looked over at me like I had called him a bad word. "What?" I asked in response. "The worst thing that could possibly happen to him just happened. In his world the sky is bloodred, and it is falling right down on his head."

I saw him visibly swallow his anger to speak normally. "One, being found out you are gay is not the worst thing that can happen to a person. He could have fallen in a hole and had to gnaw his arm off. He might have been force-fed spaghetti until his stomach was about to burst. He might have even been hit by a bus in the middle of an intersection. Only in this backward fucking town would someone think being gay is the worst of all possibilities. And two, let's pretend you're right and that somehow being gay is the worst thing in the world. Isn't that more reason to not leave him alone?"

We'd never really fought before, which meant I had never been on the receiving end of his temper. Staring down the business end of it now, I could see why people did not like arguing with him. "You can't save everyone," I said as we pulled up in front of Jennifer's house.

Kyle opened his door the moment I stopped. "I'm not interested in saving everyone. Just that one guy." And he slammed the door.

"What the fuck?" I asked as he began to walk away.

I looked back at Jennifer, who had a grin on her face. "Hey, sue me," she said, shrugging. "I'm starting to like him."

I turned off the car and jogged after him.

Kyle was serious. This wasn't a dramatic "I am going to walk away and wait for someone to stop me" kind of thing. He really was just leaving. "Come on, Kyle!" I called after him. "It's Winter Break—don't make me run!" He stopped and let me catch up to him. "Thank you," I said, trying to catch my breath.

He said nothing in return.

"So what's your plan? Go back to Kelly's and bust down his door?" I asked as we walked.

More nothing.

"Kyle, I want to help Kelly too, but he needs time."

He stopped and shot me a look. "He needs friends. He doesn't need to be alone or have space or deal by himself. I know because I spent years crying in the middle of the night for someone to hear me. He needs to know he has friends."

My response came tumbling out of my mouth before I could stop it. "You aren't his friend."

"No. His *friends* are either calling him a fag or leaving him alone. So I am the best he has." And he began walking off again.

I finally lost it. All the frustration and anger I had been holding back came flooding out. "Fine!" I shouted at him. "Do whatever you want! You have all the answers, don't you!"

He kept walking away from me.

I threw up my hands at him and stormed back to my car. Jennifer was leaning against it with a package of Pop-Tarts in her hand, a Cheshire cat grin on her face. "So did you try to lay down the Graymark law?"

"He's nuts," I replied angrily. I felt sick to my stomach because this was the first thing we ever really disagreed on, but I was too pissed to care.

"I thought he hated Kelly?" she asked, tearing off a piece and offering it to me.

I took it because I was stupid hungry. "I don't think Kyle can hate anyone, one of the many reasons I love him." I chewed as I thought on that. "Also, one of the many reasons I want to shake some sense into him. This isn't going to end well."

She nibbled on the edge of her pastry as she mused on Kyle's behavior. "So let me get this right. Kelly tried to kill him, treated him like an asshole, and pretty much made his life a living hell, and now Kyle is walking back to his house because he is worried about him?"

I nodded.

"Wow," she said finishing her snack. "He *is* too good for you." She turned and headed up her driveway. "Call me if you hear anything on Kelly."

I stood there and looked back in the direction Kyle had walked.

This was going to be the worst Winter Break of my life.

Kyle

I KNOCKED on Kelly's door, trying hard not to drop the bags in my hand.

No answer, so I knocked louder.

Still no answer, so I kicked the door a few times.

He swung open the door and glared at me. From the redness in his eyes, I could see he had been crying. "What?"

"Hungry?" I asked, holding up the two bags so that the Nancy's Diner logo showed.

"Go away," he said, starting to close the door.

I moved quickly, putting my body between the door and the jamb before it could close. "Yeah, not going to happen," I said when he glared at me furiously. Even Kelly had to admit the obvious after a minute. I wasn't going to move, so he opened the door enough to let me slip in. "Thanks," I said, making sure I didn't drop the bags.

He slammed the door behind me. "You can't take a hint, can you?"

I went into the living room and sat down on the couch. "I take hints just fine. I happen to be ignoring yours at the moment." Putting the bags down, I began to unpack the food. "Gayle said you usually ordered the chicken breast sandwich, so I got you that. If you don't want it, I'll trade my cheeseburger with you."

"I'm not hungry," he said, standing over me instead of sitting down.

"More for me, then." I shrugged as I unwrapped my burger. I turned, grabbed the remote, and turned on the TV before I took a bite. "*Teen Wolf* is on Netflix. You ever watch that show?" I asked with my mouth full.

He just stared at me like I was an alien.

"The story is nice, but the guys in it are stupid hot," I commented, ignoring the staring. "I mean it. It's on par with watching porn." I was lying since I had never watched porn, but I assumed it had to be a lot like watching Colton Haynes taking a shower.

After about five minutes, he sighed heavily and sat down next to me.

"I didn't know what you put on it, so there is mayonnaise, ketchup, and mustard in the bag," I said as he unwrapped his food.

"Why are you doing this?" he asked while he spread mustard over the bun, using the flattened packet as a knife.

"Doing what?" I asked innocently. "I missed the last season, and your TV is better than mine." Which was true of just about everything in the Aimes's house.

He gave me a "Come on" look, but I ignored him and watched the TV.

He gave up and began to watch it with me.

It was exactly forty-four minutes before he started asking questions.

"So wait, that guy is a werewolf too?" he asked, pointing.

"Yeah, he is the new alpha," I explained during the commercial.

"So he made him?" Kelly asked, confused.

"No, that was the other alpha," I began to explain and then gave up. "You know what? Let's start at Season One."

"You've already seen those," he protested.

"So? Did you see those guys?" I laughed. "Grab us something to drink, and I'll load it up."

He came back with a Pepsi in each hand. "How did you even get here? I didn't see a car outside."

I pulled up the first season of *Teen Wolf*. "I went by Nancy's, and Gayle had Pedro the busboy give me a ride."

He paused. "What did you tell her?"

I looked up at him. "I told her I had a friend who was having a shitty day, and I was bringing him some food to cheer him up." He seemed to turn that over in his head for a few seconds. "I didn't tell her anything. I wouldn't do that."

That seemed to relieve him, and he sat back down. "We're friends now?" he asked as the show started.

"Well, let's not get carried away," I said back. "It got us some free food."

He almost choked on his drink. "You got this for free?" I nodded. He shook his head. "I swear, you do not live in the same world as the rest of us."

I decided to take his statement as a compliment and just smiled.

The next few hours passed without one word about Facebook or the video, which I thought was a good thing. By the middle of the first season, the sky was darkening, and we still hadn't moved from the couch. I paused the show so we could stretch and take a much-needed bathroom break.

"You want some help cleaning up?" I asked him as we looked around the living room.

"Nah," he said, falling back into the couch. "My parents aren't going to be home until tomorrow, so there's plenty of time."

I sat down on the arm of the couch. "How do you think they are going to react?" I asked cautiously.

He began to channel surf. "Probably lose their fucking minds." I thought desperately on what to say to counter that, but honestly, his words sounded right to me. He turned the TV off and looked over at me. "You want a ride home?"

"Sure," I said, taking the hint that I was being asked to leave.

I grabbed my stuff and waited for him to find his keys. When we opened the door, what we saw caused us both to freeze in shock. Someone had taken red spray paint and written the word "faggot" over both sides of his truck. The sound of Kelly's keys falling to the ground was like a thunderclap in the silence. He just turned around and went back inside the house.

I had seen a phone in the kitchen and used it to call Brad. He answered on the third ring. "Hey."

"Hey. Someone spray-painted all over Kelly's truck." I picked up the keys and waited for his reaction.

"Fuck," he said into the phone. "I'll be right over."

"How do you get paint off a car?" I asked, realizing I had never thought about it before.

"With more paint," Brad answered sourly. "I'll see what we have in the garage."

"And hey," I added before he hung up.

"Yeah?" he asked, obviously upset.

"How long are we going to be mad at each other? I only ask because I've never actually had a boyfriend before, so I don't know how fights are supposed to go," I said bluntly.

I could hear him sigh, and I could imagine him running a hand thorough his hair in frustration. "I don't know, Kyle. I'm just pissed."

"So am I," I responded instantly.

"Well then, I guess we're going to be mad longer than this." His response was angry, but I could tell he had no idea how to handle our argument either.

"What did you do when you fought with your girlfriends?"

"I'd have no idea we were fighting, then find out, apologize for whatever they thought I did, and that was it." I could hear him pick up his keys in the background. "I'll be right over."

He hung up, and I smiled despite my frustration with him. I bet he was easily as mad as I was, yet he still dropped everything and got in his car when I called. I had a feeling no matter how pissed off we got, things would work out in the long run.

I did not feel the same about Kelly.

He wasn't in the living room, so I decided to look upstairs. I found him in front of his computer. He was cussing under his breath as he clicked the mouse. I could see there were images of his truck, posted multiple times all over his wall, no doubt by the douchebags who'd done it. "Fucking assholes," he growled. "They're bragging about it!"

"Turn it off," I said softly. He was upset, and I knew a thing or two about dealing with people who were perpetually angry. Rule one was never try to match their emotions because hate begets more hate. If you were stupid enough to engage with someone who was insanely pissed, always come in soft and quiet. Thinking about it, it was like dealing with a wild animal.

Quiet, subdued tones, show no teeth, and never turn your back on them.

"I'm just supposed to let them get away with it?" he demanded, slamming his fists down on his desk.

"Do you want to call the cops?" I asked, trying to introduce the only sane course of action open to him.

"I want to kill them!" he said, standing up, his chair falling over as he kicked it. "Why is this happening to me?"

I didn't say a word, because I was still waiting on the answer to that very same question.

He looked over at me. "Aren't you going to say I deserve it? That this is just karma or some shit?"

I shook my head.

"Why not? It's what you're thinking, isn't it?"

I shook my head again. "No one deserves this," I said, trying not to break eye contact because that can come off as sounding insincere.

He looked like he wanted to hit me, but I knew this had very little to do with me. "Why the fuck are you even here?" He walked past me and out of his room. "Just leave!" he bellowed as he went down the stairs.

I looked at his computer. More and more messages kept popping up on his Facebook page. Shaking my head, I followed him downstairs.

He was in the kitchen. I could hear running water. He was filling a bucket up with water and soap as he grabbed some towels from a drawer. "I mean it, fucking go," he raged as the water began to spill over the top of the bucket.

"You want some help?" I asked.

"*I want you to leave*!" he turned and screamed at me.

"I can carry the bucket," I offered, ignoring his shouting.

He looked like I had finally pushed him too far as he turned off the water and took a step toward me. Thank God Brad walked in and interrupted us. "Jesus, dude, I can hear you in the driveway," he said to Kelly. "Calm the fuck down."

"Awesome. And the other one shows up," he said to himself. "Take your damn boyfriend and get out of here!" he said, pointing at me.

Brad stood there for a few seconds and then said to me, "Okay. Come on, Kyle."

"He needs help with his car…," I began to explain.

Brad walked up and put a hand on my shoulder. "He's fine. Come on."

I shrugged him off. "He's not fine," I snapped at Brad.

"That may be so, but that's his choice," Brad said, pointing to Kelly. "Not yours." He was pretty pissed because he had started to yell. "You did everything you could. Now let's go."

"You don't get to tell me what to do," I said, not even sure where inside me my anger was coming from.

"And you don't get to decide what is or is not good for someone else." The words were like cold water being thrown in my face. "Seriously, he wants to be alone."

I looked back at Kelly, who was staring at the two of us like we were speaking a foreign language. "You really want us to leave?" I asked him.

He took a deep breath and closed his eyes. "Thank you for the food and the company," he said in a more subdued tone. "But yeah, I just want to get that shit off my car and then go to sleep."

"Okay," I said, not sure what to do. "You're going to be okay?"

Kelly laughed. "Dude, you earned your good-guy badge or whatever you were shooting for today. Yeah, I'm fine."

I looked back at Brad. "Can I get a ride?"

Brad shook his head and smiled. "You gonna stay in the car this time?"

I ignored that and walked over to Kelly. I looked him straight in the eye. "Those people are fucking assholes and not worth the air they breathe. They do not and will never define who you are as a person. Please, turn your computer off."

He looked at Brad and then back to me. "Are we going to hug now? 'Cause I think Brad would be pretty jealous if he saw you—"

"I'm serious," I said, bypassing his bravado. "Turn the computer off."

He stopped and nodded. "Okay, I promise to turn it off."

I knew he was lying, but it was the best I was going to get.

"Okay, then. I will see you later," I said to him, turning back to Brad.

"Wait, what?" Kelly asked.

"I'll see you tomorrow," I said, walking out of the kitchen. "Count on it."

Brad

KELLY GAVE me a look like he was asking me if Kyle was serious.

I nodded and followed him out the door.

Kyle was sitting in my car, not looking happy. I got in and fastened my seat belt. "You want to eat, fight some more, or just have me drop you off?"

He didn't say anything for a few seconds as he stared forward.

"Come on," I said, smiling. "You know you are always hungry." Which was true for both of us, but I did know was truer for him than me.

He sighed. "Fine, food." And nothing more.

I tried to hide my grin as I backed out of Kelly's driveway and headed toward Starr's, a local drive-in that usually was only crowded on the weekends when the high school kids in Foster cruised. We pulled up to a stall and looked over the menu they had posted. I saw Kyle look at the menu and then try to slyly pull out his wallet. I looked back at my menu and said, "Just 'cause we're fighting doesn't mean I can't pay for you."

He slowly put his wallet away. "Okay, but I refuse to change my feelings based on how hungry I am or how much food you buy me."

I had to laugh at that. "Are you saying I would try to bribe you with a chili dog?"

He didn't answer, but I saw him force back a smile of his own.

I ordered us a ton of food and then turned on my radio while we waited. Well, I waited, and I knew he was stewing. I counted silently in my head.

When I got to forty-seven, he broke.

"Why is what I am trying to do wrong?" he demanded of me.

I turned the music down. "It's not wrong; it's just not the right thing in this case," I tried to explain.

"Why?" he asked.

"For a few reasons." I began to count off on my fingers. "One, Kelly doesn't want you to. Two, you aren't Kelly's friend, and even if you were, he wouldn't want someone to do that. He is deathly embarrassed, and having someone like you around makes it worse for him."

"Like me?" he asked, his voice dropping the temperature in the car a few degrees.

"Yeah, someone he actively picked on, like, five minutes ago. I have no idea how you are able to just let it go, but I assure you, Kelly hasn't yet." He didn't like that answer at all, but he knew it was the truth.

"So you're telling me that because Kelly has shitty friends coupled with the fact he treated me like crap means I should leave him alone when he needs people the most?" I was pretty sure I hadn't said any of that, but the calm and collected way he said it made me think back over my own words.

"You know I am not going to leave him alone," he said in the silence.

I nodded.

"And there is nothing you or Kelly can do about that."

More nodding.

"And you're okay with that?" he asked, sounding kind of shocked.

"Of course not, but I am not going to stop you," I answered, laughing. "I've learned a few things since we started dating, and one of them is never try to stop Kyle when he has his mind set. I think you're wasting your time and that you are going to end up getting hurt, but I am your boyfriend, and I'll support you no matter what." It was an odd thing to say since I hadn't realized I felt that way until the words came out of my mouth. My anger was gone, and I understood I had been more worried about him than mad.

"You mean that?" he asked, unsure if my words were a verbal feint.

"I think I do," I said, sounding more surprised than he did. "You are aware Kelly is still a complete asshole?"

He cocked his head and asked me back, "Do you think I got hit on the head or something?"

"Hey, I was wondering," I said, laughing. "I worry he is going to end up telling you to fuck off."

"So he tells me to fuck off," he answered as the carhop came rolling up to my window, holding a tray of food. "Not the first time

I've heard those words. Hell, not the first time I've heard him say those words to me."

The girl looked at all the food we had ordered and then at the two of us. "Did you guys need some bags to go with this?"

I shook my head as I took the tray of food from her. "Nope, this is fine." I handed it to Kyle as I dug some money out of my pocket. "Keep the change," I said, shooting her a smile. She looked in the back seat to make sure and then skated off. I looked over to Kyle, who was already three bites into his burger. "You know she thinks we have an eating problem now, right?"

He said something back with his mouth full.

I answered him as I grabbed my own food. "I don't care what she thinks. I'm just saying."

We ate in relative silence as we both agreed the fight was over.

Kyle

AT TEN the next day I knocked on Kelly's door.

It took him almost five minutes before he appeared at the door, his hair standing straight up and his eyes barely open. Once his vision focused on me, he let out a wail. "Oh fucking come on!"

I held up a bag and announced cheerfully, "I brought donuts."

He stared at me silently for almost a minute.

Then, sighing, he stepped out of the way. "Fine, come in."

And that was how I became friends with Kelly.

We finished watching the first season of *Teen Wolf*, cleaned up his house, and spent an afternoon scrubbing the paint off his truck. We ended up sanding it down to metal, which made it look like shit, but at least "faggot" wasn't in glowing red letters on the side of it. I left earlier than the day before because his parents were coming home, and he wanted to deal with them alone.

I totally understood that.

Monday morning I showed up at Robbie's place, ready to work. The door was locked, so I sat down and waited. And waited.

And waited. It was almost eleven by the time he pulled into the parking lot, the soundtrack of *Mamma Mia!* blaring from the open windows. "I know, I know!" he screamed as he parked the car. "I ended up on the phone with a friend from back home who kept threatening she was going to cut her hair because of a bad breakup, and I had to talk her down." He got out and ground his cigarette butt into the sidewalk. "I should have just let her cut the damn stuff and get it over with." He rushed past me and began rummaging through his keys. "But *no*. I have to be her official drama enabler, and to be honest it was better than anything on TV last night, but she went on and on, and I fell asleep on the couch." He pushed the door open. "But I am here now, and we are open," he declared, flipping the sign on the door proudly.

And then he saw the look on my face.

"What happened?" he asked, his whole attitude changing.

I explained what happened to Kelly.

I went into the whole conversation, the video, the truck, everything. I also added I had been worried about him and had been trying to keep him in good spirits, but I hadn't talked to him since yesterday and was worried.

He just stood there behind the counter, not saying a word.

Finally he asked, "Why?"

I was confused by the question. "Why what?"

"Why are you worried?" he elaborated.

"Um, because he got outed and people are attacking him," I explained slowly, in case he was still half-asleep.

"Yeah, people just like him are attacking him. Even sharks will attack other sharks if there is enough blood in the water. Why do you care?" His voice was so… I don't know, emotionless? Cold? I stared at him, shocked.

"Because he needs friends right now." I felt like I was having the conversation with Brad all over again.

"So? Why you? Isn't this the guy who pretty much outed you?" he asked, and I wondered how much Jennifer had told him about what happened.

I shrugged. "Why not?"

"Because he is a self-loathing homophobe. Isn't that enough?"

The words moved down my spine like ice water. "He's a human being. Isn't *that* enough?"

"No," he said, turning away from me while he put the till in the register. "I thought this wasn't about you," he said, counting silently. "I thought it was just a party?"

"It became more," I said slowly.

"Well, sounds like this guy got what he deserved. But bully for you for standing up for him." He didn't sound the least bit convincing, but I wasn't going to call him a liar to his face. "So, you ready to get started?"

I nodded, not trusting myself not to say something out loud that I was going to regret.

He showed me the boxes and boxes of clothes that were stored in the back room. "We need to sort through these, see what, if anything, is worth selling, and put the rest in a donation box," he explained. "So go through them, see if there is anything that is too tragic to wear, toss them over there." He gestured to the left. "The ones you think are worth something, put over there." He gestured to the right. "And anything you think you might want to wear, keep by you, and we'll go over it at the end of the day. Got it?"

I nodded, unsure of what too tragic to wear meant but willing to give sorting a try.

"Okay, yell if you have a question," he said and walked back to the front of the store. He paused at the door, and I thought he might say something, but he just shook his head and walked out, leaving me to my chores.

I took a deep breath and opened the first box.

Two hours later, I was through my third box and had found nothing I thought would look good on me. But then, I hadn't thought what Robbie had picked out for me would look good until I tried them on. I was about to open my fourth box when Brad walked into the back room. "So the guy in front said this is where I should go if I was looking to get a cute guy."

I stood up and gave him a hug. "What are you doing here?"

He chuckled. "You said to meet you for lunch. It's after one."

"Holy crap," I said, looking at my phone to check. "I kinda lost track of time."

He looked at the piles of clothes and asked, "So what's the criteria?"

"I have no idea. He told me to use my best judgment, so I just imagined if I could see someone on TV wearing it. If I could, I put it over there, if not, over there." I paused. "Wait, no that one is the keep…." I picked up a few shirts and looked under them. "Oh crap."

Brad began to laugh as he came to the same realization that I had. At some point I had completely spaced out on which pile was which and now they were mixed up. "It's not funny," I said to him, even though it was a little funny. He tried to stop laughing, but there was no use as I looked through the other pile to see if I could make some sense of them.

"Let's go to lunch, and you can take care of this when we get back."

I sighed, stepping away from the clothes. "I think I wasted four hours of work."

Brad called out to Robbie, who was sitting behind the counter reading a book. "I'm stealing him for lunch."

He didn't look up but waved his hand at us. "Try not to eat him all in one bite."

"He's not eating me for lunch!" I protested.

"Oh," he said, looking up over the book at me. "Then you are having a far less exciting lunch than I imagined."

I was about to say something back when Brad led me out of the shop. "Man, he likes winding you up," he said as we got in the car.

"He just pissed me off earlier," I said, putting on my seat belt. I turned and asked him, "Have you heard from Kelly?"

"Nope," he said as we turned onto East Avenue. "Why?"

"His parents got home last night, and I want to know what happened," I explained.

"Ouch," he said, pulling onto First Street. "That couldn't have been a good talk."

"But why?" I asked. "They leave and let him have a wild party with no adults, but the fact he might like guys is when they decide to care?"

"It isn't that easy." We parked in front of Nancy's. "Kelly's parents are all about status. The party is just a way for them to buy themselves popularity. If being gay made Kelly popular, I assure you they would have outed him years ago." He looked over at me and grabbed my hand. "Can we have a meal without worrying about Kelly? This is our Christmas break, and I really wanted to spend it with you." He gave me the puppy-dog eyes, which was an especially nice touch. "One meal, no drama?"

I took a deep breath and nodded. "I'm sorry. It has me freaked-out."

He leaned over and kissed me. "I know, and that is why I'm in love with you. I'm not asking you to change, just pause for one meal."

"Fair enough," I said, smiling back at him.

"Last one in pays for lunch," he said, throwing open his door and jumping out of the car.

"*Unfair*!" I screamed as I wrestled with my seat belt.

Brad

I WAITED by the diner door for him to catch up.

I was worried, had been worried a while now, about how caught up he'd become with Kelly's drama. I understood that Kelly was in trouble and that this had to be the most excruciating thing he had ever gone through, but I wasn't comfortable with Kyle in the middle of it. Things were going to get worse when school started up again, and I knew Kyle wouldn't back off on trying to help Kelly.

Which meant more crap for everyone all around.

I held the door open for him, and he gave me a look. "I thought we were racing," he asked.

"You won," I said, smiling.

"One of these days you're going to let me pay," he warned before he walked in.

I slapped his ass as I followed. "You can pay in other ways." I liked watching him blush slightly as he looked back at me and told me to behave.

"Grab a seat where you can," Gayle called to us from behind the counter. She was filling a glass with Coke as she asked us, "You two want the usual?" I nodded as Kyle found us a booth.

"So what did Robbie piss you off about?" I asked, knowing he wanted to talk about it.

He made a dismissive gesture with his hand. "You don't want to know."

Which I took as his way of saying it was about Kelly.

"Isn't that going to make working there weird?" I wondered.

"It's already weird, trust me."

Gayle brought me a Coke and Kyle a tea. "We're backed up, but I put your cheeseburgers in. How you guys doing?"

"He's working over at Twice Upon a Time," I said proudly. "He's a working man."

Gayle looked over at Kyle. "You're working with Robbie?" He nodded. "You should be drinking something stronger than tea," she joked. "But congratulations."

Kyle mumbled something as he looked down at the table.

"You working with your dad at the dealership?" she asked me.

I rattled off a quick "Fuck no!" before I realized who I was talking to. "Excuse my language."

She laughed. "Brad, the day you say a curse word I haven't heard is the day you don't have to pay for your meal."

"Fucktard?" I tried. "Shitface? Shitfuckcrap?"

She shook her head. "Nice try," she said, walking away. "Food will be up soon."

"You're crazy," Kyle said once she was gone.

I grabbed his hands across the table. "About you," I said as cheesily as I could.

He rolled his eyes and laughed. "I like this," he admitted. "Being alone with just you."

Which was when someone pushed me over in the booth and slid in.

I looked over and saw Mr. Parker sitting there out of breath. "I need some help," he panted before taking a drink of my Coke.

"Hey," I said, scooting over to give him some room. "Um, help yourself."

He nodded as he finished it. "Thanks." He looked across the table. "Hey, Kyle."

Kyle waved back, still half-shocked.

"So what's up?" I asked, wondering what was wrong. I'd known Mr. Parker for a while, but we had kind of become friends a couple of months ago when I was coming out. He was really the only gay adult I knew in Foster, so I had turned to him a few times for advice. Him coming to me was a new experience.

"My mom is trying to set me up with someone," he said once he caught his breath.

"Your mom?" I asked, lost. "I thought she lived in Florida."

He paused for a moment. "She does, but she still owns a phone."

Wow, he was wound up. "Okay, so who is she trying to set you up with?"

"Matt Wallace," he said, picking a piece of ice out of my glass.

"I don't know him. He's from here?" I asked, wondering if a new gay guy had moved into town.

"He's from here, but he doesn't live here," he corrected me. "We kind of went to high school together. He lives in San Francisco."

"Your mom is trying to set you up with a guy who lives in another state?" Kyle asked.

Mr. Parker nodded. "Well, he's coming back for Christmas; his parents still live here."

"So she is setting you up for casual sex?" I asked. Both of them looked at me like I had suddenly sprouted horns. "What? It's not like you're going to date him for a week." Neither one said a word. "Come on! Like I'm the only one here who knows what a hookup is."

Mr. Parker shook his head slowly. "I am pretty sure my mom is not trying to set me up with a hookup."

I shrugged. "Okay, so then what's your problem?"

"I don't know if I should meet him," he said as Gayle brought our food to us.

"Oh hey, Tyler, you eating?" she asked, surprised to see him sitting with us.

"I'm not staying that long, but thanks," he said, flashing her a thousand-watt smile. When I got older, I wanted to be able to smile like that.

"Okay, well, here are your burgers. Holler if you need anything," she said, walking to another table. I tried to grab my glass to ask her for a refill, but Mr. Parker started talking again.

"I mean, you're right. I can't date him for a few days, but God, it sucks being gay here," he said, eating one of my fries absently.

"Have you tried online?" Kyle asked, putting ketchup on his burger.

"Ugh," Tyler said, eating another fry. "Complete waste of time."

"So then meet him," I said, trying to steal my plate back from him.

"But what if I like him?" he asked me.

Good question.

"So then don't meet him," I suggested, yanking my burger off the plate before he could eat that too.

"But God, Christmas sucks when you're alone," he said, sighing.

"So then meet him, but as a friend," Kyle suggested brightly. "There's nothing saying you have to date or have sex with him. But you can make a new friend and see where that goes."

"Yeah, that's an idea," I agreed between bites. "Actually, a real good idea."

Tyler pondered Kyle's words and ate another five fries, I might add. "You know? You're right. I am overthinking this, aren't I?" He was thinking out loud, not really asking either of us a question. "I mean, who said it has to be all or nothing?"

"Well, you did," Kyle countered bluntly. When he saw us both half glaring at him, he added, "You did! All your mom is saying is there is going to be another gay person in Foster over Christmas. You're the one imbuing it with more importance than it deserves. To be honest, that says more about you than it does about your mom."

Tyler looked over at me and asked, "You date someone this smart? You're a braver man than I am." He ate the last fry in silence while I looked longingly over at Kyle's plate. "But you're right; my mom is trying to be nice, and I completely misread it." He looked at Kyle and asked him seriously, "Do I seem that lonely?"

Without a moment's hesitation, which I would have given him out of pity, he answered, "Yes."

Tyler leaned back and took a deep breath.

I kicked Kyle under the table and gave him a "Go easy on him" look. Kyle just shrugged and went on eating.

"Yeah, maybe meeting this guy isn't such a good idea," he said after a while. "If I'm this wound up, I'm going to mess up meeting him." He looked at Kyle. "Good call."

"Thanks," Kyle said, taking a drink of his tea. "Let me ask you something. Why not go out with Robbie?"

Tyler's face hardened for a moment. I couldn't tell what the emotion was exactly, but it was pretty serious. "He isn't my biggest fan. Besides, I don't think we're each other's type."

Kyle leaned forward. "What type is that?"

Mr. Parker paused for a second. "What did he tell you about me?"

"Kyle is working for him," I interjected quickly. "At his store."

"Oh," he said cryptically. "Well then, I'm sure you've heard a lot about me so far."

Kyle was about to say something back when Tyler looked out the window. "Dammit, I knew I couldn't leave the store for more than five minutes." He got up. "We've been swamped, and I've had zero time to think about this." He threw down a twenty on the table. "That's to make up for me eating all your food." He turned to walk out and then looked back at me. "Hey, you need a job?"

"Me?" I asked.

Tyler laughed and said, "Well, he already has one," pointing to Kyle.

"Um, yeah, I guess," I said, surprised he'd ask me.

"Awesome, come by after lunch and I'll start training you." He looked at Kyle and then back at me. "And you were right; this one is a keeper." He headed out the door.

Kyle jumped up. "Mr. Parker, wait!" He hurried over to him and asked him a question.

I watched them talk for a second; out of nowhere I felt a pang of jealousy, even though I knew Tyler would never hit on Kyle. Kyle asked something and Tyler shook his head and then walked out. Kyle walked back to our table.

"What was that?" I asked him, trying not to sound like a douchebag who gets mad when his boyfriend talks to another guy.

He shook his head as he went back to his burger. "Asking him something, not important."

I felt like pushing it, but then I figured that was the wrong way to go.

Gayle walked over to refill my Coke. "Oh, you're already done?" she asked me, surprised. "You must have been real hungry."

I had been about to order more fries, but now I just felt I'd end up looking like a pig. Instead I smiled and nodded. "Yep, I'm a growing boy." I sighed.

When she walked away, Kyle slid his plate of fries over to me. "Here, growing boy." He grinned. "I'll share."

I ate a fry, and all was forgiven in my mind.

Kyle

BRAD DROPPED me off at work. I gave him a kiss and waved bye, smiling at his excitement. He hurried off to the sporting goods store to start his own workday.

My thoughts, however, were a million miles away. Okay, not a million, just as far as Kelly's house. I had tried texting him on Brad's phone while Brad finished my fries, but I hadn't received an answer, and that worried me. I had asked Tyler if he had heard anything about Kelly; his answer would help me figure out how far the word had spread.

If everything was still limited to Facebook posts and people online, then I felt I could still talk Kelly down off the mental ledge he was on.

Luckily Mr. Parker hadn't heard a word. In fact, he wasn't quite sure who Kelly was until I brought up he was a football player. "Oh yeah, the big guy who used to follow Brad around?" I nodded. "Nope. Why? What happened that I should have heard about?"

I shrugged and dropped the subject fast. The last thing I needed was to spread the news to more people.

"How was lunch?"

I spun around. Robbie lounged against the building, smoking in the shadows under the awning. "Jesus! Wear a bell!" I said, holding my chest.

He stepped on the cigarette butt. "Not my fault you were in a Brad coma and didn't notice me."

I could hear the fight just waiting on the edge of his voice. Robbie was using the same sarcastic baiting tone my mom used when she was pissed but didn't want to deal with the actual topic.

"I'll be in the back," I said, walking into the shop, ignoring his attitude altogether.

I began going over the clothes I had sorted before lunch, knowing our argument wasn't over. Sure enough, about ten minutes later, he strolled in and leaned against the door frame. "So explain it to me."

I sighed and looked up. "Explain what exactly?"

"Why you would care about some homophobic asshole who made your life hell!" he snapped, frustrated.

"Why wouldn't I?" I asked him back.

"You need a list?" he blurted out. "How about because he is a bully, a closet case, and if anyone deserves to deal with being outed against their will, it's him."

"You're wrong," I said, keeping the emotion out of my voice. "You are completely wrong."

"Prove it," he demanded.

"No one deserves that. No one at all. And by saying a person deserves the way they are treated for one thing or another is how other people justify treating gay people the way they do. It's okay if they get beat up because they are gay, and they deserve it. It's okay if we say they are an abomination and going to hell because they are gay and deserve it." My voice got louder as I lost control of my emotions. "No one deserves it, Robbie. *No one*! And the fact you think this guy, who is a human being just like the rest of us, deserves to go through what's happening to him shows what kind of person you are."

"And what kind of person is that?" he asked, his voice seething with fury.

"You're a bigot," I said, standing up. "Acting the same way the people who hate us act doesn't make you right. It makes you the same type of person." I couldn't take any more of this. "There is a human being out there who is being attacked. Just because he is straight or gay or whatever doesn't make it right." I rushed past him and headed toward the door. "I'm done for today."

"Don't bother coming back!" he screamed after me.

"*Fine*!" I yelled, looking back at him.

"*Fine*!" he yelled back.

I had no idea what to say after that, so I slammed the front door of the store shut and headed toward Kelly's house.

It was a pretty long walk, but I needed the time to calm down.

I don't understand why adults automatically assume because they're old that they're right. It was like at some point a person turns in his common sense and ability to reason and falls back on some version of "Because I said so." Whatever you think is right is all that matters. It doesn't matter if logic says you are wrong or that you're contradicting yourself; if you read it in a book somewhere, then it has to be the only way it can be. There is just no room in their head for a new idea, no matter how much sense it makes.

"You know he's right," Billy said, walking down the street beside me.

"No, he's not."

"He is. Shitty things happen to shitty people, and one of life's small pleasures is watching them have it happen to them."

"So I am a shitty person?"

"You said it, not me," it muttered.

"That is what you're saying, right?"

"Did I say that? Did those words drop out of my mouth? No, they came out of yours."

I did not even want to get into it with Billy that all of this was coming out of my mouth, so I pressed on.

"Kelly attacked me, he tortured me at school, so I am a shitty person because shitty things happened to me."

It said nothing.

"I mean, come on. You love telling me how useless I am, so go for it. Tell me I deserved for all of that garbage to fall down on my head. Do it."

It said nothing.

"Right, so then if I didn't deserve it, neither does Kelly. Shitty things happen, fact. But it doesn't matter if the person brought it upon themselves. They are in pain and they just want some help. I know this because I've spent the last eighteen years waiting for someone to help me, so I am not going to not help him. And if you have a problem with it, go play in traffic and leave me alone."

I looked over and it was gone.

As I came up on Kelly's house, I saw an expensive-looking black whale of a town car was parked in the driveway, but his truck was nowhere to be seen. I considered not knocking on the door, but I had come all this way. I was cold and worried about Kelly. I knocked. The door was opened by a woman who looked like she saw a real nice dress in the catalog and then got it and realized she wasn't anything like the model who had been wearing it but put it on all the same. She had on so much makeup it looked like she'd decided to store all her makeup in one place in case the house caught on fire and she had to evacuate. There was a point when makeup doesn't help anymore and actually detracts from beauty. She hit that limit and then kept applying stuff for another hour.

In her left hand, she clutched a tumbler of something dark brown with no ice, meaning she was drinking for real. And though Mrs. Aimes looked nothing like my mom, all I saw was what my mom would look like if she'd had money.

"Yes?" she more slurred than asked.

The smell of booze hit me like a wall of hot air. "Um, is Kelly here?" I asked, trying not to make a face.

She seemed to ponder the name for a few seconds, as if she couldn't remember who Kelly was, before it clicked. "Kelly! Door!" she bellowed before stumbling back into the house.

I stood in the doorway, not sure if she'd meant I should come in.

Looking far worse than he had a couple of days ago, Kelly thudded listlessly down the stairs. There were black circles under his eyes, and he looked like he hadn't slept in forever. "Oh, hey," he said waving me in. "I'm upstairs." Every word he said and move he made were efforts. Slowly making his way back up the stairs, plodding along as if he was a condemned man walking to the electric chair, he led me to his room. His shoulders were slumped, and he stared intently at the floor. I followed him up without saying a word.

When we got to his room, he fell face-first onto his bed, silent.

I closed the door behind me and sat down at his desk. A quick glance at its littered surface told me a lot.

His phone was dead. He obviously hadn't charged it in a few days, which was a good thing in its own way. His computer was off, and his keyboard looked like it had been run over by a car, it was missing so many keys. "So, how are you doing?" I asked, turning back to Kelly, who hadn't budged.

He flopped over and stared at his ceiling.

"My parents are freaking out. My dad is talking about moving, and my mom hasn't stopped drinking since they got home." He sounded like a victim of a natural disaster, voice a monotone, words sounding as if he had memorized them so he wouldn't have to work at speaking. "They got home and asked what happened to my truck. I started explaining, and my dad screamed, 'Why didn't you hide it in the garage?' I think he had it towed away. I haven't gone downstairs in a while." He looked over at me and attempted a facial expression. "How's your day?"

"I'm sorry," I said, not sure what else to do. "I'm sure they are just in shock. Give them some time."

He laughed bitterly and went back to staring at the ceiling. "Yeah, because not enough time is what's preventing them from being real parents my whole life."

I knew that feeling all too well.

"I don't think the word has spread around to the rest of town yet," I said hopefully. "I asked Mr. Parker if he had heard anything, and he said no."

Kelly shot up like he had been tasered. He was off his bed in a flash and grabbing my shirt with both hands before I registered the fact that he'd moved in the first place. "What did you tell him?" he roared.

I wasn't the least bit scared, which is weird, because I should have been. "Nothing, I didn't tell him a thing, Kelly. I just asked he if had heard anything." I then said in a more reassuring tone, "I promised you I wouldn't tell anyone, and I meant it."

He stood over me, his hands trembling as he was literally overcome with emotion.

"I mean it, Kelly. I won't tell a soul," I repeated.

He didn't so much let me go as he deflated into himself, his hands dropping to his sides. "I know," he mumbled. "I'm sorry…." His voice trailed off to nothing as he shambled back to his bed and sat down.

"I'm going to help you," I said, trying to impart some kind of positive feelings his way.

He stared across at me, and the look of defeat on his face was crushing. "Okay. Can you reverse time and unrecord that video? Can you make everyone who has seen it forget it? Can you convince my parents that I'm not some kind of deviant freak? Go ahead, Kyle. Help me."

It reminded me way too much of my speech to Mr. Raymond when I came out.

"Things will get better," I tried to convince him. "It just looks bad now."

"It looks bad now because it is bad," he replied frankly. "And it is going to be worse tomorrow and then worse the day after. It isn't going to get any better, dude."

I had nothing to say in return. Thankfully, I didn't have to conjure up something. The sound of footsteps crashing up the stairs was followed by someone crashing Kelly's bedroom door open. An older and fatter version of Kelly stood there glaring. "Why is this door closed?" he had begun to ask before he even saw into the room. When he saw we were fully clothed and not on top of each other, his whole attitude changed. "Kelly, your friend should be going," he said, not even looking at me.

I stood up and held my hand out. “Hi. My name is Kyle Still—”

He gave me a look that would have caused Medusa to wither. “I know who you are. It’s time you leave.”

I lowered my hand. “I’ll see you tomorrow, Kelly,” I said, not breaking eye contact with his dad.

“I don’t think Kelly is going to be up for company.” Mr. Aimes said it as a suggestion, but the expression on his face made it clear it was anything but.

“And I think I will still be here tomorrow,” I “suggested” right back.

Mr. Aimes looked like he was about to argue, but Kelly blurted out, “Jesus, Dad, it’s not like he gave me the gay or something. I’ll see you tomorrow, Kyle.”

I looked back at him and nodded. “You can call anytime. My mom won’t mind.” I glanced back at his dad. “Pleasure to meet you too,” I said and stalked out.

It was going to be a long couple of weeks.

Brad

THE NEXT week blurred by.

Between trying to figure out how to help Mr. Parker survive the Christmas rush at the store and trying to make time to see Kyle, I felt like each day was getting shorter and shorter. My days were spent helping people find something to buy for a Christmas present. My nights were spent with Kyle as he described Kelly’s descent into hell.

Since he had quit working at the clothing store, he had thrown all his effort into turning Kelly’s mood around. From what he told me, it wasn’t an easy task. Kelly’s dad, even at his best, was a dick. I remembered the way he had tried to insinuate himself into any conversation he saw us having in a lame-ass effort to seem cool and hip. The old guy was tragic on an epic scale. Of course, since coming home and finding his only son a social outcast, he was nowhere near his best.

Kyle was pretty sure the old man blamed him in some way for making his son gay. I had told him it sounded about right, since Mr. Aimes never thought he was to blame for anything. The only reason Kyle was even getting into the house at all was Kelly's mom. She had taken to talking to Kyle at length about being gay and how horrible it must be for us. Kyle had tried to tell her it wasn't, but she talked over him, saying she could only imagine how terrible our lives must be since we came out.

After the third day, Kyle just sat there and nodded. Things were getting worse. The news was no longer confined to the people on Facebook. The video had over a hundred thousand hits on YouTube, and the comments were the worst things you could imagine. It was like people out there waited for videos like this, then crawled out from under their rocks to spout hatred. Kyle had even found it on Tumblr, where the video was being passed around faster than he could follow.

"It is, like, days away from showing up on people's For You page on TikTok," Kyle said, using my laptop. "And once that happens, it is going to go viral."

I shuddered at the thought of a video like that being passed around about me.

"The internet sucks, man" was all I could add to the conversation.

"Not everyone," he said, showing me the comments of support for Kelly as well. They were few compared to the haters, but there were some. "It's easier to be a bastard when no one knows who you are."

"Tell me about it," I agreed, remembering how vicious we could be when the person we were ridiculing wasn't around. I'd seen this kind of thing before, but never on this scale. Someone had caught Billy Jackson making out with a girl who definitely wasn't his girlfriend at an away game and had sent the clip to everyone in their phone. Of course, one of those people posted it on Facebook, where Billy's girlfriend saw it. That got ugly, but it was nowhere near this.

"It's just this town," Kyle said, closing the laptop in frustration. "It's like the world starts and ends here, and there is no way to get Kelly to see past that."

"But it is the beginning and the end for some," I tried to explain. "Some people have lived in Foster for generations; to them, this is the entire world. They are born here, go to school here, fall in love and die here. Not everyone thinks it's a bad place."

He stared at me for a long time. "Is that how you feel?"

All I saw was that stupid robot from *Lost in Space* throwing his arms up screaming, "Danger, Brad Graymark, danger!"

"Well, no, I can't wait to get out of here, but I understand their point of view," I answered carefully.

"Then explain them to me," he stated plainly. I wasn't sure if he was mad or not.

I took a deep breath and plunged in. "To some people, the world changes too fast, Kyle. There was a black president and gay people getting married and people wearing dresses made out of meat, and those people don't get it. Places like this are safe to them, and they like that. I'm not saying it's all right, but I am saying they just aren't ready for change. Here they can change more at their own speed."

He thought about it for a moment.

"Tough" was all he said in return. I laughed, but I got the impression he wasn't making a joke. "I mean it. Life doesn't wait until people catch up. What's wrong is wrong, and if people can't wrap their minds around it, then they can go to hell. We didn't wait until everyone was ready to pass civil rights. We did it because the way human beings were being treated was wrong. And places like this, they aren't safe, they're ignorant. They are little hidey-holes of bigots and hatred, and the people who hide here know they would be laughed right out of a real city." His face grew redder as he went on. "I'm sick of it. I'm sick of these people acting like monsters and then having the audacity to call other people immoral."

This was pretty angry, even for Kyle. There was something else in play here. "What happened?" I asked, digging right under his tirade.

He shook his head. "I'm just tired."

I moved closer to him. "Kyle, what happened?"

"They want to send him away," he finally admitted, breaking down.

"Who?" I asked, worried.

"They want to send Kelly away to some straight camp," he said as he started to cry. "His parents want to send him to some brainwashing camp where they are going to try to pray the gay out of him." He was shaking now. "He'll die in there, Brad. He already hates himself enough. One of those places will just…."

And that was all he was able to say for the rest of the night.

I held him long after he had cried himself out and fallen into a fitful sleep. I stared up at my ceiling and began to think as he curled up next to me on my bed. I had hated myself too, once I figured out I was gay, which was the main reason I tried so hard to hide it. It was only after seeing how fearless Kyle was about it that I found the strength to follow his lead. That day I kissed him in front of everyone wasn't so much about defending him as it was about saving me from a life of self-loathing. I could see that same self-loathing in Mr. Parker when no one else was around. The way he talked about being single and lonely, even though he tried to laugh it off as a joke. There was a sadness in his eyes that made me so very glad I had escaped that fate.

Kelly didn't have a Kyle, and if his parents had their way, he never would.

I hated seeing Kyle so upset, and I was really scared for him because I had a feeling that Kelly's life was about to get worse, and Kyle was going to take that personally. I didn't know what to say to him because I knew if I tried to bring up the possibility that Kelly might not be able to be rescued, Kyle would think I wasn't behind him. I didn't know how to help him or Kelly, and that was driving me nuts. I couldn't do anything about it.

But I knew some guys who could.

Kyle

THAT MONDAY I woke up to my mom telling me I had a guest.

It was still before ten in the morning, which meant she was no more alive than I was. She stumbled to her room while I headed off to the front door. I have to admit I wasn't that shocked to see Robbie standing there, cigarette in hand.

"You know my kind can't enter unless invited, so come on," he said, putting it out. I stepped aside and let him enter. "I'm going to admit, I really thought I had you figured out." He sat down on the couch. "I really thought you'd be back the next day, wanting to talk and to work it out. But here it is a week later and nothing." He pulled a pack of smokes out of his pocket. "Okay to smoke in here or what?"

I sighed and sat down across from him. "Everyone else does. Help yourself."

He tapped the pack against his wrist, a motion I didn't understand but had seen real smokers do all my life. "So, either you are stubborn as hell or it's something else."

"It's something else," I replied without a pause.

"Oh, share with the rest of the class, then," he said, lighting up.

"I didn't come back because I didn't do anything wrong. But more than that, I didn't come back because I don't know if I want to or not. Still don't, in fact." I said it as calmly as possible, but there was no way to keep the anger out of my voice.

"You didn't do anything wrong?" he asked, almost choking on the words. "You're kidding, right?"

"Nope," I answered curtly.

"And here I thought you were smart," he snarked as he flicked his ashes into one of Mom's already overloaded trays.

"And here I thought you weren't a bigot." I mimicked his tone and inflection the best I could.

I was pretty sure if I had slapped him, I would have received almost the same look from him.

"Excuse me?" he asked, one eyebrow arching up as far as it could go.

"You heard me." I sighed and stood up. "We done?"

He tossed the cigarette into the ashtray as he got up from the couch. "Oh no, ma'am. You do not get to say some shit like that and then ask if we're done. I am a bigot?"

I was done.

"Yeah, you are a full-fledged bigot. Did I stutter?" This I did not need. I had enough on my plate with everything else. Sitting there yelling at Robbie was not my idea of entertainment.

"I am not the one who sat there saying people being beaten up and killed wasn't my problem. I was not the one who refused to take a stand when asked." He looked mad, but honestly, I had seen better attempts.

"And I am not the one who said a guy who got outed against his will, is being publicly mocked, and whose parents are thinking of sending to a straight camp deserved what he got because he wasn't ready to admit he was gay yet. No, I believe it was you who thought just because this guy wasn't waving a pride flag, everything he got was okay. If that was me or Brad or anyone you considered a 'real' gay, you would have been ready to stage a march down First Street in protest. Thinking that some people deserve to be targeted for violence because of their sexuality is being a bigot, Robbie."

"He practically beat you up!" he roared back.

"Yes. Me," I said, tapping my chest. "He almost beat *me* up." I paused for a second before adding, "He had nothing to do with the past." I hadn't wanted to say what I said, but something told me it was time.

"Fuck you," he spat out.

"He wasn't the one driving the car; he wasn't the one who yelled faggot; he wasn't the one who drove off," I said as calmly as possible. "You said you stayed here because leaving would diminish his death somehow. I say you stayed here because you are still looking to punish the town that let it happen." I saw his eyes grow red, but he said nothing more. "Kelly didn't do it. I know you want to think he is one of *those* guys, but he isn't. I am not a victim, he is not just a bully, and you need to realize that straight people are not the enemy."

We sat there staring at each other for what seemed like hours. Finally my mom opened her door and looked out at us. "Can you guys stop yelling, please?" She looked hungover, and I was grateful that was all she said; I'd heard a lot worse.

"I need to go, anyway." Robbie grabbed his cigarettes. "Sorry about that," he said to her. "Won't happen again," he said to me.

"Yeah. I don't think it will," I agreed. I opened the door and held it for him.

He stormed out without another word.

"Jesus, you two fight like the world is ending," Mom commented before she tottered back into her room.

All I could think was that to Kelly, the world was ending. I decided to get dressed and head over to make sure he was all right.

The weather had, apparently, determined that December had indeed arrived. Overnight, everything had been clamped down by the cold. Real cold. It always cracked me up when people automatically assumed Texas is always hotter than hell. They have obviously never been to North Texas around Christmas. The air was cold enough to sting my face when I walked out of the apartment building, but I knew the walk would warm me up, and Lord knew I needed time to get my thoughts back in order.

The windows on the cars and stores were all frosted over as I passed by. A small group of people from school shivered as they hung out in front of the Vine. Seeing them reminded me that Winter Break had started. I had a vague memory of thinking that my break was going to be like that, just days and days of hanging out with Brad. Now I was hoofing it across town to make sure the guy who tried to kick my ass a few months ago didn't get sent off to straight camp.

What a difference a week makes.

Another car, some sort of sedan, had been parked next to Mr. Aimes's comic attempt at a midlife crisis. On both sides, bright yellow letters proclaimed The Right Way. The *T* was a crucifix, which I guess was their attempt to be clever or something. I honestly thought I would have more time to prepare for this, but once again what I thought would happen had zero bearing on what was actually occurring. However, I'd done my homework; if I didn't have my shit together by now I never would.

I knocked on the door and steadied myself.

Mrs. Aimes answered the door, and from the look on her face, I was not who she had been expecting. "Oh, Kyle, um…." She looked behind her into the living room and then back to me. "This isn't the best time, sweetie," she tried to explain with her overly syrupy voice.

"I know," I said, sounding as pathetic as I could manage. "But it was way too cold out here. I started out for a walk, and I need to get a ride home. Since I don't have a phone with me, can I come inside and call my mom for a ride?" I widened my eyes to look as innocent as possible. If Kelly's dad had opened the door, my performance would have never worked. He would have told me to freeze and slammed the door. "I promise I will stay in the hall."

I tried to shiver, but it came off more like I was a Chihuahua in a stiff breeze.

"All right. Come in," she said, whispering. "But stay here, and keep it down."

I nodded and she let me in. The house was stifling, so I took my coat off before I burst into flames. I could hear a male voice talking in the living room; it wasn't Kelly or his dad. She handed me a cordless phone and I pretended to dial convincingly enough that

Mrs. Aimes returned to the living room. I hung up and concentrated on the conversation.

"...teach and try to explain the scripture and how it affects your life." The man sounded kindly, but his voice was so deep it carried a sense of authority that reminded me of Coach Gunn. "We aren't here to tell you what's wrong with you, Kelly; we just want to fix what's broken."

"See?" I heard Kelly's dad say. "This isn't a punishment."

My ass it wasn't.

I took the phone and tossed it toward the living room. It hit the floor and bounced twice down the hall. I pretended to run after it, stumbling into the living room with what I hoped was a completely embarrassed look on my face. "Um, I'm sorry," I said, picking the phone up. "Got away from me."

Kelly's dad looked accusingly at his wife. Kelly shook his head at me and hid a smile. The stranger in the room looked over at me and gave me a beaming smile. He was a huge rock of a man, over six feet tall and built like a cage fighter. He wore the short-sleeved black shirt of a reverend that only showed off the gun show he called his arms. He held a Bible in one of his huge paws, but it looked so small in comparison it seemed fake. I saw the trailing edge of a snake's tail peeking past the end of his left sleeve. A couple of other marks might have been the *C* in USMC. If he ever decided to get out of the preaching business, he would kill as a male stripper.

"Why, hello there," he said, reaching out to help me up. "Are you a friend of Kelly's?"

"He is not welcome here," Mr. Aimes said, standing. "This is the one who got him into all of this."

"Dad, he didn't...," Kelly began to argue, but he stopped when his dad glared at him.

"Ah, so you're the serpent in the Garden of Eden?" the preacher said to me jokingly. "I am Father Tim. You are?"

I resisted the urge to answer "A godless heathen" and instead opted for "Kyle."

"Hello, Kyle," he said, gesturing toward an empty chair. "Would you like to join us?"

"He has to go," Mr. Aimes growled at me. "Don't you?"

I ignored him and looked at Father Tim. "If it's okay," I said, sitting down. "I have a few… doubts."

"Well, doubts are the Lord's way of trying to impart wisdom despite our own stubbornness." He sounded like he was going off a speech, from the effortless way the words rolled off his tongue. "I was just explaining our camp to Kelly here. Have you heard of us?"

I nodded. "Some, not a lot."

"Well, as you know, homosexuality is a sin." He said it the same way I would say the sky is blue or I breathe air. It wasn't a concept, wasn't a belief. It was The Way Things Were.

"Leviticus 20:13," I added.

He nodded. "Chapter and verse." His smile got larger. "Impressive."

"If a man also lie with mankind, as he lieth with a woman, both of them have committed an abomination: they shall surely be put to death; their blood shall be upon them," I quoted for him. He nodded again, looking like he was watching a dog dancing on his hind legs for a treat.

"Yes, that is exactly it." He was almost laughing.

"I read that. Can I ask you some questions, then?" I framed my question as innocently as possible.

"Of course," he prompted.

"Leviticus is a set of rules, right?" He nodded. "And so the rules have to be followed. That's why the church is antigay, not because the church is bigoted or hateful, right?"

"See?" Father Tim said to the Aimeses. "This young man gets it. The church doesn't hate anyone; it is just following the rules."

"So because I'm gay, I'm going to hell unless I change my ways, right?"

His face got serious. "I'm afraid so, Kyle, but it doesn't have to be like that. Jesus can forgive you for your past sins."

"I understand that. What I wanted to know was, when you end up in hell too, are you going to be mad?" I made sure I sounded as pure as the driven snow as I asked my question.

Mr. Aimes shot up screaming, "Okay, that's enough, young man! Get out of my house right now!" He looked to Father Tim. "I am so sorry, Father. He is just…."

Tim waved him off. "Why do you think I am going to hell, Kyle?" He seemed more amused than angry.

"Well, Leviticus 19:28 says, 'Do not cut your bodies for the dead or put tattoo marks on yourselves.' And I can see your ink from here, so I was curious."

He looked down at his arm and smiled. "The tattoo it refers to in the Bible is a completely different kind of—" he began to explain.

"Yes, I know it refers to the marking that people like the Hindus did for religious practices. 20:13 actually says, 'And a man who will lie down with a male in beds of a woman, both of them have made an abomination; dying they will die. Their blood is on them.' It doesn't say the act is sinful, only that doing it in a woman's bed is. In fact, biblical scholars have said this refers to the hiding of one's sexuality more than the act itself." I paused and then gave him a puzzled look. "I mean, if we were going for original interpretation."

His smile seemed to dim slightly. Both of Kelly's parents looked from me to him. "That is one way of looking at it…," he began.

"In fact, aren't all of us in this room going to hell? Leviticus 19:19 says 'Do not wear clothing woven of two kinds of material.' Pretty sure we are all guilty of that right now. And there is also Leviticus 19:27, which is 'Do not cut the hair at the sides of your head or clip off the edges of your beard.' Your high and tight is kinda sinful, isn't it?"

Kelly's mom looked over at her husband. "Is what he is saying true?"

Mr. Aimes looked from her to Father Tim, his anger giving way to confusion. "No, of course not, right, Father Tim?"

He gave me a grin that looked more like a threat than an actual smile. "We are told that even the devil can quote scripture for his own good."

I smiled back at him. "Yes, we are told that by Shakespeare in *The Merchant of Venice*. Not quite the Bible, but close."

His eyes narrowed, his smile wearing thin now. "Maybe you're right, Mr. Aimes. Maybe Kyle here should leave."

"Is what he said right?" Mrs. Aimes asked, her voice now close to panic. "Did he make those up, or are they from the Bible?"

He sighed and looked away from me. "They are, but he is misinterpreting them for his own purposes."

"Isn't that the whole business of religion, Father Tim?" I asked, dropping the pretense of innocence now. "Interpreting a two-thousand-year-old book for its own uses?" I waited while Father Tim lost his cool. Spectacularly.

"Listen, you little queer." Father Tim's voice had lost whatever congeniality it had held when we started talking, and I detected a slight drawl in his words. "I am not going to stand here and get lectured on the Bible by some faggot teenager who doesn't know a thing about what he's talking about." He gave me a snide grin. "No offense."

"You call me queer and faggot like those words are supposed to hurt me," I said, unfazed by his outburst. "I can imagine far worse things in the world to be, sir. An intolerant, inbred, hate-spewing hillbilly comes to mind." His eyes looked like they were going to bug out of his head, so I added a curt "No offense."

That was when all hell exploded.

Brad

I WAS through my second cup of coffee when I got a text from Kelly.

Kelly: Your boy is crazy!

That didn't make any sense to me, so I checked it twice before sending a text back.

Brad: Huh?

A few seconds later I got:

Kelly: Dude, he is here laying down the smackdown!

That didn't sound good at all. Kyle was there?

Brad: To who?

Kelly: Preacher guy, better come quick, they might throw hands.

"I need to go!" I hollered toward Tyler, who was in the storeroom, and I raced out the door. I drove as fast as I could with the roads as icy as they were. Luckily it wasn't like we had a ton of traffic in Foster, so I pretty much had the road to myself. Five minutes later, I pulled onto Kelly's street and gaped at what I saw. It looked like two people were scuffling on the front lawn; then I saw Kyle crash down on his back.

I almost destroyed my car sliding it in front of the Aimes's. I grabbed my practice bat from the back seat and jumped out of the car.

It looked like that Russian dude from *Rocky IV* was beating the fuck out of Kyle on Kelly's lawn. I could see Mrs. Aimes holding Kelly back with both hands as he tried to charge into the fight. Mr. Aimes stood aside, staring. I didn't know why what was going on had started, and I didn't much care. Some stranger-asshole was beating my boyfriend. I set myself and swung with every bit of power I had and hit a good, solid double into the center of his back.

The guy gagged and dropped Kyle in a hurry. Panting and trying to get himself breathing regularly, he slowly turned to face me.

"Oh fuck" was all I could muster as he looked down at the bat and then back up at me.

"You're dead," he hissed. Just as the man-mountain started to jump at me, Kyle kicked his foot into the back of the guy's knee. He buckled forward in shock, and I used the opportunity to land a foul tip into the guy's gut. He fell down, his arms wrapped around his belly, groaning. I stood over him, both hands gripped tightly around my bat, and a red curtain of rage slowly descended over my vision.

"I am going to kill you," he gurgled at me, trying to get up.

"You're new here, so let me explain things to you," I said, putting the bat up to his face and fighting off the insane urge to do to him what he'd done to Kyle. "That boy is my everything, and if you've hurt him, I will dedicate the rest of my life to ruining the rest of yours. If you don't believe me, look into my eyes."

We locked eyes. He was listening, but he looked unimpressed and he started to stand.

"I bat .245 and can hit a ball so hard it literally lands the next block over. Stand up and you're going to feel a stand-up triple up close and personal."

He stopped moving.

I ignored him and moved over to Kyle, whose face was swelling. "You okay?" I asked, kneeling down. No answer. "Kyle?" A confused, wandering gaze finally focused on my face. "Kyle, are you all right?"

"Depends," he replied distantly. "Do you have an identical twin you never told me about?"

I chuckled despite the seriousness of the moment. "No."

"Yeah, then not doing okay." He closed his eyes.

I heard the guy get up behind me, and I turned around, putting myself between him and Kyle. He didn't look all that hurt, to be honest. "You think you can put your hands on a United States Marine?"

"I didn't." I sneered back at him. "I put my bat on your back and in your gut and I'm about to knock your front teeth out."

Everything was about to flare up again. The arrival of a police car saved me from going to prison for homicide.

Jennifer's dad and his partner exited the squad car. I was actually glad he'd arrived so I could get back to Kyle. The sheriff took in the scene and then looked back to G.I. Joe. "Step away from the boys," he ordered. One of his hands rested on his Taser.

"He hit me!" the guy shouted.

"You hit that poor boy first!" Mrs. Aimes called out. "Stephen, he's a monster! Get him off my property!" A little shakily, she pointed at the man in black.

The sheriff looked over at us. "You wanna press charges, Kyle?"

Kyle shook his head. "No, thanks, just sugar for me."

"What if I want to press charges?" the man demanded.

Jennifer's dad walked right up to him. "Well, I would then have to ask why in the world you were beating up on a high school kid. And if I did that, then I'd need to take you down to the station, and there would be paperwork and a lot of crap." He gave the man a chilling look, and I prayed he never knew that Jennifer and I had been intimate. "Or I can take off this badge, and you can try that shit with a grown-ass man."

The big guy in the black shirt took a step back. "I'm done here." He glowered over at Kelly and his parents. "Unless you repent, you too will all perish." The way he said it made it come off like a quote of some kind.

Kyle, still on the ground with his eyes closed, responded with "If you do not forgive men their sins, your Father will not forgive your sins." He opened his eyes to look at his attacker and added, "Matthew 6:15."

I had no idea what that meant, but it seemed to piss the man off even more. He hauled his car door open and rammed himself into the driver's seat. He barreled out of Kelly's driveway and almost lost control of the car when it hit the icy road. The sedan did a lovely set of fishtailing until he finally slowed down and crept off in low.

I helped Kyle to his feet slowly, taking a mental inventory of every wound on his body in case I ever met the "Reverend" again. "Can we get him inside? Good," I said to Mr. Aimes as I walked past him. I wasn't really interested in his answer at the moment. Kelly followed me in and helped me settle Kyle down on the couch.

"Dude, you should have seen him," Kelly explained to me excitedly. "That guy looked like he could take apart our entire front line by himself, and Kyle here didn't even blink! It was crazy brave. Mad props."

"Was any of that good?" Kyle asked me as I knelt beside him.

"In Kelly talk that was a five-star rating," I clarified, touching the side of his face gently. The way he moaned made it pretty clear that he was in pain. To Kelly I said, "Grab me an ice pack."

Kelly nodded and rushed to the kitchen.

"You know, when I call you my superhero, I don't mean you should go out and, like, physically fight crime, right?"

He smiled over at me. "Oh. *Now* you tell me that. I had a costume picked out and everything."

"Is he going to be all right?" Mrs. Aimes asked, touching down in the living room, a tornado of worry. "That man hit him pretty hard."

"I'm a superhero, ma'am," Kyle said from the couch. "It's all part of the service."

I nudged him to be quiet. Fortunately Kelly's mom looked at him like he had suffered a concussion. "He seems pretty okay," I answered for him. "Just a couple of bruises."

"A man of God hitting a teenager, what is the world coming to?" she asked out loud. "And to think we were considering sending Kelly to his camp."

"He doesn't need a camp," I said to her. "There's nothing wrong with him."

She looked like she was going to say something more, but Mr. Aimes walked in, and that killed the whole conversation. "Well, he's gone, and the sheriff thinks he won't be back," he reported gruffly. He looked at Kyle on the couch and me kneeling next to him, and his face blanched a little. "He going to live?"

"No thanks to you," Kelly answered him, bringing me the ice pack.

"How was I supposed to know…," Mr. Aimes began to argue and then realized there were strangers listening to them fight. "This is not the time or place, Kelly."

Kyle put the ice pack to his face and sat up slightly. "You're wrong, Mr. Aimes, this *is* the best time." The older man looked like his head would explode, but Kyle pressed on. "Kelly isn't broken, and he doesn't need to be saved. There is nothing wrong with him, and the sooner you realize that, the better it is going to be."

Mr. Aimes shot back with "This is a family matter, young man."

"That's why you called the Punisher in, right?" Kyle snarled back. "Because he's part of the family?"

Kelly's dad looked at me and said, "Brad, maybe it's time for you and your friend to leave."

I agreed, but I wasn't giving up without a fight. "Kyle's right, and you know it, sir. I've known Kelly all my life, and I think he is a great guy." I looked over at Kelly and saw the shock and surprise on his face. "I know I wasn't the best friend all the time, but Kyle is right. Kelly isn't broken, and he isn't wrong. All you have to do is look past yourself to see that."

Mr. Aimes didn't say a thing, but you could tell my words had hit home.

"Come on, Batman," I said, helping Kyle up. "Let's get you home."

"Batman? Really?" he asked as he stood up, more than a bit wobbly. "You think I could pull a cape like that off?"

Despite the seriousness of the situation, I had to laugh at that.

"Here, I'll help," Kelly said, taking Kyle's other arm. We walked him slowly to my car. Once we were out of earshot, Kelly said, "Thanks for being here, Kyle. I didn't know what to say to that guy."

Kyle nodded to him and then winced. "Ouch. No problem. I told you, I'm on your side in this. You are not alone, Kelly."

Kelly looked over Kyle at me and shook his head with a smile, which pretty much said it all. I couldn't believe I was dating Kyle either. We got him in the car and closed the door. I turned to Kelly. "You going to be able to handle them?" I asked, gesturing back toward his house.

"I don't know, man," he replied, looking down at his feet. "I wasn't even sure I liked guys, and now I'm outed to the whole town. I can't blame them for not handling it when I'm just as fucked-up about it as they are."

"It gets better," I said, putting a hand on his shoulder. "Not all at once and not in huge leaps, but slowly, it does. Trust me."

He looked at Kyle and back to me. "It's easier with someone."

I gave him a smile, but I knew it had no meaning. "You have us."

He didn't return the smile. "Yeah, thanks." He put his arms around himself. "Damn, it's cold out here! Get him home!" he said, pointing at Kyle, and ran back into the house.

There was something very wrong with him, but I couldn't put my finger on it yet.

Kyle

BRAD DROPPED me off at home and took off back to work.

He had wanted to call Tyler and tell him he was taking the day off, but I told him not to worry. I was sore, but there was nothing broken. All I needed was some rest, and it wouldn't matter if he was hovering over me watching me sleep or not.

My mom was off to her job at Better Buy, which was a godsend.

I took a long, hot shower and curled up in my bed, trying to find a position that didn't hurt so much, and fell asleep.

I had a dream that Kelly and I were falling from an airplane, hurtling toward the ground at terminal velocity. He was looking up at me with his hand outstretched, begging me to save him. I was reaching out as far as I could, trying to force my arm to get longer to grab his hand.

As the seconds turned to minutes, the dots below us began to grow into houses, and I realized we were going to crash into Foster. I don't know how, but I forced myself to bridge the gap between Kelly and me; the space between our hands grew smaller and smaller. I could almost feel my fingertips brush his when something grabbed my other hand and pulled me back. I looked up and saw Brad clutching me close when he pulled the ripcord on his parachute. As the two of us slowed our descent, Kelly fell away from me. His screaming rang in my ears like church bells.

I buried my face into Brad when he hit the ground.

The ground came up and hit me in the face when I fell out of bed. My covers were tangled around my feet, and I screamed in panic as the terror of falling hit me full force. Because life sucks, I fell on the bruised side of my face, which sent ice picks of pain through the side of my head.

"That looked like it hurt," Billy said from the chair.

"Shut up."

"*Shut up*," it mocked. "You need to get new material.

"Kill yourself with a Drano enema and leave me alone," I raged at it.

It arched one eyebrow at me. "Well, someone has her panties in a bunch."

I got to my feet. "Look, I don't have time for this anymore."

"For what? A little tea and wisdom?"

"For your six-minute stand-up on self-loathing and how I am a horrible person. This is exactly what is poisoning Kelly, and I'm not going to let you drag me down that path."

It just stared at me for a long time before speaking.

"Well. one, my stand-up is flawless, thank you. Two, you aren't a horrible person, you only think you are, and three… I'm not dragging *you* anywhere. You're the only one who drives this trash fire of a life. I'm just the designated queen to make witty comments you're afraid to say out loud."

I was about to argue the point when the sound of someone pounding on my front door made me jump out of my skin.

I untangled my legs and stood, every motion hurting and making me nauseated. I hobbled toward the front door, trying not to moan with each step. I didn't even get halfway there when the pounding came again. The hammering was loud and obnoxious, like the heroes do on crime shows where the police are trying to scare the criminals into opening the door. I half expected to find the cast of a CBS procedural drama glaring at me from the other side.

Instead I came bruised face-to-face with Robbie and Jennifer.

"Oh my God," Robbie said, rushing in, not touching me but hovering his hands over my bruises. "Oh my fucking God!"

I stared at Jennifer, who looked tired and sad. "My dad told me what happened," she explained as she closed the door. To Robbie, she snapped, "He's not dying, you queen. Stop trying for the Oscar and give the boy some space."

Robbie took a step back and gave her a disgusted stare. "If I was going to win anything, it would be a Tony. When I do, I will be sure to thank the bitch I used to know in Podunk, Texas." Back to me he said, "So some Bible thumper did this?"

"Robbie, help me get him to the couch," Jennifer ordered curtly. I knew I was really hurting when I didn't tell both of them I could cross the five-mile-wide living room on my own.

Two minutes later, I gingerly sat down on the couch and sighed. "I don't think he knew much about the Bible, to be honest. He was there from the straight camp thing." I closed my eyes and tried to find a place where pain didn't exist. "Oh, he'd been a Marine too."

"No, he wasn't," Jennifer corrected me. "My dad ran a background check on him. He got kicked out after boot camp for fighting."

"All the ones I know do," Robbie said darkly.

"Get out," I responded instantly. Both Jennifer and he gave me shocked looks. "I just got my ass kicked for standing up to one bigot. I'm sure as hell not going to let another one into my home!" I grated furiously. "That guy's problem wasn't that he believed in God or was straight or was a Marine or any of that. His problem was that he was a small-minded, hateful person who has issues. Period. Just him, not all Marines, not all religious people, and certainly not all straight people. So take that straight-hating bullshit and get out."

Robbie jumped up. "I do not hate straight people!"

"Yes, you do," Jennifer interjected.

He looked down at Jennifer like she had turned into a cockroach.

"Don't give me that look. You do hate straight people," she repeated.

"I do not," he argued.

"Sure you do," she answered frankly. "How many times did you tell me that Brad and his friends were just pussy-chasing douches, and that none of them were worth a thing? But once you found out Brad liked guys, he was okay suddenly. You think everyone in this town from my dad down to the guys I go to school with are homophobic assholes, and you have said that multiple times."

"That guy beat him up!" Robbie countered, pointing at me. "A straight guy beat him up, and it was the same straight guy who wanted to take Kelly to a straight camp to 'cure' him! Straight people—"

"Straight people called the cops, a straight cop who threatened to kick that fake reverend's ass for beating me," I cut in. "So out of four straight people, that jackass was one who wasn't on my side. In the diner it was Tony's father making the scene. A straight woman, Tony, and half a dozen straight customers told him to go fuck off. So the ratio gets even worse if you want to add them." I could see the growing realization on his face.

"There are more people on this planet who will be nice to you than won't," I said, ignoring my aching face. "The only difference is the ones who are loud and obnoxious are the only ones we tend to see. The hatred and seething fury gets all the press, while the quiet acceptance seems to fade into the background. Sure, there are twenty news stories about how many people showed up to get their free chicken dinner because they don't believe in gay rights, but how many people *didn't* show up? How many people voiced their protest? How many people just simply decided never to shop there again?" I shook my head, which was a mistake, but I forced myself to go on. "All you're doing is focusing on the bad things. You've forgotten everything else. You forget that you have a place where people shop, spend money, and do so happily. You have a house that people don't picket or try to burn down, and you drive a car that I haven't seen defaced or had the tires slit. This is not a great town, but it is not filled with the hatred you seem to think it is."

"What you don't know—" Robbie began to explain, but I cut him off.

"I know that people showed up to defend Brad from the school board. There were people who argued against what they were doing. If this town was as bad as you say, then every single person who was there would have been a foaming-at-the-mouth homophobe screaming for his head. Where were you? Where were your words of unity?"

He mumbled something.

"Come again?"

"I was there!" he screamed suddenly. "I did show up."

"I didn't see you," I said, not believing him. "Why didn't I see you?"

He sighed deeply as he sat down and began to search for a cigarette. "I left."

Jennifer looked at him in confusion. "Wait, you were there? You said you didn't go."

He pulled out a smoke and lit it. "I lied. I went and even got into the building." He took a long drag. "And then I turned around and left."

"Why?" she asked.

He didn't say anything for a long time as he nursed his cancer stick. Finally he ashed it and said, "Because I saw Tyler there and invoking Riley's name. He has no right to say that name out loud."

"Why?" I asked again.

"Because I don't like him," he hissed at me in response.

"So you don't like him? Why? What could he have done that was so bad that…?" I began to ask.

"He was there the night Riley died," he answered over my question. "He was there and did nothing about it. He didn't try to help me, he didn't come to the funeral, and he certainly hasn't talked to me since." He flicked another ash. "You say this town isn't as bad as I say it is. I say you haven't lived here long enough for it to show you its true face." He put out the cigarette and got up. "Anyway. Maybe you're right. Maybe I do hate straight people, but unlike those ignorant homophobic assholes you hear about, I wasn't born hating them. I learned the old-fashioned way." He looked at Jennifer. "You coming or staying?"

She looked at me, and I waved her off. "It's okay, I feel better than I look."

Hesitantly she grabbed her purse and moved toward the door. "Keep your phone by your bed? Call if you need anything."

I smiled and regretted that too. "I will."

"Oh, and Robbie," I called out as he opened the door. He looked back at me. "I think it is important to note, the guy who beat me up, he isn't from Foster."

He gave a small laugh. "Kyle, they are all from Foster—if not physically, in spirit." And he left.

I felt worse than I did when I woke up. I took an eon to stand up and then went back to bed, praying I could get at least a little rest before the next thing hit me.

Brad

THE DAYS leading up to Christmas were crazy.

Not only did the traffic in the store triple, but the amount of garbage that Kelly, and Kyle as well, had to deal with became almost overwhelming. One night a group of assholes dumped some kind of chemicals over Kelly's front lawn so that the grass turned brown and died and spelled out the word FAG. His parents had to tear up most of the yard to get rid of it.

Another night someone kept calling for hours and hours asking if they could get their dick sucked. The Aimeses finally took the phone off the hook. The number turned out to be a disposable cell phone and wasn't traceable. Mr. Aimes changed their number and got it unlisted. It took Kyle two days to get the new number so he could check up on Kelly.

I wanted to help Kyle as much as possible, but Tyler really needed me at the shop, and to be honest, I wasn't sure what I could do. The one thing I had set into motion hadn't done any good so far, and I was beginning to wonder what going back to school would be like for Kelly.

I was closing one night when Kelly knocked on the store's front window.

Tyler had received a phone call from someone, and he had left early, saying he needed to get over to the Better Buy before he "missed him." I wasn't sure who he was talking about, but the way he took off, it sounded like it was important. I had the radio turned up while I counted the drawer when I heard knocking. I almost didn't recognize Kelly from the way he was bundled up with a cap, scarf, and gloves. It was cold outside, but he looked like he was ready to ski.

Or he was trying hard to conceal his identity.

I unlocked the door and hurried him inside. "What are you doing out?" I asked, looking behind him to see if anyone had recognized him.

"I had to walk around," he said, unwrapping himself. "I was going fucking crazy being locked up in the house."

"Well, yeah," I said, closing the blinds to the front windows. "I would have been climbing the walls by now."

"I was climbing the walls a long time ago," he said, tossing off his jacket. "I am way closer to losing my mind."

Once I was sure no one could see in the shop, I gestured for him to take the stool behind the counter. "You want a Coke?" I asked, going into the back room. "Tyler keeps it stocked with the ones in the bottles. I think I'm addicted."

"Sure," he called back to me as I grabbed us two bottles. "So Tyler, huh? Sounds like you made a new friend."

I walked back in and handed him one of the bottles. "That better not be a crack, because he is just a friend."

He gave me a half smile. "Hey, I'm saying, for an old guy he still has it going on."

I sighed as I went back to the money. "Tell me about it. But I got Kyle," I said, meaning it. "But I can't deny I enjoy the view around here sometimes."

Kelly almost spit Coke through his nose as he laughed. "Dude! I am trying to drink here."

"Hey, you're the one who brought it up," I said, writing the totals down. "I was just making an observation."

In silence, he watched me fill out the deposit slip and lock up the money bag. When I was done, I looked over at him. "You wanna grab some food?"

He looked glanced at the window, and I could tell that was a bad idea. "Um, I'm not really hungry."

That was bullshit because Kelly was always hungry. "I have an idea," I said, pulling out my cell phone. I dialed Nancy's Diner, and Gayle answered. I explained to her that I was stuck across the street at the store and wondered if she could bag up two burgers, and I'd run over and grab them real quick. She said she'd do me one better and bring them over, which I tried to talk her out of. But she insisted and hung up before I could stop her.

I put my phone away and said to Kelly, "I think food is coming to us."

He got off the stool, looking slightly panicked. "Someone is coming here?" he asked, looking around. "Can I wait in the back room?"

I could not believe this guy who was afraid of his own shadow was the same Kelly Aimes I had known my whole life. "It's okay, dude," I said, trying to calm him down. "No one is going to try any shit here."

He didn't look convinced, but he didn't run out the back door, which I took as a compromise.

I grabbed a stool from the back room and brought it out front. "So, how does it feel?" I asked.

"How does what feel?" he asked, confused.

"Well, you had your first openly gay conversation with someone," I said, smiling. "Though Tyler is hot enough to turn straight guys' heads. You did admit he was hot."

He blushed slightly and took a long drink of Coke to cover it. "I did say that, didn't I?" he marveled after a few seconds. "It feels good to say it to someone out loud."

I held up my Coke in toast. "To feeling good."

He clinked my bottle, and I could see him relax slightly.

We began talking about the football season, and he visibly became more excited as he talked. If there was one thing Kelly loved, it was football, not just playing the game but everything about it. He knew more about the players and the teams' stats than anyone I had ever known. I liked baseball, but I had to admit that, outside of the Rangers, I didn't know squat. We talked about Tom Brady some, and when I said he was hot as well, I could see Kelly redden and then hesitantly agree.

That was when someone knocked at the door.

He almost fell off his stool as he scrambled for the back room. "Calm down," I said, walking toward the door. "It's okay." I used the same tone I would if I was trying to convince a nervous horse not to trample me to death getting away from a snake. I unlocked the door and cracked it open. Ten seconds later, Gayle pushed the door open the rest of the way and walked in carrying a cardboard box filled with Styrofoam containers.

"You didn't say you wanted anything to drink, but I brought Kyle a tea in case...," she began to say and then saw Kelly half crouched behind the counter. "Kelly? Kelly Aimes?" she asked, not believing her own eyes. "I thought you were in here with Kyle."

I shook my head as I locked the door. "Nope, just us."

She put the box down on the counter and walked over to Kelly. "Kelly Aimes, get over here." He froze, not sure what to do, so she walked right up to him and gave him a huge hug. Kelly stood there, dumbfounded. "Kelly, do not listen to what those ass hats are saying. I mean it. Greatness is always met by hatred. The true test is overcoming it." Kelly's arms moved around her as he hugged her back. I had to admit, I should have thought of doing that earlier.

When Gayle pulled back, I could see both of them were a bit teary. "You know you can eat across the street anytime you want. I mean it." He nodded, no doubt not sure if he could speak without his voice cracking. "I've thrown more than my share of idiots out before and am always ready to do it again."

Kelly laughed. "I was one of those assholes not so long ago."

Gayle shushed him with a gesture. "What happened in the past stays in the past." She turned and looked at me. "And if you start to pull your wallet out, I am going to hurt you right here in the store."

I slowly stopped reaching for my money.

"If you boys need anything, call." She moved toward the door. "And Kelly?" she asked, looking at him. "Anytime at all."

Kelly smiled and waved goodbye to her. I locked the door after she left. "See?" I said, walking back toward the food. "Not everyone is out to get you."

He didn't say anything, just nodded and grabbed his burger. I took him home once we were done.

The next day Andy and the library crew came into the shop. Tyler had asked me to cover for him. He said something about getting his computer worked on. He sounded *way* too happy to be getting computer work done, but I didn't question him.

Andy set his laptop down on the counter. The look on his face told me he had found the information I had been looking for.

When I had been feeling helpless about being able to help Kyle, I had asked my role-playing friends, who were much smarter than me, if they could find out where Kelly's video had come from. Besides Facebook and IG, I didn't know a thing about the internet, and I had been hoping there was a way for them to find it.

"You found out who?" I asked hopefully.

"Yeah," Andy answered cautiously. "But you aren't going to like it."

I made a face. "Someone is responsible for making my friend's life a living hell. I can't imagine liking anything about this."

"Well, you are going to not like this even more," he added cryptically. He looked over to Jeff.

"We ran a search on the video, trying to find out where it had started." He pushed a couple of buttons on the laptop. "It's been shared a lot, but it's still essentially the same file over and over again. So we looked at the first indication when it popped up on the web, and we found a YouTube account it had been uploaded to the night of the party."

Mike stepped forward. "Which was very cool, by the way. Thanks for inviting us."

I smiled and nodded but looked back at the laptop. Jeff kept talking. "It looks like someone took the file from that account and uploaded it again under a new account that was created the next morning. So if we are going by time, whoever uploaded it that night is the person who started all this."

"So then who is it?" I asked, getting impatient.

"Well, someone started a YouTube account and then deleted it once it took off; we went to the Wayback machine and found the original post."

I gave him a blank look. "You know I don't understand a word of what you're saying."

He ignored me and kept going. "It wasn't hard from there to find the person who posted it first." He turned the computer around and showed me a screen capture of the page.

The account belonged to BluehairedgirlinTx. Kyle's friend Sammy stared out at me from the profile box.

I barely remembered to thank the guys, and before they left we made plans to start gaming right after Christmas, but I honestly wasn't paying a lot of attention. I sat there, mindlessly helping customers while I tried to figure out what to do with this information. Did I confront her, or did I tell Kyle? Better question, did I tell Kelly?

I literally had no idea what to do, and as the day went on, I became more and more upset by what I'd learned.

It wasn't like Sammy was a big fan of mine. The fight we had the day Kyle took off was proof enough of that. And to be honest, I had no idea what to say to her. Walking up and knocking on her door just seemed like a waste of time to me because as far as I could figure it, her next move would be slamming the door in my face.

Finally, I decided I had to tell Kyle. One, because if I didn't and he found out, he'd kill me. Two, because I hated keeping things from him. And three, because he's like a million times smarter than I am, and he would know what to do. I texted him to see if he wanted to meet me at the shop when I closed. I had been stopping by his place when I got off work instead of having him come to me because he lived so far from the store.

He showed up around four in the afternoon, a worried look on his face.

"What's wrong?" he asked without even a hello as a preamble.

I began to explain what Jeff had explained to me. His expression got darker and darker as I went on. When I told him Sammy had uploaded the file, he didn't even look like he was breathing. I waited for him to react, to say something, even blink, but I have seen more expressive statues. Finally he asked, "What time do you close up?"

"Um, five if there is no one in here," I answered, confused.

"I'll be back," he said, turning around and walking out.

Even a lifetime season ticket to the Rangers' ballpark wouldn't have been enough for me to want to be Sammy.

Kyle

As I charged down First Street, I didn't even notice the cold, I was so mad.

"Mad?" Billy asked, wearing a red jumpsuit, cowboy hat, and white earmuffs. Which is from a Bond Girl in *For Your Eyes Only.* I wondered sometimes where my brain picks this shit up from. "Girl, you left mad at the last station. You're pulling into Fucking Raging Stop in about ten minutes."

"How could she do this?" I asked, again to myself, but Billy will answer any question asked around it.

"How could she not? You didn't think you made actual friends, did you?"

I said nothing.

"Hold up, you don't think you know what actual friends are?"

That made me hesitate, which was all the opening it needed.

"See, here's your problem." My cynicism began to explain, "You spend so long playing the Boy in the Bubble you don't have any actual experience when it comes to friends. You think friends either go to a high school and kill vampires together, do nothing for employment and just spend all their time in a coffee shop, or wander around all day showing off their abs and solve crimes and shit." Under its breath it exclaimed, "God, that show is trash."

"Leave. Riverdale. Alone," I said so coldly that my fogging breath had nothing to do with the temperature outside.

"Right, let's talk about your obsession with in-shape redheads," Billy chimed in.

"Get to the point," I growled.

"Right," my complete lack of social skills said, "the point is, you have no earthly clue what an actual friend is, so how can you be mad that a supposed friend broke your trust? I mean, honestly, there was no way she could like you all that much. Have you met yourself?"

I tried to get my anger under control as I walked up to her front door, but I wasn't doing a very good job of it. When she answered the door and made eye contact, I could see the look of guilt in her eyes. "Why?" I asked her, not even bothering trying to work up to the point.

She took a step out into the cold and closed the door behind her. "Does it matter?" she said in a completely lifeless voice. I had heard more emotion out of a GPS than what came out of her mouth.

"Of course it matters," I snapped. Something in the back of my mind began to bother me. "You ruined someone's life!"

"Yeah, well, he deserved it." Again, her words held none of the feeling they should have. She was almost reciting a script rather than actually speaking to me.

"You think anyone deserves what he is going through?" I asked, outraged. "His entire life is ruined, and you think that's okay?" She stared intently at the ground, refusing to keep eye contact with me. "Was this your way of getting back at him for something?"

She looked up, and I saw a small spark of anger in her eye, but it faded almost immediately. "Sure, let's go with that," she agreed sarcastically.

"That's not right," my faith in humanity commented, and then was immediately jumped and beaten by Billy and his cronies.

Nevertheless, there was something there, so I started being purposely mean. "So you're such a petty lowlife that you wouldn't be happy until you got back at Kelly for—for what? Something he did months ago?" She glared at me again, and I saw that same spark. I didn't let up. "You are so small-minded that instead of trying to bury the hatchet and enjoy the party, you went to get revenge?" I could see her anger flaring, but she still refused to say anything. "You must have been pretty mad, to carry around that anger for so long. And what about Brad? He was there too. Why not get him also?"

If looks could kill, I'd be six feet under right now, but she hadn't denied anything I said, so I decided to see if my theory was right.

"I mean if I'm being honest, the whole thing sounds petty for you. I'd have thought you'd go for something with a little more style."

More nothing from her.

"It was you, right? Who else would have your phone?"

Her expression changed.

"Why would anyone even need your phone? Unless their phone was busy doing something else."

She looked down.

"Like playing the music."

She shook her head a little, and I could tell she was crying.

"Did you give your phone to Jeremy that night?"

She peered at me through the tears in her eyes and nodded.

"Why would you cover for him?" I asked, pissed. "Why would you let me think you'd done that?"

She shrugged. "Because. If I was in your shoes, I wouldn't believe me either." A tear ran down her cheek. "When I saw what he'd put on my phone, I freaked. I didn't know what to do." She sighed, resigned. "Somehow I knew you'd figure it out. And you did." A strangled mix of ironic laugh and broken sob escaped her. She wiped her cheek, although the tears kept leaking out of her eyes. "What are you going to do?"

That was when I realized I was being a complete asshole.

My self-esteem problems and my overriding pessimism got off my faith in humanity, while Billy shouted that I was still wrong and I should trust no one.

Way to remind myself I was still broken.

"I don't know," I finally admitted. "It's not like confronting him will do any good."

"Not even a little," she agreed. "Jeremy's angry. He thinks the world hates him."

"Hard to see why," I said bitterly, then, more calmly, "I shouldn't have been so quick to think you did it."

She gave a small unfunny laugh. "If I was you, I would have thought I did it."

"I should have trusted a friend," I said as earnestly as I could.

"And I should have told you he did it," she countered. "So we're both idiots." She held her hand out. "Do-over?"

I nodded and shook her hand. "Total do-over."

"You want to come in out of the cold?" she asked, rubbing her arms. "I'm about to get frostbite out here."

"I need to get back to the shop," I replied, wishing I could get inside. "Brad's waiting for me." At the mention of Brad's name, she went wide-eyed.

"You know if you tell Brad about Jeremy, he will beat him senseless."

I did know that, which was why I hadn't planned on telling him what I had figured out.

"I'll think of something," I answered instead.

"How is Kelly?" she asked, worried.

"Bad," I said. "But I think he is going to be okay." I wanted Kelly to be okay. I wanted it so much, I tried to convince Sammy that he would be.

"I wouldn't be," she said, opening the door and stepping back inside.

I waved to her as I ran back to the shop, wondering what exactly I was going to say to Brad.

He had already locked the front door by the time I got back. I knocked to get his attention, and he let me in. "So how bad was it?"

"Someone hacked her phone," I said, trying to stay as close to the truth as I could.

"What?" he asked, locking the door again.

"Her phone got hacked, and someone used it to upload that video to her account. She didn't do anything." Again, everything I said was the truth.

"Does she know who?"

"She didn't say," I said, sitting down on the counter, soaking up the store's warmth.

"And you believe her?" He frowned, clearly unconvinced.

"I do," I said, telling the truth. "I am sure she didn't do this to Kelly."

"Then who the hell did it?" he asked rhetorically.

"Could have been anyone at the party." Which was true; anyone could have hacked Sammy's phone. But anyone hadn't. Someone had.

He thought about it for a moment and then shook his head. "Well, I'm glad it wasn't her," he said, going back to counting the money. "I know you like her as a friend."

"I do," I said, trying not to breathe a sigh of relief when he changed topics. I hated lying to him, but confronting Jeremy wouldn't help, and kicking his ass would just confirm for him that the world was out to get him and justify what he had done. I decided to keep the information close and see if there was anything I could do with it in the future.

"So you wanna order a pizza and watch movies at your house?" he asked, closing the register.

I banished the thoughts of Jeremy and smiled back at him. "You read my mind."

Brad

THIS WAS going to be my first Christmas as an adult.

Okay, let me rephrase that. This was going to be my first Christmas not being a little kid. I had a job, which meant a paycheck, so I actually had gone out and bought people presents with my own money.

When you're a kid, Christmas seems like one big party because you never have to give presents; you just sit on the floor and receive them. Your parents put your name on something they bought and your aunt or your grandfather or your cousin pretends it is from you, sure, but they know it's not. For a kid, Christmas is all about getting and not giving.

Mine were a little different. Christmas morning we'd all get up, my mom would pass out presents and videotape me opening them, all smiles and hyper. And then my dad would commence to tell me how much the thing I was holding cost and that I better take care of it because I was not getting another.

It's a magical time of the year.

I bought my mom some perfume and my dad a set of golf tees, not the best presents but about all I could afford with my paycheck and still have enough to buy something special for Kyle. Then, out of nowhere, Tyler gave me an envelope the Monday before Christmas, saying I had been a lifesaver this year, and he was very grateful.

It had five hundred bucks in it!

I had never had so much money that was all mine in my entire life! Half a dozen things I *could* buy for Kyle went through my mind before it came up with what I should buy. I went to Better Buy and talked with Kyle's mom on her break, and we agreed on a plan.

I hadn't said a word to Kyle about any plans for Christmas, so on Christmas morning, when I knocked on Kyle's front door bright and early, he looked a little sleepy and a lot confused to see me standing there so early.

"Brad?" he asked, rubbing his eyes. "What time is it?"

"Does it matter?" I asked, wrapping my arms around him and kissing him. "It's Christmas; that's the only thing that counts."

He closed the door. "What about your parents?"

I laughed and plunked down on the couch. "My dad's dealership had their Christmas party last night. They won't be moving until noon." I patted my lap. "Now come over here and tell me what you want for Christmas."

He glanced nervously over at his mom's closed bedroom door. "Brad, we can't do anything out here," he said quietly.

I reached up and grabbed his hand, pulling him into my lap. "Relax, we aren't going to do it right here." He laughed as he fell into me.

"You're crazy!" he exclaimed, realizing I wasn't going to let him up.

"I believe we have covered that," I said, kissing his neck. "Several different times, if I am not mistaken."

He sighed as he leaned into my mouth on him for a moment before pushing off. "Brad, don't start!" he complained. "She can walk out at any moment!"

"Okay, okay," I laughed. "How about we trade presents?" Instantly, Kyle's expression went serious.

"Mine is lame," he said, sounding depressed. "I'm just warning you now."

"How about you give me those boxers you're wearing and we call it even?" I asked with an evil grin.

He slapped my chest again. "Who worked you up this morning?"

I ran a hand over his hair. "It's this bedhead; I swear it turns me on." I saw the blush working up from his chest to his forehead. He tried to pat the unruly locks down. "Okay, then… me first," I said, reaching into my jacket pocket.

"No!" he said, stopping me. "Because yours is going to rock, and then I'll be too embarrassed to give you mine. Let me go first."

I put the package back, sighing. "You, sir, are a few beers short of a six-pack. Anyone tell you that?"

"No. To be fair, though, I didn't know anyone who spoke fluent douchebag before we started dating," he explained. He half stood, half crab walked to the small Christmas tree near the end of the couch.

I put a hand over my chest as if I had been shot. "I speak English!" I mock protested.

Kyle paused in midsearch for my present. "Uhm… English as translated by a spastic golden retriever, maybe."

And I started to laugh.

He grabbed a small box and handed it to me. "You can say if you hate it," he added.

I shook it slightly before starting to unwrap it. Inside was one of those ball chains, like the ones dog tags come on. I pulled the chain from the box and came to a dead stop, midmotion.

Five coins, each pierced by a small hole, dangled from the chain: three quarters, a nickel, and a penny.

My eighty-one cents.

The same eighty-one cents I had left when we got into our first fight, the same eighty-one cents he brought back to me when we made up. Our entire relationship could be measured in these coins.

"Oh my God," I whispered, instantly choking up. My present was stupid compared to this. Each coin had been polished and sealed in lacquer, making them look like precious gems instead of plain pieces of money.

"You don't have to wear it," Kyle explained quickly. "I just couldn't think of anything to get you."

I undid the chain and put it around my neck. The coins jingled faintly when I let them drop in place onto my chest. "I'm never going to take it off," I said, looking down at the coins and touching each one tentatively, completely thrown by the gift. When I thought about what I had for Kyle, I suddenly felt like a complete asshole.

"You really like it?" he asked, still not believing my reaction.

"No, I really like baseball," I explained quietly, looking over at him. "I love this." Because there were no words left in me, I kissed him to say "thank you" and "I love you" and a lot of other things I knew I couldn't even begin to describe.

Suddenly, he pulled back a little and, eyes alight, asked, "So what did you get me?" His grin and his excitement made him look like a little kid.

"Um, now I feel lame," I said, wishing I had put more thought into my gift.

"Oh come on, you were all fired up a second ago," he teased. "Show me."

I slowly pulled the box out of my pocket and handed it to him. "I'm going to get you something real now too," I added quickly.

He tore off the wrapping paper and stared at the box, speechless. He said nothing, looking like he was trying to wrap his mind around what he was seeing. He asked, "Are you serious?" I nodded, gesturing for him to open it.

Fingers shaking, he removed the box top and pulled out a brand-new iPhone. He held it with a reverence I had seen mothers use to handle their babies. He pushed the Unlock button, and the screen lit up to reveal a picture of the two of us on our date at Nancy's. Gayle had shared it with me a couple of weeks ago, and I had begged her for a copy. He just stared at the phone and shook his head. "I… I can't take this," he said, pushing it back to me. "It's way too expensive."

I pressed the phone back into his hands. Firmly. "Well, one, it's paid for, and two, no it isn't."

"How did you even afford this?" he asked, his voice somewhere between anger and amazement.

"Tyler gave me a bonus," I answered, smiling. "And I know how much you hate your phone." I unlocked the screen, and his eyes lit up as the icons sparkled back at him.

He shook his head again and locked the phone down. "No. I can't afford a phone like this. The data plan alone is more than I can afford." Reluctantly, he put it back in the box and tried to close the lid.

I put a hand over his and stopped him. "I already talked to your mom, and it's taken care of." I opened the box again. "Merry Christmas, Kyle."

He stared at me, and even I could see he was overwhelmed by the gift. "You spent your whole bonus on me?"

"I bought my boyfriend a Christmas present," I said, leaning over and giving him a kiss. "Just accept it and tell me thank you."

He threw his arms around me and hugged me tight. I hugged him back and kissed him again. A lot.

But between you and me? His gift was much better than mine.

Kyle

I SUPPOSE you could say I got an iPhone for eighty-one cents.

I wasn't looking at it that way, but every time I thought I knew Brad and what he was capable of, he did something like this and floored me. We stayed on the couch thanking each other for our gifts for about an hour before my mom woke up. She marveled over my new phone and then over the perfume I had bought her as a present. Around eleven, Brad's mom called and asked where he was, which meant he had to get home for his own Christmas.

I asked my mom if she had anything planned for us, and she shook her head, which was not a surprise since we didn't celebrate holidays a lot. I asked Brad for a ride to Kelly's because I wanted to check up on him and see how he was doing. I could tell Brad wasn't fired up about me going to the Aimes's, but he didn't say anything and just nodded.

The whole town was shut down for the day.

The roads between my apartment and Kelly's house might as well have been in Siberia, there was so little traffic. Foster looked like it had been hit by a zombie attack while we slept. Not one store was open, and there wasn't a soul to be seen on the streets. It was honestly half-creepy and half-beautiful with no one around.

"So do you want me to wait?" he asked as he pulled into the neighborhood where Kelly lived.

"Nah, I'll just walk home," I assured him.

"It's freezing outside," he argued. "If you won't let me wait, will you at least call me when you're done?"

"But you'll be with your folks doing the whole Christmas thing," I tried to reason.

He leaned in. "Call. Me," he insisted.

I rolled my eyes and nodded. "Fine, I'll call on my *new* phone!" I said, holding it up in front of him. He laughed in reply and put the car in Park for a minute. "Merry Christmas," I said to him, giving him a kiss. He paused and looked past me at the front of the house. A frown settled on his lips, and he cocked his head to one side, confused, so I looked over my shoulder.

Kelly balanced precariously on a footstool and reached up to grab one of several things hanging all around the front porch. I couldn't tell what they were from where we were. "Is he taking down decorations already?" Brad asked, squinting.

"I don't know," I replied, equally confused. "I'll check."

Brad was about to turn off the car to go with me when his phone rang again. "Fuck," he said, looking down at the screen. "I need to go. You okay?"

I waved him off. "Go already! I'm fine."

He stuck his tongue out at me before he slipped the car into gear and drove off.

I jammed my hands into my jacket pockets and walked toward Kelly. He was still trying to pull whatever they were off the gutter of the porch's roof. They were long, and for a second I thought maybe they were fake icicles.

When I got closer, I saw they were clear jelly dildos.

Someone had hung a dozen of them all around the front porch, and Kelly was trying his best to pull them down. He didn't even look back at me. "If you think I bought you a present, you're nuts," he said, yanking on one of them.

"Who did this?" I asked, disgusted.

He shrugged as he hauled at the sex toy again. "Who knows? Some guys with way too much time on their hands." The dildo broke, and Kelly almost tumbled backward off the footstool. I grabbed his legs and steadied him as he clung to the porch roof. "Thanks," he said, hurling the plastic dong to the side. "So, making sure I am still sucking air?"

I looked up at him. "What?"

He grabbed the next one. "Nothing. So what brings you to my house on Christmas Day?"

"I can't stop by and check up on you?" I asked as I held him in place.

"You make me sound like I'm on death watch. I'm fine," he said, pulling the next one free.

"I know, you just need friends right now," I said as he stepped off the stool and set it farther down the porch so he could work on the next. "Whether you like it or not."

He tossed another one onto the lawn. "Well, I don't."

"Nice to know," I said, ignoring him.

"Man, you do not give up, do you?" he said, yanking on the last one.

"Nope."

He climbed down, the last offensive piece of silicone in his hand. "Well then, you might as well come in and warm up." He handed it over to me. "And Merry Christmas."

I threw it back at him, and he ran away trying to dodge it.

I am pretty sure we then engaged in Foster's first dildo fight.

About an hour later, we threw them all away and went inside. The whole house smelled of food, and I actually heard my stomach grumble. Kelly paused, taking off his jacket, and looked back at me. "Hungry much?"

I blushed as I put my coat up next to his. "Sorry. I didn't eat before I left."

He looked at me strangely. "You really came over on Christmas Day to make sure I was okay?" I nodded. He gave me a small grin. "Queer."

He laughed as I pushed him down the hall.

They had made enough food to feed the Russian army. I just thought Mrs. Aimes had overestimated her cooking abilities until Kelly explained that all the people who had been invited over for a Christmas meal had canceled. Most were from their church and had called only that morning to say they weren't going to make it, knowing the food was already cooking.

"They sound like assholes," I commented as we sat upstairs in Kelly's room, waiting for the food.

He nodded. "Yeah, but they're church assholes, so it matters to my parents." He sounded bitter as he turned his computer on.

"Um, what are you doing?" I asked as it booted up.

"Checking my email," he said without turning around. "That okay?"

Kelly checking his email wasn't even close to okay with me, but I couldn't push him out of the way.

His mailbox was full of hate mail. The subjects had "fag," "queer," or "burn in hell" in them. I was shocked, but he went on deleting them one at a time. "How do they know your email?" I asked, not believing how many there were.

"Someone posted my email on one of the links. It's been like this for a while now. I like to clear it out every couple of hours before my mailbox goes insane."

My mouth dropped open. "That is just a few hours?"

He looked back and nodded. "I checked it before I went outside to get those things down."

"Who does this crap?" I asked myself, not even aware I had asked it out loud.

"I used to," he said, turning his computer off. "If this was anyone else, I probably would have been one of these guys. Hanging dildos on a front porch? That's pretty funny if it isn't happening to you."

I looked him in the eyes. "Do you really think it's funny?"

He looked down. "I would have a couple of weeks ago."

We would have continued to talk about it, but his mother called us down to eat. If there is one thing you can always count on with teenage boys, it's this: No matter how important a football game or a conversation or anything else may seem, we can always pause for food.

His dad had left once he realized no one was coming over, and from what Kelly had said, he wasn't going to be back soon or sober. So after the three of us sat down to eat, she held out her hands and asked if we'd join her in prayer. I held mine out, not sure how this was done.

She closed her eyes, and I saw Kelly do the same. After about thirty seconds they opened them and said, "Amen."

"Oh," I said surprised, "that was it?"

"A prayer is a conversation between you and God," Mrs. Aimes explained. "It's a private conversation; what you ask and say is between His ears and your mouth."

I glanced over at Kelly. "What did you pray for?"

He didn't say anything as he grabbed some turkey and piled it on his plate.

Brad

A COUPLE of days before the New Year, Tyler took off.

He had hit it off with the guy his mom set him up with, but then something happened, and the guy went back to California. Less than an hour later, Tyler followed him. I woke up to a semi-intelligible voicemail that said he had screwed up and was going to get Matt back, and could I handle the store for the next day or so, in case anyone had any returns. After that he said if he didn't come back, I should leave the store closed.

Still no idea who the fuck Matt was.

I had started Christmas break without a job, and now I was running a sporting goods store. Not bad for a guy who couldn't pass history without his boyfriend coaching him.

When I called Kyle and told him what had happened, he said he already knew. I asked him how he knew, and then he admitted having had something to do with it. He told me how Tyler had come over to his house drunk because Kyle's mom and he were friends from school and he'd needed a shoulder to blubber all over. Kyle had found him passed out on the couch. They had a talk about love and what a person should be willing to do to get it, and the next thing he knew, Tyler was racing to the airport to catch a flight.

I should have known better than to expect something positive to happen in Foster without Kyle's fingerprints all over it.

"I remember a time in the distant past where you just wanted to be invisible, and now you're making grown men race across the country? What do you call that?" I asked over the phone as I opened the store.

"Mad skills?" he answered, which made me crack up.

With Kyle's help, we kept the store open up to New Year's Eve without incident. A couple of people asked where Tyler had taken off to, and we told them he had a family emergency out of state.

New Year's Eve was him and me in this huge oversized chair his mom had. We watched *Pretty in Pink* and *Some Kind of Wonderful*, his choices, not mine, and ate so much pizza we might have been close to throwing up. As the night got later you could hear firecrackers and people cheering outside, the normal debauchery as midnight grew closer.

While Kyle changed the DVD, I heard the celebrating outside and realized I didn't care what was going on.

I know that doesn't sound groundbreaking or anything, but New Year's Eve was always a big thing for me. Since junior high, me and the guys would steal some booze, get loaded, and then run around town setting off firecrackers or just generally getting into trouble. It was a night of drunken chaos, and damn the regrets we'd have the next day. That was who I used to be, a guy who counted the seconds before he could get wasted and break some laws to have fun.

But here I was, sitting in a chair, no booze, no friends, just Kyle and a movie and I was completely at peace. Not just at peace, but insanely happy. As Kyle looked back at me and asked if I wanted another Coke, I knew, I could feel it in the moment.

I could do this for the rest of my life.

Now I know you're going to say something like "Brad, you are barely eighteen, and Kyle is the first guy you've dated. How can you be so sure that you can make a statement like that?" For those people out there who have not gone through that moment yet, let me assure you. When you know, you know.

I had always lived a life about wanting and wanting more. I had always felt a pull inside me that was never satisfied with anything I knew, which was one of the many reasons I wanted out of Foster. I wanted more than this tiny town in the middle of nowhere, more than these same blank faces, just *more*. It wasn't like I was biding my time so I could go out and have a lot of sex or whatever. I just felt an urge that made me want what I didn't have yet.

It had been there every time I kissed Jennifer; it had been part of every home run I hit. There hadn't been a moment in my life up to this point that wasn't colored by that wanting-for-more in some way. I had always assumed it was because I couldn't be myself in Foster, or that I had known deep down I would someday want to be with a man, but I had been wrong. What I felt had nothing to do with that.

I hadn't been searching for more. I had been searching for Kyle.

When I was with him, my heart slowed, my breathing became normal, and my mind just settled. I didn't feel drugged or sleepy when he looked at me or kissed me; I felt complete. Sitting there in that chair with him in my lap, I realized I didn't want to be at some party or in Times Square or anywhere else that didn't include Kyle next to me. And if for the next sixty years we sat in a chair like this and kissed the New Year in, then I was looking at sixty incredible years.

He had to have sensed me staring at him, because he looked at me and asked, "What? Do I have something on my face?"

I shook my head and kissed him again. I was going to tell him what I'd suddenly understood, but we had all the time in the world, and I didn't want to freak him out with all that. I pulled him into the chair and waited for the countdown to begin.

At midnight I kissed him and knew there was no better way to start the year.

Kyle

WAY FASTER than I thought possible, the last weekend before school started arrived.

In some ways it felt like we had just got out of school yesterday; in others it seemed like a year ago. I had tried to get over to Kelly's more, but between taking care of Tyler's store, spending time with Brad, and getting ready for school, I had no time left.

I hadn't even been really aware how close the first day of school was, until the UPS guy woke me up the Friday before our first day back.

I wasn't even sure who he was until he handed me his clipboard and made me sign. I scribbled something and handed it back to him. He stepped to the side and revealed a box that came up to the middle of my thigh. "All yours," he said, walking away.

"Wait! What?" I asked as he got into his truck. He waved and drove off, leaving the box on my doorstep. I went to move it, and it barely budged. "What the fuck?" I asked out loud. I looked at the return address. The box was from Robbie's store. For a second, I thought it might have rocks in it but rejected that idea. He'd never pay for shipping just to be mean when he could show up at my doorstep and do that in person. I pulled the tape off the box and looked inside.

It was filled with clothes. It was a box filled with neatly folded clothes with an equally neatly folded note on top. I sat there on my front step and read:

> *Dear Princess Aurora (look it up),*
>
> *Before we get into the sappy shit, let's go over a few reasons why you're wrong. One, you're like five and a half years old, so you know nothing about life—keep that in mind whenever you think about talking out loud. Two, you've known me like fifteen seconds, which means you know nothing about me. Three, because I said you are wrong. Four, see number three.*
>
> *I in no way want you to look at these clothes as a backhanded admission that you might have been a little right. These clothes count as your second wish granted. The first was me agreeing to be your fairy godmother, of course. Your third and still unspoken wish is still under consideration.*
>
> *Your last year of school is when everything changes, and no, this is not a speech that has anything to do with your changing body; ask Brad about that. Everything changes because you are standing in the wings of what will be your finest performance.*

Real life.

High school is just a really long dress rehearsal about who you are going to be. Now, of course, some people are background characters (you) and some are born stars (me), but everyone has to play their part to the fullest, because I assure you, there is only one show. Since this is your last chance to practice, I am providing some wardrobe for you. And again, that is all this is, not me even considering your words might have some merit. So there.

In a few months you are going to get to exit this town stage right and never look back. That means you have to start dressing like a real live boy and not run around in red shorts and that idiotic cap with the feather in it. If you didn't laugh at my Pinocchio joke, then you have no hope of understanding earth humor, my alien friend.

By the way, I don't hate all straight people. I hate all stupid people, and the difference is not only negligible but sometimes nonexistent.

So, anyway. Enjoy the clothes and have fun at school and don't run with scissors and all that crap. If you are waiting for me to ask you to come back to work, then you have another thing coming because you were in no way right, and I was in every way not wrong. Just saying.

The Indigo Fey

(You're so smart, figure that *out!)*

I had never hated anyone I liked so much in my life.

With some effort—okay, a lot of effort—I hauled the box into the apartment and on to my room. Then, with unadulterated glee, I began rummaging through it. There were shirts and sweaters and jeans and slacks and on the very bottom four different pairs of shoes, none of them sneakers. There were blazers and ties and suspenders and… well, I'm sure you don't need an itemized list, but it was pretty fucking cool to me.

I spent the rest of the morning tossing my old clothes out of my closet and replacing them with my new ones. Not only were these clothes way cooler than anything I had ever owned before this, but they were literally more clothes than I had ever owned, period. At some point, I was slipping blazers on over shirts because I had run out of hangers and refused to set them down where they might become wrinkled.

When Brad came over to pick me up for lunch, I was still trying to find room for everything. He just stared at the clothes in amazement and asked, "Did you rob an A&F when I wasn't looking?"

"Robbie," I explained, changing the shirts around so they were sorted by colors.

He scratched his head. "I thought you guys were, like, fighting."

I nodded, placing the ties next to the blazers I thought they went with. "I think this is his way of apologizing or him trying to convince me I was wrong. Either way… *clothes*!" I screamed.

He laughed and sat down on my bed. "I can see that. Hmmm, maybe I should have bought you clothes instead of that phone."

I looked over at him with a fake panicked look. "My phone? *My preciousss*?" I pulled the iPhone out of my pocket and clutched it close to my chest. "My precious."

He burst out laughing and held his arms open to me. "Come here, Gollum."

I fell into his arms and forgot about everything else for the next couple of days.

The next time I was able to find some free time for myself was the Sunday before school started. I was setting out clothes to wear when I remembered.

"Kelly!" I realized I still hadn't talked to him about going back to class.

I changed and hightailed it over to his place. By the time I knocked on his door, it was late afternoon. His dad opened the door, and the look on his face warned me I was the last person he wanted knocking on his door. "What?" he asked bluntly.

"Is Kelly here?" I asked, trying to keep the sarcasm out of my voice. Honestly, did Mr. Aimes think I had another reason to be there?

"It's a school night," he said, not looking like he was going to budge. I almost said something along the lines of "Kelly's not twelve. He doesn't have a curfew." But I avoided confronting Kelly's dad as much as I could.

"Well, technically not yet," I pointed out. "This is still vacation time."

His eyes narrowed in anger, and he looked like he was going to yell at me, but Mrs. Aimes screamed from inside the house, "Just let him in!"

He sighed and stepped aside. I tried to keep the smugness out of my expression, but I'm not sure I pulled it off.

I climbed the stairs and paused in Kelly's bedroom doorway. He sat at his computer, staring. "Hey," I said, closing the door behind me.

He turned the computer off and turned around to face me. "Why am I not surprised to see you here?"

"So, I had an idea," I said, ignoring the agitation in his voice.

"Again, why am I not surprised?" He looked two parts exhausted and two parts pissed. The combination was scary.

"So you are probably all weirded out about tomorrow, with good reason!" I added quickly when I saw him getting angry. "I mean, who would want to walk into school after all this? But I had an idea how to make it better."

He didn't say anything, but I could see he was not in a place to be open and honest about suggestions.

Taking a deep breath, I forged on. "Sit with us," I said quickly. He gave me a confused look, and I explained. "Sit with Brad and Jennifer and all of us on the band hall steps for lunch. That way you aren't alone, and you can show people you have friends." He didn't say anything, so I kept talking. "Because at first it sucked for Brad and me, but now we have this little group, and I'm betting there are more people out there who still think you're a cool guy even after this." Still nothing from him. "This doesn't have to be the end of the world for you."

"It is the end of the world for me," he said expressionlessly. "It is the end of the world I lived in for eighteen years."

"So then make a new one!" I urged him.

He laughed bitterly and looked away, dismissing me completely. "God! You don't give up, do you?" He glared back at me, and I could see the pain in his eyes. "Why do you care? Why are you so on about this? I have been *nothing* but a dick to you since the very moment we met, and now you're, like, my best friend. Why? What do you get out of this?"

Confused, I blinked a couple of times at him. I really didn't understand the question. "I don't get anything out of this," I answered slowly. "I just want to help you."

"Why? Because I'm a pathetic loser who needs help? Is that it, Kyle? Am I such a charity case that you're going to try to nurse me back to health? Am I some Adopt-a-Fag project you have to do to earn a Fag Scout merit badge? Am I so fucking weak that I look like I need help from a loser like you?" He was raging now, trying to cover the fact he was losing it.

"I don't think you are weak at all, Kelly." I kept my voice low and steady, trying not to show any emotion he could pick up on to amplify. "I think you need a friend right now."

"And you're it?" He kicked his chair back as he stood up. "You're going to be my friend?" I nodded slowly. "Why? Why would I want to be your friend?" he demanded, angry tears running down his face.

I shrugged. "I don't know. I was just offering."

He wanted me to say more so he could attack it, but I had done this dance one too many times with my mom to take that bait. I sat there and waited for his next attempt. "Do you honestly think I can walk back into that school after all this?" he asked. "You can't be that stupid."

"I don't know, I am pretty stupid," I said with no humor in my voice. "I know what you have gone through sucks, and the things people have done to you are bullshit, and I think you will get through it better if you have people standing next to you."

"You think me standing by a pack of losers like you guys will even matter?"

"It's better than standing alone," I answered.

We stared at each other for almost a minute before he shook his head and looked away. "After everything I just said to you, you'd still want me to sit with you guys at lunch?"

Now I stood up. "I don't give a fuck what you say to me, Kelly. I am not saying we need to be blood brothers. I'm saying I'm a person who is on your side. Not because you're weak or because you're down, but because what happened to you isn't fair. Period. I would offer anyone who had been tortured like you have over Christmas break a place to eat lunch. Not out of pity, but in some small attempt to counterbalance the shittiness that is your life right now."

He didn't say anything, so I tried again. "So when you get to school tomorrow, stick with us. I promise you, it won't be as bad as you think."

He let out a laugh that sounded more like a sob as he picked up his chair and sat down. He looked up at me three times, and each time I thought he was going to say something, but he stopped himself and looked away. On the fourth try, he looked at me and gave me a strained smile. "You know, I can see what Brad sees in you."

That took me back a few steps. "Is that a compliment? From you?"

"Don't piss yourself, Pee-wee Herman. We aren't picking out bridal patterns yet," he said, sneering. "I just said I can see why he would go out with you now."

"So sit with us," I pleaded now. "It isn't that bad."

He sighed and looked down. I heard him mumble, "Yeah, it is," but he looked back before I could comment on it and said, "If I say yes, will you leave me alone?"

"For tonight," I said, smiling.

He rolled his eyes. "Fine. Yes."

"You'll do it?" He nodded. "For real?" He nodded again. "Because if you're not convinced, I can explain to you the benefits of being in a crowd when it comes to—"

"Hey! Nerd boy!" he shouted at me, stopping me cold. "I said yes; don't push it."

"Awesome," I said, trying not to get too excited. "So meet us in the parking lot before school? I'll make sure the place next to Brad's car is open." I paused. "Do you need a ride instead? I mean, if you don't want to take your truck…."

He held up a hand to stop me. "I don't need a ride. And fine, save me a space next to Brad."

I almost jumped up and hugged him, I was so happy, but I refrained because there was no way he would be okay with that. "Okay, so then before first period?" He nodded. "Promise?"

He held up his right hand and said, "May God strike me down if I am lying."

We both looked up for a moment, waiting for a lightning bolt.

He sighed and asked me, "Convinced?"

I was and left before he could change his mind. I knew it wasn't going to be easy, but I knew if we all worked on it, Kelly could get through the first day of school. I just knew it.

Brad

THAT MONDAY, I did not want to wake up.

I wanted to lie there and wish this Christmas break could continue forever. A lifetime of working at the sporting goods store, loving Kyle, and no school was about the closest to perfect I was going to get. It still looked like winter outside, and I just added that to the list of reasons I should not have to get up. The sky was a slate gray that looked like it was one massive cloudbank over the entire city.

"Brad, school," my mom said, rapping on my door.

With an audible groan, I got out of bed.

I showered and dressed on autopilot as I wondered how bad today was going to be. Kyle had called me last night and told me his plan for Kelly and then asked me what I thought about it. I thought it was a horrible idea, but I told him I would back anything he wanted to do because I knew that's what he needed to hear. Kelly was poison, and his life was going to get much worse before it got better.

The part Kyle didn't get was that all of this fallout wasn't because Kelly got outed. It was because he had been a dick most of his life, and people were itching to pay him back. If everything that had happened to him was only about sexuality and coming out, then it would have blown over that week after the party, at least here in town. The internet crap was just people looking for someone new to hate, and Kelly fit the bill nicely.

The vandalism of his stuff, the dildos, all of that came from the fact that more people in Foster disliked Kelly than liked him, and for the first time since, well, since forever, he was alone. Like a wounded lion, he had been left behind by his pride. The hyenas he had hunted his entire life could sense he was defenseless and were moving in for the kill. I felt bad about it, of course, but I was more worried about Kyle getting caught in the crossfire than I was about Kelly.

On one level, Kelly had brought this on himself. If I could help, I would, but Kyle was ready to go to the mat for him, and that scared me.

It also made me love Kyle even more, but that goes without saying.

I went over all this driving to his house and wondering if there was a way to get him to understand what I was thinking. Then I sighed when I realized that Kyle, no doubt, had thought of the same things already and just didn't care. I pulled up in front of his house and honked twice because I knew if I went inside, I wouldn't be able to keep my hands off him. We didn't need to be late the first day back.

He walked out, and he looked perfect.

Robbie had given him some damn good-looking clothes, and I had to be honest, Kyle was wearing the shit out of them. Gone was the shaggy-headed nerd who had stalked the halls, invisible. In his place stood a sharp-looking, vest-wearing stud who took my breath away.

He waved to me as he walked to the car, and I could only stare in wonderment.

"What's that look for?" he asked, closing the passenger door. "Do I have something on my face?"

I nodded mutely. He went to look in the vanity mirror on the front visor, but I stopped him. "You have hotness all over you," I said, leaning over to kiss him. He laughed and then kissed me back.

He held my hand as we drove to school, and it reminded me of the first day we went back after coming out when all we had was each other. Somehow it felt like that all over again, except this time it was Kelly who was alone, and all he had was us. And just like that, I understood why Kyle was fighting so hard.

"I love you," I said to him before we got to school.

He chuckled and looked over at me. "What was that for?"

"What? I can't just say I love you?" I asked, sounding like I was offended.

"Usually you have a reason," he countered.

"Well, this time I just love you. So there," I huffed.

"Make sure you park where there's an empty space," he reminded me as we turned into the parking lot.

I nodded and looked for two open parking spaces. I found a pair over by the history building and parked in one of them, then opened my door and left it open so there was no way for someone to take the space next to me. "This good enough?" I asked him.

He leaned over and kissed me quickly. "You're my knight in a letterman jacket."

I got out and pulled my books from the back seat. They hadn't moved since the Friday Christmas break started. I silently hoped I hadn't accidentally left a sandwich in my backpack. Kyle started looking around the parking lot. "Do you see his truck?" he asked. "He might have changed his mind."

"Dude, not everyone loves school like you," I said, putting the pack down on my trunk. "We're lucky if Kelly is even awake right now."

"It's the first day back," he said, still searching the parking lot. "Who doesn't show up early on the first day?"

"Everyone who doesn't want to come back to school after a few weeks of vacation," I suggested as I cautiously opened the zipper.

He walked over and opened my pack up all the way. "I emptied it out the weekend of the party," he said, sighing. "What if he doesn't show up?"

I wanted to tell him, "I wouldn't blame Kelly one bit for blowing off school," but that would just upset Kyle even more. "Well, that's up to his parents and him, isn't it?" He didn't like my answer, but he couldn't argue with it.

"Let's wait a little longer," he said, looking around again.

"As you wish, Buttercup," I said, quoting from one his favorite movies.

He looked back at me with a smile and replied, "I am no one's fairy princess."

"Tru dat," I said, laughing at the look of annoyance on his face.

"Look," he said, pointing. "Maybe Jennifer knows if he's here."

I looked over and saw Jennifer coming from the quad. She had her phone in her hand, and she looked like she was hurt, she was walking so slowly. Kyle waved at her, and she looked up and saw us. Something was wrong. I could tell from where we stood. She did not look normal. Halfway to us, I could see she was crying.

My stomach dropped, and I suspected something far, far beyond "wrong" had happened.

"Jennifer!" Kyle called out to her when he noticed the tears on her face. "What's wrong?"

Jennifer got to us, and we could tell she was openly sobbing now.

"What happened?" Kyle asked, concern in his voice.

Jennifer looked over at me and shook her head subtly. I felt the air rush out of me, but I knew I had to be sure, had to know. I reached over and snatched her phone from her. She lunged after it, but she couldn't move fast enough.

I almost dropped it when I read the text message.

"What's wrong?" Kyle asked both of us now. "Brad?"

He looked at me, and I looked away as I tried to comprehend the words I'd just read. He looked to Jennifer and then back to me. "Where's Kelly?" I couldn't look at him, and he asked again, "Brad, where is Kelly? Is he not coming?" He sounded like a little kid suddenly as his mind began to race toward a conclusion he couldn't begin to accept.

I forced myself to move past my shock. "We need to go," I said to him, trying to put some urgency in my words. "Come on." I tried to maneuver him toward the car. "Let's go talk somewhere."

He pulled away from me. "What's it say on the phone?" he asked, terror in his voice.

Phone? I looked down and was surprised to see I was still holding Jennifer's phone. I tried to hand it back to her, and Kyle tried to snag it from me. Some part of me must have been expecting his reaction because I pulled my hand away. "Brad, what's it say?" he pleaded. He looked at Jennifer. "Where's Kelly?"

I looked at her, and she wiped her eyes.

"Guys, where is Kelly?" he asked, already knowing the answer.

"Let's just go," I said to him again.

He pulled away from me. "Where is Kelly?" he demanded.

"He's not coming," I said cryptically. "Come on, Kyle…."

He lunged at me and grabbed the phone. I tried to pull it back from him, but I wasn't ready for the speed and power he used to pull it away from me.

He looked down at the screen before I could stop him.

My heart sank as his eyes went over the text Jennifer had got from her dad.

Dad: School is going to be canceled. Kelly shot himself last night. Go straight home. Kyle let the phone drop from his hand.

Kyle

I DROPPED the phone like it was a snake.

Brad came toward me, but I couldn't hear him. I backed away from both of them. He tried to put his hands on my shoulders, but I shrugged them off. I mentally screamed as loud as I could. I could hear the blood rushing in my ears, and it sounded like a demonic roar from a legion from hell charging over the horizon.

My mind would not process the fact Kelly was dead.

The text message was like a math problem that kept coming out wrong no matter how many times I tried to solve it. There was no way he could have.... I couldn't even think it. I couldn't form the words in my mind. My thoughts went from shock to sorrow to rage in about three seconds flat.

And from that rage came action.

I pushed past Brad and Jennifer and ran toward the quad. I could hear them behind me, but I ignored them completely. There—over there. Tony and his pack of friends sat at the Round Table, laughing and talking as if nothing had happened. Tony was drinking a Coke, laughing about something one of his friends had said when I walked up to him. Something about the look on my face must have warned the pack because an uneasy silence fell. When Tony looked over his shoulder and up at me, I batted the can out of his hand.

"Are you fucking happy?" I screamed at him. His eyes went wide in shock while he tried to figure out what was going on. I didn't plan on giving him that chance and kept screaming. "Is this what you wanted? You just couldn't leave him alone, could you?" He looked at me, confused. "What the fuck did he do to you?"

I accented my last words by pushing him with both hands.

He came off the table, pushing me back. "What the hell are you talking about?" he asked, ready to push me again.

"Kelly! What did he do to you?" I roared. I could feel Brad trying to pull me back. "What was so bad about him liking guys that you had to torture him all break?"

He gave me a sneering laugh. "Fuck that fag." He looked back at his friends and laughed. "He got what was coming to him. Why? Are you mad we picked on your boyfriend?"

Brad stepped in front of me. "I'm his boyfriend, and Kelly killed himself, you douche."

Everyone at the table froze at those words. Everyone but me.

I moved around Brad and pushed Tony as hard as I could. "Is *that* what you wanted? Did you want him dead? Because that's what he is, and it's *your* fault!" I could hear the tears in my voice as I slammed my fists into Tony's chest. "Why couldn't you just leave him alone?" Dumbfounded, Tony gave way and backed off, but I kept coming.

Brad tried to pull me into his arms, but I spun away from the table. The rest of the ghouls in the quad were, of course, standing around watching us. "Every single one of you fucking vultures who posted something on his wall is responsible! You killed him! You all fucking killed him!"

I saw Mr. Raymond running across the quad, but I was done, mentally and physically.

"What's going on here?" Mr. Raymond shouted, assuming there was a fight happening.

Just looking at him made me even madder.

"I told you this would happen!" I said, pointing my finger at the principal. "I told you that this was going to get worse, and you did nothing! Are you happy? One less abomination in the world now."

His entire face paled at the accusation. "Mr. Stilleno, Kelly died during Christmas break. The school is in no way responsible—"

"You did nothing to change things," I said, cutting him off. "You created an environment where this kind of hate isn't just tolerated, but it's silently encouraged. What did you think would happen?"

He knew I was right, and I could see it in his eyes. There was no way he could admit it out loud, but he knew I was right. "There is no school today," he said loudly enough for the entire quad to hear. "If you do not have a ride home, please go to the office and call your parents. We will have the gym open for people to wait." In a much lower voice, he said to me, "I think you should go home, Kyle."

"Or what?" I said, getting right up in his face. "Am I going to go to hell for that too? Is that where Kelly is? Come on, sir, tell me how this is all God's plan and not just your seeds of intolerance finally bearing fruit."

Brad grabbed me harder this time and pulled me back. "Come on, Kyle, come on," he pleaded. "It's over; let's go."

"Mr. Stilleno, I don't like what you're implying—"

"Implying? I am not implying anything. I am saying." I looked around at the mass of people in the quad, now watching. "*You all killed him! Every single person who posted that video, you're a fucking murderer!*"

Brad came up behind me and wrapped his arms around me as he fought me.

"*Murderers! Are you happy? Another faggot gone.*" I looked at Tony. "Your dad's going to be so proud of you."

Tony looked like he'd been kicked in the nuts.

I let Brad lead me away as I muttered, "All of you fucking killed him."

I didn't save him. I didn't save anyone at all.

Brad

WE WENT to Jennifer's house, since there was really nowhere else for us to go.

Kyle was withdrawn and sullen. He hadn't said one word on the car ride over, and he was equally silent when Jennifer and I began talking about the first time we'd met Kelly. We both ended up crying, and I felt like shit for treating him like I had. But no matter how upset I was, one eye was always on Kyle.

About an hour later, Robbie came bursting into Jennifer's house, a tornado of skinny jeans and spiked hair.

"Oh my God, what happened?" he asked Jennifer, not even noticing Kyle sitting in the chair behind him.

For the first time since we got here, Kyle looked up. "What do you think happened?" he asked in a seething voice. "The big, bad homophobe got what he deserved."

Robbie spun around, half in shock since he didn't know Kyle was there and half in anger at his words. "Oh, so this is my fault now?"

Kyle came off the chair so fast I thought he was going to hit Robbie. "This is a lot of people's fault. But you did absolutely nothing, so I guess you're off the hook, right?"

Robbie opened his mouth as if he wanted to say something and then closed it again as he looked down.

"Where was your all-for-one talk with Kelly?" Kyle pressed on. "What happened to the community and looking out for one another? You know why you didn't do anything? You want the answer?" Robbie looked up at him. "Because he wasn't gay enough for you. He didn't pass your internal gay test, and that meant he wasn't eligible for compassion or help."

It looked like Kyle was going to keep snarling at him, but Robbie slipped out a quiet "You're right" that punched through Kyle's pain and fury. I could see Kyle's mental gears grind to a halt when Robbie's words sank in. "What else do you want me to say? It is partly my fault? I should have helped him? I am a horrible person? Fine, I just said it."

Kyle stood there with his mouth open, not sure what to say next.

"So now what?" Robbie asked Kyle. "You plan on holding it against me for the rest of my life? Use it as a reason to hate me?"

Kyle shrank in on himself and sat down. "I don't hate you; I hate me." And he meant it. No melodramatics, no fishing for rescue. He meant it.

That brought me off the couch. "What?" I asked, moving past Robbie. "You did everything you could." I moved him over and sat on the chair with him. "This isn't your fault."

He began to cry as he leaned into me. "I told him I'd make it better," he sobbed. "I promised him!"

I held him as he sat there and cried. I literally had no words that would make him feel better.

Robbie went and sat down next to Jennifer. "So then Foster wins again."

Kyle's entire body went stiff in my arms. "No." He looked up. "No, not this time," he said, his voice becoming hard as steel. "Not this time."

We all looked at him as he stood up. I was the only one who could see his knees knocking, an aftershock reaction to the horror that had swept over us.

"I made a promise to Kelly, and I am not breaking that," he said.

Jennifer wiped her eyes. "What can we do about it?"

He looked over to me and asked, "Where is your laptop?"

"Um, at home," I replied hesitantly.

"Go get it," he snapped, his voice tough as a drill sergeant's. He looked at Jennifer. "You have a printer here, right?" She nodded. "We're going to need to use it."

I got up slowly. "What are we doing?"

He looked toward me, but I wasn't sure he saw me clearly. "Not letting Foster get away with it."

I didn't ask anything else. Two minutes later, I went home to get my laptop.

Although it was Monday and the holiday season had ended, Foster stood mostly empty. The buildings, the trees, even the wind seemed to be holding its breath. I didn't realize until I forced myself to breathe that I had been holding mine as well. First Jennifer's neighborhood, and then all of Foster that I drove through looked empty. Maybe it was my imagination, but it felt like Foster was a ghost town. People hid inside or stood huddled against doors in the shadows of their front porches.

I argued with myself for a few blocks about driving by Kelly's house or just going straight to my house. Even though I knew there would be nothing to see, part of my brain wanted proof he was gone, that this wasn't some sick dream I was having.

My curiosity won over my caution, and I turned left, toward Kelly's house.

A couple of police cars and an ambulance stood in front of it, and two cops were standing by the front door talking. No lights flashing, no EMTs racing in or out with a gurney— There was no need. The emergency had ended before they arrived. The front door was open, and I strained to look inside as I drove by slowly. I could see Kelly's mom being held by Mr. Aimes. Jennifer's dad spoke to them. I suddenly felt like some kind of ghoul voyeur and drove off fast toward my house.

Seeing all that had not made Kelly's death any more real to me.

I got out of my car and went into the house; my hands shook uncontrollably as I closed the door behind me. I leaned against it, just for a second, just to have something solid to fall against because the rest of the world had gone nightmarish. Grimly, I forced myself not to cry. Not yet. Kyle—I had to get back to Kyle.

I was so engrossed in my own sorrow I didn't even notice my mom walking out of the kitchen.

"Brad," she exclaimed, rushing toward me. She put her arms around me and hugged me close. "I just heard…."

The smell of booze was like a blanket wrapped around her.

I pulled back, disgusted, and she stumbled forward, unable to keep her balance. "Are you kidding me?" I asked her. "You think this is the best time to get wasted?"

"I was worried…," she began to explain, her words slurring slightly.

"If you were worried, then you wouldn't be smashed. What if I needed you?" I demanded. "What if I was in trouble? Goddammit, I need a mother all the time. Not just when you decide to sober up and remember you have a son!"

She stood there, gaping at me as if I had slapped her.

"This is the most important time of my life; the choices I make in the next six months are going to decide the rest of my life!" I felt the wave of the future threatening to crash down on me. "I need help. I need parents!" I didn't say the rest of what I thought: "I need Kyle. I need Kelly not to be dead." Because hearing myself say those words would break me.

She shook her head. "You're just upset about Kelly." She put her hand up to stroke my face.

I batted it aside.

"Yes, I am upset. But that isn't about this," I raged at her, pointing at the glass in her hand. "If you don't change, if you and Dad don't get your shit together—" I took a deep breath to steady myself. "—don't expect to hear from me after I move away."

She looked at me, half-sauced, boozily shocked at my words.

I ignored her and ran up the stairs to my room. I grabbed my laptop and the charger off my desk and headed back downstairs. I passed my mom halfway down the stairs. "Brad!" she called out to me. "Where are you going?"

I didn't even turn around. "Why does it matter? You aren't going to remember this anyway!" I slammed the door behind me, tossed the laptop on the passenger's seat, and forced myself to calm down. The calm lasted until I'd slid behind the steering wheel. Then I screamed as loud as I could as I pummeled the steering wheel with both fists. Angry tears ran down my face, and I honestly didn't know if I was crying for Kelly or for me anymore.

I was just crying.

Who knows how long I might have sat there if my phone hadn't beeped. Kyle had sent a text message, asking me if I was okay.

I took a deep breath and started the car. If I wasn't going to keep it together for me, I'd keep it together for Kyle. I drove straight back to Jennifer's house, knowing I would never drive by Kelly's house again.

Kyle

I HAD outlined my plan to Jennifer and Robbie while Brad got his laptop.

Both of them were looking at me like I was nuts. Robbie, in fact, just came out and said it. "You're nuts," he said after a few minutes of silence. "You'll get kicked out of school."

I shrugged at him. "So? I don't care anymore. I'm sick of this."

Jennifer looked over at me. "He's right. They'll expel you the second they find out it was you."

"And I don't care," I repeated.

"What about college?" Robbie asked. "You think you can snag a scholarship after being expelled from school?"

"I *don't care*!" I screamed, losing my patience. They both looked at me with wide eyes, and I tried to calm down. "Don't you see? This is more important than me and fucking college. This is about not letting those people get away with what they did. I know I can get expelled, and I know that can cost me college. But I do not care."

Brad walked in with his laptop; he looked like he had been crying. I took my cues from his movements, standing near, not crowding him. Reminding him I was there. "Here," he said, handing it to me. "Now, what's going on?"

I plugged it in. "Jennifer, catch him up, okay?"

Jennifer began explaining the plan to him while I booted up the computer. I pulled up Facebook and logged Brad out. Then I started to put Kelly's email into the login field; the second I pushed the letter *K,* his email popped up in the box. When I clicked it, the browser automatically put his password in.

I'd noticed this last time I was using Brad's laptop to see what people were saying about Kelly. I could only guess he had used the laptop in the past, and it had saved his password with auto-complete. Since Brad never logged out of Facebook, he had never even noticed. I logged Kelly on and opened his messages.

"Bingo," I said, looking up at Jennifer. "I'm going to need that printer."

She went into her bedroom to grab her printer, and I looked at Robbie. "Can you handle this?" I asked him.

He nodded and hooked up the laptop. "Why? What are you going to do?"

I pulled out my phone. "Making sure I can get into the building before school starts."

Jennifer came out with her printer and hooked it up to Brad's laptop as the phone rang in my ear. On the third ring, Sammy picked up; she sounded like she had been crying. "I didn't know if you'd call me," she said.

"This isn't your fault," I assured her, and I meant it. Because everything was my fault. "I need a favor."

She sniffled a little bit. "Anything."

"Do you still have keys to the drama department?"

"Yeah, why?" she asked, curious now.

"I need you to lose them," I told her as the first pages began to print up behind me. "Actually, I need you to lose them in front of me."

"What's going on?" she asked, not sounding the least bit depressed now.

"Come over to Jennifer's house. I'll explain everything."

She agreed and hung up. I slipped my phone into my pocket and began to think.

"Can I talk to you alone, Kyle?" Brad asked me. I could have said he looked concerned, but he really looked scared. He walked us over to a corner away from everyone else. "Jennifer told me what you were planning. You can't do it."

"I can, and I'm going to," I said frankly. "And before we get into an argument about it, I need to do this."

"Because you think you let Kelly down?" he asked.

"Because I am not going to let the same people who got away with bullying us get away with torturing Kelly." I could see he was upset, but my mind was made up. "Brad, I need to do this. I know the risks."

"What if you get kicked out?" he asked, sounding as lost as I had ever heard him.

"Then I get a job at Nancy's and meet you for lunch every day," I said, hugging him. "Nothing is going to get between us. Nothing at all."

He hugged me back, and I felt him lean into me as he started to cry again. After a few minutes, he pulled himself back together, until the next storm overwhelmed him. This time it was my turn to help Brad sit down. I kissed him and told him how much I loved him. I was done crying.

Sammy showed up, and we explained what I was planning to do. She just smiled and handed her keys over to me. "I haven't seen them since Christmas break," she said.

I took them and put them in my pocket. "You rock. Thank you."

"So, can I help?" she asked, looking as Jennifer and Robbie went to work at their tasks. Robbie was huddled over the laptop, typing, while Jennifer was taking the pages the printer spat out and sorting them. "You can help Jennifer gather them up."

She nodded and moved over to help them.

"I need a ride to Kelly's house," I said, trying to keep my expression neutral.

"What? Why?"

I started to explain what I wanted to do.

Brad

WE DROVE over to Kelly's house…where Kelly used to live. Fuck it. I went to the place I said I never wanted to see again because Kyle needed something. The ambulance was gone and the police were about to leave. Kyle got out and Mr. Aimes saw him.

"You little faggot," he roared, running at Kyle like a wild bull.

Kyle paused and I got in front of him and yelled, "Mr. Aimes, don't do this."

He slowed down. "Get out of the way, Brad."

"Make me," I said, balling my hands into fists.

He stopped in front of me and looked at Kyle. "Get off my property."

Kyle ignored him and looked at Mrs. Aimes. "I am so sorry…."

She began to sob, and Kyle moved over to her while I made sure Mr. Aimes did nothing.

I heard them talking and she hugged Kyle tightly, and they both cried on the lawn for a few minutes.

"Get your guy out of here," Mr. Aimes said. "He's making a scene."

That brought me up cold, and I just stared at him. "You son is dead and you care about a scene? Jesus Christ, man, do you even possess a fucking soul?"

He blanched at my words and then began to retreat back into his house.

I followed and saw Kyle and Mrs. Aimes talking.

She finally nodded and said, "Let me go get some."

"Thank you, ma'am," Kyle said sadly.

Once we were alone, I asked him, "She go for it?"

He nodded and moved over to hug me.

I knew how he felt.

Kyle

IT WAS close to six in the evening when Brad pulled up in front of the house.

"You sure this is it?" he asked me.

I clutched the book to my chest and nodded.

"You want me to come in too?" he asked, knowing I was close to chickening out.

Yes, very much yes.

"No," I said with a sigh. "I need to do this alone."

He put his hand on my arm and gave me a smile. "No, you don't."

I put a hand over his and smiled back. "Thanks. Wait for me?" He nodded, and I got out of the car.

I knocked on the door and an older man wearing a ratty T-shirt answered. He shook his head at me. "You're the most normal person he's ever had over." He stepped back and pointed to a door halfway between the entry and the kitchen. "He's down in the basement."

I hadn't even asked to come in, but he sat back down in front of the TV and ignored me completely, which I took as an invitation. I closed the door and walked over to the one that led down to the basement. For a second, I considered knocking and decided against doing it. I just opened it up and walked downstairs.

Jeremy sat in front of a computer that was hooked up to a couple of digital turntables. He seemed lost in another mash-up and hadn't heard me at all. I walked up behind him and tossed the book down on the keyboard in front of him. Jeremy jumped and then looked up at me. "Kyle? What are you doing here?"

Nothing came out of my mouth.

"Kyle?"

I was frozen. My mind was just too emotional, too much in shock to do it. I stood there, unable to speak.

"Here," Billy said, moving in front of me. "Let me."

And I began to talk.

"I brought you a present," I said, gesturing to the book. "We're going to take a little trip."

"What the hell are you…."

Surprised, Jeremy tried to move away, but I grabbed his neck and held him in place. "We start, of course, at the beginning."

I opened the book and there were baby pictures, dozens of them.

Of Kelly.

"He was a big kid, his mother said fifteen hours of labor to get him out." I turned the page. "Look at him; that's his first birthday."

He tried to stand up again, but I wouldn't let him.

"That's his fifth," I said, turning the page again. "That was his first football. See? These are pics of him that day, playing with it. Doesn't he look happy?"

He tried to squirm away, but he was too surprised to resist. "I don't know what Sammy told you, but she—"

"Shut up!" I barked. "We aren't to the Q&A part yet. We're moving on to elementary." Another page turn. "This is his third-grade picture. He insisted on wearing that jersey. His fourth, see his missing tooth? Pop Warner, he made a touchdown that week. Oh, and look at sixth grade. He had just gotten his braces off; look at that smile."

"I don't know…," he began to say.

"You know all that work at straightening his teeth? Wasted now, the impact of the gun broke most of them when he fired."

He pushed me off him, and the chair he had been sitting in kicked away as he took a few steps back. "What do you want me to say? I posted it? Fine! I did, but he deserved it!"

I grabbed the book. "This is junior high, Jeremy. This was his first boy-girl dance. He insisted on wearing sneakers with his khakis because he didn't want it to be too serious."

He glanced over at the pictures and looked away quickly. "I didn't mean for him to do that!" he tried to reason. "He was an asshole! He picked on both of us! You know that!"

"This is football camp," I said, turning the page. "You see this? You see that smile?"

Jeremy was backing away from the book now.

"He had thought Brad and him were a thing, and were at the very least friends. Brad threw him under the bus for fooling around with him, and the other guys all snubbed him for the rest of the summer. Look at that smile!"

He glanced at the picture.

"That is a guy who is dying inside because he is in love with a guy who doesn't love him back. Sound familiar? You think somewhere in your life you can relate?"

Jeremy's mouth hung open.

"You have a picture like this, Jeremy? A picture where your heart is breaking but you have to smile anyways, because to tell people what was actually wrong would get you killed? Do you?"

He nodded.

"Cool, then I have an idea." I closed the book.

He just sat on the floor.

"Put a gun in your mouth and pull the trigger, because that's what Kelly did. He had all this pain and suffering and humiliation, he had his whole world fall down on him, and he couldn't handle it."

"I didn't want that!"

"But that's what happened. You thought you'd be cute and get back at him, by doing the thing that if it happened to you, would cause you to blow your brains out too."

He looked like he was about to cry.

"He was like us!" I screamed, "He was gay too, and you fucking pushed him to this."

"You don't know the things he did to me," Jeremy sobbed.

"Bad things?" I asked.

He nodded.

"Cruel things?"

Another nod.

"Things that made you want to kill yourself?"

Slow nod.

"Well, then congratulations, Jeremy, you were just like him."

He began to openly cry. I took one of the photos out of the book and held it up to him. "Take a good look, Jeremy, because this is the human being you helped kill. You are directly responsible for his death, and that's a fact you will live with for the rest of your life."

I tossed the picture at him. "Have fun living with that."

I turned to walk out and stopped at the bottom of the steps. "By the way, you asked if I would have ever gone out with you. The answer is no. I don't date bullies."

I heard him break down as I walked out of his house. I knew exactly how he felt.

I got into Brad's car and cried all the way home.

I am so sorry, Kelly.

Brad

EARLY TUESDAY morning Kyle, Jennifer, Sammy, and I used Sammy's keys to get into the school. We had a lot to do, and we went about it quietly, driven to finish before the first bell rang.

It took almost three hours to get everything done, but as we looked up and down the halls, a strange sort of grim satisfaction filled my mind. "Okay. You guys need to get out of here," Kyle said, turning to us. "The janitor is going to unlock this hall, and once he sees all this, he's going to call every single number he knows."

Jennifer glanced over at me, and we both nodded. I looked over to Sammy, and she nodded as well.

"Yeah," I said, looking back at Kyle. "That isn't going to happen."

I thought his eyes were going to bug out when he saw the three of us refusing to move. "This isn't funny, guys," he said, looking around in case any adult was coming. "You have to go."

"We knew Kelly too," Jennifer said.

"He was our friend too," I added.

"And we didn't do anything about it," Sammy finished.

"So you're stuck with us," I told him.

"What about baseball? What about a scholarship?" he asked me.

"What about yours?" I replied. "If you're willing to climb out onto that ledge, least we can do is climb out with you."

"Please go?" he begged us.

Jennifer sat down in the hall, leaning on the locker doors. "It's a good day to die," she announced.

Sammy sat down next to her. "Can't agree more."

"Brad!" he pleaded at me.

I got as close to him as I could and explained, "You were the one who went and made friends. This is the price of having them." I hugged him, and he reluctantly hugged me back. When I didn't let him go, he relaxed against me. I swore I could feel him pulling strength from me, although I didn't know if I had any.

The janitor walked up the steps, looked inside, and saw our work. He dropped his keys as he scrambled to pull his phone out of his pocket.

We sat and waited for the sparks to fly.

About ten minutes later, Mr. Raymond's car screeched to a halt in the parking lot. He looked like he was about to spit fire.

He strode toward the building as far as the doors. He looked in at us. "Stilleno, open these doors right now!" he ordered.

Kyle shook his head. "I don't think so."

Mr. Raymond looked over to the janitor and told him to unlock the door. The other man turned his key in the lock and tried to pull the doors open. They didn't move. Both of them tugged at the doors, but they refused to open. The principal looked down and saw the bike chain we had used to lock the doors from the inside.

"Those aren't coming down until people show up for class," Kyle informed him. "Do me a favor, please call the cops." He held up his phone. "Because the second you do, we call Channel Three."

"I am not going to let you vandalize school property," Mr. Raymond threatened us.

"We aren't vandalizing anything," Kyle said, pulling one of the papers out of his jacket. He slapped it against the glass so Raymond could read it. "We're making sure everyone knows who said what. We're just giving their words back to them."

Mr. Raymond read the paper and then looked down the hall.

The paper was a printout of a message sent to Kelly over the Christmas break, with the name of the person who sent it. Raymond looked and saw papers taped on over half the lockers. He looked down at Kyle, who just smiled back at him. "Call the cops," he said. "I dare you."

And that was how the entire school found out how hateful they all were.

Kyle

NINETY MINUTES later, we were all in the principal's office, waiting for our parents to show up.

Mr. Raymond refused to call my bluff and didn't try to get the cops. The janitor and he tried everything short of breaking and entering themselves to get into the building, but there was no way in. People started showing up for class, and the crowd outside the door began to grow. Mr. Raymond was joined by the vice principals, who threatened us as well but also chose not to call the cops.

When it was almost time for first period, we undid the chain and the kids came rushing into the hall.

The adults tried to pull the notes down off the lockers, but there were just too many of them. Both people who had tortured Kelly and those who hadn't got to read what people had said. Most people tore the paper off and crumpled it up, but it didn't matter. We had made an IG account and posted a pic of the posts and tagged who each had been from. By third period, everyone knew they couldn't hide anymore.

We were locked in an office while they tried to round up all our parents.

"You guys should have run while you had the chance," I told them.

Brad looked over at me. "Hey, I didn't want to go to class anyway. This is a vacation to me."

Jennifer nodded. "I promise you, that *is* how he feels."

I rolled my eyes as Sammy looked at her phone. "Well, the shit hit the fan," she said, looking up at us. "People are posting links on Facebook of what people said. By the end of the day, no one will be able to deny anything." She closed her phone and smiled at me. "You did it."

"I wanted to do it without you guys getting in trouble too," I muttered.

Brad came and sat down next to me. "Maybe we can all work at Nancy's?" he asked, smiling.

"How can you be so happy about this?" I asked him, confused.

He shook his head and just grinned. "We did the right thing," he replied. "It feels pretty fucking cool."

I looked over at Jennifer, and she nodded, Sammy joining her.

I rolled my eyes. "You guys are nuts."

"That's my dad," Jennifer exclaimed, looking at the office. We all got up and looked out the window in the door as our parents showed up. I saw my mom, a guy who must be Sammy's dad, Jennifer's dad in his sheriff's uniform, and finally Brad's mom.

Brad shook his head and looked away. "Never thought I would want my dad to show up somewhere," he muttered, sitting back down.

I was about to say something to him, but Sammy called out, "Someone is coming!" and we all got away from the door.

One of the office secretaries opened the door and told us, "They want you all now."

She led us into Mr. Raymond's office, where our parents waited along with Mr. Adler and Mr. Davis, proving to me this was as bad as I feared. "Have a seat, kids," Mr. Raymond told us. It sounded to me like he was saying "Please put this blindfold on" as they loaded their rifles.

"Thank you all for coming," Mr. Davis began. "We had a serious problem this morning before school started, and I am afraid we were forced to take action."

"Action?" my mom asked, sounding none too pleased. "I swear, this school is about one step away from wearing Klan robes."

Mr. Raymond looked like he was about to scream at her, but Davis cut him off. "Ms. Stilleno, that kind of talk is not helping."

"That kind of talk isn't so far off," Brad's mom shot back.

"What do the messages have to do with the school?" That was Jennifer's dad, using his police-officer voice, which really didn't open the room up for idle conversation.

"It was a serious violation of several school policies, not counting actual laws," Mr. Davis explained, sounding like he was sad about everything. Mr. Davis was a rotten actor.

"Excuse me?" Sammy's dad asked. "What laws?"

"That's a good question," the sheriff asked. "What laws do you think they broke?"

Mr. Adler looked over at him. "Well, breaking and entering, vandalism, not to mention the invasion of privacy issue."

It was the wrong thing to say to the sheriff. "One, they didn't break anything; they had keys. Two, taping stuff to a locker is not vandalism. If that was true, the booster club would be in trouble every time they decorated a player's locker for game day. As for the invasion of privacy, is the school speaking on behalf of Facebook now, since Facebook is the only entity that can claim that?"

All three men looked uncomfortable. Belatedly, they had begun to realize our parents weren't going to just sit there and listen to them expel us.

Brad's mom asked, "Are we going to ignore the fact that my son told you there needed to be a change in the attitude of the administration toward bullying at this school?"

Mr. Davis looked at her with anger on his face. "Kelly did not get bullied on school grounds—"

"What does it matter, since my son was, and you did nothing about it then?" my mom interrupted him. "You said it was his problem for coming out, so you're saying this is Kelly's?"

"We didn't say that," Mr. Adler answered.

"What *are* you saying?" Sammy's dad asked.

"I am saying your children are no longer welcome at this school," Davis said, trying to grab control of the meeting again. "As of now, they are expelled."

Brad's mom leaned forward. "I wouldn't do that if I were you."

Mr. Davis returned her glare. "Or what? Your husband is going to come in and threaten us with a lawsuit again?"

"I don't need my husband to do that," she said, standing up. "You have one student who was verbally abused on campus, and you did nothing. My son was assaulted in *your* locker room, and you did nothing. You want to expel these kids for doing *something* after one of their friends killed himself because he was tortured by bullies, be my guest. But if you think for one second I will not bury you in the press, you are sorely mistaken. I am tired of this school not taking responsibility for its actions. Or in this case, its inaction. You want to expel my son? Then you can explain everything that has happened at the press conference." She looked over at the other parents. "You know, the one we're going to have the second we walk out of here."

They all nodded back at her.

"A young man took his own life, and you want to punish the only people who were trying to do something about what caused him to commit suicide? I don't know what passes for logic in your world, Mr. Davis, but whatever it is, I can assure you it won't hold up to public scrutiny."

Mr. Davis stood up now. "I will not be blackmailed again by a group of kids! Or their parents!"

"You can try that," Kyle warned. "But you really think in a cancel culture this story is going to play well on Twitter? How long before the entire country knows how shitty a school you run?"

"I am not afraid of Twitter," Raymond insisted.

"That's fine," Brad's mom said, opening her purse. "But it isn't Twitter you should be scared of." She pulled out a stack of papers and tossed it on the desk. "It's the federal government."

Mr. Raymond picked the papers up and browsed through them as Jennifer's dad nodded and smiled. "You're talking about Title Nine again," the sheriff said. Brad's mom nodded. Everyone else looked on, confused. He began to remind them of what I'd pointed out at the meeting. "If a school receives federal money, it cannot discriminate against people based on gender."

"Title Nine is about sports," Mr. Adler argued.

"It was, but in some states it has been argued that it also covers discrimination against sexual orientation as well." The three men didn't look convinced. "The law was enacted to create a safe place where all students can learn and grow. It focused on sports, but it refers to all schools receiving federal money."

"Expel my son," Brad's mom said. "He will graduate from Granada, and you can explain to the school board why you lost all of your funding." She leaned on the desk to look directly into Davis's face. "This school is for all the students. Not just the ones you like."

"This will never hold up," Raymond blustered.

Mrs. Graymark gave him a smile that made me promise never to piss her off. "Davis versus the Monroe County Board of Education. Federal funding was withheld because the funding recipient was held liable for student-on-student harassment. The harassment was severe, pervasive, and objectively offensive; the school district had actual knowledge of the harassment, and it acted with deliberate indifference to the harassment." She turned around and said to Brad, "I looked it up when I was sober." She turned back to the principals. "If that doesn't sound like what you have done to these kids, I don't know what does. I don't need my husband to threaten you. I can do it fine all by myself."

It looked like all the blood had drained out of Mr. Raymond's face.

Sammy's dad stood up. "I am taking my daughter home. She will be back at school tomorrow." He paused for a moment. "If it's not this one, you better tell me now so I can call my lawyer."

Jennifer's dad took a step closer to Mr. Raymond. "Here's an easy fix. Pass the antibullying codes you all have been sitting on for months now. You will say it is because you realize there is a problem, and you want to address it. We know it is because we have your feet over the fire. You slap these kids on the hand for what they did"—his voice got real angry—"and try to do the right thing for once."

The principals looked like they were about to throw up.

My mom motioned for me to leave with her, and we all walked out as one. As soon as we were out of earshot, she said, "You know, if you don't want to go here anymore, I will transfer you to Granada today." Brad and the others paused and looked at us.

I had the feeling they were waiting for me to say something.

If we left, Davis and the rest of the school board would be thrilled. Without us pressuring them, they would let the school slide back to the same way it had always been. People like Sammy, the library crew, and everyone else who wasn't lucky enough to be cool would have to suffer through what we all had the past four years. Brad looked at me, and I could see in his eyes that he would transfer with me in a second.

Even if that meant he couldn't play baseball.

They were all looking at me, waiting for me to make a decision. They were going to follow me. Whatever I chose right now, they would do the same thing. A familiar panic rose up in the pit of my stomach as everyone paused and looked at me to speak. It would be easy to just say yes, transfer, and fuck this school. They didn't want us here; no one did. I wasn't sure if Granada wanted us, but anything would have to be better than this place.

I saw Raymond and the other principals looking at me too. They were waiting as well.

"So then leave," Billy said, putting down the copy of *Vogue* it was skimming through. "You transfer to Granada and away from these fucks and it isn't your problem anymore, is it?"

Time stopped and I looked at it. "So you want me to keep going to this school?"

It took a few steps toward me. "What I want is for you to stop being so fucking scared all the time!"

I tried not to take a step back.

"This, this is what Robbie was warning you about. This exact thing, and you wanna get all pissy at Jeremy, hike up your skirt and change schools? Fine, do it! But do you think one thing gets better if you do? You think these three white assholes give a fuck that some queer kid killed himself? Do you think their crusty asses will lose one second of sleep over it?"

I said nothing.

"Right, so then you and your merry men over here bail, what happens to the next queer kids who come through here? Oh, that's right; that isn't your problem. You aren't Rosa Parks. You aren't a hero. Know how I know that?"

I closed my eyes and could feel the heat of Billy's breath on my face.

"Because you haven't saved one motherfucker."

When I opened my eyes, time had started again and everyone was looking at me.

When I opened my mouth, it wasn't Billy who spoke. It wasn't my guilt or my fear or even the bottomless chasm of despair I was teetering over because I had failed Kelly. No, when I opened my mouth, it was none of them.

It was all me. "No, I want to stay, if for nothing else, just to make them change things. I'm not going anywhere, and if they want us to sit in the back of the bus, they better bring more than a couple of middle-aged principals to make us. I am not going anywhere; none of us are." I locked eyes with Mr. Raymond. "You'll be gone before I am."

And I meant it.

EPILOGUE
I WILL FIX YOU

Brad

THE DAY of the funeral was miserable.

The sky was a dirty gray that made it look like all creation was in mourning. My mom had set out my suit the night before, and as I sat there staring at it, I couldn't bring myself to put it on. We hadn't talked since school, but she knew I was proud of the way she handled herself. I was sure we would have a real talk later, but right now I had to put on this suit, which I couldn't bring myself to do.

Putting it on would mean that everything was real, that Kelly was gone. If I stayed in my room and refused to move, then the world would stop as well. He would be alive somewhere, safe in his house, and everything would be okay. Nothing would have happened. Somehow time would be turned backward and he would be waiting for us at school. I would tell him I was sorry, and he would call me a fag.

Except he wouldn't.

Sighing, I got up and began to get dressed. Each new piece of clothing made me feel a thousand pounds heavier.

I hadn't even realized my mom was standing in my doorway until I heard her say, "You look like your father did in high school." Startled, I turned around. She was wearing a black dress I had never seen her wear before. I wondered distantly if she had an outfit just for funerals. Was that what growing up meant? Having a set of clothes ready to say goodbye to fallen friends? If it was, I didn't want to grow up any more than I had.

"Is that a good thing?" I asked, trying not to sound too bitter.

She came in, nodding. Her hands fiddled with my tie. "You father may have many, many faults as a human being, but as a man, he was… he is a very handsome man."

"Is that why you went out with him?" I asked.

Her hands paused for a moment. "Maybe. Maybe I saw there was a better man inside of him trying to get out. A man Kyle seems to have found in you." She patted my lapels down. "Are you riding with us?" she asked, stepping back.

I shook my head as I slipped my shoes on. "I'm picking up Kyle. I don't think his mom is going."

"Lucky her," she mumbled, looking around my room. "I know we haven't talked much about everything that happened. But you do know if you are having any problems…."

I looked up at her. "Mom, it can wait. We have time."

She seemed relieved and nodded quickly. "I know, but I'm a mom. It's time I started acting like one."

I stood up and checked myself in the mirror. "We'll figure it out." I walked over to her and kissed her forehead. When had I gotten so much taller than her? I forced the confusing thought out of my mind. The morning was moving too fast, and I just wanted to scream at it to slow down.

"Don't be late," she said, walking out of my room.

I looked at my feet and willed them to take me downstairs to my car so I could get going. They refused to move. I uttered another sigh that came from the very core of my being and made me feel even more exhausted than I had felt before. With the enthusiasm of a condemned man turning to face a firing squad, I marched to my car.

The entire town seemed to be deserted as I drove down First Street. Most of the shops had a sign in the window that said Closed for Funeral. I wished Kelly had seen this, how many lives he had touched, how many people knew him and were missing him. My vision began to blur, and I wished Kelly was here for anything. When I pulled into Kyle's parking lot, I sat there for a few seconds and forced myself to calm down. I'd gotten halfway to the door when Kyle came out.

I had to give Robbie credit; he knew how to dress my boy.

The black suit seemed to have been tailored for Kyle's frame. I couldn't imagine it was secondhand. He walked up to me and put his arms around me, and I felt myself breaking down again. "I'm so sorry," he said as I rested my head on his shoulder.

I had no words as I clung to him and let myself go for the first time since I had heard the news.

"I was such an asshole to him," I said, the guilt clawing at my conscience like a feral cat in a bag, trying to get out. "He deserved better than me…." My whole body shook as I was wracked with sob after sob.

"Hey," Kyle said softly. "Hey, listen to me," he repeated when he saw I was still crying. "Kelly did what he did because of other people, not you. He loved you, Brad. He always loved you, and that is because he could see the same thing I do. A guy who's worth loving, no matter what." His words were like a slap in the face, and I wiped my face with the back of my hand. "You want to honor his memory? You want to respect his death? Honor his life. Do what he couldn't. Live."

My sorrow was now mixed with complete and absolute awe of the guy in front of me.

"Come on," he said, giving me a smile. "Let's get going."

He began to walk me toward the car, but I pulled him back into another hug, my arms wrapped around him tightly as I tried to will my love and dedication into him. "I love you so much." I felt him hug me back.

"It's going to be okay, Brad. I promise."

I wished I believed him.

The funeral home was on the other end of town. I had never been there myself, but as the only mortuary in town, everyone knew where it was. When we arrived, the parking lot was packed, and I saw a ton of people walking into the small chapel. Kelly's dad stood at the entrance. Next to him was a picture of Kelly, probably taken for his senior class portrait. Something else he would never see. I swallowed hard and tried to force my emotions down as we got out of the car.

My hope that this day would get better vanished when Kelly's dad saw Kyle and me walking toward him.

If you have never seen actual hate on someone's face when they look at you, let me tell you, it is not something you just shrug off. There is an almost physical wall of emotion pushed toward you, making your steps slow no matter how sure you are that they won't hit you. To his credit, though, Kelly's dad didn't so much as skip a beat.

When we got up to him, he said through gritted teeth, "I don't think you boys want to be here." There was still a smile on his face, and those who were at a distance probably thought he was simply greeting us. Anyone closer would be able to see the murder in his eyes.

"We're here to pay our respects," Kyle said, not even blinking. "We're not here to cause trouble."

"Then leave," Mr. Aimes said, his hands balled into fists.

Kyle and he stared at each other for several tense seconds before Kyle asked, "Or what? You going to take a swing at me again? Try to beat me up? You sure you want everyone here to see what you really think of gay people?" I gave Kyle a double take as the older man's face reddened with fury.

"I loved my son," he growled.

"So much so you were going to send him to a straight camp? You loved him so much that you demeaned him and his sexuality?"

"My son was not gay." He took half a step toward Kyle, and I moved between them.

"Keep telling yourself that," Kyle shot back. "If that's what lets you sleep at night, then you scream it from the rooftops, but we both know it's not true." I really thought Kyle was going to take the first swing.

"Do you think you were doing anyone any favors with that stunt at school?" he asked. "Embarrassing us like that? After that crap, you expect me to let you in?"

Kyle laughed sarcastically. "Incredible. Kelly is dead, and you are still more worried about what other people think. You know what?" he said, his voice changing. "You're right; I don't want to be here. I don't want to be anywhere near you."

"Good. Then leave," Mr. Aimes commanded.

"Your son is in a better place," Kyle continued, ignoring him completely. "He is in a place where there is no fear or hatred or any of that. He is beyond that now, and that makes me feel good because I know it's where he belongs. But you know what makes me feel even better? The fact that you will never see him again." I actually gasped, but Kyle just kept talking. "See, you're not going to get to that place, Mr. Aimes. You are going to spend the rest of your miserable life with the knowledge that you helped cause your son to kill himself. And when you die, you won't be sharing heaven with him. You don't deserve to."

"Get the fuck out." Now it looked like Kelly's dad was going to hit Kyle.

Kyle grabbed the photo from the pedestal and turned back to me, "I need a ride." And he walked away.

I fumbled for something to say to Mr. Aimes, but everything that came to mind all boiled down to the same sentiment. "Fuck you," I said and followed after Kyle.

He already sat in the car, as angry as I had ever seen him. I got in the car and looked over at him. "Where are we going?"

"Drive out East Avenue," he answered, staring straight ahead.

"What's out there?" I asked, confused.

He looked at me, and I could see he was barely holding on. "Please, Brad, just drive?"

Without another word, I turned the key, backed out of that horror of a funeral, and did as Kyle had asked.

Once we left the city proper, the world around us could have been the surface of the moon. So much of Texas was made of up these open, barren places where no one lived. We huddled together in our cities and towns, small groups of humans clinging to one another like survivors from a shipwreck. We should have been able to work together to make sure we didn't really die on a reef, but we couldn't. Surrounded by a gigantic world bent on its own business, we wasted our time snarling and clawing at one another. I had no idea anymore where all this hate came from. What did it prove? What did it accomplish?

Besides killing people.

We drove for almost an hour. He had taken the picture out of the frame and was holding it like a talisman. He looked up and said, "Over to the right."

And out in the middle of nowhere, there stood a bar.

"What is this place?" I asked. The parking lot was full of cars and trucks. I could not imagine a place like this being a big attraction.

He didn't answer as he got out of the car, Kelly's picture clutched in his fist.

"Kyle, wait up!" I said, running after him. "We're underage. We can't go in there."

He stopped, looking toward me but not really seeing me. "We can go in there; trust me." He put a hand on the door and looked back at me. Wherever his mind had been, it had returned, because he saw me clearly. "Come on." He gave me a ghost of a smile, and he cocked his head toward the open door.

I took a deep breath and walked in.

The bar was full of guys who turned to stare at us. I froze. Most of them were dressed somberly, and they looked like we had interrupted something extremely serious. "Kyle?" one of them asked, and I realized it was Robbie.

"Take his picture," Kyle said, jerking a thumb at me. He walked over to the bar and told the bartender, "I need a tack."

The guy behind the bar, a bear of a man, considered the request for a moment and then handed him over a thumbtack. Kyle turned to face the other side of the room and began walking. The people parted like the Red Sea as Kyle made his way through the group. I heard a couple of people let out a strangled sob when Kyle reached that wall full of pictures.

He put the picture of Kelly up and tacked it right in the center of all of those faces.

Robbie sobbed quietly as he watched Kyle staring at the wall for a long time. No one talked as they waited for him to finish. He touched one fingertip to Kelly's picture and hauled in a deep breath.

Then Kyle turned around. His expression made his face look as if it had been carved out of stone. He looked around the bar and then at Robbie. "I was wrong. I was wrong about everything. I have six months before I leave this town and go to college." He paused for a moment before he asked, "How do I fix Foster?"

That was the moment Kyle began to change our world forever.

AUTHOR'S NOTE

REAL LIFE can suck.

I really don't have a follow-up to that statement, just stating a fact. Real life, at times, can suck. The problem, as I see it, is that we can't skip to the end of the book. I think life could be made better if, in the middle of a crappy day where everything is going bad, I could open a magical Kindle and skip past this part and see what happens next. I mean, sure, I got ragged on, and I looked like a homeless person, and I am pretty sure when I was talking to that one guy I had something in my teeth, and my cat is giving me attitude, and of course the cable went out the night the show I wanted to watch was on....

But what happens next?

With a wave of my finger, I could scroll into the future and see that the people who ragged on me were actually just having a bad day themselves and apologized by buying me a smoothie, and that the boy I was talking to with something in my teeth liked the fact I looked like I made no effort to dress up and asked for my number, and the show I wanted to watch was a rerun anyway, and my cat... well, my cat always has an attitude, so that is never going to change.

If I could see what comes next, I might be able to get through what is right now.

Of course, it doesn't work that way. Even though we might be able to skim through our own story just to cheer ourselves up, we would not resist the urge to test the limits, and we would end up abusing that power in, like, fourteen different ways. It's human nature: give us an inch, we want a mile; give us a rope, and we think we're a cowboy. Still, being able to skip ahead to see tomorrow would be very cool.

I have found life is a lot like a rat running through a maze without having an idea whether or not there is cheese at the end.

The walls are high, it's almost impossible to turn around in, and no matter how far I go, everything looks like everywhere else I've been. It can be daunting, it can be overwhelming, and as I previously stated, it can suck. At this point I'm not sure what kind of cheese is at the end of the maze, but I swear to you, it better be some real good cheese or someone is in trouble.

The only time I find myself not worried about the maze and the possible lack of cheese is while I read. There's nowhere I can get lost in like a book—not even a good book, just *a* book will do it for me. Books are safe, they are comfortable, and above all else, they are not me. I like not being me for a little while. It's refreshing.

So if you have gone through this book and find yourself sad, or upset, or even a little betrayed, I understand.

If you went in wanting a nice little vacation with Kyle and Brad, you might feel like this was not the trip you wanted to take. And while your feelings are completely valid, and I am in no way going to try to change your mind about that, I want to point out one small fact.

For some kids out there, what is in this book is their real life.

There are kids out there right now walking around thinking about killing themselves. You may never know it, they may never even let on about it, but they are seriously thinking about it.

I know because I was one of those kids.

I walked around for years thinking about killing myself because I was so utterly depressed about my life. I had a boyfriend who had a girlfriend. He didn't want anyone to know we were together. I had friends who had no idea who I really was. My home life sucked, and there was no way out for me. I was miserable, and I spent every night crying and hoping for one of two things to happen.

For things to get better or for me to gain the courage to kill myself.

I tried and failed three times. Three times in my life I worked up the courage to go ahead and end my life. Each time I failed and was given a second and then a third chance.

Looking back now, I think someone on high was on my side. (For some of you that is God. I myself like to think that Thor was on my side. No, I am not Norse, nor do I pray to Thor, but the thought that someone who looks like Chris Hemsworth is watching out for me makes me happy. Very happy. So very happy that maybe you should stop laughing and give me a break, huh?) If you asked me even five years ago if there was a reason why someone like God (Thor) would spare my life, I would tell you no, I am just a guy.

But… recently I have begun to think differently.

You see, I wrote these books, and people like you read them, and some people have written me and told me how much they meant to them. They say things like it made them happy, it made them realize that they weren't the only ones out there, and one reader even said it made him realize that though life might suck right now, there might be a Kyle or Brad out there waiting for him. Those are heady words, and I take each and every one of them to heart. I really do.

So maybe there was a reason Thor didn't let me die.

Maybe I was always supposed to write these books, and maybe you were always supposed to read these books, and maybe, just maybe, it all makes sense in some cosmic way. Maybe I was supposed to write these words to save your life and in doing so you saved mine. Maybe. I don't know. Chris Hemsworth works in mysterious ways.

But I can tell you this with absolute certainty.

I wish I had had that magical Kindle back then to skip to now and see what was going to happen. If Past Me could see Now Me and look at the difference these books have made….

Anyway, just a thought.

Now about the book. Everything that has happened in the Tales from Foster High series has happened to someone. Every event has been taken from real life and has happened to a real person. Bullying is very real and cyberbullying doubly so. Teen suicide happens all the time, and not just to gay and lesbian teens. All of this happens all the time. That is a fact.

What is also a fact is there are ways you can deal with it.

There are organizations out there that can and will help you. There are people out there who want to help so bad it hurts. People who hate and hurt others may make the most noise and, therefore, get the most press. For every hateful person who is trying to push you down, there are three caring people who would gladly extend a hand to help you up in a second. And if you think killing yourself is the answer? I am sorry, friend. You are not just wrong, but you are stupid as well.

Your story is as, if not more, important than the one you just read. You cannot let the people whose hearts are filled with hate beat you down. You just can't. We are all people, and we are all deserving of respect. And you can't let anyone take that away from you. Ever.

I posted these in the last book, but I am going to repost them again in case you missed them.

If you are being bullied in high school, regardless of your sexuality, you can find help at http://stopbullying.gov, and if you are a gay or lesbian student being bullied in high school, you can contact the It Gets Better Project at http://www.itgetsbetter.org.

If you are a parent of a gay or lesbian teen and want information or resources on talking to them about it, please go to http://www.pflag.org.

You are not alone, and it *does* get better. There is always another choice out there, and if you think you are alone, you are not. If you are feeling suicidal, please visit http:// www.suicide.org/gay-and-lesbian-suicide.html for help.

I am not going to lie to you and say that all stories have a happy ending. I hated to hear that when I was a kid, and I hate it now. It's not true. Some stories end horribly, so it is just an untrue statement. Instead I say this: happy endings are for people who make their own. If you sit around the house, waiting for some lady to appear with a magic wand and make things all better, you have a long-ass wait ahead of you. People can and will hate you for any reason they can think of. I don't know why they do it, but they do, and it sucks.

What sucks worse, though, is when you let those people make you hate yourself. Don't do that. Why would you hate yourself? I like you. I bet my friends would like you… I am not so sure about my cat because he is a dick, but he would fake liking you if you had tuna.

Life isn't about what other people think of you. It's about what *you* think of you. If you are going to let other people cloud the way you think about yourself, then you are going to be miserable for most of your life, and there is nothing I can do to help. But if you like yourself despite what people around you say and don't give in to the hatred and darkness that seems to be everywhere…

Then let me be a magic Kindle for you, if only for a few seconds.

You're going to end up just fine.
Don't give up, not yet.
John Goode
Sitting by the second
window at Nancy's
with my laptop open.

JOHN GOODE is fifty years old and was found in his floating crib by a strange man… wait, no that's Baby Yoda. I am a cat that gets constantly screamed at by a blond woman while I'm trying to eat… wait, no, not me. I am inevitable, nope. I am Iron Man? More no. I'm not bad, I'm just drawn that way? I can't pull that dress off. Okay, I am and shall always be your friend. Sigh, I think I stole that from somewhere. Let me try again. WHEN I WAS A YOUNG WARTHOG! Too much? I agree. Okay, how about a little Fosse, Fosse, Fossee, a little Martha Graham, Martha Graham, Twyla, Twyla, Twyla and then some Michael Kidd, Michael… I lost you, huh? Well whoever he is, I can assure you he isn't a black cat that wears glasses. Okay, how about this?

He is this guy who lives in this place and writes stuff he hopes you read.

Twitter: @fosterhigh
Facebook: www.facebook.com/TalesFromFosterHigh

JOHN
GOODE
TALES FROM
FOSTER
HIGH

Tales from Foster High: Book One

Kyle Stilleno is the invisible student even in his nothing high school in the middle of Nowhere, Texas. Brad Graymark is the baseball star of Foster High. When they bond over their mutual damage during a night of history tutoring, Kyle thinks maybe his life has changed for good. But when you're gay and falling for the most popular boy in school, the promise of love is a fairy tale, not a reality. Isn't it?

A coming-of-age story, *Tales from Foster High* shows an unflinching vision of the ups and downs of teenage love and what it is like to grow up gay.

LAST DANCE
WITH MARY JANE

JOHN GOODE

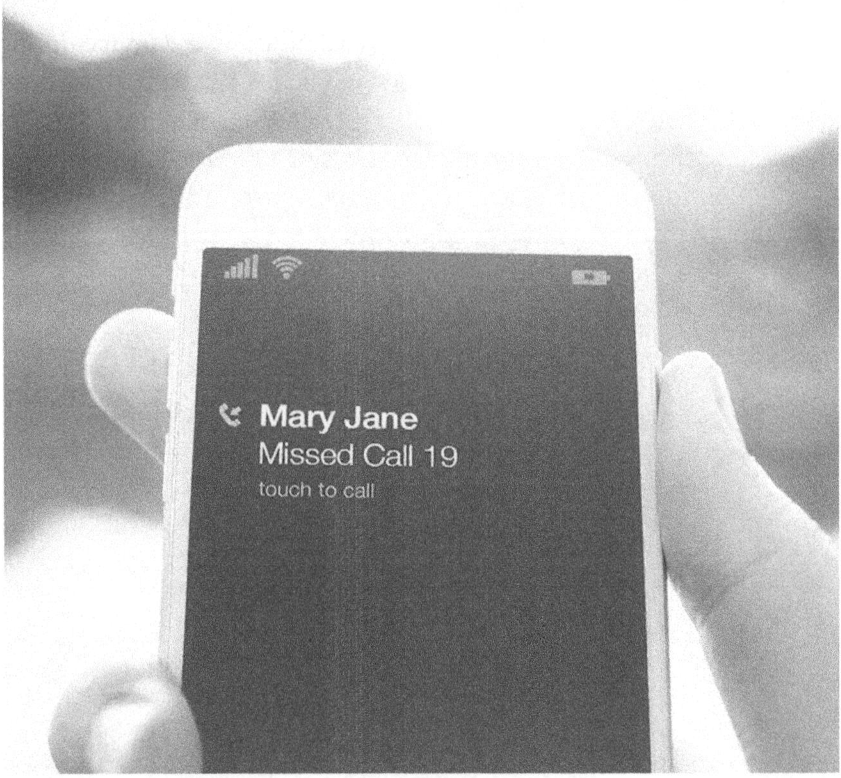

Peter was devastated when he lost his love, Shayne, in a car crash. Though he knows nothing will bring Shayne back, Peter takes solace in listening to Shayne's voice mail, just to hear his voice one last time. He's not prepared when one night, Shayne answers the phone.

www.dreamspinnerpress.com

Also from Dreamspinner Press

www.dreamspinnerpress.com

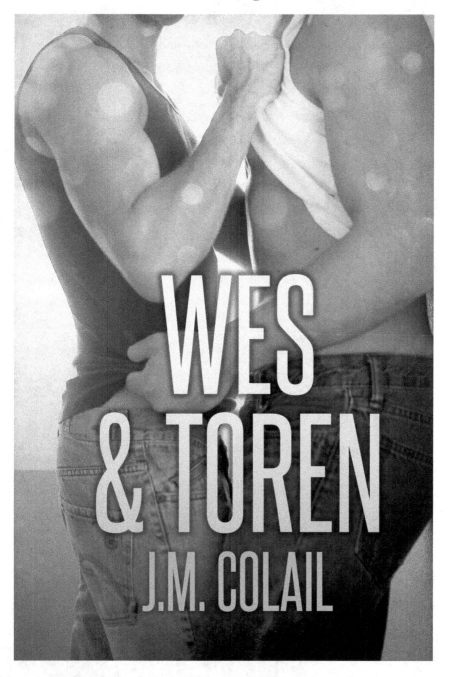

Printed in the USA
CPSIA information can be obtained
at www.ICGtesting.com
LVHW021741131023
761031LV00037B/725

9 781644 058404